WIZARD

ROGER ZELAZNY

WORLD

BAEN

WIZARD WORLD

A Baen Books Original

Baen Publishing Enterprises
P.O. Box 1403
Riverdale, NY 10471

ISBN: 0-671-72057-0

Cover art by David Mattingly

First Printing, October 1989
Second Printing, November 1990

Printed in the United States of America

Distributed by Simon & Schuster
1230 Avenue of the Americas
New York, NY 10020

Young man, do you think you are the first to come here, to seek the rod?

The figure raised both arms, spreading them. The light Pol had summoned trebled in intensity. Dim forms, which he had taken for rubble—on the floor, in corners, near the statues—were suddenly clearly illuminated. He saw many strewn bones. He counted four skulls.

All those who came remained.

Pol felt his fingers twitch toward a yellow strand, but he suppressed the impulse to seize it. It drifted nearer.

The strand doubled and redoubled, looping back upon itself, hovering near his shoulder.

Uh—is it possible, Pol inquired, edging foward, *simply to borrow it and bring it back later? I've an excellent guitar I could leave for security—*

This is not a pawnshop! I am a guardian and you are a thief!

That is not true. It belonged to my father.

There came another pulse of light, and the beast to his right and ahead began to move, slowly at first, taking a step toward him. The other blinked and twitched its ears.

Now it belongs here, came the reply.

Pol reached up and seized the bunched yellow strands. With a jerk and a burst of power that ran along his arm, he tore them down and back, then brought them forward like a lash across the face of the advancing beast. It snarled and cried, drawing back, and he struck again. The third time that he hit it, it cringed, lowering its belly to the floor. At that moment, he noticed that the second jackal was about to spring.

Even as he turned and drew back his arm, he realized that he would not be able to strike in time . . .

WIZARD WORLD

CHANGELING

This book is for Devin

I

When he saw old Mor limp to the van of the besiegers' main party, the Lord of Rondoval realized that his reign was about over.

The day was fading fast behind storm clouds, a steady drizzle of cold rain descended and the thunder rolled nearer with each beat, with each dazzling stroke of light. But Det Morson, there on the main balcony of the Keep of Rondoval, was not yet ready to withdraw. He patted his face with his black scarf and ran a hand through his hair— frost-white and sparkling now, save for the wide black band that passed from his forehead to the nape of his neck.

He withdrew the finely wrought scepter from his sash and held it with both hands, slightly above eye-level, at arm's distance before him. He breathed deeply and spoke softly. The dragon-shaped birthmark on the inside of his right wrist throbbed.

Below, a line of light crossed the path of the attackers, and flames grew upward from it to wave before them. The men fell back, but the centaur archers stood their ground and unleashed a flight of arrows in his direction. Det laughed as the winds beat them aside. He sang his battle-song to the scepter, and on the ground, in the air and under the earth, his griffins, basilisks, demons and dragons prepared themselves for the final assault.

Yet, old Mor had raised his staff and the flames were already falling. Det shook his head, reflecting on the waste of talent.

Det raised his voice and the ground shuddered. Basilisks emerged from their lairs and moved to stare upon his enemies. Harpies dove at them, screaming and defecating,

3

their claws slashing. Werewolves moved in upon their flanks. On the cliffs high above, the dragons heard him and spread their wings. . . .

But, as the flames died and the harpies were pierced by the centaurs' shafts, as the basilisks—bathed in the pure light which now shone from Mor's staff—rolled over and died, eyes tightly shut; as the dragons—the most intelligent of all—took their time in descending from the heights and then avoided a direct confrontation with the horde, which was even now resuming its advance, Det knew that the tide had turned, his vultures had come home to roost and history had surprised him in the outhouse, so to speak. There was no way to employ his powers for deliverance with old Mor out there monitoring every magical avenue of egress; and as for Rondoval's physical exits, they were already blocked by the besiegers.

He shook his head and lowered the scepter. There would be no parlaying, no opportunity for an honorable surrender—or even one of the other kind. It was his blood that they wanted, and he had a sudden premonition of acute anemia.

With a final curse and a last glance at the attackers, he withdrew from the balcony. There was still a little time in which to put a few affairs into order and to prepare for the final moment. He dismissed the notion of cheating his enemies by means of suicide. Too effete for his tastes. Better to take a few of them along with him.

He shook the rain from his cloak and hurried down the hallway. He would meet them on the ground floor.

The thunder sounded almost directly overhead now. There were bright flashes beyond every window that he passed.

Lady Lydia of Rondoval, dark hair undone behind her, turned the corner and saw the shadow slide into the doorway niche. Uttering a general banishing spell, appropriate to most unhuman wights likely to be wandering these halls, she made her way up the corridor.

As she passed the opening, she glanced within and realized immediately why the spell had been somewhat less than efficacious. She confronted Mouseglove the thief—a small, dark man, clad in blackcloth and leather—whom she had, until that moment, thought safely confined to a cell beneath the castle. He regained his composure quickly and bowed, smiling.

"Charmed," he said, "to meet m'lady in passage."

"How did you get out?" she asked.

"With difficulty," he replied. "They make tricky locks in these parts."

She sighed, clutching her small parcel more closely.

"It appears," she said, "that you have managed the feat just in time for it to prove your undoing. Our enemies are already battering at the main gate. They may even be through it by now."

"So that is what the noise is all about," he said. "In that case, could you direct me to the nearest secret escape passage?"

"I fear that they have all been blocked."

"Pity," he said. "Would it then be impolite of me to inquire whence you are hastening with— Ah! Ah!"

He clutched at his burned fingertips, immediately following an arcane gesture on the Lady Lydia's part when he had reached toward the bundle she bore.

"I am heading for a tower," she stated, "with the hope that I can summon a dragon to bear me away—if there still be any about. They do not take well to strangers, however, so I fear there is nothing for you there. I— I am sorry."

He smiled and nodded.

"Go," he said. "Hurry! I can take care of myself. I always have."

She nodded, he bowed, and she hurried on. Sucking his fingers, Mouseglove turned back in the direction from which he had just come, his plan already formed. He, too, would have to hurry.

As Lydia neared the end of the corridor, the castle began to shake. As she mounted the stair, the window on the landing above her shattered and the rain poured in. As she reached the second floor and moved toward the winding stairway to the tower, an enormous clap of thunder deafened her to the ominous creaking noise within the walls. But, had she heard it, she might still have ventured there.

Partway up the stair, she felt the tower begin to sway. She hesitated. Cracks appeared in the wall. Dust and mortar fell about her. The stairway began to tilt. . . .

Tearing her cloak from her shoulders, she wrapped it about her bundle as she turned and rushed back in the direction from which she had come.

The angle of the stair declined, and now she could hear a roaring, grating sound all about her. Ahead, a portion of the ceiling gave way and water rushed in. Beyond that, she could see the entranceway sliding slowly upwards. Without hesitation, she drew back the bundle and cast it through the opening.

The world gave way beneath her.

As the forces of Jared Klaithe pounded into the main hall at Rondoval over the bodies of its dark defenders, the lord Det emerged from a side passage, a drawn bow in his hands. He released an arrow which passed through Jared's armor, breastbone and heart, in that order, dropping him in his tracks. Then he cast the bow aside and drew his scepter from his sash. He waved it in a slow circle above his head and the invaders felt an invisible force pushing them back.

One figure moved forward. It was, of course, Mor. His illuminated staff turned like a bright wheel in his hands.

"Your loyalty is misplaced, old man," Det remarked. "This is not your fight."

"It has become so," Mor replied. "You have tipped the Balance."

"Bah! The Balance was tipped thousands of years ago," said the other, "in the proper direction."

Mor shook his head. The staff spun faster and faster before him, and he no longer appeared to be holding it.

"I fear the reaction you may already have provoked," he said, "let alone what might come to pass should you be permitted to continue."

"Then it must be between us two," said Det, slowly lowering the scepter and pointing it.

"It always was, was it not?" said Mor.

The Lord of Rondoval hesitated for the barest moment. Then, "I suppose you are right," he said. "But for this, be it upon your own head!"

The scepter flared and a lance of brilliant red light leaped from it. Old Mor leaned forward as it struck full upon the shield his spinning staff had become. The light was instantly reflected upward to strike against the ceiling.

With a roar that outdid the thunder, great chunks of masonry came loose to crash downward upon the Lord of Rondoval, crushing and burying him in an instant.

Mor straightened. The wheel slowed, becoming a staff again. He leaned heavily upon it.

As the echoes died within the hall the remaining sounds of battle came to a halt without. The storm, too, was drifting on its way, its lightnings abated, its thunders stilled in that instant.

One of Jared's lieutenants, Ardel, moved forward slowly and stood regarding the heap of rubble.

"It is over," he said, after a time. "We've won. . . ."

"So it would seem," Mor said.

"There are still some of his men about—to be dealt with."

Mor nodded.

" . . . And the dragons? And his other unnatural servants?"

"Disorganized now," Mor said softly. "I will deal with them."

"Good. We—what is that noise?"

They listened for several moments.

"It could be a trick," said one of the sergeants, Marakas by name.

"Choose a detail. Go and find out. Report back immediately."

Mouseglove crouched behind the arras, near to the stairwell that led to the dark places below. His plan was to return to his cell and secure himself within it. A prisoner of Det's would be about the only person on the premises likely to receive sympathetic treatment, he had reasoned. He had succeeded in making it this far on his journey back to duress when the gate had given way, the invaders entered and the sorcerous duel taken place. He had witnessed all of these things through a frayed place in the tapestry.

Now, while everyone's attention was elsewhere, would be the ideal time for him to slip out and head back down. Only . . . His curiosity, too, had been aroused. He waited.

The detail soon returned with the noisy bundle. Sergeant Marakas wore a tense expression, held the baby stiffly.

"Doubtless Det planned to sacrifice it in some nefarious rite, to assure his victory," he volunteered.

Ardel leaned forward and inspected. He raised the tiny right hand and turned it palm upwards.

"No. It bears the family's dragon-mark of power inside the right wrist," he stated. "This is Det's own offspring."

"Oh."

Ardel looked at Mor. But the old man was staring at the baby, oblivious to all else.

"What should I do with it, sir?" Marakas asked.

Ardel chewed his lip.

"That mark," he said, "means that it is destined to become a sorcerer. It is also a certain means of identification. No matter what the child might be told while it was growing up, sooner or later it would learn the truth. If that came to pass, would *you* like to meet a sorcerer who knew you had had a part in the death of his father and the destruction of his home?"

"I see what you are getting at . . ." said Marakas.

"So you had best—dispose of—the baby."

The sergeant looked away. Then, "Suppose we sent it to some distant land where no one has ever heard of the House of Rondoval?" he asked.

" . . . Where one day there might come a traveler who knows this story? No. The uncertainty would, in many ways, be worse than a sureness of doom. I see no way out for the little thing. Be quick and merciful."

"Sir, could we not just cut off the arm? It is better than dying."

Ardel sighed.

"The power would still be there," he said, "arm or no arm. And there are too many witnesses here today. The

story would be told, and it would but add another griev-
ance. No. If you've no stomach for it yourself, there must
be someone in the ranks who—"

"Wait!"

Old Mor had spoken. He shook himself as one just
awakening and moved forward.

"There may be a way," he said, "a way to let the child
live and to assure that your fears will never be realized."

He reached out and touched the tiny hand.

"What do you propose?" Ardel asked him.

"Thousands of years ago," Mor began, "we possessed
great cities and mighty machines as well as high magics—"

"I've heard the stories," Ardel said. "How does that
help us now?"

"They are more than just stories. The Cataclysm really
occurred. Afterwards, we kept the magic and threw much
of the rest away. It all seems so much legend now, but to
this day we are biased against the unnatural tech-things."

"Of course. That is—"

"Let me finish! When a major decision such as that is
made, the symmetry of the universe demands that it go
both ways. There is another world, much like our own,
where they threw away the magic and kept the other. In
that place, we and our ways are the stuff of legend."

"Where is this world?"

Mor smiled.

"It is counterpoint to the music of our sphere," he said,
"a single beat away. It it just around the corner no one
turns. It is another forking of the shining road."

"Wizards' riddles! How will this serve us? Can one
travel to that other place?"

"I can."

"Oh. Then . . ."

"Yes. Growing up in such a place, the child would have
its life, but its power would mean little. It would be
dismissed, rationalized, explained away. The child would
find a different place in life than any it might have known
here, and it would never understand, never suspect what
had occurred."

"Fine. Do it then, if mercy can be had so cheaply."

"There *is* a price."

"What do you mean?"

"That law of symmetry, of which I spoke—it must be satisfied if the exchange is to be a permanent one: a stone for a stone, a tree for a tree . . ."

"A baby? Are you trying to say that if you take this one there, you must bring one of theirs back?"

"Yes."

"What would we do with that one?"

Sergeant Marakas cleared his throat.

"My Mel and I just lost one," he said. "Perhaps . . ."

Ardel smiled briefly and nodded.

"Then it *is* cheap. Let it be done."

With the toe of his boot and a nod, Ardel then indicated Det's fallen scepter.

"What of the magician's rod? Is it not dangerous?" he asked.

Mor nodded, bent slowly and retrieved it from where it had fallen. He began to twist and tug at it, muttering the while.

"Yes," he finally said, succeeding in separating it into three sections. "It cannot be destroyed, but if I were to banish each segment to a point of the great Magical Triangle of Int, it may be that it will never be reclaimed. It would certainly be difficult."

"You will do this, then?"

"Yes."

At that moment, Mouseglove slipped from behind the arras and down the stairwell. Then he paused, held his breath and listened for an outcry. There was none. He hurried on.

When he reached the dimness of the great stair's bottom, he turned right, took several paces and paused. They were not corridors, but rather natural tunnels that faced him. Had it been the one directly to the right from which he had emerged earlier? Or the other which angled off nearby? He had not realized that there were two in that vicinity. . . .

There came a noise from above. He chose the opening on the extreme right and plunged ahead. It was as dark as the route he had traversed earlier, but after twenty paces it took a sharp turn to the right which he did not recall.

Still, he could not afford to go back now, if someone were indeed coming. Besides, there was a small light ahead. . . .

A brazier of charcoal glowed and smoked within an alcove. A bundle of faggots lay upon the floor nearby. He fed tinder into the brazier, blew upon it, coaxed it to flame. Shortly thereafter, a torch blazed in his hand. He took up several other sticks and continued on along the tunnel.

He came to a branching. The lefthand way looked slightly larger, more inviting. He followed it. Shortly, it branched again. This time, he bore to the right.

He gradually became aware of a downward sloping, thought that he felt a faint draft. There followed three more branchings and a honeycombed chamber. He had begun marking his choices with charcoal from the body of the torch, near to the righthand wall. The incline steepened, the tunnel twisted, widening. It came to bear less and less resemblance to a corridor.

When he halted to light his second torch, he was aware that he had traveled much farther than he had on the way out earlier. Yet he feared returning along the way he had come. A hundred paces more, he decided, could do no harm . . .

And when he had gone that distance, he stood at the mouth of a large, warm cavern, breathing a peculiar odor which he could not identify. He raised the torch high above him, but the further end of the vast chamber remained hidden in shadows. A hundred paces more, he told himself. . . .

Later, when he had decided not to risk further explorations, but to retrace his route and take his chances, he heard an enormous clamor approaching. He realized that he could either throw himself upon the mercy of his fellow men and attempt to explain his situation, or hide himself and extinguish his light. His experience with his fellow men being what it had been, he looked about for an unobtrusive niche.

And that night, the servants of Rondoval were hunted through the wrecked castle and slain. Mor, by his staff and his will, charmed the dragons and other beasts too difficult to slay and drove them into the great caverns beneath. There, he laid the sleep of ages upon everything within and caused the caverns to be sealed.

His next task, he knew, would be at least as difficult.

II

He walked along the shining road. Miniature lightnings played constantly across its surface but did not shock him. To his right and his left there was a steady flickering as brief glimpses of alternate realities came and went. Directly overhead was a dark stillness filled with steady stars. In his right hand he bore his staff, in the crook of his left arm he carried the baby.

Occasionally, there was a branching, a sideroad, a crossroad. He passed many of these with only a glance. Later, however, he came to a forking of the way and he set his foot upon the lefthand branch. Immediately, the flickering slowed perceptibly.

He moved with increased deliberation, now scrutinizing the images. Finally, he concentrated all of his attention on those to the right. After a time, he halted and stood facing the panorama.

He moved his staff into a position before him and the progression of images slowed even more. He watched for several heartbeats, then leaned the tip of the staff forward.

A scene froze before him, grew, took on depth and coloration. . . .

Evening . . . Autumn . . . Small street, small town . . . University complex . . .

He stepped forward.

Michael Chain—red-haired, ruddy and thirty pounds overweight—loosened his tie and lowered his six-foot-plus frame onto the stool before the drawing board. His left hand played games with the computer terminal and a figure took shape on the cathode display above it. He studied this for perhaps half a minute, rotated it, made adjustments, rotated it again.

13

Taking up a pencil and a T-square, he transferred several features from the display to the sheet on the board before him. He leaned back, regarding it, chewed his lip, began a small erasure.

"Mike!" said a small, dark-haired woman in a severe evening dress, opening the door to his office. "Can't you leave your work alone for a minute?"

"The sitter is not here yet," he replied, continuing the erasure, "and I'm ready to go. This beats twiddling my thumbs."

"Well, she is here now and your tie has to be retied and we're late."

He sighed, put down the pencil and switched off the terminal. "All right," he said, rising to his feet and fumbling at his throat. "I'll be ready in a minute. Punctuality is no great virtue at a faculty party."

"It is if it's for the head of your department."

"Gloria," he replied, shaking his head, "the only thing you need to know about Jim is that he wouldn't last a week in the real world. Take him out of the university and drop him into a genuine industrial design slot and he'd—"

"Let's not get into that again," she said, retreating. "I know you're not happy here, but for the time being there's nothing else. You've got to be decent about it."

"My father had his own consulting firm," he recited. "It could have been mine—"

"But he drank it out of business. Come on. Let's go."

"That was near the end. He'd had some bad breaks. He was good. So was Granddad," he went on. "He founded it and—"

"I already know you come from a dynasty of geniuses," she said, "and that Dan will inherit the mantle. But right now—"

He shook himself and looked at her.

"How is he?" he asked in a softer voice.

"Asleep," she said. "He's okay."

He smiled.

"Okay. Let's get our coats. I'll be good."

She turned and he followed her out, the pale eye of the CRT looking over his shoulder.

Mor stood in the doorway of a building diagonally across the street from the house he was watching. The big man in the dark overcoat was on the doorstep, hands thrust into his pockets, gazing up the street. The smaller figure of the woman still faced the partly opened door. She was speaking with someone within.

Finally, the woman closed the door and turned. She joined the man and they began walking. Mor watched them head off up the street and turn the corner. He waited awhile longer, to be certain they would not be returning after some remembered trifle.

He departed the doorway and crossed the street. When he reached the proper door he rapped upon it with his staff. After several moments, the door opened slightly. He saw that there was a chain upon it on the inside. A young girl stared at him across it, dark eyes only slightly suspicious.

"I've come to pick something up," he said, the web of an earlier spell making his foreign words clear to her, "and to leave something."

"They are not in just now," she said. "I'm the sitter. . . ."

"That is all right," he said, slowly lowering the point of his staff toward her eye level.

A faint pulsing began within the dark wood, giving it an opalescent hue and texture. Her eyes shifted. It held her attention for several pulsebeats, and then he raised it slowly toward his own face. Their eyes met and he held her gaze. His voice shifted into a lower register.

"Unchain the door now," he said.

There was a shadow of movement, a rattling within. The chain dropped.

"Step back," he commanded.

The face withdrew. He pushed the door open and entered.

"Go into the next room and sit down," he said, closing the door behind him. "When I depart this place, you will chain the door behind me and forget that I have been here. I will tell you when to do this."

The girl was already on her way into the living room.

He moved about slowly, opening doors. Finally, he paused upon the threshold of a small, darkened room, then entered softly. He regarded the tiny figure curled within the crib, then moved the staff to within inches of its head.

"Sleep," he said, the wood once again flickering beneath his hand. "Sleep."

Carefully then, he placed his own burden upon the floor, leaned his staff against the crib, uncovered and raised the child he had charmed. He lay it beside the other and considered them both. In the light that spilled through the opened door, he saw that this baby was lighter of complexion than the one he had brought, and its hair was somewhat thinner, paler. Still . . .

He proceeded to exchange their clothing and to wrap the baby from the crib in the blanket which had covered the other. Then he placed the last Lord of Rondoval within the crib and stared at him. His finger moved forward to touch the dragonmark. . . .

Abruptly, he turned away, retrieved his staff and lifted young Daniel Chain from the floor.

As he passed along the hallway he called into the living room, "I am going now. Fix the door as it was after me—and forget."

Outside, he heard the chain fall into place as he walked away. Stars shone down through jagged openings among the clouds and a cold wind came out of the east at his back. A vehicle turned the corner, raking him with its lights, but it passed without slowing.

Tiny gleams began to play within the sidewalk, and the buildings at either hand lost something of their substantiality, became two-dimensional, began to flicker.

The sparkling of his path increased and it soon ceased to be a sidewalk, becoming a great bright way stretching illimitably before and behind him, with numerous sideways visible. The prospect to his right and left became a mosaic of tiny still-shots of innumerable times and places, flashing, brightening and shrinking, coming at last to resemble the shimmering scales of some exotic fish in passage by him. Overhead, a band of dark sky remained, but cloudless and pouring starlight in negative celestial image of the road below. Occasionally, Mor glimpsed other figures upon the sideways—not all of them of human form—bent on tasks as inscrutable as his own.

His staff came to blaze as he picked his way homeward, lightning-dew dripping from his heels, his toes.

III

In lands mythical to one another, the days passed.

When the boy was six years old, it was noted that he not only attempted to repair anything that was broken about the place, but that he quite often succeeded. Mel showed her husband the kitchen tongs he had mended.

"As good as Vince could have done at the smithy," she said. "That boy's going to be a tinker."

Marakas examined the tool.

"Did you see how he did it?" he asked.

"No. I heard his hammering, but I didn't pay him much heed. You know how he's always fooling with bits of metal and such."

Marakas nodded and set the tongs aside.

"Where is he now?"

"Down by the irrigation ditch, I think," she answered. "He splashes about there."

"I'll walk down and see him, tell him he was a good boy for mending that," he said, crossing the room and lifting the latch.

Outside, he turned the corner and took the sloping path past the huge tree in the direction of the fields. Insects buzzed in the grasses. A bird warbled somewhere above him. A dry breeze stirred his hair. As he walked, he thought somewhat proudly of the child they had taken. He was certainly healthy and strong—and very clever. . . .

"Mark?" he called when he had reached the ditch.

"Over here, Dad," came a faint reply from around the bend to his right.

He moved in that direction.

"Where?" he asked, after a time.

17

"Down here."

Approaching the edge, he looked over, seeing Mark and the thing with which he was playing. It appeared that the boy had placed a smooth, straight stick just above the water's surface, resting each of its ends loosely in grooves among rock heaps he had built up on either side; and at the middle of the stick was affixed a series of squarish—wings?—which the flowing water pushed against, turning it round and round. A peculiar tingle of trepidation passed over him at the sight of it—why, he was not certain—but this vanished moments later as he followed the rotating vanes with his eyes, becoming a sense of pleasure at his son's achievement.

"What have you got there, Mark?" he asked, seating himself on the bank.

"Just a sort of—wheel," the boy said, looking up and smiling. "The water turns it."

"What does it do?"

"Nothing. Just turns."

"It's real pretty."

"Yeah, isn't it?"

"That was nice the way you fixed those tongs," Marakas said, plucking a piece of grass and chewing it. "Your mother liked that."

"It was easy."

"You enjoy fixing things and making things, making things work—don't you?"

"Yes."

"Think that's what you'd like to do for a living some day?"

"I think so."

"Old Vince is going to be looking for an apprentice down at the forge one of these days. If you think you'd like to learn smithing, working with metals and such—I could speak with him."

Mark smiled again.

"Do that," he said.

"Of course, you'd be working with real, practical things." Marakas gestured toward the water-spun wheel. "Not toys," he finished.

"It isn't a toy," Mark said, turning to look back at his creation.

"You just said that it doesn't do anything."

"But I think it could. I just have to figure what—and how."

Marakas laughed, stood and stretched. He tossed his blade of grass into the water and watched the wheel mangle it.

"When you find out, be sure to tell me."

He turned away and started back toward the path.

"I will . . ." Mark said softly, still watching it turn.

When the boy was six years old, he went into his father's office to see once again the funny machine Dad used. Maybe this time—

"Dan! Get out of here!" bellowed Michael Chain, a huge figure, without even turning away from the drawing board.

The little stick figure on the screen before him had collapsed into a line that waved up and down. Michael's hand played across the console, attempting adjustments.

"Gloria! Come and get him! It's happening again!"

"Dad," Dan began, "I didn't mean—"

The man swiveled and glared at him.

"I've told you to stay out of here when I'm working," he said.

"I know. But I thought that maybe this time—"

"You thought! You thought! It's time you started doing what you're told!"

"I'm sor—"

Michael Chain began to rise from his stool and the boy backed away. Then Dan heard his mother's footsteps at his back. He turned and hugged her.

"I'm sorry," he finished.

"Again?" Gloria said, looking over him at her husband.

"Again," Michael answered. "The kid's a jinx."

The pencil-can began rattling atop the small table beside the drawing board. Michael turned and stared at it, fascinated. It tipped, fell to its side, rolled toward the table's edge.

He lunged, but it passed over the edge and fell to the

floor before he could reach it. Cursing, he straightened then and banged his head on the nearest corner.

"Get him out of here!" he roared. "The kid's got a pet poltergeist!"

"Come on," Gloria said, leading him away. "We know it's not something you want to do. . . ."

The window blew open. Papers swirled. There came a sharp rapping from within the wall. A book fell from its shelf.

" . . . It's just something that sometimes happens," she finished, as they departed.

Michael sighed, picked things up, rose, closed the window. When he returned to his machine, it was functioning normally. He glared at it. He did not like things that he could not understand. Was it a wave phenomenon that the kid propagated—intensified somehow when he became upset? He had tried several times to detect something of that sort, using various instruments. Alway unsuccessfully. The instruments themselves usually—

"Now you've done it. He's crying and the place is a shambles," Gloria said, entering the room again. "If you'd be a little more gentle with him when it starts, things probably wouldn't get so bad. *I* can usually head them off, just by being nice to him."

"In the first place," Michael said, "I'm not sure I believe that anything paranormal really happens. In the second, it's always so sudden."

She laughed. So did he.

"Well, it is," he said finally. "I suppose I had better go and say something to him. I know it's not his fault. I don't want him unhappy. . . ."

He had started toward the door. He paused.

"I still wonder," he said.

"I know."

"I'm sure our kid didn't have that funny mark on his wrist."

"Don't start that again. Please. It just takes you around in circles."

"You're right."

He departed his office and walked back toward Dan's room. As he went, he heard the sounds of a guitar being softly strummed. Now a D chord, now a G . . . Surprising, how quickly a kid that age had learned to handle the undersized instrument · . . . Strange, too. No one else in either family had ever shown any musical aptitude.

He knocked gently on the door. The strumming stopped.

"Yes?"

"May I come in?"

"Uh-huh."

He pushed the door open and entered. Dan was sprawled on the bed. The instrument was nowhere in sight. Underneath, probably.

"That was real pretty," he said. "What were you playing?"

"Just some sounds. I don't know."

"Why'd you stop?"

"You don't like it."

"I never said that."

"I can tell."

He sat down beside him and squeezed his shoulder.

"Well, you're wrong," he said. "Everybody's got something they like to do. With me, it's my work." Then, finally, "You scared me, Dan. I don't know how it happens that machines sometimes go crazy when you come around—and things I don't understand sometimes scare me. But I'm not really mad at you. I just sound that way when I'm startled."

Dan rolled onto his side and looked up at him. He smiled weakly.

"You want to play something for me? I'll be glad to listen."

The boy shook his head.

"Not just now," he said.

Michael looked about the room, at the huge shelf of picture books, at the unopened erector set. When he looked back at Dan, he saw that the boy was rubbing his wrist.

"Hurt your hand?" he asked.

"Uh-uh. It just sort of throbs—the mark—sometimes."

"How often?"

"Whenever—something like that—happens."

He gestured toward the door and the entire external world.

"It's going away now," he added.

He took hold of the boy's wrist, examined the dark dragon-shape upon it.

"The doctor said it was nothing to worry about—no chance of it ever turning into anything bad. . . ."

"It's all right now."

Michael continued to stare for several moments. Finally, he squeezed the hand, lowered it and smiled.

"Anything you want, Dan?" he asked.

"No. Uh . . . Well—some books."

Michael laughed.

"That's one thing you like, isn't it? Okay, maybe we can stop by a bookstore later and see what they've got."

Dan finally smiled.

"Thank you."

Michael punched his shoulder lightly and rose.

" . . . And I'll stay out of your office, Dad."

He squeezed his shoulder again and left him there on the bed. As he headed back toward his office, he heard a soft, rapid strumming begin.

When the boy was twelve years old he built a horse. It stood two hands high and was moved by a spring-powered clockwork mechanism. He had worked after hours at the smithy forging the parts, and on his own time in the shed he had built behind his parents' place, measuring, grinding and polishing gears. Now it pranced on the floor of that shed, for him and his audience of one—Nora Vail, a nine-year-old neighbor girl.

She clapped her hands as it slowly turned its head, as if to regard them.

"It's beautiful, Mark! It's beautiful!" she said. "There's never been anything like it—except in the old days."

"What do you mean?" he said quickly.

"You know. Like long ago. When they had all sorts of clever devices like that."

"Those are just stories," he said. Then, after a time, "Aren't they?"

She shook her head, pale hair dancing.

"No. My father's passed by one of the forbidden places, down south by Anvil Mountain. You can still see all sorts of broken things there without going in—things people can't make anymore." She looked back at the horse, its movements now slowing. "Maybe even things like that."

"That's—interesting . . ." he said. "I didn't realize—and there's still stuff left?"

"That's what my father said."

Abruptly, she looked him straight in the eye.

"You know, maybe you'd better not show this to anybody else," she said.

"Why not?"

"People might think you've been there and learned some of the forbidden things. They might get mad."

"That's dumb," he said, just as the horse fell onto its side. "That's real dumb."

But as he righted it, he said, "Maybe I'll wait till I have something better to show them. Something they'll like. . . ."

The following spring, he demonstrated for a few friends and neighbors the flotation device he had made, geared to operate a floodgate in the irrigation system. They talked about it for two weeks, then decided against installing it themselves. When the spring runoff occurred—and later, when the rains came—there was some local flooding, not too serious. They only shrugged.

"I'll have to show them something even better," he told Nora. "Something they'll *have* to like."

"Why?" she asked.

He looked at her, puzzled.

"Because they have to understand," he said.

"What?"

"That I'm right and they're wrong, of course."

"People don't usually go for that sort of thing," she said.

He smiled.

"We'll see."

When the boy was twelve years old, he took his guitar with him one day—as he had on many others—and visited a small park deep in the steel, glass, plastic and concrete-lined heart of the city where his family now resided.

He patted a dusty synthetic tree and crossed the unliving turf past holograms of swaying flowers, to seat himself upon an orange plastic bench. Recordings of birdsongs sounded at random intervals through hidden speakers. Artificial butterflies darted along invisible beams. Concealed aerosols released the odors of flowers at regular intervals.

He removed the instrument from its case and tuned it. He began to play.

One of the fake butterflies passed too near, faltered and fell to the ground. He stopped playing and leaned forward to examine it. A woman passed and tossed a coin near his feet. He straightened and ran a hand through his hair, staring after her. The disarrayed silver-white streak that traced his black mop from forehead to nape fell into place again.

He rested the guitar on his thigh, chorded and began an intricate right-hand style he had been practicing. A dark form—a real bird—suddenly descended, to hop about nearby. Dan almost stopped playing at the novel sight. Instead, he switched to a simpler style, to leave more attention for its movements.

Sometimes at night he played his guitar on the roof of the building where birds nested, beneath stars twinkling faintly through the haze. He would hear them twittering and rustling about him. But he seldom saw any in the parks—perhaps it was something in the aerosols—and he watched this one with a small fascination as it approached the failed butterfly and seized it in its beak. A moment later, it dropped it, cocked its head, pecked at it, then hopped away. Shortly thereafter, the bird was airborne once again, then gone.

Dan reverted to a more complex pattern, and after a time he began singing against the noises of the city. The sun passed redly overhead. A wino, sprawled beneath the level of the holograms, sobbed softly in his sleep. The park vibrated regularly with the passage of underground trains. After several lapses, Dan realized that his voice was changing.

IV

Mark Marakson—six feet in height and still growing, muscles as hard as any smith's—wiped his hands on his apron, brushed his unruly thatch of red back from his forehead and mounted the device.

He checked the firebox again, made a final adjustment on the boiler and seated himself before the steering mechanism. The vehicle whistled and banged as he released the clutch and drove it out of his hidden shed, heading down toward the roadway along the path he had smoothed.

Birds, rabbits and squirrels fled before him, and he smiled at the power beneath his hands. He took a corner sharply, enjoying the response to the controls. This was the sixth trial of his self-propelled wagon and everything seemed to be functioning perfectly. The first five expeditions had been secret things. But now . . .

He laughed aloud. Yes, now was the time to surprise the villagers, to show them what could be wrought with thinking and ingenuity. He checked the pressure gauge at his side. Fine . . .

And it was a beautiful morning for such an expedition— sunny, breezy, the spring flowers in bloom at either hand . . . His heart leaped within him as the hardwood seat pounded his backside and thoughts of suspension systems danced through his mind. It was indeed a day for great undertakings.

He chugged along, occasionally feeding the flames, trying to imagine the expressions on the people's faces when they got their first sight of the contraption. A farmer in a distant field let up his plowing and stared, but he was too far removed for his reaction to be visible. Mark wished suddenly that he had thought to install some sort of whistle or bell.

As he neared the village, he drew back on the brake, slowing. He planned to halt right in the middle of town, stand on the seat and give a little talk. "Get rid of your horses," it would begin. "A new day is dawning . . ."

He heard the cries of children from a nearby field. Soon they were racing along beside him, screaming questions. He tried to answer them, but the noises of the machine destroyed his words.

As he turned onto the only street through the village, slowing even more, a horse bolted and ran off between two houses, dragging a small cart. He saw people running and heard doors slamming. Dogs snarled, barked and backed away. The children kept pace.

Reaching the town's center, he braked to a complete halt and looked about.

"Can we ride on it?" the children shouted.

"Maybe later," he replied, turning to check that everything was still in good order.

Doors began to open. People emerged from homes and stables to stand staring at him. Their expressions were not at all what he had imagined they would be. Some were blank-faced, many seemed fearful, a few looked angry.

"What is it?" a man shouted from across the way.

"A steam wagon," he yelled back. "It—"

"Get it out of here!" someone else called. "We'll all be cursed!"

"It's not bad magic—" he began.

"Get it out!"

"Out with it!"

"Bringing that damned thing into town . . ."

A clod of earth struck the side of the boiler.

"You don't understand!"

"Out! Out! Out!"

Stones began to fly. A number of men began moving toward him. He singled out the one he knew best.

"Jed!" he shouted. "It's not bad magic! It's just like boiling water to make tea!"

Jed did not reply, but reached out with the others to seize hold of the wagon's quivering side.

"We'll boil you, you bastard!" one of the others shouted, and they began to rock the vehicle.

'Stop! Stop! You'll damage it!" Mark cried.

Top-heavy, it quickly responded to their pressures with a swaying motion. When he realized that it was beginning to tip, it was too late to jump.

"Damn you!" he cried, and he fell.

He landed rolling and struck his head but did not pass out. Dazed, he saw the boiler burst and the firebox come open, scattering embers. Several droplets of hot spray struck him, and he continued to roll. The waters streamed off toward the main ditch, missing him.

"Damn you, damn you, damn you, damn you," he heard himself repeating, and then he blacked out.

He smelled the smoke and heard the flames when he came around again. The wagon had taken fire from the embers. People stood about watching it burn. No one made an attempt to extinguish it.

" . . .Have to get a wise man to exorcise the demon now," he overheard a woman saying. "Don't no one touch it. You kids stay away!"

"Fools!" he muttered, and he struggled to rise.

A small hand on his shoulder pushed him back.

"No! Don't draw attention to yourself! Just lie still!"

"Nora . . . ?"

He looked up. He had not at first realized that she was there, holding a compress to his head.

"Yes. Rest a moment. Gather your strength. Then come back this way between the houses." She gestured with her head. "We'll move quickly when we do."

"They didn't understand. . . ."

"I know. I know. It was like the horse, when we were children . . ."

"Yes."

" . . . Something you just thought up because you think that way. I understand."

"Damn them!" he said.

"No. They just don't think the way you do."

"I'll show them!"

"Not now you won't. Let's just get ready and slip away.

After that, I think it might be a good idea for you to stay out of sight for a time."

He stared at the burning wagon and at the faces beyond it.

"I suppose you are right," he said. "Damn them. I'm ready. I want to get out of here."

She took hold of his hand. He winced and drew it back.

"I'm sorry. It's burned," she said. "I hadn't noticed."

"Neither had I. It will be all right, though. Let's go."

She clasped his other hand. He rose quickly and moved with her, past shrubs, beyond the houses.

"This way."

He followed her down a lane, through a barn.

When they paused to rest, he said, "Thank you. You were right. I'm going away for awhile."

"Where?"

"South," he hissed.

"Oh, no!" she said. "That's too wild, and—"

"I've got the name," he stated.

She stared into his eyes.

"Don't," she said.

He reached forward and embraced her. She was stiff for a moment, then relaxed against him.

"I'll be back for you," he told her.

The trees were smaller, the land was drier here. There were fewer shrubs and more bare areas. This land was rockier and much, much quieter than his own. He heard no birdcalls as he walked and climbed, no insect-noises, no sounds of running water, rustling boughs, passing animals.

His hand had stopped throbbing several days ago, and the skin was peeling now. He had long since discarded the bandage from his head. His tread was firm despite weariness, as he neared the anvil-shaped peak through lengthening shadows. He wore a small backpack, and several well wrapped water bottles hung from his belt. His garments were dirty, as were his face and hands, but he smiled a tight smile as he looked upward and plodded on.

He did not feel that there were demons and assorted monsters in the area, as some people believed. But he bore a short sword across his pack—one he had forged himself years before, when he had been shorter and lighter. It seemed almost a toy now, though he could wield it with great speed and dexterity. He had spent months practicing with blades to obtain the feeling for edged weapons which alone would insure his producing a superior product when he came to forge them. He had picked his up at the smithy when he had returned there for the supplies for his flight. Now, hiking closer and closer to the forbidden area, he felt no great need for the blade in what he took to be a dead place, but its presence made him think of the effort which had gone into its manufacture, yet had still produced an item inferior in quality to some of the strange fragments of metal he discovered imbedded in the ground here.

He carried such a scrap in his hand and studied it now and again. He saw it to be some sort of tough, light alloy, once he had scraped and rubbed the dirt from it, uncorrupted after all these years. What were the forces that had formed it? What heats? What pressures? It told him that something peculiar had once existed nearby.

That evening he walked through the still standing shell of a large building. He could not even guess what might once have been transacted within it. But twice he thought that he heard scurrying sounds near at hand as he explored. He decided to camp at some distance from the ruin.

He could not decide whether a fire would attract or repel anything that might dwell nearby. Finally, the lack of sufficient kindling materials to keep a blaze going for very long persuaded him to do entirely without. He ate dry rations and rolled himself into his blanket on a ledge eight feet above the ground. He placed his blade within easy reach.

How long he had slept, he could not say. Several hours, it felt, when he was awakened by a scratching noise. He was alert in an instant, hand moving toward the weapon. He turned his head slightly, muscles tensing, and beheld the thing which moved over the rocks below, coming in his direction.

Its dark, segmented body gleamed in the moonlight as it crept over the rocks on numerous tiny feet, its front end

sometimes raised, sometimes lowered. It was three or four
times his own size, and it resembled nothing so much as a
gigantic, metallic caterpillar moving along the trail he had
followed to this place. Mounted near the forward end was
something small and twisted and vaguely man-shaped,
clutching what appeared to be reins in its left hand and
the shaft of a long spear in the other. The beast reared,
rising as high as the ledge, swayed, then dropped to the
ground once more and proceeded as if sniffing out his
path.

Hackles risen, a cold lump in the pit of his stomach,
Mark eyed a possible escape route among the rocks below
and to the right. If he moved quickly enough there might
still be a sufficient margin. . . .

He breathed deeply, vaulted to the ground and twisted
his ankle beneath him. Rising, limping, he headed toward
the rocks. He heard a sharp whistling noise behind him
and an increase in the scratching sounds. He dodged as
best he could, thinking of the spear in the thing's hand.

He looked back once and saw that he seemed to be
holding his own. The spear-arm was cocked, but the rocks
were right before him now. He dove and heard the shaft
clatter on stone behind him. Recovering immediately, he
continued on, heading obliquely back in the direction of
the ruin he had visited earlier.

The noises behind him did not diminish. Apparently,
the monstrosity could move at a faster pace than that at
which he had first seen it coming.

He darted among rocks, keeping the sounds to the rear
and the ruin roughly ahead. There had been places to
climb, places to hide there—places better suited for defense than the open ground of this rock maze.

He rounded a huge boulder, froze, and barely had time
to bring his blade into play. Another of the things, also
bearing a rider, appeared to have been searching or waiting for him. It was reared upright only feet away, and the
spear was already descending.

He parried, driving the shaft aside, and swung a back-
handed cut toward the swaying creature. It rang like a bell
and dropped forward. He stepped aside, feeling a sharp
pain in his right ankle, then thrust upward toward the

gnarled rider. There came a scream as his blade connected and entered, somewhere. He dragged it free, turned, ran.

There were no sounds of pursuit, and when he glanced back he saw the beast, now riderless, groping aimlessly among the rocks. He began to draw a deep breath, and then the world gave way beneath him. He fell a short distance through darkness and landed shoulder-first on a hard surface. The blade fell from his hand with a clanging sound, and he immediately retrieved it. There came a sharp, slamming noise from overhead, and dust, gravel and pieces of earth fell about him. Suddenly then, there was light, but his eyes did not immediately adjust to it.

When the effects of the brightness had passed, he still did not understand what lay before him.

A table . . . Yes, he recognized that—and the chairs. But where was the main light source? What was that large gray thing with the glassy rectangle at its center? And all those tiny lights?

Nothing moved about him, save for the settling dust. He got to his feet, advancing slowly.

"Hello?" he whispered.

"Yes, hello, hello!" came a loud voice. "Hello?"

"Where are you?" he asked, halting and turning in a slow circle.

"Here, with you," was the reply. The words had an archaic accent to them, like that of the Northlanders.

"I do not see you. Who are you?"

"My, you speak strangely! Foreigner? I am a teaching machine, a library computer."

"My words may seem strangely accented and assembled because of the passage of time," Mark said, with a sudden insight concerning the age and function of the device. "Can you make allowances, adjust for this? I am having a difficult time understanding even your simplest statements."

"Yes. Talk a lot. I need a good sample. Tell me about yourself and the things that you wish to know."

Mark smiled and lowered his blade. He limped to the nearest chair and slumped into it. He rubbed his shoulder.

"I will," he said, moments later. "But how is this place lighted?"

The screen glowed before him. Beneath a heavy layer of dust, a wiring diagram suddenly appeared upon it.

"Is that what you mean?" asked the voice.

"Maybe. I'm not certain."

"Do you know what it is?"

"Not yet," he said, "but I intend to. If you will instruct me."

"I have the means to provide for your well-being for so long as you wish to remain here. I will instruct you."

"I think I may have just fallen into the very thing I sought," Mark replied. "I'll tell you about myself, and you tell me about power sources. . . ."

V

Daniel Chain—a junior at State, working on his certificate in Medieval Studies; slim and hard, after two years on the boxing and fencing teams; less than happy at the subtle pressure still exerted by his father for him to change his History and Linguistics major and join him in the business—sat upon the tall stool, thinking of all these matters and others, after the fashion of half-controlled reverie which informed his mind whenever he played.

The club was dim and smoky. He had followed Betty Lewis, who sang torch songs and blues numbers accompanied by piano rolls and a deep decolletage and who always drew heavy applause when she took her bows. Now he was filling the room with guitar sounds. He played on Saturday nights and alternate Fridays, doing as many instrumentals as vocals. The people seemed to like his music both ways. Right now, he was in a nonvocal mood.

Tonight was the other Friday, and the place was considerably less than packed. He recognized several familiar faces at the small tables, some of them nodding in time with the beat.

He sculpted the swirls of smoke as they drifted up toward the lights, into castles, mountain ranges, forests and exotic beasts. The mark on his wrist throbbed slightly as this occurred. It was strange how few of the patrons ever looked up and noticed his music-shaped daydreams hovering above their heads. Or perhaps the ones who did were already high and thought it normal.

Improvising, he moved an army across a ridge. He attacked it with dragons and tore it to pieces. Troops fled in all directions. Smiling, he upped the tempo.

33

In time, he saw an elbow strike a mug of beer. It slowed in midair as he played, twisting upright, retaining much of the beverage. It came to a stop inches above the floor, then descended the final distance gently. By the time its owner found it there and exclaimed upon the miracle, Dan had returned to his world of open spaces and trees, mountains and clear rivers, prancing unicorns and diving griffins.

Jerry, the bartender, sent up a pint. Dan paused to sip from it, then in a small fit of self-awareness began the tune to which he had set "Miniver Cheevy." Soon, he was singing the words.

Somewhere past the halfway point, he noticed a frightened look on Jerry's face. He had just taken a step backward. The man immediately before him was leaning forward, hunched over his drink and looking ahead. By leaning back on the stool and craning his neck, Dan could just make out the lines of the small handgun the man held, partly wrapped in a handkerchief. He had never tried to stop one from firing and wondered whether he could. Of course, the trigger might well remain untugged. Jerry was already turning slowly toward the cash register.

The pulse in his right wrist deepened as he stared at a heavy mug and watched it slide along the bartop, as he shifted his gaze to an empty chair and saw it begin to creep forward. For those moments, a part of him seemed also to be a part of the chair and the mug.

Jerry rang up NO SALE and was counting out the bills from the register. The chair found its position behind the hunched gunman and halted, soundlessly. Dan sang on, castles fallen, dragons flown, troops scattered in the white haze about the lights.

Jerry returned to the counter and passed the man a wad of bills. They vanished quickly into a jacket pocket. The weapon was now completely covered by the handkerchief. The man straightened and slid from the stool, eyes and weapon still upon the bartender. As he moved backward and began to turn the chair lurched to reposition itself. His foot struck it and he stumbled, throwing out his hands to save himself.

As he sprawled, the mug rose from the counter and sped toward his head. When it connected, he lay still. **The** weapon in its white wrapping sped across the floor to vanish beneath the performer's platform in the corner.

Dan finished his song and took another drink. Jerry was beside the man, recovering the money. A knot of people had already formed at that end of the room.

"That was very strange."

He turned his head. It was Betty Lewis who had spoken. She had left the table near the wall where she had been sitting, sipping something, and approached the platform.

"What was strange?" he said.

"I saw that chair move by itself—the one he tripped on."

"Probably someone bumped it."

"No."

Now she was looking at him rather than the scene across the room.

"The whole thing was very peculiar. The mug . . ." she said. "Funny things seem to happen when you're playing. Usually little things. Sometimes it's just a feeling."

He smiled.

"It's called mood. I'm a great artist."

He fingered a chord, ran an arpeggio. She laughed.

"No, I think you're haunted."

He nodded.

"Like Cheevy. By visions."

"Nobody's listening now," she said. "Let's sit down."

"Okay."

He leaned his guitar against the stool and took his beer to her table.

"You write a lot of your own stuff, don't you?" she said, after they had seated themselves.

"Yes."

"I like your music and your voice. Maybe we could work out a thing where we do a couple of numbers together."

"Maybe," he said, "if you've no objection to the strange things you say happen."

"I like strange things." She reached out and touched his hair. "That's real, isn't it—the streak?"

"Yes."

"At first I thought—you were a little weird."

". . . And now you know it?"

She laughed.

"I suppose so. Someone said you're still in school? That right?"

"It is."

"You going to stay with music when you get out?"

He shrugged.

"Hard to say."

"You've got a future, I'd think. Ever record anything?"

"No."

"I had a record. Didn't do well."

"Sorry."

"The breaks . . . Maybe bad timing. Maybe not, too. I don't know. I'd really like to try something with you. See how it sounds. If it works, I know a guy . . ."

"My material?"

"Yeah."

He nodded.

"Okay. After the show, let's go somewhere and try a few."

"My place isn't far. We can walk"

"Fine."

He took a sip of beer, glanced over and saw that the man on the floor was beginning to stir. In the distance, he heard the sound of a siren. He heard someone ask, "Where's the gun?"

"It's a funny feeling I get when I hear you," she resumed, "as though the world were a little bit out of kilter."

"Maybe it is."

". . . As though you tear a little hole through it and I can see a piece of something else on the other side."

"If I could only tear one big enough I'd step through."

"You sound like my ex-husband."

"Was he a musician?"

"No. He was a physicist who liked poetry."

"What became of him?"

"He's out on the Coast in a commune. Arts and crafts, gardening . . . Stuff like that."

"He up and leave, or he ask you to go with?"

"He asked, but I didn't want pig shit on my heels."

Dan nodded.

"I'll have to watch where I step if I ever step through."

The police car pulled up in front, its light turning, blinking. The siren died. Dan finished his drink as someone located the weapon.

"We'd look pretty good on an album cover," she said. "Especially with that streak. Maybe I could . . . Naw."

The man with the sore head was led away. Car doors slammed. The blinking stopped.

"I've got to go sing something," he said, rising. "Or is it your turn?"

She looked at her watch.

"You finish up," she said. "I'll just listen and wait."

He mounted the platform and took the guitar into his hands. The pillars of smoke began to intertwine.

VI

The giant mechanical bird deposited Mark Marakson on the hilltop. Mark brushed back the soft green sleeve of his upper garment and pressed several buttons on the wide bracelet he wore upon his left wrist. The bird took flight again, climbing steadily. He controlled its passage with the wristband and saw through its eyes upon the tiny screen at the bracelet's center.

He saw that the way ahead was clear. He shouldered his pack and began walking. Down from the hill and through the woods he went, coming at last to a trail that led toward more open country. Overhead, his bird was but a tiny dot, circling.

He passed cultivated fields, but no habitations until he came within sight of his father's house. He had plotted his return route carefully.

His work shed stood undisturbed. He deposited his pack within it and headed toward the house.

The door swung shut behind him. The place seemed more disarrayed than he had ever before seen it.

"Hello!" he called. "Hello?"

There was no reply. He went through the entire house, finding no one. Dust lay thick everywhere. Marakas could well be in the field, or tending to any of the numerous chores about the place. But Melanie was usually in the house. He looked about outside, investigating the barns and work sheds, walked down to the ditches, scanned the fields. No one. He returned to the house and sought food for lunch. The larder was empty, however, so he ate of his own provisions. But he operated the wrist-control first,

38

and the speck in the heavens ceased its circling and sped southward.

Disturbed, he began cleaning and straightening about the place. Finally, he went out to the shed and set to work assembling the unit he had brought with him.

It was on toward evening, his labors long finished, when he heard the sound of the approaching wagon. He departed the house, which he had set back in order, and awaited the vehicle's arrival.

He saw Marakas drive up to the barn and begin unhitching the team. He walked over to assist him.

"Dad . . ." he said. "Hello."

Marakas turned and stared at him. His expression remained blank for an instant too long. During that instant, it struck Mark what had troubled him about his father's movements, his reaction time: he was more than a little drunk.

"Mark," he said then, recognition spreading across his face. He stook a small step forward. "You've been gone. Over a year. A year and a half . . . Almost two. What—happened? Where have you been?"

"It's a long story. Here, let me help with that."

He took over the unhitching of the team, the rubbing down of the horses in their stalls, their feeding.

" . . . So, when they destroyed my wagon, I had to leave. I was—afraid. I headed south."

He barred the barn door. The sun was just losing its final edge.

"But so long, Mark . . . You never sent us word or anything," Marakas said.

"I couldn't. How's—how's mother?"

Marakas looked away and did not reply. Finally, he pointed toward a small orchard.

"Over there," he said at last.

After a time, Mark asked, "How'd it happen?"

"In her sleep. It wasn't bad for her. Come on."

They walked toward the orchard. Mark saw the small, rocked-over grave, a part of the shadows and rootwork near one of the larger trees. He halted beside it, looking down.

"My going away . . ." he finally said. "That didn't have anything to do with it—did it?"

Marakas put a hand on his shoulder.

"No, of course not."

"You never appreciate . . . Till they're gone."

"I know."

"That's why the place is—not the way it used to be?"

"It's no secret I've been drinking a lot. Yes. My heart hasn't been in things around here."

Mark nodded, dropped to one knee, touched the stones.

"We could work the place together, now you're back," Marakas said.

"I can't."

"They've got another smith now. New fellow."

"I didn't want to do that either."

"What will you be doing?"

"Something new, different. That's a long story, too. Mother—"

His voice broke, and he was silent for a long while.

Finally, "Mark, I don't think too clearly when I've been drinking," Marakas said, "and I don't know whether I ought to tell you this now, later or never. You loved her and she loved you, and I don't know . . ."

"What?"

"I guess a man should know, sometime, and you're a man now, and things'd of been a lot different without you. We wanted a kid, see?"

Mark rose slowly.

"What do you mean?"

"I'm not your father. She's not your mother. Natural-like, I mean."

"I don't understand . . ."

"We never had any of our own that lived. It was a sad thing. So when we had a chance to make a home for a baby, we took it."

"Then, who were my natural parents?"

"I don't know. It was right after the war—"

"I was orphaned?"

"I don't think so. I couldn't understand all the wizard's fancy talk. But they couldn't bring themselves to kill old Devil Det's kid, so they sent him someplace far away and got you in exchange. He called you a changeling. That's all I know. We were so glad to take you. Mel's life was a lot happier than it would have been otherwise. Mine, too. I hope that doesn't change anything between us. But I felt it was time for you to know."

Mark embraced him.

"You wanted me," he said, a little later. "That's more than a lot of people can say."

"It's good to see you again. Let's go back to the house. There's some food and stuff in the wagon."

After dinner, they finished a bottle of wine and Marakas grew sleepy. Shortly after he had retired, Mark returned to his shed. They should all be circling high above now, he realized, bearing the additional equipment he needed, awaiting the signal to bring it to him. He carried the unit he had assembled earlier to a large, open area, from which he transmitted the necessary orders.

The dark bird-shapes began drifting down out of the sky, blotting out stars, their outlines growing to vast proportions. He smiled.

It took him several hours to unload the equipment and convey most of it to the barn. He was bone-tired when he had finished. He sent all but one of these products of his assembly lines flying back to his city in the south. That one he set to circling again, at a great altitude.

He returned to his shed to sleep, pausing in the orchard a final time.

The following day, Mark assembled a small vehicle which, he explained to Marakas, drew its energy from the sun. He could not convince him that this was not a form of magic. That he did not wish to explain from where the parts had come only added to this impression. Mark gave up when he saw that it did not seem to matter to Marakas, and he went on with the installation of special features. That afternoon, he loaded it with equipment and drove off along the trail that followed the canal. He returned several times for additional tools and equipment.

For the next five days, he remained away from the farm. The afternoon that his work was completed, he drove toward the village. He headed the car down its street and halted it at the same spot where his steam wagon had been destroyed. He activated several circuits and picked up the microphone.

"This is Mark Marakson," he said, and his voice rang through the town. "I've returned to tell you some of the things to which you would not listen before—and many new things, as well. . . ."

Faces appeared at windows. Doors began to open.

"This wagon, like the other, is not powered by a demon. It uses natural energies to do work. I can build planting and plowing and harvesting devices of similar design which will function faster and more efficiently than any a horse can draw. In fact, I already have. I propose to furnish these for no charge to all of the farms in the area and to provide instruction in their use. I would like to turn our land into a model of scientific farming techniques, and then into a manufacturing center for these vehicles. We will all grow rich, providing them to the rest of the country. . . ."

People emerged onto the street. He saw familiar faces and some new ones. If any were shouting this time, he could not hear them above his own broadcast words.

"I also have things to teach you concerning the alternation of crops, the use of fertilizers and superior irrigation techniques. The water levels here have always been something of a problem, so I have set up a demonstration of how this can be controlled by installing a series of automatic flow-control gates along the ditches at the abandoned Branson farm above the west bend of the river. I want you to go and take a look at this—to see how they work all by themselves—after you have had a chance to think over my words. No demons there either."

Stones and pieces of dirt and dung had begun striking the vehicle while he spoke, but these rebounded harmlessly and he continued:

"I have also fertilized, plowed, tilled and seeded one of the old fields there. I want you to see how smoothly and evenly this was done, and I want you to watch and see what the yield from that plot comes to. I believe that you will be impressed. . . ."

Four men rushed forward and set hands upon the side of the car. They immediately leaped or fell back.

"That was an electrical shock," he stated. "I am not foolish enough to give you the same opportunity to harm me twice. Damn it! We're neighbors, and I want to help you! I want my town to be the center from which the entire country receives the benefits I wish to bring it! I have amazing things to teach you! This is only the beginning! Life is going to be better for everyone! I can build machines that fly and that travel under water! I can build weapons with which we can win any war! I have an army of mechanical servants! I—"

The pelting had become a steady hail, and larger, heavier objects were now falling.

"All right! I'm going!" he cried. "All that I want you to do is to think about the things that I have said! They may seem a lot more reasonable later, when you have cooled off! Go and look at the Branson place! I'll be back another time, when we can talk!"

The vehicle moved slowly forward. A few people chased after for a time, hurling some final rocks and words. Then they fell behind. He left the village.

As he swung to the left, climbing about the side of a small hill, he saw a slim figure in a blue blouse and gray skirt, standing by the side of the trail, waving to him. He slowed immediately when he recognized Nora.

Coming to a stop, he leaned over and opened the door.

"Get in," he said.

She studied the car through narrowed eyes, then shook her head slowly.

"No," she said. "I thought you'd come this way, and I came on ahead to warn you—not to go for a ride in the thing."

"Warn me?"

"They're angry—"

"I know that."

She struck her fist against her palm.

"Don't interrupt! Listen! Could you hear what they were saying?"

"No. I—"

"I didn't think so, over all that noise. Well, I could, and

I don't think that they are going to calm down and see things your way. I think that the only reason you're alive right now is that they couldn't break into this thing. . . ." Gingerly, she reached out and touched the door. "Don't go back to the village. You probably ought to leave again—" Her voice broke and she turned away. "You never got in touch," she managed later. "You said that you would, and you never did."

"I— I couldn't, Nora."

"Where were you?"

"Far away . . ."

"Far? As far as Anvil Mountain, or one of the other forbidden places? That's where you got this thing, isn't it?"

He did not reply.

"Isn't it?" she repeated.

"It's not the way you think," he answered then. "Yes, I was there, but—"

"Go away! I don't want to know you any more! I've warned you. If you value your life, leave here again—and this time, don't come back!"

"I can convince you you're wrong—if you'll listen, if you will let me show you some—"

"I don't want to listen and I don't want to see anything!"

She turned and ran off through the trees. He would have pursued her, but he feared leaving the car there, should any villagers be following.

"Come back!" he called.

But there was no answer.

Reluctantly, he closed the door and continued on. A puzzled centaur peered after him from the hilltop.

VII

The synthetic caterpillars crisscrossed the streets of the reviving city, removing trash and rubble. Their superintendent, a short, wide-shouldered mutant with heavy brow-ridges, followed their slow progress, occasionally leaning upon his hooked driving-prod. The skies were sunny today, above the shining spires about which laborers clambered, building. Terraces were spreading under the care of a company of robot attendants. The steady throbbing of the restored factories filled the air as other-styled robots, flying machines, cars and weapons moved down the computerized assembly lines. Far below, a line of passing mutants genuflected as they passed the white-stone monument above the entranceway to the old teaching machine's quarters, which their leader had caused to be erected there and had designated as a shrine. Giant bird-like forms departed from and returned to flat-roofed buildings, moving into and out of their enormous patrol patterns. The superintendant uttered a cry, swung his goad and smiled. Life had been growing steadily better, ever since the arrival of the suncrowned one, with his power over the Old Things. He hoped that the leader fared well on his latest quest. Later, he would visit the shrine to pray for this, and that they might spread the blessings of warmth at night and regular meals across the land. A virtuous feeling he could now afford possessed him as he swung the goad again.

*   *   *

Michael Chain, florid-faced, hair thinning now, sat across from Daniel in the small, quiet restaurant, trying to seem

45

as if he were not studying his reactions. Dan, in turn, uncomfortable in his best suit, poked at his melting dessert and sipped his coffee, trying to seem as if he were not aware of the surreptitious scrutiny. Occasionally, his wrist throbbed and somewhere a dish shattered. Whenever this occurred, he would hastily apply the biofeedback technique he had learned to suppress it.

"The record isn't doing too well, eh?" Michael said.

Dan raised his eyes, shook his head.

"I seem to go over better in person," he replied. Then he shrugged. "Hard to tell what you're doing wrong the first time around, though. I can already see a number of things I should have done differently—"

"It was good," Michael surprised him by saying. "I liked it." He flipped a palm upward and gestured vaguely away. "Even so," he went on. "A small outfit, no promotion . . . Do you have any idea how many songs are recorded each year?"

"Yes, I do. It's—"

" . . . And you know something about statistics, even with a liberal arts background. It's practically a lottery situation."

"It's rough," Dan acknowledged.

The hand turned over and struck the tabletop.

"It's damn near impossible to make it, that's what it is."

A sound of breaking crockery emerged from the kitchen. Dan sighed.

"I suppose you're right, but I'm not ready to give it up yet."

The elder Chain called for an after dinner drink. Dan declined one.

"Still seeing that Lewis girl?"

"Yes."

"She strikes me as kind of cheap."

"We've had some good times together."

Michael shrugged.

"It's your life."

Dan finished his coffee. When he looked up, Michael was staring at him, smiling.

"It is," the older man said. He reached out and touched Dan's hand. "I'm glad your mind's your own. I know I sometimes push hard. But listen. Even without the degree, there'll always be a place for you in the firm. If you should ever change your mind, you can learn what you need on the job—pick up some night courses . . . No sales pitch. I'm just telling you. There'll still be a place."

"Thanks, Dad."

Michael finished his drink and looked about.

"Waiter!" he called. "The check!"

The chandelier began to quiver, but Dan recognized the feeling and quelled it in time.

*   *   *

Mor stood, leaning against the bedpost for support. He inserted a knuckle into an eye-socket and rubbed vigorously. It seemed that all he did these days was sleep. And his ankles, swollen again . . .

He raised the water bottle from the bedside table and took a long drink. He coughed, then swallowed a potion he had left ready, washing it down with another gulp of water.

Crossing the chamber, he drew back the long, dark drape and opened a shutter. Stars sparkled in a pale sky. Was it morning or evening? He was not certain.

Stroking his white beard, he stared out across the hushed land, realizing that something other than physiology had troubled his slumber. He waited for the dream, the message, the feeling to recur, but it did not.

After a long while, he let the drape fall, not bothering to close the shutter. Perhaps if he returned to bed, it might come back to him . . . Yes, that seemed a good idea.

Shaking his head slowly, he retraced his steps across the room. Human bodies are so much trouble, he reflected.

An owl hooted several times. The mice scurried within the walls.

*   *   *

Deep beneath the ruin of Castle Rondoval, weighted by the heavy spell of sleep that filled the cavern, Moonbird, mightiest of the dragons, assumed a stiff, heraldic pose upon the floor and relaxed it with equal suddenness, his sigh moving like a warm wind across the forms of his mates. His spirit fled ghostly across the skies, passing the forms of giant, dark birds with bodies like sword metal at heights only his kind had once held. Invisible, he threatened, then attacked. The creatures passed along their ways, unaffected.

Raging in his impotence, Moonbird retreated to the dark places of sleep, narrowly missing a smaller form nearby as he tossed, his claws raking furrows along a stony ledge.

VIII

Mark was not awakened by the distant cries. He slept on long after they had begun and was only aroused when a figure entered his shed, seized hold of his shoulder and shook him violently.

"Wake up! Please! Wake up!" came a sharp whisper.

"What—" he began, and he felt a hand cover his mouth.

"Keep your voice down! It's me—Nora. They'll get this one soon enough, just for good measure. You must flee!"

The hand came away from his face. He sat up and reached for his boots, began drawing them on.

"What are you talking about?" he asked. "What is happening?"

"I tried to get here in time to warn you, but they were too fast," she said. "I remembered you sometimes slept in this shed . . ."

He seized his swordbelt and buckled it on.

"I've weapons in the barn to stop anything," he said. "I wish I'd kept some here—"

"The barn is burning, too!"

"Too?"

"The house, the small stable and the two nearer sheds are also on fire."

He sprang to his feet.

"My father was in the house!"

She caught hold of his arm, but he shook her off and made for the door.

"Don't!" she said. "It's too late! Save yourself!"

He flung the door wide and saw that she had spoken the truth. The house blazed like a torch. Its roof had already caved in. A number of townfolk were headed in his direction, and a cry went up as they sighted him.

He took a step backward.

"Get out through the rear window," he whispered, "or they'll know you were here. Hurry!"

"You come, too!"

"Too late. They've spotted me. Go!"

He stepped out, shut the door behind him and drew his blade.

As they approached, faces dirt-streaked and sweaty in the firelight, he thought of his last sight of old Marakas, passed out on his pallet in the loft. Too late, too late . . .

Father, they will pay for this!

He moved forward to meet them. As he advanced, he saw that some of them were armed with other than makeshift weapons. Old blades—some that he might have forged himself—had been freshly oiled and honed. Several of these shone in the midst of the mob. He did not slow his pace.

"Murderers!" he cried. "My father was in there! You all knew him! He never hurt anyone! Damn you! All of you!"

There was no reply, nor did he expect one. He fell upon them, swinging his blade. The nearest man, Hyme the tanner, cried out and dropped to the ground, clutching at his opened belly. Mark swung again, and the butcher's brother screamed and bled. His next attack was parried by one of the blades, and a staff struck him upon the left shoulder. He beat down a thrust toward his chest and fell back, swinging his blade in a wide arc, severing an extended hand clutching a club.

Ashes fell about them, and a line of fire moved through the long grasses toward the orchard. The barn shuddered and a wall gave way, crashing and spraying sparks off to his left.

He was struck upon the chest by something hard-thrown. He staggered back, still swinging the blade. A staff caught him again, this time upon the thigh, and he stumbled. They were all about him then, kicking, pushing. His blade was wrenched from his grasp. Immediately, his hand moved to the bracelet upon his left wrist. He pressed several of the studs . . .

A blade was swinging toward his head. He twisted aside, felt it cut into his brow, slip lower . . .

He screamed and covered his face.

And another voice also carried above the cries of his attackers. Beyond the pain, behind the blood, he recognized Nora's near-hysterical shout: "You'll kill him! Stop it! Stop it!"

Someone kicked him again, but it was the last blow that he felt.

A frightened scream arose nearby, soon to be echoed by many others, as a dark form dropped from the sky and plunged into the midst of his assailants. Its wings were like twin scythes and its metal beak rose and fell among them.

Mark drew a deep breath and staggered to his feet, his body a network of pain, his left hand still covering that half of his face, blood trickling between the fingers, running down the arm, filming the bracelet toward which his right hand now moved.

A number of men lay still upon the ground, and the dark bird stalked those who stood . . .

His fingers danced across the metal band.

The bird-thing halted, drew back, hopped, beat with its wings, rose into the air, circled . . .

"You have decided your own fates," Mark cried hoarsely.

The bird descended, seized hold of him by the shoulders, bore him aloft. His left hand was now entirely red and seemed firmly fixed to his face.

"I give those of you who still stand your lives—for now—that memory of this night shall remain among you, that witnesses be available," he called down to them. "I shall return, and all shall be done as I said it earlier in town—but you will be subjects, not partners in the enterprise. I curse you for this night's work!"

The bird picked up speed, gained altitude.

" . . . Save for you, Nora," he shouted finally. "I will be back for you—never fear!"

He vanished into the sky above. The wounded moaned and the fires crackled. Countercurses followed him across the night. His blood was a small rain over fields he had once worked.

IX

After knocking and waiting—several times—she had just about given up on his being at home. She had also tried the door and found it to be secured.

She was tired. It had been a long walk up to the place, after an absolutely horrible night. She leaned against the door frame, eyes sparkling, but she simply did not feel like crying. She drew back her foot and kicked the door as hard as she could.

"Open up, damn you!" she cried, and she heard a click and the door swung inward.

Mor stood there, wearing a faded blue robe, blinking at the light.

"I thought I heard someone scratching," he said. "You seem familiar, but I don't—"

"Nora. Nora Vail," she told him, "from the east village. I'm sorry I—"

Mor brightened.

"I remember. But I thought you were just a little girl . . . Of course! Excuse me. It flies." He stepped back. "Come in. I was just making some tea. Don't mind the litter."

She followed him through one curiously furnished room and into another. There, he cleared a chair for her and turned his attention to a boiling pot.

"It's terrible . . ." she began.

"It will wait until tea is ready," he said sternly. "I do not like terrible things on an empty stomach."

Nodding, she seated herself. She watched the old sorcerer, as he put out bread and preserves, as he brewed the tea. There was a trembling in his hands. His face,

52

always deeply lined, was now unnaturally pallid. He had been correct, though, in that he had not seen her for years—she had been but a small girl when he had last stopped by for dinner, on his way to or from someplace. She recalled a surprisingly long conversation. . . .

"There," he said, setting a plate and a cup on the table beside her. "Refresh yourself."

"Thank you."

Partway through the meal, she began talking. The story poured out in disjointed fashion, but Mor did not interrupt her. When she looked at him, she realized that some color had returned to his cheeks and the hand that held his cup seemed steadier.

"Yes, it is serious," he agreed when she had finished. "You were right to come to me. In fact—"

He rose and slowly crossed the chamber to stand before a small, dark mirror set within an iron frame.

"—I had best look into it immediately," he finished, and he passed his fingertips near the glass and muttered softly.

His back was to her and his right shoulder partly blocked her view of the glass, but she saw images dance within the exposed portions, and something like a section of a strange skyline appeared in the upper right quadrant, a vaguely disturbing silhouette circling above it. The entire prospect seemed to rush forward then, and she could not tell what it was that Mor was now regarding. Changes in lighting seemed to indicate several more scene shiftings after that, but she could not distinguish the details of subsequent images.

Finally, Mor moved his hands once again, across the face of it. All action fled, and darkness filled the glass like poured ink.

Mor turned away and moved back to his seat. He raised his teacup, sipped, made a face and dashed its tepid contents into the fire. He rose and prepared fresh tea.

"Yes," he repeated when he had returned and served them. "It is very serious. Something will have to be done about him. . . ."

"What?" she asked.

He sighed.

"I do not know."

"But could not you, who banished the demons of Det—"

"Once," he said, "I could have stopped this changeling easily. Now, though . . . Now the power is no longer in me as it was in the old days. It is—too late for me. Yet, I am responsible in this."

"You? How? What do you mean?"

"Mark is not of this world. I brought him here as a babe, after the last great battle. He was the means whereby I exiled Pol Detson, the last Lord of Rondoval, also then a child. It is a strange feeling—knowing that the man we got in exchange is now a far greater menace than anything we had feared. I am responsible. I must do something. But what, I cannot say."

"Is there someone you could ask for help?"

He touched her hand.

"I must be alone now—to think," he said. "Return to your home. I am sorry, but I cannot ask you to remain."

She began to rise.

"There must be *something* you can do."

He smiled faintly.

"Possibly. But first I must investigate."

"He said that he would come back for me," she persisted. "I do not want him to. I am afraid of him."

"I will see what can be done."

He rose and accompanied her to the door. On the threshold, she turned impulsively and seized his hand in both of hers.

"Please," she said.

He reached out with his other hand and stroked her hair. He drew her to him for a moment, then pushed her away.

"Go now," he said, and she did.

He watched until she was out of sight amid the greenery of the trail. His eyes moved for a moment to a patch of flowers, a butterfly darting among them. Then he closed and barred the door and moved to his inner chamber, where he mixed himself powerful medicines.

He took a quarter of the dosage he had prepared, then returned to the room where he had sat with Nora.

Standing before the iron-framed mirror once again, he

repeated some of his earlier gestures above its surface, as well as several additional ones. His voice was firmer as he intoned the words of power.

Some of the darkness fled the mirror, to reveal a dim room where people sat at small tables, drinking. A young man with a white streak through his hair sat upon a high stool on a platform at the room's corner, playing upon a musical instrument. Mor studied him for a long while, reached some decision, then spoke another word.

The scene shifted to the club's exterior, and Mor regarded the face of the building with almost equal intensity.

He spoke another word, and the building dwindled, retreating down the street as Mor watched through narrowed eyes.

He gestured and spoke once again, and the glass grew dark.

Turning away, he moved to the inner chamber, where he decanted the balance of the medicine into a small vial and fetched his dusty staff from the corner where he had placed it the previous summer.

Moving to a cleared space, he turned around three times and raised the staff before him. He smiled grimly then as its tip began to glow.

Slowly, he began pacing, turning his head from side to side, as if seeking a gossamer strand adrift in the air. . . .

X

Dan turned up his collar as he left the club, glancing down the street as he moved into the night. Cars passed, but there were no other pedestrians in sight. Guitar case at his side, he began walking in the direction of Betty's apartment.

Fumes rose through a grating beside the curb, spreading a mildly noxious odor across his way. He hurried by. From somewhere across town came the sound of a siren.

It was a peculiar feeling that had come over him earlier in the evening—as if he had, for a brief while, been the subject of an intense scrutiny. Though he had quickly surveyed all of the club's patrons, none of them presented such a heavy attitude of attention. Thinking back, he had recalled other occasions when he had felt so observed. There seemed no correlation with anything but a warm sensation over his birthmark—which was what had recalled the entire matter to him: he was suddenly feeling it again.

He halted, looking up and down the street, studying passing cars. Nothing. Yet . . .

It was stronger now than it had been back at the club. Much stronger. It was as though an invisible observer stood right beside him. . . .

He began walking again, quickening his pace as he neared the center of the block, moving away from the corner light. He began to perspire, fighting down a powerful urge to break into a run.

To his right, within a doorway—a movement!

His muscles tensed as the figure came forward. He saw that it bore a big stick. . . .

"Pardon me," came a gentle voice, "but I'm not well. May I walk a distance with you?"

He saw that it was an old man in a strange garment.

"Why . . . Yes. What's the matter?"

The man shook his head.

"Just the weight of years. Many of them."

He fell into step beside Dan, who shifted his guitar case to his left hand.

"I mean, do you need a doctor?"

"No."

They moved toward the next intersection. Out of the corner of his eye, Dan saw a tired, lined face.

"Rather late to be taking a walk," he commented. "Me, I'm just getting off work."

"I know."

"You do? You know me?"

Something like a thread seemed to drift by, golden in color, and catch onto the end of the old man's stick. The stick twitched slightly and the thread grew taut and began to thicken, to shine.

"Yes. You are called Daniel Chain—"

The world seemed to have split about them, into wavering halves—right and left of the widening beam of light the string had become. Dan turned to stare.

"—but it is not your name," the man said.

The beam widened and extended itself downward as well as forward. It seemed they trod a golden sidewalk now, and the street and the buildings and the night became two-dimensional panoramas at either hand, wavering, folding, fading.

"What is happening?" he asked.

"—and that is not your world," the man finished.

"I do not understand."

"Of course not. And I lack the time to give you a full explanation. I am sorry for this. But I brought you this way years ago and exchanged you for the baby who would have become the real Daniel Chain. You would have lived out your life in that place we just departed, and he in the other, to which you now must go. There, he is called Mark Marakson, and he has become very dangerous."

"Are you trying to tell me that that is my real name?" Dan asked.

"No. You are Pol Detson."

They stood upon a wide, golden roadway, a band of stars above them, a haze of realities at either side. Tiny rushes of sparks fled along the road's surface and a thin, green line seemed traced upon it.

"I fail to follow you. Completely."

"Just listen. Do not ask questions. Your life does depend upon it, and so do many others. You must go home. There is trouble in your land, and you possess a power that will be needed there."

Dan felt constrained to listen. This man had some power himself. The evidence of it lay all about him. And his manner, as well as his words, compelled attention.

"Follow that green line," the man instructed him. "This road will branch many times before you reach your destination. There will be interesting sideways, fascinating sights, possibly even other travelers of the most peculiar sort. You may look, but do not stray. Follow the line. It will take you home. I— Wait."

The old man rested his weight upon his staff, breathing deeply.

"The strain has been great," he said. "Excuse me. I require medication."

He produced a small vial from a pouch at his waist and gulped its contents.

"Lean forward," he said, moments later.

Dan inclined his head, his shoulders. The staff came forward, issuing a blue nimbus which settled upon him and seemed to sink, warmly, within his skull. His thoughts danced wildly, and for a long moment he seemed trapped in the midst of an invisible crowd, everyone babbling without letup about him.

"The language of that place," the man told him. "It will take awhile to sink in, but you have it now. You will speak slowly at first, but you will understand. Facility will follow shortly."

"Who are you? What are you?" Dan asked.

"My name is Mor, and the time has come for me to leave you to follow that line. There has to be an exchange of approximately equivalent living mass if the transfer is to be permanent. I must depart before I lose one of the qualifications. Walk on! Find your own answers!"

Mor turned with surprising energy and vanished into the rippling prospect to the right, as if passing behind a curtain. Dan took a step after him and halted. The shifting montage that he faced was frightening, almost maddening to behold for too long. He transferred his gaze back to the road. The green line was steady beneath the miniature storms.

He looked behind and saw that the glittering way seemed much the same as it did before him. He took one step, then another, following the green line forward. There was nothing else for him to do.

As he walked, he tried to understand the things that Mor had told him. What power? What menace? What changeling step-brother? And what was expected of him at the green line's end? Soon, he gave up. His head was still buzzing from the onslaught of voices. He wondered what Betty would think when he failed to show up at her place, what his father would feel at his disappearance.

He halted and gasped. It only just then reached the level of realization that if this strange story were true, then Michael was not his father.

His wrist throbbed and a small, golden whirlwind rose, to follow him, dog-like, for several paces.

He shifted the guitar case to his other hand and continued walking. As he did, he was taken by a small pattern in the mosaic ahead and to his left—a tiny, bright scene at which he stared. As he focussed his attention upon it, it grew larger, coming to dominate that entire field of vision, beginning to assume a three-dimensional quality.

Coming abreast of it, he saw that it had receded without losing any of its distinction. A side road now led directly toward it, and he realized that he could walk there in a matter of minutes.

He saw bright green creatures playing within a sparkling lake, blue mountains behind them, orange stands of stone rising from the water, serving as platforms upon which they rested and cavorted before diving back in again, brilliant sunlight playing over the entire prospect, giant red dragonflies wheeling and dipping above the lake's surface with amazing delicacy of motion, floating flowers, like pale, six-pointed stars. . . .

He found his feet moving in that direction. The call of the place grew stronger. . . .

Something yellow-eyed, long-eared and silver-furred passed him on the right, running bipedally, nose twitching.

"Late again!" it seemed to say. "Holy shit! She'll have my head, sure!"

It looked at him for an instant as it went by, its glance sliding past him along the way to the lake-scene.

"Don't go there!" it seemed to yell after him. "They eat warmbloods alive!"

He halted and shuddered. He looked way from the lake and its denizens, sought the green line, located it, returned there. By then, his informant was out of sight.

He tried to keep his eyes on the line as he continued, avoiding the sideshows as much as possible. It took an unexpected turn after a dozen paces, and he felt as if he were moving downhill for a time. Something like a red skateboard, bearing a large green scarab beetle, streaked by him. From time to time, he seemed to hear a chorus of voices singing something he could not distinguish.

He walked down this branch, and a piece of the action to his right seemed to beckon after his gaze. This time, he resisted, only to discover that the green line curved in that direction. A side road grew there as he advanced, and it seemed to lead on toward a forest.

The downhill sensation continued, and a breeze seemed to be blowing toward him. It smelled of leaf mold and earth and flowering things. He hurried, and the scene moved toward him at more than a reciprocal pace. The tiny storms began to diminish underfoot, the green line was widening. . . .

Suddenly, he heard bird-notes. He reached out and touched a tree trunk. The green line lost itself amid grasses. The world widened into a single place of forest and glade. The stars went out overhead, to be replaced by blue sky and clouds, crisscrossed by leafy boughs. He looked behind him. There was no road—only, for a moment, what seemed a golden strand of webbing, tossed by the wind toward his right, gone.

He began walking across the glade. Abruptly, he halted. He could wander lost for a long while if this were a sizable wood, and he had a feeling that it might be.

He removed his jacket, as the day was pleasant enough, placed it upon the trunk of a fallen tree, hoisted himself up and sat upon it. Better to stay right where he was until some plan of action suggested itself. This spot might in some way be significant as the terminus of his peculiar journey.

He opened the case to check on his guitar, which seemed intact. He raised it and began strumming upon it as he thought. It sounded all right, too.

He might locate a tree that looked more climbable than the giants which surrounded him, he decided, and see whether he could spot a town or a road from higher up. He looked about, without breaking his rhythm. Yes. That appeared to be a good one, a few hundred meters right rear. . . . He faced forward again and almost missed a beat.

The tiny creature which cavorted before him looked exactly like what it was—a centaur colt. Its small hands moved in time with the rhythm, and it pranced.

Fascinated, he turned his attention to what he was playing, switching to a more complicated righthand style. Softly, he began singing. His wristmark grew warm, throbbed. Shortly, two more of the small creatures emerged from the woods, to join the dancer. As a number of leaves blew by, as he felt they must—as he had half-consciously willed it—he caught these in the net of his playing and swirled them about the laughing child-faces, the rearing pony-bodies. He drew birds to spin after them, and a deer he had somehow known was present to join in the movements which were now taking on a pattern. The day seemed to darken, as he willed it—though it must only have been a cloud passing over the sun—to transform the spectacle into a twilit scene, which somehow struck him as most appropriate.

He played tune after tune, and other creatures came to join in—bounding rabbits, racing squirrels—and somehow he knew that this was right and proper, exactly as it should be, in this place, with him playing, now . . . He felt as if he might go on forever, building walls of sound and toppling them, dancing in his heart, singing . . .

He did not become aware of the girl until sometime after her arrival. Slim and fair, clad in blue, she appeared beside a tree, far to the left of the clearing, and stood beneath it, unmoving, watching and listening.

When he did notice her, he nodded, smiled and watched for her reaction. He wished to take no chance of frightening her away, making no sudden movements. When she returned his nod, with a small smile of her own, he stopped playing and placed the instrument back in its case.

The leaves fell, the animals froze for an instant then tore off into the woods. The day brightened.

"Hello," he ventured. "You live around here?"

She nodded.

"I was walking the trail back to my village when I heard you. That was quite beautiful. What do you call that instrument? Is it magic?"

"A guitar," he answered, "and sometimes I think so. My name is Dan. What's yours?"

"Nora," she said. "You're a stranger. Where are you from? Where are you going?"

He snapped the case shut and climbed down to the ground.

"I've come a great distance," he said slowly, seeking the proper sentence patterns, locating words with some hesitation, "just wandering, seeing things. I'd like to see your village."

"You are a minstrel? You play for your keep?"

He hauled down his coat and shook it out, draped it over his arm.

"Yes," he said. "Know anybody who needs one?"

"Maybe . . . later," she said.

"What do you mean?"

"There have been a number of deaths. No one will be in a festive mood."

"I am sorry to hear that. Perhaps I can find some other

employment for a time, while I learn something of this land."

She brightened.

"Yes. I am sure that you could—now."

He picked up the guitar case and moved forward.

"Show me the way," he said.

"All right." She turned and he followed her. "Tell me about your homeland and some of the places you've been."

Best to make something up, he decided, something simple and rural. No telling yet what things are like here. Better yet, get her to talking. Hate to start out sounding like a liar . . .

"Oh, one place is pretty much like another," he began. "Is this farming country?"

"Yes."

"Well, there you are. So is mine. What sorts of crops do you grow?"

They came to the trail and she led him downward along it. Whenever a bird passed overhead, she looked upward and flinched. After a time, he found himself scanning the skies, also. He was able to direct the conversation all the way into town. By the time they got there, he had learned the story of Mark Marakson.

XI

The old man in the faded blue robe walked the streets of the drowsing city, past darkened storefronts, parked vehicles, spilled trashcans, graffiti that he could not read. His step was slow, his breathing heavy. Periodically, he paused to lean upon his staff or rest against the side of a building.

Slowly, light began to leak through the dark skyline before him, a yellow wave, rising, putting out stars. Far ahead, a shadowy oasis beckoned: trees, stirred by the faintest of morning breezes down a wide thoroughfare.

His stick tapped upon the concrete, more heavily now, as he crossed a side street and negotiated another block with faltering steps. His hand trembled as he reached out to grasp a lamppost. Several vehicles passed as he stood swaying there. When the street was clear, he crossed.

Nearer. It was nearer now, the place where the boughs swayed and the songs of birds rose in the early morning light. He strode clumsily ahead, the faintest of blue flickers occasionally dancing at the tip of his stick. The breeze brought him a weak, flower-like aroma as he bore toward the final corner.

He rested again, breathing heavily, almost gasping now. When he moved to cross this street, his gait was stiff, awkward. Once he fell, but there was no traffic and he recovered and staggered on.

The sky had grown pink beyond the small park which now lay before him. His staff, from which the final light had faded, swung clumsily through a patch of flowers which closed immediately, undisturbed, behind it. He did not hear the faint hiss of the aerosols as he crossed the fake

64

grass to slump against the bole of a standard model midtown park area tree, but only breathed the fragrance he had hoped might be there, smiling faintly as the breezes bore it to him, eyes following the dance of the butterflies in the still fresh light of the new-risen sun.

His staff slipped from his fingers and his breath came short and rushed as unnumbered mornings past joined with this one to smear all colors and smells into a greater reality which finally told the story he had always wondered at, through to its vision past objects. One of the butterflies, passing too near on its beam, was overtaken by his life's final throb, to settle, fluttering, upon his upturned wrist near to the dragonmark it bore.

With a blare and a rattle, the city came alive about him.

XII

Strange feelings came and went. Each time that they came they were a little stronger; each time they departed some residuum remained. It was difficult to pin them down, Dan thought, as he drove a peg into a fence post, but perhaps they had something to do with the land itself—this place that felt so familiar, so congruent to his tastes. . . .

A cow strayed near, as if to inspect his work.

No, go that way, he willed. *Over there*, and his wrist felt warm, as with power overflowing, spilling from his fingertips, and the cow obeyed his unspoken command.

. . . *Like that*, he decided. *It feels right, and I get better at it all the time.*

A peg shattered under a hammer blow and a splinter flew toward his face.

Away! he commanded, without thinking.

Reflex-like, something within him moved to stop it, and the fragment sped off to the right.

. . .*And like that.*

He smiled as he finished the work and began collecting his tools. Shadows were growing across the pasture as he looked back along the lengths of fencing he had repaired. It was time to wash, to get ready for the dinner, the performance.

For three days now he had stayed at Nora's uncle's place, sleeping in the barn, turning his hand to odd jobs the old man had been unable to get to. In that time, his familiarity with the language had grown, just as Mor had said it would, almost as if he were remembering. . . .

Mor . . . He had not thought of him for a time. It was as if his mind had locked away the entire experience of his journey to this place in some separate, off-limits compartment. It was just too bizarre, despite the fact that he walked where he now walked. But now, the effects of distancing made him cast back, examining that magical walk, wondering how his absence was being taken in his own world. He was surprised to find that his own past, now, was beginning to feel dream-like and unreal. Whereas this land . . .

He drew a deep breath. This was real, and somehow it felt like home. It would be good to meet more of the neighbors.

As he cleaned the tools and stored them in their places, he thought about the evening's steer roast at the field in toward town. Real country living this, and he was enjoying it. He could think of worse places to be stuck for life. And afterwards, of course, he would play for them. . . . He had been itching to get his hands on his guitar all day. There seemed peculiar new effects—para-musical, as it were—that he could manage in this place, and he wanted to experiment further. He wanted to show these things off, for the neighbors, for Nora. . . .

Nora. He smiled again as he stripped off the heavy workshirt belonging to her Uncle Dar and walked back to bathe in the creek before donning his own garments. She was a pretty little thing. It was a shame to see her so frightened by the local inventor of a few mechanical toys. . . .

And if this—Mark Marakson—were indeed Michael's son . . . He could almost see some genetic factor operating both in the aptitudes and the total lack of appreciation for possible reactions to their operation. Too bad he wasn't back home and in the business. He and Michael would probably have gotten along well.

But, as he washed the sweat and dust from his body, another thought came to trouble him. Why was he here? Mor had spoken with some urgency, as if his presence were a necessary thing. For what? Something involving Mark's creations. He snorted. It did seem to have been something of the sort, mentioned only in the vaguest of terms. But what mechanical menace could a society this simple turn out in a single generation? And why call upon *him* to combat it? No. He felt under-informed and the subject of an enigmatic old man's alarmist fantasies. But he did not feel victimized. When he got his bearings, he would learn more about this place, though he already felt it to be in many ways preferable to the society from which he had strayed. Why, he might yet become a genuine minstrel. . . .

He dried himself with a piece of rough sacking and donned the loose, long-sleeved white shirt he had worn upon his arrival. He changed back into his black denim tousers, but retained the boots he had been given. They fit him well and seemed functionally superior to the shoes he had worn on his hike between the worlds.

He combed his hair, cleaned his fingernails and grinned at his reflection in the water. Time to get his guitar and meet Nora and her uncle. Things were looking up. He whistled as he walked back toward the house.

There were bonfires and lanterns casting impressive shadows. The remains of feasting were even now being gathered up from about the field. At first, Dan felt as if he should not have had those extra glasses of wine, and then he felt that he should have. Why not? It was a festive occasion. He had met a great number of the villagers, anxious for some diversion after the unpleasant events of several days past, and he had succeeded with some grace in parrying questions concerning his homeland. Now he was ready to perform.

He dallied a little longer, until the bustle had ceased and people began seating themselves about the low hill he was to occupy. The lanterns were moved nearer, encircling it.

He made his way forward then, breaking the circle, mounting the rise, the instrument case a familiar weight in his right hand. There came a soft flutter of applause and he smiled. It was good to feel welcome after only a few days in a new place.

When he reached the top, he removed the guitar from its case and put on the strap. He tuned it quickly and started to play.

Partway through the first tune, he began feeling at ease. The good mood grew within him as he played several more and began singing in his own tongue. Then he attempted the first of a group he had tried translating into theirs. It was well-received, and he swung immediately into another.

Looking out over his audience, he could only distinguish the expressions on the nearest faces—smiling or concentrating—in the lantern light. The listeners farther back were partly hidden by shadows, but he assumed similar attention from their immobility, from their joining in the applause whenever he rested. He saw Nora off to the left, seated near her uncle, smiling.

He broke into a virtuoso number of his own composition, a rousing piece which kept increasing in tempo. He suddenly wanted to show off. He rocked back and forth as he played. A breeze tousled his hair, rippled his garments. . . .

It must not have been the first gasp, which reached him during the first lull. He would not have heard any earlier exclamation over his playing. But there were also murmurs, where before there had been only applause or silent attention. There came an indistinguishable cry from the back of the audience. He looked all about, attempting to ascertain its cause.

Then, "Devil!" he heard distinctly from nearby, and something dark flew past his head.

"The mark! The mark!" he now heard, and a stone struck him on the shoulder.

"Dragonmark!"

He realized that his right sleeve had been drawn back almost to his elbow during the last number, exposing his birthmark. But still, why should it cause such alarm?

"Detson!"

A shock went through him at that last word. He instantly recalled old Mor's telling him that his name was actually Pol Detson. But—

The next stone struck him on the forehead. He dropped the guitar into the case and snapped it shut, to protect it. Another stone struck him. The crowd was on its feet.

He felt a terrible anger rise within him, and his wrist throbbed as it never had before. Blood was running down his brow. His chest was sharply struck by another cast stone.

He stumbled as he attempted to raise the case and turn away. Something struck him on the neck, something sounded against the case's side. . . .

The crowd had begun to move forward, past the lanterns, up the hill, slowly, stopping to grope for missiles.

Away! He was not aware whether he had shouted it or sounded it only in his mind, accompanied by a broad, sweeping motion of his right arm.

People stumbled, fell, tripped over lanterns. All of the other lanterns seemed to topple spontaneously. There were dark shapes in the air, but none of them struck him. The grasses at the foot of the knoll began to take fire. The cries that now came up to him seemed less angry than frustrated, or frightened.

Away!

He gestured again, his entire arm tingling a sensation of warmth flowing through his hand, out his fingertips. More people fell. The flames spread about them.

Clutching his guitar case, he turned and fled down the rear of the hill, leaping over sprawled forms and low fires, his breath almost a sob as he tore across the field, heading toward the dark wood to the north.

The anger subsided and the fear grew as he ran. His last glance back before he entered the trees seemed to show him the beginnings of pursuit. Supposing they fetched horses? They knew their own country and he had no idea where he was headed. There might be all sorts of places where they could cut him off, and then—

Why? he wondered again, dodging about trees, crashing through underbrush, wiping spiderwebs from his face, blood from his eyes. *Why had they suddenly turned on him when they had seen the mark? What could it mean to them?*

After stumbling for the third or fourth time, he halted and stood panting, resting his back against the bole of a large tree. He could not be certain how near his pursuers might be, unable to distinguish other sounds over his breathing and the heavy beating of his heart. But this wild rushing was doing him no good. He was hastening exhaustion in addition to leaving a well-defined trail. To move cautiously, to expend his energies more economically . . . Yes. He would have to proceed differently.

Mor had addressed him as the possessor of some power, and he was not blind to the fact that he had just exercised it in a wild fashion in escaping. Back home, save for mainly playful interludes in smoky, late-night clubs, he had always striven to suppress it, to keep it under control. Here, though, he already had the name of witch or wizard, and if there were some way that that power could serve him further, he was ready to learn it, to use it to the confusion of his enemies.

His thoughts turned to the obvious connection, the mark upon his wrist, as his breathing became more even. Immediately, he felt the warmth and the heightened sense of his pulsebeat.

He continued to dwell upon it in his mind. *What is it, specifically, that I need?* he wondered.

A safe way out of here, to a place of safety, he decided. *The ability to see where I am going and not run into things* . . .

As he attempted to order this, he felt the forces within him stir, then saw the dragonmark clearly, despite the darkness. It seemed to move, brightening, then drift away from his arm to hover in the air before him, glowing faintly.

It passed slowly to the left and he followed it, its pale light dimly but surely illuminating his way. He lost all track of time as he pursued its passage through the forest. Twice, it halted, when he realized how tired he had become. On these occasions, he rested—once, beside a stream, where he drank deeply.

He remembered very few details of that long first night of his flight, save that at some point he realized that his way had taken a turn uphill and that this remained his course until light began to seep through the leaves overhead. With this, a sense of fatigue and time passed came over him, and he began casting about for a place to sleep. Immediately, his firefly dragon veered to the right, heading downhill for what must have been the first time in hours.

It led him among a maze of boulders to a small, rock-shielded dell, and there it hovered. Accepting the omen, he sprawled in the grass. From somewhere nearby, there came the sound and smell of running water:

He fell asleep almost immediately.

When he awakened, it was late in the day. His ghostly guide was gone, he ached in a number of places and he was hungry.

The first thing that he did was to remove his guitar from its case and inspect it for damage. He found that it had come through the night's ordeal intact. Then he sought the water—a small stream, a hundred or so meters to the right of the rocks—where he stripped and bathed and cleaned his wounds. The water was too chill for comfort, so he did not dally there. The sun was already falling fast, and he felt he could continue in relative safety.

Continue? At what point had his flight become a journey? He was not certain. Possibly while he slept. For it did feel now that his glowing guide had been doing more than helping him escape the villagers. Now he felt, intuitively—certainly not logically—that there was a definite destination ahead for him, that his will-o'-the-wisp had been guiding him toward it. He decided to let it continue on, if it would, though first it would be nice to find some food. . . .

He repeated the process which had summoned the guide, and it came again, paler in this greater light, but sufficiently distinct to direct his course. As he followed it, he wondered whether it would be visible to another person.

It led him downhill for a time, and a little after sunset he found himself in the midst of a large orchard. He gorged himself and filled his pockets and all the odd nooks in the guitar case.

The guide led him uphill after that, and sometime during the middle of the night the trees grew smaller and he realized—looking back by moonlight—that had it been daytime, he could have seen for a great distance.

Before much longer, the way steepened, but not before he had caught a glimpse of a large building on a crest ahead. It was not illuminated and it appeared to be partly in ruin, but he had a premonition the moment that he saw it, reinforced by the behavior of the dragon-light. For the first time, the light appeared as if it were trying to hurry him along the trail.

He allowed himself to be hurried. An excitement was rising in his breast, accompanied by an unexplainable feeling that ahead lay safety—as well as shelter, food, warmth—and something else, something undefined and possibly more important than any of the others. He shifted his guitar case to his other hand, squared his shoulders and ignored his aching feet. He even forgot to wish again for the coat he had left behind, when a chill wind came down from the height and embraced him.

* * *

He would have liked to wander about the wrecked hall, surveying some of the more picturesque destruction, but the light pressed steadily ahead, leading him along a back corridor and into what could only be a pantry. The food stored all about him looked as fresh as if it had just been brought in. He reached immediately toward a loaf of bread and stopped, puzzled, his hand blocked by an invisible barrier.

No . . . Not quite invisible. For as he stared, he slowly became aware of a mesh of softly pulsing blue strands which covered everything edible.

A *preservation spell*, came into his mind, as though he had activated a mental recording. *Use the guide to solve it—selectively.*

He tried mentally calling upon the hovering image of his mark for assistance. It drifted back and merged with the original one upon his wrist, the light flowing outward, into his hand. Suddenly, he felt a gentle tugging at it and relaxed and let it move through a series of gestures which finally bore it forward into a gap now apparent in the meshing.

He seized the bread; also, some meat and cheese that were within reach. After he had withdrawn his hand for the final time, he felt the tugging again. Again, he let himself be guided, and this time he saw the gap close, returning to its initial state of taut webwork.

On another shelf, he located some wine bottles and repeated the performance to obtain one.

As he gathered together the meal, he felt a strong urge to depart. He released the light and was pleased to see that it had a route mapped out for him. It led him up a flight of stairs and into a chaotic room which once might have been a library.

He cleared a place on the writing desk and set down his supplies. Then, by dint of intense concentration, he was able to cause his drifting light to hover, successively, over the end of each taper in a heavy candelabrum which he had uprighted and repaired, causing each to spring into flame. He seemed to grow better at such heat-thinking with each effort.

When the room was thus more fully illuminated, he retired his pale guide and seated himself to dine. He noted that the chamber had indeed been a library, many of its books now in disarray upon the floor. As he ate, he wondered whether Mor's language-treatment had extended to the written word.

Finally, unable to contain himself any longer, he rose and retrieved a volume from the clutter. When he got it into the light, he smiled. Yes, he could decipher the runic lettering. This one appeared to be a travel book—though in his world it would have passed for some sort of mythology text. It described the dwellings of harpies and centaurs, salamanders and feathered serpents, it showed pyramids and labyrinths and undersea caverns, accompanied by cautionary notes as to their denizens, natural and otherwise. In the margins were penned an occasional "Very true" or "Hogwash!"

As he read, Dan—*Should he begin thinking of himself as "Pol" now?* he had wondered earlier. *Why not?* he had finally decided. *A new name for a new life. . . .*

As he read, Pol felt his attention being constantly drawn toward the middle shelf across the room to his left. At one point, he put down his book and stared at it. There was almost something there. . . .

Finally, when he had finished eating, he rose and moved

to inspect the shadowy section of shelving. As he did, three faint, red threads seemed to be fluttering at its rear. They were possessed of the same insubstantial quality as the blue ones in the pantry. Was this land—or this place, in particular—causing him to develop a kind of second sight?

He cleared the remaining books from the shelf and stacked them near his feet. Then, slowly, he extended his hand, waiting for a guiding impulse. His left hand trembled at his side. Two hands seemed required then, or just the left. Very well . . . He raised it and advanced it. Then the middle fingers of his left hand caught the lower thread between them and raised it. The index finger hooked the upper strand and drew it downward, twining the two. His right hand was then drawn forward, all fingers and the thumb bunching to seize the tip of the third thread, to wrap it three times counterclockwise about the twisted pair . . .

He drew the bunch down, released it and struck it twice with his left fist.

"Open. Open," he said.

The panel at the rear dropped forward, revealing a hidden compartment. He began to reach and recoiled instantly. There lay another spell, hidden, coiled like a smoky snake, an interesting knot at its tail, designed to trap the unwary. He smiled faintly. It was going to be an intriguing problem. The working out of the previous one had become something of a conscious process as he had labored over it, gaining some small understanding of the thought and effort that had gone into its casting. Moving his left hand cautiously crossbody, two fingers extended, he reached forward. . . .

Later, he sat back at the desk, reading a history of the Castle Rondoval and its illustrious if somewhat eccentric inhabitants. Several volumes of personal observations on the Art were stacked before him, along with his father's journals and notebooks on sundry matters. He read through the entire night, however, before he realized his own connection with the inhabitants of the place. Light had already spilled into the world when he came across a

reference to the dragon-shaped birthmark inside the right
wrists of the children of Rondoval.

But this excitement spent the balance of his energy.
Shortly, he began to yawn and could not stop. His garments became a heavy weight upon him. He cleared a
couch at the room's far end, curled up upon it and was
soon asleep, to dream that he wandered these halls in a
state of full repair and more than a little glory.

*   *   *

During the next afternoon, he ate a large meal and later
solved the spell for a sunken tub on the ground floor,
bringing him water for a bath (diverted, it seemed, from a
nearby river, though he could not understand the twist-
ings of the yellow and orange threads which appeared to
govern its temperature). He committed these things to
memory as he filled and drained the pool repeatedly,
scouring it for his use. Then he luxuriated for a long while,
wondering how Rondoval had come to achieve its present
state of decay, and what had become of the rest of the
family.

As he wandered later, uprighting furniture, tossing trash
out of windows, unscrambling and memorizing a number
of minor spells, he decided to return to the library for one
of the secret books he had thumbed, which had partly
mapped the place.

The books now returned to their shelves, the room
dusted after a fashion, he poured a glass of wine and
studied the materials before him. Yes, there were many
drawings, a number of floor plans, sketches of the place at
various moments in its history and one rough outline of a
vast series of caverns below, across which someone had
penned "The Beasts." He did not know whether to chuckle
or shudder. Instead, in response to an unvoiced desire, a
blue-green thread came drifting by him. He hooked it
with the first joint of the little finger of his right hand,
twined it three times about his glass, tugged upon it twice
with his middle finger accompanied by the appropriate
image-commands, untwined it and dismissed it. Yes, now
it was properly chilled.

Rising he placed the book in the pocket of the dark

jacket he had found in a wardrobe earlier and dusted thoroughly when he saw that it fit him so well. He carried the wineglass with him as he walked out and descended the stair to the main floor. "Beasts," he said aloud, and smiled . . . Images of the villagers hurling stones through the night returned to him. "Beasts," he repeated, making his way to a small storeroom where he had discovered lanterns and fuel earlier.

Walking the dim tunnels, occasionally consulting his guidebook, the lantern in his left hand casting sharp-edged shadows upon the rough walls, he could almost smell the concentration of power ahead. Whenever he looked in that certain way, he could see great multicolored bunches of streamers in the air. Nowhere else had he yet witnessed signs of such massive workings. He had no idea what it represented, other than that it must be something of great importance. Nor had he any notion whether his newly awakened powers could have any effect whatsoever upon it. As he brushed his fingertips against the strands, it seemed almost as if he could feel the mumble of mighty words, echoing infinitely, slowly, along a vast convoluted circuit. If he tried very hard . . .

Several minutes later, he found his way barred by a huge slab of stone. Strands led around it, wrapped it, crisscrossed it. There had to be a spell involved, but he wondered whether he would also need a dozen men with pry bars to dislodge it, once any magical booby traps had been defused. He moved nearer, studying the pattern of the strands. There did seem something of a method to their positioning. . . .

The strands faded as his eyes slipped back into more normal channels of perception. Then he saw what it was that had distracted him. He raised the lantern and moved nearer, to read the inscription he now beheld:

PASS AT YOUR PERIL. HERE SLEEP THE HOR-RORS OF RONDOVAL.

He chuckled. They may be horrors, he thought, but I'm going to need a little muscle in this world. So, by God! now they're *my* horrors!

He set down the lantern and shifted his attention back to the colored strands.

. . .Just like unwrapping a very peculiar present, he thought, reaching forward with both hands.

He felt the tangles of power and began the motions that would unlock them. As he worked, the subaural mumbling returned, growing, intensifying, until words burst into his consciousness and he cried them out at the same time, whipping his hands back from the final threads and taking three timed paces backwards: "Kwathad! . . . Melairt! . . . Deystard!"

The slab shuddered and began to topple away from him. He realized then that the spell must have been infinitely more difficult to lay than it had been to raise. All of that power had had to be channeled from somewhere and bound up here. His own work had been more on the order of figuring out how to pull a plug.

The crash that followed echoed and reechoed until he could not help but be impressed by the enormity of the cavern that must lie behind.

He had snatched up the lantern, covered half his face with his sleeve and squinted until the reverberations and the hail of stone chips had settled. Then he moved cautiously forward, crossing the cracked monolith he had toppled.

He was about to raise the lantern to look around the vast hall, when his new key of vision registered an enormous collection of filaments, like a multicolored ball of string larger than himself, resting just off to his left. Individual strands departed it in all directions before him. He realized that it would have taken ages to work each separate spell and then, in some fashion, join them at this common center. No . . . It had to have been done the other way around . . . He could not yet conceive of the manner of its laying but he'd a sudden flash of insight into its undoing. It, too, could fall like the door before his new skill.

However . . . Could he control whatever he released. A good man had obviously spent a lot of time and energy putting the thing together. Best to have a look around before doing anything else. . . .

He raised the lantern.

Dragons, dragons, dragons . . . Acres of dragons and other fantastic beasts lay all about him, extending far beyond his feeble light. His eyes caught them at another level, also. To each of them extended one strand of the master spell.

He lowered the light. What the hell do you say to a dragon? How do you control one? He shuddered at the thought of releasing any of the slumbering horrors.

Probably wake up hungry, too. . . .

He began to back away.

Clear out. Forget this part of the family heritage. They must have bred tougher Lords of Rondoval in the old days. . . .

As he began to turn away, his attention was caught by a single green filament. Its color was slightly darker than any of the others, and it was also the thickest one in sight, almost twice the size of its mates. *What might it tether?* he wondered.

Suddenly, all the dreamlands he had ever read of or conjured in song, all the fantasy worlds he had ever sculpted of smoke or walked through at bedtime as a child rose before him, and he knew that he could not leave this place without looking upon the prodigy bound by this mighty spell. Turning back, he followed the strand among the massive sleepers, averting his eyes as well as his feet in some instances.

When he reached out to brush the strand with his fingertips, a sound like a crystal bell echoed within his head, "Moonbird . . ."—constantly fading—and he knew that to be the name of the creature toward which he was headed.

"Moonbird," he said, fingers still feeling the pulse of the cord.

Lord, I hear, beyond the depths of sleep or life. Shall we range the skies together, as in days gone by?

I am not the lord you knew, and Rondoval has come upon sad times, he thought back, still brushing the cord.

What matter? So long as there is a lord in Rondoval. You are of the blood?

Yes.

Then call me back from these ghost skies. I'll bear you where you would.

I am not even sure I know what to feed you . . .

I'll manage, never fear.

. . . And then there is the problem of this spell.

Not for one such as—

Pol halted, for he could go no further. His hand had left the strand awhile back, as it seemed tangled on an overhead ledge. For several moments, he had thought it was a huge mineral formation which confronted him—a vast mound of scaly copper bearing the green patina of age. But it had moved, slightly, as he had watched.

He sucked air between his teeth as he raised the lantern. There, there was the great crested head! How huge those eyes must be when opened! He reached out and touched the neck. Cold, cold as metal. Perhaps nearly as tough.

"How low must your fires now be, bird of the moon . . ." he said.

Back to him came a jumbled vision of clouds and tiny houses, forests like patches of weeds . . .

. . . Shall we range the skies together?

The fear was gone, leaving only a great desire to see the huge beast freed.

He moved back to the first place where the strand came within reach again. He touched it as he began to follow it back out.

Patience, father of dragons. We shall see. . . .

. . . And kill your enemies.

First things first.

He followed it back to the ball of plaited rainbows near the entrance. He traced its point of entry into the mass and noted each place where it became visible again at the surface. Would it be possible to tease out this one strand? Could he arouse Moonbird without awakening all the others?

He stared for a long while before he moved, and then his first gestures were tentative. Soon, though, his left arm was plunged past the elbow into the glowing sphere, his fingers tracing each twisting of the thick, green strand. . . .

Later, he stood holding it free, its end twisted about his

finger. He walked quickly back, to stand regarding the drowsing giant once again.

Awaken now, he willed, untwining it, releasing it.

The thread drifted away, shriveling. The dragon stirred.

Even bigger than I thought, he decided, staring into the suddenly opened eye which now regarded him. Much bigger. . . .

The mouth opened and closed in a swallowing movement, revealing spike-like ranks of teeth.

Those, too . . .

He moved nearer.

. . . Must seem bold for a little longer, establish where we both stand right away . . .

He reached out and laid his hand upon the broad neck.

I am Pol Detson, Lord of Rondoval until further notice, he tried to communicate.

The giant head was raised, turned, the mouth opened . . . Suddenly, the tongue shot forward, licking him with a surface the texture of a file, knocking him backwards.

. . . Master!

He recovered himself, dodged a second caress of the tongue and patted the neck again.

Contain yourself, Moonbird! I am—soft.

Sometimes I forget.

The dragon spread its wings and lowered them, drew itself upright, raised and lowered its head, nuzzled him.

Come, mount my back and let us fly!

Where?

Out the old tunnel, to view the world.

Pol hesitated, his courage ebbing.

. . . But if I don't do it now, I never will, he decided. I know that. Whereas if I do, I may be able to do it again one day. And I may need to . . .

A moment, he communicated, looking for the easiest way up.

Moonbird lowered his head fully and extended his neck.

Come.

Pol mounted, located what he hoped was a traditional dragon rider's position, above the shoulders, at the widening base of the neck. He clung with his legs and his arms. Behind him, he heard the vanes stir.

I sense that you play a musical instrument, Moonbird began, as they moved forward (To distract him? No—too sophisticated a concept). *You must bring it next time and play to me as we fly, for I love music.*

That might be novel.

They sprang from the ground and Moonbird immediately located a draft of air which they followed into a broader, higher part of the cavern. The light from the lantern Pol had left on the ground dwindled quickly, and they flew through an absolute darkness for what seemed a long while.

Suddenly, with a rush of cool air, there were stars all about them. A moment later, surprising himself, Pol began to sing.

XIII

Mark rolled out of his bed, drew the purple dressing gown about his shoulders and sat clutching his head, waiting for the room to stop spinning.

How long had it been—four, five, six days?—since the robo-surgeon had worked him over?

He raised his head. The room was dark. The thing which protruded from his left eye socket hummed. Finally, it grew silent and he had vision on that side.

He rose and crossed the meticulously well-kept chamber—all metal and plastic and glass—and regarded himself in the mirror above the washstand. He tapped lightly with his fingertips about the perimeter of the lens case, where it joined his brow and cheekbone.

. . . Still too tender. Impair efficiency to take too many drugs, but I'll need some more to be able to think at all. . . .

He withdrew a container of tablets from a drawer in the stand, gulped two and proceeded to wash and shave without turning on a light.

. . . It does have some advantages, though, especially if you get turned around this way. Must be the middle of the night . . .

He drew on a pair of brown trousers with many pockets, a green sweater, a pair of boots. He opened the rear door of his apartment and stepped out onto the terrace. His personal flier stood on the pad—delta-winged, compact, glassy and light. Mechanical things rose and fell in the distance, some only visible in his left field of vision. He inhaled the fragrance of imported plants, turned, crossed to an elevator hatch, dropped three levels—to a footbridge leading across the road. He crossed there, heading for the surveillance center in the lower, adjacent building.

One of the small, gnarled men, clad in a brown and black uniform, sat before a bank of glowing screens. Whether he actually watched any of them was something Mark could not tell from the rear—one of the reasons he disliked using people except in situations such as this where he had no choice.

As he approached, his optic prosthesis hummed, its lens becoming a greenish color as it adjusted to the lighting. The man straightened in his chair.

"Good evening sir," he said, not turning away from the screens.

. . . *Damned sharp senses these fellows have.*

"Anything to report?"

"Yes, sir. Two surveillance birds are missing."

"Missing? Where?"

"The village, your own—"

"What happened to them?"

"Don't know, sir. They just suddenly weren't there anymore."

"How long ago was this?"

"A little over three hours ago, sir."

"Didn't you try to maneuver any of the others to get a look at what was happening?"

"It was too sudden, sir."

"In other words, nothing was done. Why wasn't I notified immediately?"

"You had left orders not to be disturbed, sir."

"Yes . . . I know. What do you make of it?"

"No idea, sir."

"It has to be a malfunction of some sort. Pull back the others in that area for complete inspections. Send out fresh ones. Wait!"

He moved nearer and studied the appropriate screens.

"Any activity in the village?"

"None, sir."

"The girl has not been out of her house?"

"No, sir. It has been dark for hours."

"I think I may pick her up tomorrow. It depends on

how I feel. Plan B, three birds—two for safety escort. See that they're standing ready."

"Yes, sir."

The small man stole a glance at him.

"I must say, sir. The new eye-thing is most attractive."

"Oh? Really? Thank you," he mumbled, then turned and left.

What had he been thinking? The pills must be starting to work. . . . He wouldn't be in shape by tomorrow. Wait another day. Should he go back and countermand that last order? No. Let it stand. Let it stand. . . .

He wandered down to spot-check a factory, his eye humming its way to yellow.

*   *   *

Lantern-swinging shadows bouncing from his rapid step, the small man passed along the maze of tunnels, occasionally pausing to listen and to peer about abrupt corners. Usually, when he halted, he also shuddered.

It might almost have been easier without the lantern, he thought, back there. And that slab . . . He did not remember that broken slab at the cave mouth.

He thought back upon the scene he had witnessed immediately after awakening. The man acting almost as if he were talking with that monster, then mounting it and flying off, fortunately leaving his lantern behind. Who could it have been, and what the circumstances?

He turned right at the next branching, remembering his way. There seemed to be no sounds, other than those of his own making. Rather peculiar, in the aftermath of such a battle. . . .

When he finally reached the foot of the huge stair, he left the lantern. He moved soundlessly through the darkness, toward some small illumination above. When his eyes just cleared the top step, he halted and surveyed the hall.

"How long have I slept?" he asked of, perhaps, the tattered tapestry.

But he did not wait for a reply.

*   *   *

As the sun pinked the eastern corner of the sky, Moonbird descended slowly to land upon the last steady tower of Rondoval. Pol dismounted and slapped him upon the shoulder.

Good morrow, my friend. I will call you again soon.

I will hear. I will come.

The great dark form leapt from the tower and drifted across the sky, heading for one of the hidden entrances to the caverns. A green strand seemed to connect its shoulder to Pol's still upraised hand. It faded soon to join the other strands of the world, drifting everywhere.

For several moments, he watched the stars fading in the west, wondering at the strange flying things Moonbird had destroyed earlier, wondering even more at the beast's comment, *They had troubled my dreams.*

Turning, with a glance to the sunrise, he entered the tower, to make his way down and around within it, returning to the library which had come more and more to feel like home. He hummed as he walked, occasionally snapping his fingers. He finally felt that he belonged—a member of the magic-working, dragon-riding family which had lived here. He wanted to take his guitar into his hands and sing about it, watching the dust depart the surfaces in each chamber through which he strolled, the furniture move itself about, the debris roll into heaps in corners, the strands of power which controlled these operations attaching themselves to, resonating with, his instrument. Rondoval did actually feel more *his* at this moment than it had at any time before.

When he reached the library, he moved to pour himself a drink, to celebrate. He was surprised to find the bottle empty. He had thought that several inches still remained within it. For that matter, he had thought that some food also remained, though the serving board was now empty.

Shrugging, he headed for the stair. He would charm more out of the pantry. He was ravenous after the night's adventures.

XIV

He had threaded them all through Rondoval; and now, as the day slackened, he was resolved to lie in wait, to learn whether they worked, to see what they snared.

In a small sitting room he had not previously frequented, he seated himself at the center of his web and waited. He had set himself no other chore than thinking during this period, but that was all right. Fine, in fact.

The strands lay all about him, silver-gray, taut. He had strung them throughout Castle Rondoval that afternoon, like a ghostly series of trip wires. He could feel them all, knew where each one led.

By now, he had come to the conclusion that they were not visible to other people under normal conditions. Summoning them, noting them, using them, were all a part of his power—the same power that had led him to this place he now knew to be his home. The others who had dwelled here had also possessed it, along with other knowledge and aptitudes—things about which he was still learning. He wondered about them. . . .

Mor had taken him as a baby, the old man had said, and exchanged him for the real Daniel Chain. If he had been born here and removed at the time of the battle which had so damaged this place, then these depredations had occurred a little over twenty years ago—presuming that time behaved in approximately the same fashion here as it did there. Such being the case, he wondered concerning the cause of the conflict and its principals. All things considered, it would seem that his parents had been the losers and were doubtless now dead.

He wondered about them. There were intact portraits

in various rooms, one of which could have been that of the Lord Det, the author of the journals, the man he judged to be his father. The portraits were untitled, though, and he had no idea at all as to his mother's identity.

His wrist tingled slightly, but there were no signs yet from the strands he had laid. He watched the hallway darken beyond the door. He thought of the world in which he now found himself, speculating as to whether he might have been able to see threads in his own, had he known to try. He wondered what it would have been like to have grown up here. Now, now he felt a proprietory attitude toward the place, even if he did not understand its full history, and he resented the presence of the intruder.

For an intruder there was. He knew it as surely as if he had seen him lurking about. Knew it not just from the fact that everything edible and drinkable which he left about had a way of disappearing, but from dozens of small telltales—suddenly bright doorknobs which he knew to have been dusty, minor rearrangements of articles, abrupt scuff marks in unused hallways. It added up to a sense of the presence of another. Irrationally, he felt as if Rondoval itself were passing him warnings.

And he had worked this spell out carefully, partly by intuition, partly from hints in his father's books. It seemed that everything had been done correctly. When the visitor moved, he would know it, he would act—

Again, the tingling. Only this time it did not pass, and his finger jerked toward a single strand. He touched it, felt it pulse. Yes. And this one led to a ruined tower to the rear. Very well. He caught it between his fingers and began the manipulations, the sensations in his wrist increasing as he worked.

Yes. A moving human body, male, had disturbed his alarm. Even now the thread swelled, pulsed with power, was firmly fixed to the intruder.

Pol smiled. The workings of his will flowed forth along the line, freezing the man in his tracks.

" . . . And now, my friend," Pol muttered, "it is time for us to meet. Come to me!"

The man began descending the tower stair, his movements slow and mechanical. He tried to resist what he realized to be a spell, but this had no effect upon his progress. Perspiration broke out over his brow and his teeth were clenched. He watched his feet proceed steadily down the stair, then along a hallway. He tried catching at door frames and pillars as he passed them, but his hands were always torn free. Finally, they vanished beneath his cloak.

Moments later, he held a long climbing cord, which he hurriedly knotted about his right wrist. He attached a small grappling hook to its farther end and cast it up and out through a high window. He tugged several times upon it, saw that it held. Seizing the cord with both hands then, he began to pray to Dwastir, protector of thieves, as he threw his weight upon it.

Pol frowned. He realized that the other's progress had ceased. He increased his efforts, but the intruder was no longer coming toward him. Rising with a curse, he walked out into the twilit hallway, following the filament, candles flaring as he neared them. It only occurred to him after he had gone some distance that the other might also be some sort of an adept. How else could he have halted in the midst of such a summons as he had received to walk in this direction? Perhaps he should simply call Moonbird, to overwhelm the intruder with sheer force . . .

No. This act of defense, he decided, should be his own, if at all possible. He felt a need to test his powers against another, and the defense of Rondoval seemed as if it should be a personal thing now that he and the place had claims on each other.

He might have missed the small, darkly clad man, had not the angle of the silver-gray strand directed his attention upwards. There, he saw the kicking feet, as if they still strove to walk, as the figure dragged itself upward using armpower alone.

"Amazing," Pol observed, reaching out and touching the strand again. "Halt all your efforts to flee me. Climb back down. Return. Now!"

The man ceased his climbing and his boots grew still. He hung for a moment, began to lower himself. Then, at a point about ten feet overhead, in full if not proper obedience to his order, the man let go the cord at a certain moment of its sway and, heels together, dropped directly toward him.

Pol leaped backward, struck the wall with his shoulder, spun aside. The man struck the floor nearby, fulfilling the order, then began to run.

Recovering, Pol manipulated the strand so that it slipped and caught like a lariat about the other's ankles. The man sprawled.

He moved to the other's side, maintaining the tension upon the filament. The man rolled, a knife appearing in his hand, thrusting toward his thigh. Pol, already alert, danced away, a loop appearing in the strand and twisting itself about the other's wrists, tightening.

The blade fell to the floor and skidded a great distance along it, vanishing from sight in the far shadows. The man's wrists were drawn together as tightly as his ankles. His pale eyes now found Pol's and regarded him without expression.

"I must say you are extremely imaginative in executing an order," Pol remarked. "You take me literally when you choose to and take advantage of every loophole when you do not. You must have some legal background."

The other smiled.

"I have at times been very close to the profession," he said in a soft, almost sweet voice, and then he sighed. "What now?"

Pol shook his head.

"I don't know. I've no idea who you are or what you want. My security as well as my curiosity require that I find out."

"My name is Mouseglove, and I mean you no harm."

"Then why have you been sneaking about here, stealing food?"

"A man must eat—and my own desire for security demanded that I sneak about. All that I know of you is that you are a sorcerer and dragon-rider. I was somewhat reluctant to come up and introduce myself."

"Reasonable enough," Pol observed. "Now, if I knew why you are here at all, I might be in a better position to sympathize with your plight."

"Well, yes," said Mouseglove. "I am, as they say, a

thief. I came here for the purpose of stealing a collection of jewelled figurines belonging to the Lord Det. It was a commissioned thing. I simply had to deliver them to a Westerland buyer, collect my fee and go my way. Unfortunately, Det caught me at it—much as you've trammeled me here—and had me confined to one of the cells below. By the time I managed to escape, a war was in progress. The castle was under attack and the besiegers were about to break in. I saw Det destroyed in a magical contest with an old sorcerer, and I decided that the safest place for me was back in my cell. I lost my way below, however, and wound up in a cavern, where I slept. I was awakened to the sight of you flying off on a great dragon. I left there, came up here, was hungry. I couldn't get at the food in the pantry."

"I don't understand why you remained around at all."

Mouseglove licked his lips.

"I had to check," he said finally, "to see whether the figurines were still about."

"Are they?"

"I couldn't locate them. But from the growth of the trees hereabout, I began to realize that more time than I'd thought had passed while I slept . . ."

"About twenty years, I'd guess," Pol said, freeing Mouseglove's legs. "Are you hungry?"

"Yes."

"So am I. Let's go and eat. If I release your hands, will you use them to help me carry food, rather than try to knife me?"

"I'd much rather knife you on a full stomach."

"That'll do."

Pol untwisted the final loop.

"I'd give a lot to know that trick," Mouseglove said, watching him.

"Let's go to the pantry," Pol said, "and on the way, I want you to tell me how my father died."

Mouseglove rose to his feet.

"Your father?"

"The Lord Det."

"There *was* a baby," Mouseglove said.

"Twenty years," Pol replied.

Mouseglove rubbed his brow.

"Twenty . . . That is hard to believe. I don't see how it could happen."

"You were trapped in a grand sleep spell, along with the dragons. I must have released you when I awakened Moonbird. You had to have been asleep nearby."

They began to walk.

"There *were* dreams of dragons, now you mention it."

He turned and regarded Pol.

"I first saw you in your mother's arms. She burned me when I tried to touch you."

"You knew her?"

"The Lady Lydia . . . Yes. Lovely woman. I suppose I'd best start at the beginning . . ."

"Please do."

They obtained food and drink from the pantry and returned to the library, to spend most of the night talking. When they had finished eating, Pol strummed his guitar absently and listened to the other speak, occasionally pausing to sip from his wineglass. At one point, he struck a chord which made Mouseglove's hair rise and set his teeth on edge.

"*They* killed my parents?" he said softly. "The villagers?"

"I guess there were other people in the army besides villagers," Mouseglove replied. "I even saw centaurs among them. But it was another sorcerer who actually fought Det— Mor, I think he was called—"

"Mor?"

"I believe so."

"Go on."

"I think your mother was in the southwest tower when it fell. At least, that was where she was headed when I saw her with you. You were discovered alone outside the entrance to it. You were taken to the main hall. The troops wanted to kill you. Mor saved you, though, by exchanging you for another child from another place—or rather, he claimed that he could. Did he?"

"Yes. They killed my parents. . . ."

"Twenty years. They'll be older now—perhaps even dead. You could never locate all of them."

"Those who stoned me had the proper mentality—and their recognition of my dragonmark says something."

"Pol—Lord Pol—I don't know your story—where you've been, what it was like, what you've been through, how you came back—but I'm older than you. There are many things of which I am not sure, but one that I've had more opportunity than most to learn. Hate will eat you up, will twist you—more so, perhaps, if there is no longer, really, a proper object upon which to vent it—"

Pol began to speak, but Mouseglove raised his hand.

"Please. Let me finish. It's not just a sermon on good behavior. You're young and I got the impression on the way up here that you had just come into your powers. I've a feeling that this may be a pivotal point in your life. Looking back on my own, I see that there were a number of such occasions. Everyone seems to have a few. It looks to me as if you have not yet given thought to the path you intend to follow. Old Mor seemed, basically, a white magician. Your father had a reputation as one of the other sort. I know that things are never really black or white, pure and simple, but after a time one can usually judge from a preponderance of evidence in which direction a great power has led a person, if you see what I mean. If you start looking for revenge after all these years, at this time in your life—using your newfound powers to do it—I've a feeling you may in some ways be twisted by the enterprise, so that everything you touch later on will somehow bear its mark. I tell you this not only because I fear turning another Det loose upon the land, but because you are young and because it will probably hurt you, too."

Pol was silent for a time. Then he struck a chord.

"My father had a staff, a wand, a rod," he said. "You mentioned earlier that Mor broke it into three parts. Tell me again what he said he was going to do with it."

Mouseglove sighed.

"He spoke of something called—I believe—the Magical Triangle of Int. He was going to banish each segment to one point of it."

"That's all?"

"That's all."

"Do you know what it means?"

"No. Do you?"

Pol shook his head.

"Never heard of it."

"What do you think of my assessment of your position?"

Pol took a sip of wine.

"I hate them," he said, as he replaced the glass. "Perhaps my father was an evil man—a black magician. I do not know. But I cannot learn of his death by violence and be unmoved. No. I still hate them. They responded like animals in their ignorance. They treated me badly when I meant them no harm. And I recently heard the story of another man, who meant them well and perhaps went about things incorrectly, but who suffered greatly at their hands. It is not so easy to forgive."

"Pol—Lord Pol. They were afraid. You represented something they must have had good cause to fear if its memory lingered this long, this strongly. As for the other man, who knows? Could there have been some similarity?"

Pol nodded.

"Yes. I understand that he tried to force something new upon them—new, yet like something which had been rejected long ago. I suppose you are right. Have you more to tell me?"

"Not really. I would like to hear your story, though. It seems only a few days since I saw you as a babe."

Pol smiled for the first time in a long while. He refilled their glasses.

"Very well. I would like to tell someone . . ."

Daylight was trickling into the room when Pol opened his eyes. He had slept on the sofa. Mouseglove was curled up on the floor.

He rose and soundlessly made his way downstairs, where he washed and changed his garments. He headed for the pantry to load a breakfast tray. Mouseglove was up by the time he returned, grooming himself, eyeing the food.

As they ate, Mouseglove asked him, "What are your plans now?"

"A little vengeance, I think," Pol replied.

"I was afraid of that," said the other.

Pol shrugged.

"It's easy for you to say, 'Forget it.' They didn't try to kill you."

"I spent time in the hands of your father's jailers."

"But you admit to attempted larceny here. I wasn't doing a damned thing to them, except providing a free floor show. There *is* a distinction."

"You've made up your mind. There is nothing more I can say—save that I would like to leave, if it is all right with you."

"Sure. You're not a prisoner any longer. We'll make you up a food parcel."

"Just these extra loaves here, and some of those other leftovers would be sufficient. I like to travel light."

"Take them. Where are you headed?"

"Dibna."

Pol shook his head.

"I don't know it."

"A port city, to the south. Here." He turned and drew an atlas from a shelf. "There it is," he finally said, pointing.

"Fairly far," Pol remarked, nodding "A lot of dead country between here and there. I'll take you, though, if you're game."

"What do you mean?"

"Dragonback. I'll fly you down."

Mouseglove paled and gnawed his lip. Then he smiled. "Of course you jest."

"No, I'm serious. I feel indebted for all the information you've given me. I can postpone burning a few fields and barns for a day or so. I'll take you to Dibna if you're willing to ride with me on Moonbird."

Mouseglove began to pace.

"All right," he finally said, turning on his heel and halting. "If you are sure he'll permit the company of a stranger."

"He'll permit it."

They sailed south on the massive back of the coppery dragon, the sun still low to their left, the cool winds of the retreating night making human conversation difficult.

I wish you had brought the musical instrument.

It's a little crowded for it.

That human is somehow familiar. From dreams, I'd say.

*He was tangled in your sleep spell, nearby in the cavern.
He dreamt of dragons, he tells me.*

Strange . . . I almost feel as if I could talk with him.

Why not try?

HELLO, HUMAN!

Mouseglove started, looked down, smiled.

You are Moonbird? he asked.

Yes.

I am Mouseglove. I steal things.

We slept together?

Yes.

I am glad to meet you.

Likewise . . .

The small man relaxed noticeably after that, leaning
back at one point to remark to Pol, "This is not at all as I'd
thought it would be. He seems awfully familiar. Those
dreams . . ."

"Yes."

They watched the countryside dip and rise beneath
them, green wood, brown ridges, blue waters. They passed
an occasional isolated dwelling, traced a track that turned
into a road. There were several orchards, a farmhouse. To
the left, where the land sloped, Pol saw the cluster of
stones where he had slept. His mouth tightened.

Follow the road.

Yes.

The village would be coming up soon. Might as well
take another look, during daylight hours, he decided. Might
even be able to frighten a few people.

Below, he saw a centaur on a hilltop, staring upward.
What was it Mouseglove had said? "I even saw centaurs
among them?"

Dive. Give him a good look.

They dropped rapidly. The centaur turned and ran. Pol
chuckled.

"It's a beginning," he remarked, as they climbed again.

Ahead, Lord. More of the flying things. Let me smash them.

Pol squinted. The dark metallic shapes were circling
over a small area. He looked below.

Aren't there more of them on the ground?

Yes. But those in the air will be easier to get at.

He felt Moonbird's body grow warm beneath him.

But isn't there someone—human—down there with them? It looks like a girl.

Yes.

Even from this height, he could see the color of her hair. . . .

Let's go after the ones on the ground. Be careful not to harm the girl.

Moonbird sighed and wisps of a grayish gas seemed to curl from his nostrils, to be immediately dispersed by the winds.

Humans always complicate things.

Suddenly, they were diving. The scene below enlarged rapidly. Pol was certain now that it was Nora, at the center of a triangle formed by three of the flying things. These seemed more elaborately constructed than those he had encountered in the night. They had landed and were moving—hopping and crawling—along the ground, closing in on her. She, in turn, was using the rough terrain to keep them at a distance, maneuvering so that rocks and stands of shrubbery barred their ways, as she worked her way toward the fringes of the forest. Once she got in among the trees, he decided, she might well be able to elude them. Still, she might not.

He smelled an odor of rotten eggs now, as the results of some internal chemical reaction of Moonbird's seemed to fill the air about him.

Suddenly, Moonbird's wings were extended and his body was assuming a more upright position as he slowed. Pol braced himself. Mouseglove, seated before him, did the same.

The landing was even worse than he had anticipated—a spine-jolting crash that nearly threw him loose from his position. He squeezed with his legs and his knuckles tightened. It was several seconds before he realized that they had come down directly atop one of the devices.

Then Moonbird belched—a moist, disgusting sound, which was accompanied by an intensification of the odor Pol had detected during their descent. Immediately thereafter, he appeared to be regurgitating. A great stream of noxious liquid spewed from his mouth to drench the second machine nearby. It fumed for several seconds after it struck, then burst into flame.

Pol sought Nora. She now appeared to be retreating as much from them as from the final machine. Suddenly, however, she recognized him.

"Pol!"

"It's all right!" he called back, just as Moonbird advanced and began striking at the device which was now bounding about as if attempting to take flight.

The first blow damaged its right wing. The second shattered it completely. By then, however, two more had descended and a third was diving but pulled up and began to circle.

Moonbird belched again and another began to flame. The final one launched itself toward his face.

Pol crouched low, as did Mouseglove, but not so low that he could not see what followed.

Moonbird opened his mouth and raised his forelimbs. There followed a crunching sound, and then he was tearing the wings off the flier.

. . .Not at all good to eat.

He spat. The remains fell before him and began to smolder.

Pol looked up. The one remaining bird was climbing higher and higher.

Chase it?

No. I want to help Nora. Wait.

He climbed down and threaded his way through the wreckage.

"Hi," he said, taking hold of her hand. "What happened? What are they?"

"They're Mark's," she replied. "The same sort of thing that came to save him. He sent them for me. . . ."

"Why?"

"He wants me. He said he'd come for me."

"And you don't want to go to him?"

"Not now."

"Then I think we'd better go see him and straighten this out. Where is he?"

She looked at him, at Moonbird, back at him.

"South, I believe," she finally said, "at a forbidden place they sometimes call Anvil Mountain."

"Do you know how to find it?"

"I think so."

"Have you ever ridden a dragon before?"

"No."

He squeezed her hand and turned.

"Come on. It's fun. This one's named Moonbird."

She did not move.

"I'm afraid," she said. "The last dragons anyone saw were Devil Det's. . . ."

He nodded.

"This one's okay. But let me ask you whether you're more afraid of this Mark guy and his gadgets or a tame, housebroken pet I just rode in on."

She shook her head.

"Where did you find it? How do you control it? Is it true about your being related to the House of Rondoval? You said you were a traveler—"

"Too much. Too long to tell you now."

". . . .Because, if you are of Rondoval—as they said—then that probably *is* one of Det's dragons."

"He's mine now. But I won't lie to you. I didn't before, either. I just didn't know then. Yes, I'm related to that House. I'd like to help you, though. Will you show me where this guy lives? I want to talk with him."

She studied his face. He met her eyes. Abruptly, she nodded.

"You're right. He means harm. Perhaps we can reason with him. How do we mount?"

"Let me introduce you first. . . ."

As the ground dropped away beneath them, Pol leaned past Nora and told Mouseglove, "There's going to be a little detour on the way to Dibna. I want to visit the person who controls these things."

Mouseglove nodded.

"You postponing your revenge, too?" he asked.

Pol reddened.

"Revenge?" Nora inquired. "What does he mean?"

"Later," Pol snapped. "Tell me about forbidden places."

"They are areas containing leftover things from the old days when people still used that sort of equipment.

"They are supposed to be haunted," she added.

"I've heard similar stories," Mouseglove put in. "Seen

some artifacts too, in my line of work. The day you were taken away, I heard Mor speak of some sort of balance. Our world went the way that it did, the one he was taking you to went the other way. The two ways seem basically incompatible, and attempts to combine them are dangerous. I got the impression Det might have been doing something along those lines."

"So Mark could be a greater menace than is immediately obvious?"

"It seems that way."

Pol shaded his eyes and stared ahead, locating the tiny dot the bird-thing had become.

"We seem to be headed in the same direction."

"What revenge?" Nora said.

"I'm not sure. Let it go, huh?" He glowered at the small thief, who smiled back at him. "An intention is less than a deed," he said, "less even than an attempt." His gaze grew unfocussed. He seemed to pluck at something in the air. "You're a fine one to preach," he added, long moments later, as the smaller man clutched suddenly at his chest, "when you've got my figurines inside your shirt."

Mouseglove blanched, then fell into a spell of coughing "I'll deal with you later," Pol said. "I doubt you'll be running off in the meantime. Right now, though, I think I'm beginning to see what Mor meant about a menace when he was bringing me here."

"I can explain—" Mouseglove began.

"Old Mor is the one who brought you to our land?" Nora said.

"Yes."

"That is very interesting. For he is the one I told about Mark when it happened. He seemed ill at the time, though."

Pol nodded.

"He wasn't well."

The character of the land began to shift beneath them. The forest grew thinner. A large river which had followed roughly parallel to their course in the west narrowed, finally passed beneath them and vanished into the southeast. Exposed areas of land were lighter in color now, shading over toward yellow.

The dark speck that was the surveillance flier disap-

peared from Pol's sight far ahead. It was not until afternoon that they encountered more of them. They first saw
several wheeling at a great height far ahead. They dipped
lower and moved in their direction, half a dozen of them.

Pol felt a sudden tension in Moonbird's neck and it
seemed that the dragon began to grow warmer.

More to smash . . .

Wait, Pol instructed. *They don't seem to be attacking. I
think he has sent us an escort.*

Smash escort.

Not so long as they keep their distance.

. . . .Some time later.

Wait.

They continued on until the shape of Anvil Mountain
appeared low on the horizon in the afternoon light. Their
escort had maintained a regular flight about them for
hours, unvarying. As they drew nearer, they saw that
more of the birds patrolled the skies above the flat-topped
height. Below, the land had assumed a bleaker aspect—
yellow, streaked with red, dotted with gray and russet
outcrops of stone; jagged cracks ran in dry, unpatterned
profusion, as on a dropped, earthenware pot; small, scrubby
bushes, wind-twisted, clung to the slopes of hills.

The mountain stood larger now, and they could make
out a skyline atop it—white, green, gray, a reflecting
backdrop to many movements. Pol looked about as they
drew closer and he felt Moonbird stiffen, then change his
course slightly to conform with the movements of the dark
fliers.

*Go where they take us, for they are surely taking us to
him,* he ordered.

Moonbird did not reply, but altered course several times
as they neared the city on the rock, rising and swinging to
the west, beginning a gradual approach to the great flat-
roofed building near the center of the complex. Peering
downward, Pol saw a tall, red-haired man standing upon a
terrace outside what appeared to be a penthouse dwelling.
A flying machine of unusual design rested upon a gridded
landing area behind the structure. A number of man-sized
machines of unknown function moved about in the vicinity.

"More magic," Mouseglove muttered.

"No," said Pol. "Not at all."

He felt Nora's hand upon his arm then, gripping it.

"You know this guy pretty well, don't you?" he asked her.

"Know him? I've been in love with him for years," she replied. "But I'm afraid of him, too, now. He's changed a lot."

"Well, we seem to have a landing clearance. Let's go and talk with him. If you want him to stop bothering you, tell him so and I'll back you up. If you don't, now's your chance to straighten things out."

Down, Moonbird. Land in the clear area.

They descended into a much smoother landing than the previous one. His ears rang faintly as the winds finally ceased whistling about them. He climbed down and assisted Nora to descend. He heard her gasp.

"His eye! It *was* injured!"

Pol turned. The man in the khaki jumpsuit with numerous bulging pockets was now approaching a peculiar device which covered his left eye changing color as he left the shade, becoming a bright, then deep blue. A vivid scar passed down his forehead above it, emerged on his cheek below it. Pol stepped forward to meet him.

"I'm Pol Detson," he said. "Nora wants to talk to you. So do I."

Mark halted at a distance of about two meters and studied him. Finally, he nodded curtly.

"I'm Mark Marakson." He immediately turned to look at Moonbird. "I've never seen a dragon before . . . Gods, he's big!"

He returned his attention to Pol, not even glancing at Nora.

"Detson . . . Magician?"

"I suppose so."

"I don't understand magic."

"I'm still working at it myself."

Mark gestured suddenly, a sweeping motion of his left arm, apparently intended to take in the entire city.

"This I understand," he said.

"Me, too. There's a lot of it where I come from."

Mark rubbed the scar on his cheek.

"What do you mean? Where is that?" he asked.

"We are step-brothers," Pol replied. "Your parents raised me, in a land much like this place you have restored. Excuse me if I stare, but you do bear Dad a very strong resemblance."

Mark turned away, paced several steps, returned.

"You're joking," he said at last.

"No. Really. For most of my life, I bore the name you were given as a child."

"Which is?"

"Dan Chain."

"Dan Chain," Mark repeated. "I rather like that . . . But how could this be? I did learn only recently that I'd been adopted, but this— Too much coincidence! I can't believe it."

"Well, it's true, and it's not entirely coincidence. In fact— Wait a minute . . ."

Pol dug in his hip pocket, withdrew his wallet. He opened it and flipped through the card case.

"Here," he said, stepping forward, extending it. "These are pictures of Mother and Dad."

Mark reached toward him, accepted the wallet, stared.

"These aren't drawn!" he said. "There's a very sophisticated technology involved!"

"Photography's been around for awhile," Pol replied.

The lens brightened as Mark stared.

"Their names?" he asked.

"Michael Chain—and Gloria."

"I— Yes, I see myself in these faces. May I— Have you others?"

"Yes. I have some more further down. You can take those. Just slide them out. Yes, like that."

Mark passed the wallet back.

"What sort of work does he do?"

This time Pol made a sweeping gesture.

"He builds things. Designs them, rather. Much on the order of what you've apparently been doing here."

"I would like to meet him."

"I believe he'd like you. But I was thinking—as I acquired certain recent skills of my own—on the means by which I was brought to this world. It would take more research and some experimenting, but I believe I could learn to duplicate Mor's stunt in transporting me. It's occurred to me that a guy like you might not be happy here—especially after the story I heard—and I wondered whether you might be interested in going to the place from which I came. You might like it a lot better there."

Mark finally looked up from the photos and inserted them into a small thigh pocket. He stared at Nora as if seeing her for the first time.

"She told you what they did to me, to my—stepfather?"

Pol nodded.

"You have my sympathy. I received very similar treatment myself, for different reasons."

"Then you must understand how I feel." He looked again at Moonbird. "Do you have plans for them?"

"At first, I did. But now, no. I can almost understand, almost forgive. That's close enough. The longer I let it go, the less it should bother me. Let them go their ways, I'll go mine."

Mark struck his right fist against his left palm and turned away.

"It is not that easy," he said, pacing again. "For you—a stranger—perhaps. But I lived there, grew up there, knew everyone. I took them a gift. It was rejected under the worst circumstances. Now— Now I'm going to force it upon them."

"You will cause a lot of pain. Not just for them. For yourself, too."

"So be it," Mark said. "They've made their own terms."

"I think I could send you home—a place you'd probably like—instead."

For a moment, Mark looked at him almost wistfully. Then, "No. Maybe afterwards," he said. "Now it's no longer the gift, but its acceptance. In a matter of weeks, I'll be ready to move. Later . . . We'll see."

"You ought to take some time to think it over."

"I've had more than enough time. I've done plenty of thinking while recovering from our last encounter."

"If I could send you back for just a little while—and you rethought it in a different place—you might get a whole new perspective, decide that it isn't really worth doing. . . ."

Mark took a step nearer, lowered his head. His new eye hummed and the lens shone gold.

"You seem awfully eager to be rid of me," he said slowly. Then he turned and looked again at Nora. "Might she be the reason?"

"No," Pol said. "She's known you for years, me for only a few days. There is nothing between us."

"A situation you would probably like to remedy in my absence."

"That's your idea, not mine. I'd like to keep you from making a mistake I almost made. But she can talk for herself."

Mark turned toward her.

"Do you want to get rid of me, also?" he asked.

"Stay," she told him. "But leave the village alone. Please."

"After what they did?"

"They showed you their feelings. They were too harsh, but you'd scared them."

"You're on their side!"

"I was the one who warned you."

". . . And his side!" He gestured at Pol, lens flashing. "Magic! Dragons! He represents everything archaic and reactionary! He stands in the way of progress! And you prefer him to me!"

"I never said that!"

She took a step forward, beginning to reach toward him. He turned away. He waved his right fist in Pol's face.

"I could kill you with one hand. I was a blacksmith."

"Don't try it," Pol said. "I was a boxer."

Mark looked up. Moonbird looked down at him.

"You think that ancient beast makes you invincible? I, too, have servants."

He raised his left hand, peeled back the sleeve. A large control bracelet, covering half his forearm, gleamed in the space between them. His fingers danced upon the studs. The man-sized machines all turned in their direction and began to advance.

Pol raised his right hand. His loose sleeve fell back. The dragonmark moved visibly upon his pulse.

"It is not too late," Pol said, "to stop what I think I see coming."

"It is too late," Mark replied.

One by one, the machines faltered and grew still, some emitting static and strange noises, others ceasing all movement abruptly, without sound. Mark ran his fingers over his controls once again, but nothing responded.

"Dad used to call that my poltergeist effect," Pol stated. "Now—"

Mark swung at him. Pol ducked and drove a fist into his midsection. Mark grunted and bent slightly. Pol caught him on the jaw with a left jab. He'd a chance for a second blow to the other's face but pulled the punch for fear of striking the eye prosthesis. In that off-balance moment of hesitation, Mark swung his entire left arm like a club, his heavy bracelet striking Pol on the side of the head.

Pol fell to his knees, covering his head with both arms. He saw a boot coming and fell to the side to avoid it.

Squash? Burn?

He realized that he had come into contact with the great beast.

No, Moonbird! No!

But a low rumble from the dragon caused Mark to draw back, looking upward, raising his hands.

Vision dancing, Pol saw the strands all about them. That red one . . .

From the corner of his normal eye, Mark saw the fallen man gesture with his left hand. He moved to kick at him again and felt his legs grow immobile. He began to topple.

He struck and lay there, paralyzed from the waist down. As he struggled to prop himself with his arms, he saw that the other had risen to his knees again and was still rubbing his head. Suddenly, there was an arm about his shoulder. He looked up.

"Nora . . ."

"Please, Mark. Say you won't hurt our village, or any of the others."

He tried to pull away from her.

"You never cared for me," he said.

"That's not true."

"The first good-looking stranger comes along you lay your claim and send him to get rid of me. . . ."

"Don't talk like that."

He turned into a sitting position.

"Flee while you have the chance," he said. "Warn the villages or not, as you choose. It will make no difference. I will be coming. I will take what I want. That includes you. What I bring with me will be more than sufficient to deal with a dragon—or a whole family of them. Go! Tell them I hate them all. Tell them—"

"Come on, Nora," Pol said, rising. "There is no reasoning with the man."

He held out his hand. She rose and took it.

"I suppose I would be wise," he said to Mark, "to kill you. But she would never forgive me. And you are the son of the only parents I knew. So you have some time. Use it to reconsider your plan. If you come, as you said you would, I will be waiting. I've no desire to be the villagers' champion. But there is a balance you would upset which could bring great danger to us all."

As he helped Nora to mount Moonbird, he saw that Mouseglove had vanished. He looked about the rooftop, but the man was nowhere in sight.

He climbed up behind her. He looked down at Mark.

"Don't come," he said.

"I feel your magic," Mark said softly. "I will find a way to stop it. It must be a wave phenomenon, tuned by your nervous system—"

"Don't lose any sleep over it."

Moonbird, home!

He felt the great muscles bunch beneath him. Moonbird was running, hopping, gliding. They sailed out over the edge of the roof and began to climb.

"He will not be paralyzed for good, will he?"

Pol shook his head.

"An hour or so. The strands are tangled, not knotted."

"Strands? What do you mean?"

"He's a prisoner inside himself. His body will recover soon."

"He will destroy us," she said.

"He's got quite an impressive base," said Pol, looking down. "You may be right. I hope not."

The sun had begun its long slide westward. Once more, the winds sang about them. Below and behind, Mark's

mechanical servants began to move long before he did. He
had not really paid attention to the third person to regard
him from the back of Moonbird. Now, the shadowy image
of the small man was submerged by the torrent of his hate
for the other, passing altogether into oblivion.

Clouds passed. His lens darkened. The bracelet began
to function once again.

XV

The prototype blue-bellied, gray-backed tracer-bird with the wide-angle eye and the parabola ear followed the dragon-riders north. A series of the larger fliers followed it at well-spaced intervals, to serve as relay points for the spy broadcasts. So far, however, the tracer-bird had not yet gained sufficiently upon its objective that it had anything to transmit. Had it been nearer, it would have overheard portions of the story Pol had recently recounted to Mouseglove. But as it was not, it did not even hear Nora's questions:

"I am surprised that you realized this much of your heritage so quickly, so fully. But even so, Mark has had time to build his strength and you have not. How would you oppose a large flight of those birds, and a mass of the ground machines? And I thought that I saw men back there, too. Or dwarves . . . Supposing he has a large army? Have you any plan at all?"

Pol was silent for a time, then, "There was an instrument of power which had belonged to my father," he said. "With it, I think I might be able to command all of the, uh, resources of Rondoval. If I could get hold of it before Mark begins to move, I would have something formidable to throw against him. I'm still hazy on the geography and the political setup of this land, though. I don't know how much territory and how many population centers he would be moving against, or what the local defense apparatus is. All of the books I have are older than I am. . . . I have maps, too, but I'm not sure what goes where."

"I can show you," she said, "and tell you about it, when we get to the maps."

"But I'll be dropping you in your village."

"No! You can't do that! I'm afraid. He might come for me again. Who would stop him this time?"

"You might not like Rondoval."

"It's got to be better than Anvil Mountain. You don't know any magic that could change him back, do you? To the way he was a few years ago?"

"I don't think any magic can undo what life has done to a person, or a person to himself. I'm sorry."

"I thought you'd say that. The wise folk all seem to talk the same way."

She began to cry softly, for the first time that day. Though it was gaining, the tracer-bird did not hear this either. Pol did, but he was not certain what to say. So he stared ahead and said nothing.

It was dark when they passed above Nora's village and by then Pol had placed his cloak about her shoulders. The stars had come forth in profusion and shone with great brilliance. Pol realized for the first time that he did not recognize any constellations. Moonbird, looking down rather than up, noted the locations of all visible cattle against his return for a late night snack.

*   *   *

He awoke in a dirty room far below ground level. It seemed to be one of the original ancient chambers in the rock, which the new occupants had not yet gotten around to refurbishing. Possibly it had been some sort of store-room. It was full of junk, dust and stale air. This was why he had chosen it. It was far from the throbbing, or even the humming of the great machines, and none of the lesser ones had rattled by. As for the small, long-armed, slope-shouldered men with the low brows—they seemed to avoid this quarter.

He ate some of the food he had brought with him. He secreted the parcel of figurines beneath a trash heap.

. . . Had to leave at this stop, he reflected. Once the kid caught on, it was all over. Damned scary, the way he'd plucked the information out of the air. Good thing there was a distraction . . .

. . . How many days' walk to Dibna? Could take the

better part of a week, he guessed. Therefore, he needed a good supply of food before he set out. . . .

. . .What time was it? Probably the middle of the night, judging by his internal clock. With any luck at all, he'd have the supplies by morning and be ready to move the following night. . . .

He opened the door slightly and stared out upon the dim corridor. Empty. He was out, along it and up a ramp in a matter of seconds. The air grew somewhat fresher as he advanced, but was still warm. Keeping to the darkest ways available, he mounted until he was several stories above the ground. He heard the distant noises of the factories now, the nearer ones of servant machines passing on mysterious errands.

He stepped out beneath stars. There was that low structure he had not investigated earlier, some illumination within it now. Off to the left and standing higher was the building from which he had descended that afternoon. Yes. There was the bridge above the avenue by which he had crossed over. . . .

He had seen Pol and Nora fly off, heading back to the north. Good that they had gotten free. He wished them no ill, particularly at the hands of that tall, red-haired man with the glowing eye. He had a fear of something even worse than magic should he fall that one's prisoner, and he resolved to avoid him at all costs.

They may keep the food someplace around here. . . .

He was attracted again by the small, dimly lighted structure. It was probably not a supply house, but it might be prudent to know what it was—situated in such a prominent position—in case any threats resided there.

He moved nearer, circling to place a blank wall between his advance and whoever was inside. His tread was soundless. He was alert for trip-wires, sentries.

Finally, he touched the gray wall, slid his hand along it, flattened himself and waited a moment. Then he edged his way to the corner, peered around it, passed beyond it, moved toward the window near the door.

Nothing. The view was blocked by some sort of equipment. He dropped and passed beneath it, hastily passed the door. He tried the next window.

Yes. There were two men, off toward the right, rear, seated before what appeared to be a group of glowing windows which he knew did not penetrate the wall. But the angle was too sharp here, and the window through which he peered was closed.

He passed on, turned the next corner, advanced even more cautiously toward an opened window. Reaching it, he dropped to one knee and looked in toward the right.

He heard an occasional voice, though it took him several moments to realize that the figures within were not speaking. The words seemed to emerge from the wall before them. He squinted, he concentrated, he breathed a few words to Dwastir.

Suddenly, he recognized one of the scenes on the wall. The peripheral screens held strangely accented aerial views of countryscape, not unlike some over which he had passed earlier on dragonback. But the central one, toward which the two men were leaning, showed, in much sharper detail, the library at Rondoval, where he had spent so many hours. It was as if he were peering in through the end windows. There was Pol at the desk, candles flickering near at hand, a number of books opened before him. Nora was dozing on the couch.

Abruptly, he realized that the larger of the two men viewing the screen was Mark Marakson. He fought an impulse to flee. Both men seemed too involved with the display to be exceptionally wary. So, checking about him periodically, Mouseglove continued to stare. The men's attitudes, the surreptitious quality of the enterprise, both convinced him he must be witnessing something important.

Time slipped by, with Pol occasionally muttering something about the points of a triangle. Once or twice, this drew a sleepy reply from Nora.

An hour, perhaps longer, passed before Pol spoke again. He was smiling as he looked up.

"A pyramid, a great labyrinth and the Itzan well," he said, "in that order. That's the Triangle of Int. Nora?"

"Mm?"

"Can you find them for me in the big atlas?"

"Bring it here." She raised herself upright and rubbed

her eyes. "I've never been anyplace far, but I always liked
geography. What were they, again?"

Pol was rising, a book in his hands, when the view was
suddenly blocked by a movement of Mark's.

Mark half-rose to scrawl something on a writing sheet,
which he folded and inserted into one of his pockets. Pol's
and Nora's voices had resumed, partly muffled now. Mark
leaned forward, moving his face close to the screen.

"I've got you," he said softly. "Whatever the weapon
you seek to use against me, you shall not have it. Not
when I have three chances—"

His voice broke. He raised a hand as if to cover his
eyes, forgetting for a moment the red lens that he wore.

"Damn!"

He turned away and Mouseglove ducked quickly, but
not before he had glimpsed the screen and what might
have been an embrace.

*   *   *

Moonbird drowsed, riding a thermal to a great height,
then dropping into a long glide. When he lowered the
night-membrane over his eyes, he saw another thermal,
like a wavering red tower, ahead and to his left. Uncon-
sciously, he shrugged himself in that direction. He'd a full
belly now, and it was pleasant just to drift home, watching
the dreams form in the other chamber of his mind.

He saw himself bearing the young master and the lady
across a great desert, heading toward a mountain that was
not a mountain. Yes, he had passed that way once before,
long ago. He remembered it as very dry. He saw a gleaming bird pass and lay an egg which bloomed into a terrible
flower. This, he felt, he should remember.

He glided into the next thermal and rose again. It was
good to be out of the cavern once more. And he saw that
they would be leaving for the dry place tomorrow. That
was good, too. Perhaps he would sleep in the courtyard,
where he could show them the carrier and the saddle
come morning. They would be up early, and they would
be needing them. . . .

Near to the tower's top, he spread his wings and com-

menced a long glide. Somewhere in his dreams, the one
with the strange eye moved, but he was difficult to follow.

*   *   *

The sun was already high when Pol finished packing the
gear. Again, Nora's argument that she would be in greater
danger alone than with him prevailed. He packed two
light blades, along with the food, extra clothing, blankets
. . . No armor. He did not want to push Moonbird to the
limits of endurance, or even to slow him with more than
the barest of essentials. Besides, he had learned to fence
in a different school.

How did he know? he wondered, hauling the parcels
out to the carrier the great beast had located for him.

Crossing the courtyard, he placed his hands upon
Moonbird's neck.

How do you know what is needed?

I—know. Now. Up high. Look!

The massive head turned. Pol followed the direction of
its gaze.

He saw the small, blue-bellied, gray-backed thing upon
the sill overhead. It was turned as if watching them. A
portion of its front end caught the sunlight and cast it
down toward them.

What is it?

Something I do not know. See how it watches?

*It must be something of his. I wonder how much of my
plans it has learned?*

Shall I upchuck firestuff upon it?

No. Pretend that it is not there. Do not look at it.

He turned and crossed to the castle, entering there. He
had come upon a description of an effect in one of his
father's volumes and had been meaning to try it when he
had the time.

He hurried up the stair, to halt outside the library
where Nora sat sketching some final maps. Peering in, he
saw that she wore a pale tunic, short gray breeches, a
metal belt and sturdy boots she had located in one of the
upstairs wardrobes. Her hair was bound back by a black
strap.

She looked up as Pol entered.

"I am not entirely finished," she said. "There's another page."

"Go ahead."

She completed a drawing she had been making, took up another writing sheet, turned a page, began another map. She glanced up at Pol and smiled. He nodded.

"Soon," she said.

She worked for several minutes. Finally, she sighed, closed the book and took up the papers.

"Would you step outside for just a moment, please?"

"Your voice sounds strange."

"Yes. I talked too much. Please."

She crossed to the door. He waited beside it. His face was expressionless. She paused.

"Is something wrong?" she asked.

"No. Go out."

His lips, now that she looked closely, did not seem to move in proper time with his words. She passed through the doorway and halted. In the corridor, Pol stood off to the right, fingers to his lips.

"How?"

"This way," he whispered, taking her hand.

She followed him.

"It is a simulacrum spun of magical strands, my likeness laid upon it. I don't know how long it will last. Maybe all day, maybe only a little while." He began gesturing, slowly at first, then more rapidly. Something took shape between his hands, a faint glow to it. "This one is yours," he said. "It will go back in there and keep mine company, to distract the spy device, while we depart. He's been watching us. I want as good a lead as possible."

Later, Nora seemed to stroll back into the room, taking the hand of Pol, who still stood beside the door. They crossed slowly to a pair of chairs and sat facing one another.

"Lovely weather."

"Yes."

Periodically, one of them would rise and walk about the room. There were a number of things they would do, together and apart, taking perhaps an hour before the sequence began again.

The prototype blue-bellied, gray-backed tracer-bird followed their every step, hung upon their words. It did not turn away at the noises below, or as Moonbird rose above the flagstones, drifted over the far wall, pivoted on the point of a breeze, bore east and vanished.

* * *

As the night progressed, Mouseglove had slowly come to feel as if he were a prisoner. Despite several near-disasters, he had remained undetected, gradually enlarging his mental map of the area and developing an awareness of the city's peculiar defenses. But he could find no way off of Anvil Mountain. The perimeters of the plateau were extremely well-patrolled, both by the small men and the half-mechanical caterpillars, as well as being subject to the scrutiny of fixed mechanical eyes and those of the circling birds. It seemed that not even an insect could pass undetected.

Picking lock after lock, he had finally located stores of foodstuffs and transferred what he judged a sufficient quantity to his hiding place. He memorized every niche, every unfrequented passage he came upon. With a thief's eye, he studied the various fixed detection devices from a distance and finally close up, coming to appreciate their functions and some of their weaknesses.

It was only by chance—chance, and Mark's immediate decision to bolster his combat forces above the level he had formerly felt adequate—that Mouseglove happened upon a newly formed ground school for the preliminary training of pilots for a series of manned fliers on which production had been stepped up.

Lying flat on the roof, blocked from overhead detection by an angled air duct, he could hear the words and view the training machine through a grating he had exposed by removing a small panel.

He listened to the entire lecture. When it was over, he had convinced himself. If he could audit just a few more sessions, he would be willing to steal a flier by night and take his chances in the air. Short of finding a hidden tunnel through the rock itself, it seemed the only way to manage an escape.

Feeling a grudging respect for the red-haired man who

had brought this city back to life, he returned to his quarters to rest until evening when he intended spying upon the surveillance center once again and later breaking into the classroom to study the trainer's controls at closer range.

Following a full meal, he slept deeply; one hand upon his dagger, a stolen grenade he knew was some sort of weapon beneath the other.

*   *   *

Statue-like, an old female and two young stallions stood on a crag in the midst of a stand of dwarf pines, regarding Castle Rondoval.

"There is nothing out of the ordinary," she said.

"I saw lights last night, Stel, and I heard noises. Bitalph, in the south, did report a dragon."

"The place is probably haunted," she said. "Enough has gone on there."

"And what of the dragon?" asked the younger stallion.

"If one has come awake, it will be dealt with—eventually—by those it most oppresses. It could also be a foreign beast."

"Then we should do nothing?"

"Let us watch here, a day and a night. We can take turns. I've no desire to enter the place."

"Nor I."

It was much later in the day that they saw the dragon rise and drift eastward.

"There!"

"Yes."

"What do we do now?"

"Alert the others. It may never return. But then, again, it may."

"It appeared that there were two riders."

"I know."

"You were there on the day of the battle, Stel. Was that one of the old dragons of Rondoval?"

"All dragons look alike to me. But the riders . . . One of them looked like Devil Det himself, younger and stronger than I ever saw him."

"Woe!"

"Alas!"

"Go and spread the word among the folk. And we had best talk with the men of the villages, and with old Mor."

"Mor is gone. A Wise One—Grane—said that he walked the golden road and will not return."

"Then things are becoming difficult. Go! I will investigate further."

"You would enter the castle yourself?"

"Go! Do as I say! Now!"

The youths obeyed her. They knew the look in her eye, and they still feared her hoofs.

*   *   *

During his evening explorations, Mouseglove was attracted by a series of screams emerging from a small, barred window. Approaching, he ventured one quick glance through the opening, then ducked into a pool of shadow to digest what he had seen and, if possible, to eavesdrop.

The first impression had shaken him. But upon reflection, he wondered whether the small man in the reclining chair had indeed been covered with snakes. The black things did seem overlong to qualify for serpenthood, and their farther ends did all appear to be attached to the large metal box nearby. Also, their movements could have been a result of the man's own thrashings. Mark had stood nearby with a small metal case in his hand, turning something on the face of the unit.

He listened to the shrieks a little longer, wondering for what offense the man might be undergoing discipline. Wondering, too, whether anything was to be gained by remaining, or by venturing another look.

There was silence. He waited, but the cries did not resume. He decided to remain. There came faint sounds of movement from within.

Finally, he could bear it no longer. He rose for another glimpse.

Mark, facing away from the window, was detaching what now appeared to be a series of shiny black ropes from the suppine form, coiling them and placing them in compartments within the large box. The smaller man's eyes were open, staring up at the ceiling. When the last of the leads were removed, he stirred weakly. Mark passed him a glass of something pink and he drank from it.

"How do you feel?" the large man asked.

"Shaky," the other replied, flexing his arms, his legs. "But everything's all right again."

"Did it hurt?"

"No. Not really."

"You screamed a lot."

"I know. Some were blue, but most were red."

"The screams?"

"Yes. And I could smell them."

"Excellent. You were a brave man to volunteer for this, and I want to thank you."

"I was happy to serve."

"Tell me more about it."

"I tasted the colors, too—and the sounds."

"It was a fine mix, then. Pity it only has such a short range. There are all sorts of problems in scaling it up, too . . . I wish I had more time."

"What do you call the—thing that did it?"

Mark hefted the small unit.

"For want of a better name, I call it a jumble box. It smears your sensory inputs, mixes them. Instant synesthesia."

The man gestured toward the huge unit to his right.

"That didn't do it? Just the little one you're holding?"

"That's right. The other just recorded what was happening. If you didn't hurt, tell me why you cried out so much?"

"I—I couldn't understand what was happening. Everything was still there, but it was changed . . . It scared me."

"No pain?"

"No one place that hurt. Just a—feeling that disaster was coming. Most of the time, it kept getting worse. Sometimes, though—"

"What?"

"There were moments of great pleasure."

"You were able to count all right."

"Yes . . . Most of the numbers were yellow. Some tasted sour."

"Did you feel you could have gotten up, walked about?"

"Maybe. If I'd have thought of it. It was hard to think. Too much was wrong."

"You are a brave man, and I thank you again. I will not forget this service. Now, let's test your reflexes."

Mouseglove heard some instruments being shifted about. Silently, he slid off through the night.

                    *   *   *

It was difficult for Stel to place her hoofs quietly on stone and tile unless she moved very slowly. This she did, however, with the patience of a huntress and former commando.

Memories returned to her as she passed through the great hall where she had stood dripping blood and sweat that final day of the battle. Ah! the stallions had had much work that night . . . She recalled the sorcerers' confrontation, and her eyes automatically sought that ruined area of ceiling which had settled Det for good, before he could call upon his hidden powers. Much of the rubble beneath had been cleared for the removal of his body. She recalled how Mor had borne it away into the west. . : .

She paused periodically and stood listening. Her ears pricked forward. There were voices. Somewhere up higher, to the left.

She crossed the gallery, came to the foot of the stair, halted again. Yes, up there . . .

Slowly, keeping near to the wall, she began to climb. The place appeared to be in better condition than she had remembered.

As she made her way along the hall, the voices came louder. To her right now, that third door . . .

She noted that the door was ajar. Approaching, she stopped directly beside it. She heard nothing from within, not even the sounds of breathing. Venturing farther forward, she looked around the corner, then drew back in puzzlement.

The couple had just seated themselves, facing one another—the young man with the white streak through his hair and the slim blonde girl. But . . . These were the same people she had seen departing on dragonback. She had not seen them return. Strange . . .

She looked again.

More than strange . . .

The girl's face seemed to be melting, pieces of it falling, drifting away, decomposing in the air. The man—who still bore a striking resemblance to old Det—seemed totally oblivious to the fact that portions of his left arm and right thigh appeared to be unravelling, as though he were composed of thin strips of cloth wound about nothing.

Fascinated, Stel did not retreat, but stared in frank astonishment as the couple came apart. Finally, she moved forward and entered the room. What was left of the pair paid her no heed whatsoever.

"Lovely weather."

"Yes . . ."

The man's face now began to melt, the girl's garments ran from her body like liquid, drifted in the air currents like strands of silk. Their conversation continued.

". . . Though it could rain."

"That is true."

The man rose to his foot and crossed to the girl.

"You have lovely eyes."

She rose slowly.

Stel watched them embrace, losing larger and larger pieces of themselves every moment, to drift tinsel-like before her, fading from view as they crossed the room.

"I-arrooowarnn . . ."

The words slowed and deepened, the mouths were gone, the hair went up like smoke. Another half-minute, and they had intertwined and vanished. Stel whinnied and backed away. She had never before seen the like of it. Superstitious dreads rose to harry her.

The prototype blue-bellied, gray-backed tracer-bird now focussed its attention upon her as she circled the room, studying it carefully without paying real attention to the opened atlas, as she retreated out the door and into the corridor beyond, her hoofs clattering rapidly as she passed down the corridor.

*   *   *

Mouseglove heard the great doors opening below and made it to an appropriate vantage in time to see the metal

birdforms launched like blown leaves into the dark sky,
where they rose to swirl beneath stars, then assumed a
formation which tightened itself as it wound and unwound,
took its course and passed in a direction he deemed to be
roughly southeast. This troubled him as he made his way
to the surveillance center. He managed the approach once
more and heard Mark within, cursing and giving orders.
The one glimpse he got of the screens showed nothing of
interest.

He did not understand Mark's, "They're gone! More of
that magic, I suppose. That damned centaur had something to do with it! Bring me a centaur!"

Mouseglove decided to leave it at that. Less now than at
any other time, did he desire to fall into the hands of the
ruddy giant the small men treated like a god. As he
backed away, though, the words, ". . . At the triangle's
point!" reached him from within. It would not be until
later, however, that these would set off lengthy trains of
speculation.

Instead, immediate considerations occupied him for the
better part of several hours: Time to get out. Things are
getting more frantic and life gows less certain. The longer
I stay, the worse my chances. . . .

The lock on the training room door barely halted his
stride. Slowly and carefully, his fingertips found the controls in the model cockpit. He was afraid to make a light.

. . . Funny if I can only fly it with my eyes closed, he
reflected. It's scary up there, but it's worse down here.
Anyway, better this than a dragon. What did he say about
this little lever? Oh, yes. . . .

Batteries fully charged, the dark birds fled across the
night, the land, the water.

XVI

East and south. They traveled until fatigue overcame them. Night was rising when they located the island they had marked, and there they slept unmolested. The following day, before the night was fully departed, they crossed over the waters to the land, to sweep above mountains, dwindling rivers, desert. The next night was spent among chilly hills, where Pol reviewed all that he knew concerning their route and destination. The geography here was not congruent with that of his previous world. In that place, the larger land mass he had departed did not even exist, and that over which he was crossing, while similar in places, was not a true match. Distances varied radically between locales which seemed to possess some reconcilability on maps of the two worlds. But they both had pyramids in several places, though the one he sought had the way to its entrance flanked by rows of columns alternating with sphinxes, many of them fallen, damaged, but most still visible. Something in the description he had read seemed to indicate that he should commence his entrance at the end of that way.

*   *   *

The dark birdforms dotted the mountaintops like statues of prehistoric beasts, wings outspread. Had there been an eye to observe them, it might not even have noted their minute, tropism-like pursuit of the sun across the sky as they recharged their batteries for the night's flight.

The day had beaten its way well on toward evening before they stirred, almost simultaneously, as if shaken by a sudden breeze. They began to flex their wings.

123

Soon, one by one, they dropped from the heights, caught the air, rose, found their way, found their patterns, resumed their journey. . . .

*   *   *

Pol's wrist began to itch some time before their goal came into view. He felt that it was not just the now-darkening sunburn, and increased his surveillance of the bright and wavering horizon. Minutes later, a pointed dot resolved itself before him and he licked his dry lips and smiled.

Your internal compass seems to be working fine.

I do not know what you mean.

That seems to be it up ahead.

Of course.

"Nora!" His voice came out as a croak. "I see it!"

"I think I do, too!"

It grew before them until there could be no doubt as to its nature. There were no signs of movement anywhere about the dark stone structure. The plain before it was dotted with columns and statues.

Moonbird took them down near the far end of the approach, and Pol's joints creaked as he alighted.

"I can't persuade you to wait here?" he said, as he helped Nora down.

She shook her head.

"If anything happened to you, I'd be in to investigate later, anyway. Waiting would just defer things."

He turned to Moonbird.

Wish I could take you with—but the entrance is too small.

I will guard. You will play sweet music for me later.

I appreciate your confidence.

Pol turned and looked up the sand-scoured roadway, pylons and beasts converging upon the dark rectangle of the structure's entranceway.

. . . Walking into a vanishing point, he mused.

"Okay, Nora. Let's go," he said.

His vision blurred and cleared again as they advanced. For a moment, he thought it was an effect of the brilliant sunlight or the sudden activity after hours of sitting crouched. Then he saw what he took to be flames pouring forth from the opening before them. He flinched.

Nora took hold of his arm.

"What is it?"

"I—oh, now I see. Nothing."

The flames resolved themselves into great billows of what he had come to think of as the weft of the world. He had never seen them bunched so thickly before, save in the great ball in the caverns of Rondoval—and here they were flapping and drifting freely.

"You must have seen something," she said as they continued on.

"Just an indication of sorts, showing a concentration of magical power."

"What does it mean?"

"I don't know."

She loosened her blade in its scabbard. He did the same.

His right wrist, which had not stopped its itching and tingling was now throbbing steadily, as if that special part of him which was best suited to deal with such matters was now fully alert.

He brushed his fingertips across the massed strands and felt a surge of power. He tried to locate some clue as to its nature, but nothing suggested itself.

The rod, the rod . . . he concentrated. Somewhere among you . . .

A pale green strand, like milky jade, drifted toward him, separating itself from the mass. As he raised his hand, it seemed drawn toward his fingertips. Once he touched it, he willed it to adhere and held it, knowing that this was the one.

"Now," he told Nora, advancing to the threshold, "I know the way—though I know nothing of what it will be like."

He entered the narrow passage and halted again. The dimness about them deepened to an inky blackness only a few paces ahead.

"Wait," he said, commencing the mental movements which had summoned the phantom dragon from his wrist the night he had fled her village.

It rose and drifted before him again, exactly as it had on that earlier occasion.

Is this a phenomenon I am destined never to use in the absence of danger? he wondered.

Behind him, Nora drew her blade. His chuckle rang hollowly.

"That is my doing," he told her. "It is our light. Nothing more."

"I believe you," she said, "but it seems a good time to have a weapon."

"I can't argue," he replied, beginning to move once again, following the pale thread through the new light.

They came to a flight of steps where they descended perhaps ten meters, the air growing pleasantly cool, then clammy about them. From the foot of the steps, passages ran to the right, the left and straight ahead. The thread followed the one before them. Pol followed the thread.

After several paces, the passage began to slant downward, its angle of steepness seeming to increase as they continued. The air was thick now, and stale, with a scent of old incense or spices buried within its dampness.

The light danced before him. The walls vanished. At first, he thought that they had come to another set of side passages. As he willed his light to brighten and move, however, he saw that they had come into a room.

He sent the dragon-light darting before him, outlining the chamber, revealing its features. The walls were decorated with a faded frieze, the ceiling was cobwebbed, the floor dusty. At the far end of the room was a stone altar or table, a band of carvings about its middle. A dark rectangle stood behind it. The strand at Pol's fingertips ran directly across the block of stone and vanished into the shadowy oblong.

Pol listened but heard nothing other than their own breathing. He moved forward, Nora at his side, their footsteps muffled. For him, the air was alive with strands, as if they passed through a three-dimensional web woven of rainbows. Still, the milky green strand could not be lost. Eyes open or closed, he knew precisely where it hung.

They separated to pass around the altar, and Pol increased his pace to reach the small doorway first, duck his head and pass within, a mounting feeling of anticipation hinting at some climax beyond its threshold.

The light shot in before him and, on his willed command, rose to a level above his head and increased in brilliance.

This room was smaller than the outer one and it, too, possessed something resembling a low altar at its farther end. Flanking this was a pair of stone or stuffed jackals, eyes fixed forward. A great mass of the strands, all of them of the darker shades, were woven into strange patterns about the altar and the jackals. No doorway was visible behind this carved block, but rather a tall, shadowy figure, roughly man-shaped save for its head which resembled those of the jackals. Something small and glowing rested upon a dark green cushion atop the stone before it.

Pol swept his arm backward, halting Nora.

"What do you see?" he asked her.

"Another table and two statues," she said. "Something on the table . . ."

"According to the description and the sketch, that appears to be what I'm after," he said. "I want you to wait here while I go and try to take it. I expect to meet some sort of resistance and I'll probably have to improvise. All those braided areas look menacing."

"Braided areas? What do you mean?"

"There is some sort of spell protecting it. You stand guard while I find out what it does."

"Go ahead. I'm ready."

He took a single step forward. A pulse of light raced about the loops, the knotted junctions, leaping from figure to figure. He took a second step.

Hold, came a command he was certain that Nora could not hear. It seemed to beat upon him from the sudden vibrations of all the strands, passing down them from the shadowy figure behind the stone.

Why? he sent back immediately, deciding that it was no time to be shy.

He halted, to see what the reaction would be. The figure actually seemed to deliberate for a moment. Then,

You approach a thing I guard, presumably to remove it, it replied. *I will not permit it.*

You refer to the section of rod on the stone before you?

That is correct.

I confess that I would like to have it. Does your charge permit you to make any sort of deal whatsoever for it?

No.

Pity. It would make life so much simpler for both of us.

I see that you are a young sorcerer, but recently come to the Art. If you were to live, you would probably become a great one. If you depart immediately, you will have that opportunity. I will let you go unmolested.

Pol took another step forward.

That is your answer?

I'm afraid so.

The jackal-headed figure raised its right arm, pointed a finger. The hovering dragon-light went dark. Pol felt a shock in his wrist. His vision seemed unimpaired, however, as if he viewed the chamber in the light of all the strands.

"Pol! What happened?" Nora cried.

"It's all right," he said. "Stay put."

He decided against resummoning the glowing image. That did not seem terribly imaginative, and it would probably just be put out again. It seemed that some measure of variety and originality should govern in these matters.

He sent the power that throbbed in his wrist out along the jade strand, causing the rod-section itself to begin glowing where it lay upon the table of stone. He pictured himself turning a lamp switch for a three-way light bulb, willing more wattage, raising the glow. The chamber brightened on a mundane level.

"Better?" he asked Nora.

"Yes. What is happening?"

"A conflict seems to have begun—with the forces which guard here. Hold on."

Young man, do you think you are the first to come here, to seek the rod?

The figure raised both arms, spreading them. The light Pol had summoned trebled in intensity. Dim forms, which he had taken for rubble—on the floor, in corners, near the statues—were suddenly clearly illuminated. He saw many strewn bones. He counted four skulls.

All those who came remained.

Pol felt his fingers twitch toward a yellow strand, but he suppressed the impulse to seize it. It drifted nearer. He knew that his magical sense was showing him a weapon, and for the first time he overrode it—his reason telling him that its employment had better be a matter of careful timing.

The strand doubled and redoubled, looping back upon itself, hovering near his shoulder.

Uh—is it possible, Pol inquired, edging forward, *simply to borrow it and bring it back later? I've an excellent guitar I could leave for security—*

This is not a pawnshop! I am a guardian and you are a thief!

That is not true. It belonged to my father.

There came another pulse of light, and the beast to his right and ahead began to move, slowly at first, taking a step toward him. The other blinked and twitched its ears.

Now it belongs here, came the reply.

Pol reached up and seized the bunched yellow strands. With a jerk and a burst of power that ran along his arm, he tore them down and back, then brought them forward like a lash across the face of the advancing beast. It snarled and cried, drawing back, and he struck again. The third time that he hit it, it cringed, lowering its belly to the floor. At that moment, he noticed that the second jackal was about to spring.

Even as he turned and drew back his arm, he realized that he would not be able to strike in time. . . .

*   *   *

Moonbird's view of the west was partly blocked by the pyramid, so that he did not see the bird-things dark against the brilliant sky until their van was near. Several began to dive as he raised his head, but they pulled up sharply and continued on.

Then he saw the falling object, and superimposed upon it came the image out of his dream. He spread his wings immediately to take to the air.

By the time the bombs struck, he was fifteen meters above them and climbing. He felt the heat building within his stomachs. Above him, he counted eight of the fliers. Good, he acknowledged. He had been waiting for an opportunity to meet them when he was unencumbered with passengers.

The bright flames were faded to smoke beneath him. Above, the formation had already begun its turn. Extending his neck and plowing the sky with his wings, he rose to meet them.

*   *   *

. . . And as he turned to strike at the leaping form, Pol saw Nora's blade fall upon it—a two-handed, overhead blow that landed upon its right shoulder behind the neck. Crying out, the creature twisted, giving Pol the opportunity to sidestep and bring his magical whip lashing soundlessly down upon it.

He moved ahead and to the right as it fell, writhing to the floor. The strands of his yellow weapon cut it again, across the face. Nora had withdrawn her blade and moved back to heft it for another swing. . . .

Continuing his advance into a position very near to the altar, he brought his whip-arm out and around to deliver another, heavier blow. . . .

He was almost pulled from his feet as the figure at the back of the altar extended its arm and seized the falling strands that he wielded. At that moment, it seemed that the ground shook beneath him.

The strands were torn from his grip as his momentum sent him spinning, catching at the edge of the stony table. Realizing where the fall was bearing him as he plunged before that awesome presence, and certain that its next move would be to extinguish his life if he did not act immediately, he reached out with his right hand and seized the section of rod that rested on the cushion nearby. It responded with the immediate surge of energy he had felt might be present, a force his new sensitivity recognized as utilizable.

He turned the end of the rod upward the moment he caught hold of it, channeling the power from its manifold

connections into a white, flame-like burst of power that
shot against the animal-headed figure's inclined breast.

No!

He saw it driven backward even as he slipped to the
floor. From his hand, the glow of the rod still illuminated
the entire chamber.

Rolling to the side, he saw that both jackals lay still
nearby. He felt Nora's hand take hold of his left arm,
helping him to his feet.

"You're all right?"

"Yes. Yourself?"

"Yes."

He looked back. The strands still billowed about the
stone, but were now in total disarray, their patterns undone. The shadowy figure was far dimmer but seemed in
the process of reassembling by attraction several portions
of itself which had dispersed. He held his new weapon
before him and backed away, Nora at his side.

When they reached the doorway to the next chamber,
they turned and fled through it. Rounding the altar, they
continued on. The air seemed much dustier here than it
had been earlier. When they had mounted the stair and
were traversing the forward passageway, a crashing sound
came to them from outside.

Racing toward the light, they emerged to view a crum-
pled flier beyond the first column to their left. There were
two large craters ahead and to the right. One statue was
upset and broken and a column had fallen across the way.
Farther along, there were two more wrecked fliers.

Pol heard a sound from overhead and looked upward.
There was nothing in view in the sky. Turning, he then saw
that two more of the birds were shattered against the side
of the pyramid. As he stared, another circled into and out
of view above that mountain of stone. Since Moonbird was
no longer where he had left him, he was not surprised,
moments later, to see his great green and bronze form
wheel into view over the top of the monument. Two of the
fliers then came into sight, circling, diving at the dragon.
As their positions continued to shift, Pol saw that there
was a third. He thought, too, that he detected an occasional puff and the echo of a small report from the ma-

chines. If they did have guns, they at least did not appear
to be rapid-fire automatic weapons. Their main tactic seemed
to consist of darting attempts to slash at their larger,
slower opponent with their spear-like beaks and the fore-
edges of their wings. They were closing with him again
even as Pol watched.

Not knowing what he might be able to do at this distance, he sought strands. They seemed to be everywhere,
just awaiting the proper act of discernment and manipulation
. . . Indeed! They became visible to him—an orange trail
leading upward. He reached for them and they drifted
toward him, along with an enormous feeling of separation
and the formula for electrical resistance, which he had
learned one summer while working for his stepfather. He
took this as an indication that he was not going to be able
to do much to help Moonbird. Then the rod-segment
jerked in his hand and he wondered. He studied it for the
first time in full light.

It was of a light, heavily tarnished metal—possibly an
alloy of some sort; and if so, far too technologically sophisticated for anything he had seen here, save for Mark's
creations—and this seemed old, felt old, as his special
sense measured things. It was about eight inches long and
opened at one end, presumably to accommodate the succeeding section; its other end was a simple hemisphere,
possibly of a different metal. About the shaft itself was
chased a pattern of stylized flames within which a rich
variety of demons danced and engaged in peculiar acts.

He raised it—it seemed that it might be some sort of
magical battery, or transformer—and, with a rapid twisting motion, he twined an orange strand about it. Nora,
who had been about to speak, realized from his gesture
and his intent expression that he was conjuring and she
remained silent, eyes fixed upon the shaft.

Suddenly, the distance seemed telescoped, and he found
himself working with the far end of the strand, weaving,
looping, turning it into a wide net before a diving flier. To
affect something of that mass and velocity, at that distance,
he realized that an enormous amount of power would have
to flow upward. He felt it go out of him as he willed it, and
the rod jerked within his grip.

The flier sped into the trap he had attempted to lay, and it did not seem impeded by it. It rushed on toward Moonbird's flank, as Pol felt weak from willing energy into his snare.

Then, all at once, it veered crazily—one wing held high, the other low. It seemed frozen in that position, spinning ahead, slowing in a dropping, drooping trajectory that bore it beneath the dragon, turning until it was headed downward. It rotated all the way to the ground, where it stopped. Even before it struck, another followed it, blazing, target of Moonbird's fiery regurgitations.

Pol turned his attention to the final flier, which suddenly seemed bent upon a suicide attack on the lazily turning skybeast. He knew that no time remained for the slow knottings of another spell, and he doubted that from this distance he could release an effective blast such as that which had felled the guardian in the pyramid. And even as he raised the rod for the attempt, he saw the small white puff and moments later heard the report.

Moonbird showed no sign of having been hit, however, and as the bird-thing plunged toward him, he moved to meet it, twisting in a serpentine fashion, acquiring more speed than the moment seemed to offer. As they met, he clasped the flier to him and began his descent.

Nora and Pol watched him spiral downward in a leisurely fashion, coming to rest near the rim of a nearby crater, turning so as to land directly atop the captive flier with a series of crunching noises which ceased only when he moved away from the broken device, which a final nudge sent toppling and sliding into the hole.

Well-fought, great one, he said. *You were injured . . . ?*

Hardly at all. And dragons heal quickly. You have the thing you sought?

Yes. This is it.

He displayed the piece.

I have seen it before, joined with the others. Gather your things, come mount me and let us be on our way to wherever you would go now.

You should rest after such a struggle.

A dragon rests on the wing. Let us leave this place if we are finished here.

Pol turned to Nora.

"He is able to go on now. How about you?"

"I'd like to get out of here myself."

He looked at her for the first time in a long while. Dishevelled and moist with perspiration, she still clutched the blade in her right hand. But he saw no signs of injury.

Noting his regard, she relaxed her grip on the weapon and sheathed it. She smiled.

"All right?"

"All right. Yourself?"

He nodded.

"Then let's get our stuff together and move on. Have you any idea how he knew we'd be here?"

"No," she said. "You say that the things he does are not really magic—but they do seem that way to me. It's just that he has a different style."

"I hope you like my style better."

"So far," she said.

As Moonbird lifted them above the desert and bent his course northward, the skies were clear and the sun had already begun its western plunge.

Land where you would to forage, Pol told him. *Once we hit the northern sea, we'll be island-hopping—and the maps are not all that good on distances.*

I have been this way before, Moonbird told him. *I will feed in time. Now, will you make some music to warm my cold reptilian heart?*

Pol unearthed his guitar, tuned it and struck a chord. The wind whistled accompaniment as the land unrolled like a dry and mottled parchment beneath them.

XVII

That night, as they lay listening to the sound of waves and breathing the smell of the sea on a small island far from the mainland, Moonbird sought sustenance far afield and Nora studied the rod from the pyramid.

"It does have a magical look, a magical feel to it," she said, turning it in the moonlight.

"It is that," Pol replied, stroking her shoulder, "and the other two pieces should do more than just add to its potency. Each should multiply the power of those which precede, several times."

She put it aside and reached out to touch his wrist.

"Your birthmark," she said. "They weren't really wrong—the villagers. You *are* of that tribe with your feet in hell and your head in heaven."

"No reason to throw rocks," he said. "I wasn't doing anything to them."

"They'd feared your father—once he got involved in blood sacrifices and the treating with unnatural beings who had to be paid in human lives."

Pol shrugged.

". . . And they took his life to balance accounts. Also, my mother's. And they wrecked the place. Didn't that pretty much square things?"

"At the time, yes—as I understand it. But you stirred up fears as well as leftover hatred. Supposing you'd come home to avenge their deaths? You did have that in mind, too, didn't you? That's what that Mouseglove person said."

"Not at the time, though. I hadn't even realized who I was when they attacked me. But it made it easier for me to hate them when I did learn."

"So, in a way they were right."

Pol took the rod into his hands and stared at it.

"I can't deny it," he said, finally. "But I didn't follow through on it. I've harmed none of them."

"Yet," she said.

He turned onto his side and glared at her, the covers slipping from his shoulder.

"What do you mean 'yet'? If I'd been that serious about it, it would have been my first order of business."

"But you still dislike them."

"Wouldn't you, in my position? So far as I'm concerned, they're not very likable people. And if they'd handled Mark a little differently, they probably wouldn't have him on their backs."

"They are quick to react to the unknown. Theirs is a settled way of life—traditional, slow to change. They saw both of you as threats to it and acted immediately to preserve it."

"Okay. I can see that. But I can understand something without liking it. I've called off the feud I almost declared on them. That should be enough."

"Only because you've got a bigger one on your hands. You know that if you don't destroy Mark he's going to destroy you."

"I have to operate under that assumption. He's given me every indication. The time is past for trying to talk with him."

She was silent for a long while.

"So why aren't you like the others?" he asked. "You were a friend of his and now you're hanging around with a dark sorcerer—helping me, in fact."

She remained silent. Then he realized that she was crying softly.

"What is it?" he said.

"I'm a pawn," she answered in a low voice. "I'm the reason you got involved—you were trying to help me."

"Well—yes. But sooner or later Mark and I would have met, and the results would probably have been the same."

"I'm not so sure," she said. "He might have been more inclined to listen to you if it hadn't been for me. But he was jealous. You might have become friends—you have much in common. If you had—think what an alliance that might have been—a sorcerer and a master of the old science arts—both out for revenge on my homeland. Now that cannot be, and the wheels are turning to bring you into a struggle to the death. Supposing I really hated you both? It wouldn't make a bit of difference—now."

"Do you?" he asked.

". . . And I'd be damned if I'd tell you."

"You wouldn't have to sleep with me. Once those wheels are in motion a roll in the hay wouldn't alter them."

"It might make the winner more disposed to leave us alone, out of a certain fondness."

"And telling him about it might have just the opposite effect."

"It's a good thing I'm talking principles and not cases," she replied, touching his shoulder again. "As I said, I do feel like a pawn, though, and you wanted to know why. As for your last question, I was answering it as things could be, not informing you. It was the wrong question, anyhow."

"You're too tough to be a pawn," he said, "and you know who the only woman on the board is. And we can sleep with a sword between us if you want."

"It is not cold steel that I want," she said, moving nearer.

He saw a pale blue strand drifting by, but he ignored it. *Everything shouldn't be gimmicked*, he thought. *Should it?*

* * *

He heard the voices again, in that place where he drifted between sleep and wakefulness.

"Mouseglove, Mouseglove, Mouseglove . . ."

Yes. It was not the first time he had heard them—weak yet insistent, calling to him—and on awakening he always forgot the small chorus. But this time there seemed more strength to the calls, almost as if he might come away with the memory, this time . . .

"Mouseglove!"

He began to remember his circumstances, sprawled in the secret apartment atop Anvil Mountain, unwilling guest of Mark Marakson, a.k.a. Dan Chain, taboo-breaking engi-

neer from the east village. He was trying to find a way out,
past the man's gnome-like legions and electronic spies,
trying to learn to fly one of the small craft—small, yes, not
like the battle-wagons with the six-man crews, two can-
nons and a rack of bombs he had seen take off earlier,
sailing in every which direction across the sky, rotors
whirling, wings tilting all about them—small, just right for
himself and the jewelled figurines which would make him
his fortune. . . .

"Mouseglove!"

He was moved a jot and two tittles nearer awakening yet
still the chirping cries came to him. It was almost as if . . .

He tried. Suddenly, somewhere inside himself, he
answered.

"Yes?"

"We bring warning."

"Who are you?"

Immediately, his dreamsight began to function. He
seemed to stand at the center of a low-ceilinged room,
illuminated by seven enormous candles. A figure, human
in outline, stood behind each of them. The flames obscured the faces, and no matter how he turned or stared,
nothing more of them was revealed to him.

"You sleep with the figures beneath your head," said the
one at the extreme left—a woman's voice—and immediately he knew.

Four men, two women and one of uncertain gender, out
of red metal, studded in peculiar places with jewels of
many colors . . . Somehow, they addressed him now:

"We gained power when the Triangle of Int was unbalanced by the heir of Rondoval," said the second figure—
a man.

"We are the spirits of sorcerers vanquished by Det and
bound to his statuettes," said the third—a tall man.

"We exist now mainly to serve him or his successor,"
said the fourth—a woman with a beautiful soprano voice.

"We see futures and their likelihoods," said the fifth—a
gruff-voiced man.

"We have come into your possession for a reason," said
the sixth—of uncertain gender.

". . . For we can to some extent influence events," finished the man on the right—the seventh.

"What is your warning?" asked Mouseglove. "What do you want?"

"We see a great wave about to break upon this plane," said the first.

". . . At this place," said the second.

"Soon," said the third.

". . . To settle the future of this world for some time to come," said the fourth.

"Pol must be protected," said the fifth.

". . . At this point of the Triangle," said the sixth.

A map was lying before him on the floor. It was actually a part of the floor, he now realized, cunningly inscribed. It seemed that it had been there all along. As he looked, one spot grew light upon it.

"Steal maps, steal weapons, take Mark's flier and go to that place," said the seventh.

"Take Mark's flier?" he asked.

"It is the fastest and is capable of the greatest range," said the first.

"Pol isn't a bad guy," Mouseglove said, "and I wish him no ill, but my intention is to get as far away from him and Mark as soon as I can, as fast as I can."

"Your willing cooperation would make things easier," said the second.

". . . But it is not absolutely necessary," said the third.

". . . As our power rises," said the fourth.

"I've never had booty talk back to me before," Mouseglove replied, "except for a parrot, when I was a lad. But that doesn't count. You're asking too much. I've led a dangerous life, but this was to be my last big risk. You are my retirement security. I want nothing to do with your breaking wave."

"Fool," said the fifth.

". . . To think you have a choice," said the sixth.

"You have walked a charmed line since the day you entered Rondoval," said the seventh.

"We had a part in everything that brought you to this point," said the first.

"Even our theft," said the second.

Mouseglove chuckled.

"If I have no choice, then why do you request my cooperation?" he asked. "No. Perhaps I was manipulated up to this point. Now, though, I think you need my help and your power has not risen sufficiently to insure it. I'll take my chances. The answer is no."

Silence followed. He felt himself the object of intense scrutiny.

Then, "You are shrewd," said the third, "but incorrect. The answer is merely that it would be easier for us with your cooperation. We could devote our energies to other matters than your coercion."

"We can see that you are suitably rewarded," said the fourth.

"Rewards are of no benefit to a dead man," he stated. "No deal."

"You will not like what Mark does to this world," said the fifth.

"I've never been totally happy with it the way that it is," he replied. "But I get by."

"For your own protection then, learn to use the grenades. They practice with them on the southern rim," said the sixth, neutral-voiced.

". . . And get the maps," said the seventh.

"That much I intended anyway," Mouseglove answered. "But I am not going to the place you showed me and do any fighting there."

The candles flickered, the room expanded toward nothingness and his consciousness faded. The last thing that he heard was the sound of their voices, laughing.

*   *   *

Three flying boats approached Castle Rondoval cautiously, guns loaded and swiveling in pace with the vessels' circling movements. As the circles diminished, the first battlewagon discharged a shot across the battlements. At this point, all three were poised to withdraw and regroup in the face of a severe reaction. Nothing however, followed.

The circling continued for the better part of an hour, though no more shots were fired. Finally, the vessels— very close, very low now—broke formation to drift about among the still-standing towers, to hover while their occupants peered through windows and damage gaps in the walls. Slowly, then, one of the three floated to a landing in the main courtyard. None of its occupants emerged immediately, and the other two ships moved above it, guns ready. A quarter of an hour passed, and nothing stirred but the leaves on the trees and a lizard on the wall.

At last, a large hatch at the rear fell open and five small figures emerged, weapons held ready, to rush for cover in five different directions, dropping to earth and remaining motionless as soon as it was achieved. After several minutes, they rose and began to move, entering the castle.

It was over an hour before they emerged, their attitudes more casual, their weapons slung. Their leader signalled to the other two vessels, which immediately began to descend. When they were down, five more individuals emerged from each of them.

The fifteen men stood about, conferring on the building's layout. At last, they returned to the vessels to bring forth heavier weapons for emplacement inside.

Later that afternoon, when Rondoval had been secured, one of the vessels departed, leaving behind a dozen men, one on permanent duty in each of the remaining ships, the other ten set to patrol the castle.

The departing battle-wagon spiraled outward, moving more rapidly than on its inward journey, ship's telescope sweeping the rocky heights and, finally, the forested depths of the vicinity. Still, it was nearly an hour before a small group of centaurs was detected in a distant glade.

The sky boat dropped immediately to a point near treetop-level, out of line of sight of the creatures. It descended into the first clear area it reached, where its engines died and its hatch opened. The five infantrymen emerged, moving away into the trees, the pilot remaining behind with the vessel.

They passed slowly and silently through the forest, having spent basically predatory existences before their present level of culture had been thrust upon them. Now they fanned, like a well-organized hunting team, moving to surround their prey. As they neared the glade, they communicated entirely by a kind of sign language, messages

passing from man to man about the circle they formed.
Taking up their positions, they studied the disposition of
the eight centaurs in the area and commenced a rapid and
elaborate sign discussion as to target assignments. Then
they raised their weapons.

The signal was then passed, and each of the five fired
one round. Five centaurs jerked and bled. Two fell immediately. None of the riflemen paused to reload his single-
shot weapon. Instead, they rushed forward to use the
butts as clubs, only two finally drawing the blades they
wore at their sides. There were only a few cries from the
centaurs, but the smells of sweat and urine were suddenly
strong upon the air.

One of the wounded ones rose unexpectedly, crushing
an attacker's skull with her forehoofs. She was beaten down
along with the three unwounded. The lightest of the unin-
jured had his legs bound together and hands tied behind
him. Three of the remaining attackers slung their weapons
and moved to transport him, the fourth reloading and
covering them.

They bore their burden back through the woods, encountering no resistance. They entered and secured the vessel.
Shortly thereafter, the rotors became shimmering blurs
and the ship rose slowly, took its course and drifted southward, acquiring altitude, its speed slowly mounting as it
passed above the deepening forest.

                    *   *   *

Moonbird flew above the dark, convoluted patterning—a
large, flat design within the field of rock—at the other end
of the long island from the city and its ports. Shadows cast
by the morning's sun broke the scheme in numerous places,
and the entire prospect caused a swimming effect whenever one stared for too long. Pol gestured as if to interrupt
his vision, for countless dark strands now drifted from it,
further blurring, confusing the image.

Some power lies there, beneath the ground, Moonbird
remarked. *This is the place?*

Yes.

Pol scanned the skies carefully, then looked down once
again. There was one break, at the pattern's northern

edge, where the strands billowed like an inkpot dropped
into an aquarium.

*Take us down at that far end, where the stand of trees
comes in like a spear point, nearest to the thing.*

Moonbird slowed and began his descent. Pol strained
forward, studying the terrain. Soon, he saw that the marked
area was an elaborate, monolithic construction, the dark
lines representing a continuous overhead opening presumably running the entire length of many interconnected
interior corridors for purposes of some small illumination.
The structure itself stood perhaps twice his height above
ground level. As they slowed to land, Pol saw the single
pale jade strand he sought among the masses of sable and
ochre lines. A faint bellowing noise reached his ears from
some undeterminable point.

As he touched the ground, Moonbird asked:

Play me one more song.

Do you fear that you will never hear one again?

*Humor an old sauroid servitor. Dragons have their
reasons.*

Very well.

Pol uncased his guitar, not even bothering to dismount.

"What are you doing?" Nora inquired.

"Request performance," he answered, and he began a
long, slow, nostalgic ballad.

Thank you, Moonbird replied, when it was finally concluded. *That was soothing, and you reminded me of a
story that a griffin once told me—*

*I'm afraid that I do not have the time to hear it now.
More of those metal birds with bombs could—*

Did you notice anything special as you sang?

No. What do you mean?

The bellowing sounds. They stopped.

Pol climbed down and assisted Nora in alighting. He
patted Moonbird's neck.

Thanks.

"How to you intend to approach this one?" Nora asked.

"The same way as . . ."

She had barely noticed the twirling motion of Pol's left
hand, two fingers extended, slightly bent. As they moved

near to her face, it felt as if a black bandage were sliding
across her eyes. . . .

Pol caught her as she slumped, bearing her to a spot
beneath the branches of the nearby trees, largely shel-
tered from overhead view.

Guard her while I'm inside, he told Moonbird. *If more
of those things show up, it would be better if you stay
hidden here for so long as you are undetected.*

I can break them.

*But then Nora will be unprotected. No. Only fight if
you are discovered.*

Moonbird snorted and drops of spittle fell upon the
ground and began to smolder.

Very well. I can at least listen to the music.

Pol turned away and approached the high, wide entrance. A snuffling, growling sound commenced somewhere
within—distant or near, he could not be certain. It shifted
about him, moving, growing, diminishing.

The corridor he had entered ended abruptly several
paces before him. There was a lower, narrower opening to
his right and the strand led directly into it.

He halted and hung the guitar by its strap. He began to
play, a slow, lullaby-like tune, into which he poured a
wrist-throbbing desire to calm, to charm any listener. Several strands drifted near and he caught them on the neck
of the instrument and saw them grow taut and begin to
pulse in time with the music.

Slowly, he turned, still playing, and entered the opening.

He found himself in a dim passageway, a narrow band of
sky visible high above him, running like a blue brook to
separate into several tributaries at a place where a number
of corridors met. He stood still for a time, strumming and
humming, letting his eyes adjust to the lesser light. He
realized then that the snorts and snufflings had ceased,
though there was now a sound of heavy breathing all about
him.

He moved forward, following the pale green strand. He
turned right when it did, and left and immediately left
again. Two more paces bore him into a circular chamber,
ten equidistant doorways in its walls, including the one
from which he had just emerged.

His strand led through the one to the immediate right, though another section of it crossed the chamber, stretched between two other doors. He ignored this and followed it to the right.

There came a series of left-right, left-right, then left-left, right-right turns which left him dizzy. He paused to regain control of his music. The sounds of breathing still came heavily about him, filling all the passageways, accompanied now by a strong barnyard odor. A tiny bit of cloud drifted across the blue band above him. Switching to another tune—still languid, dreamlike—he continued on.

After a time, he entered a circular chamber with ten doors, following the strand across it. He felt that it was the same one through which he had passed earlier, because of a familiar pattern of cracks in the wall, but there was no trace of the green strand passing between the adjacent doors across the way.

Then, looking behind him, he realized that the jade strand was shrinking or being gathered before him as he progressed. It was then that it occurred to him that while the force within the object he sought made it easy to describe a spell that would lead him to it, finding his way back out again might be a little more difficult without such a goal.

He ducked and squatted as he traversed a low passage—hell of a place to get caught!—and turned sideways as he negotiated a narrow one. He then entered upon a fresh series of turns, most of them doubling back upon themselves.

How long? he wondered. Surely I don't have to go through the entire thing. . . .

Shortly thereafter, he realized that the breathing sounds had grown louder. And it was not long after that that he entered the long, low hall where the minotaur paced. . . .

*   *   *

Mouseglove leaned forward again. The light in Mark's penthouse had been out for the better part of an hour, yet he had learned by observation that the sometime flashing device which had replaced the man's left eye was capable of very effective night-vision. He was also aware of Mark's restless disposition, of his inclination to pace within his

quarters, to burst suddenly forth and embark upon surprise inspections of his installations, his factories, the bar-
racks, his laboratories, his fields.

Is it better to assume that sleep has claimed him? he
wondered. *He's had a busy day. Still, he's so full of
nervous energy . . . He could come out at any time. Once
he's off and running again, it would be easy. . . .*

More maps than he really needed were folded in the
various pockets of his cloak. The package containing the
seven figurines was there, also. The grenades—about which
he felt even more uncomfortable, having earlier witnessed
their power—hung from his belt, along with one of his
daggers. He carried a parcel containing food and a pistol
he had stolen.

He leaned back behind the duct again and breathed
more deeply of the chill and smoky night air. The longer
he waited, of course, the greater the risk of discovery by
one of the gnomes or machines. He was certain that he
had spotted all of the stationary alarm devices, yet there
were mobile units.

Still, he realized that he could not enter the flier and
secure it about him without making some noise. Even if
Mark were already sleeping, it would be well to let him
drift further along into oblivion.

He looked up at the stars. The moon had not risen.
Good for stealth. Less good for one's first flight. He touched
each grenade. He checked his supplies. He had no intention of being captured. Especially after having seen what
they had done to that centaur they had brought in earlier.
And he was convinced that the poor brute had not even
understood what it was that they wanted to know.

Patience had long been a way of life with Mouseglove.
He commenced massaging major muscles, pausing periodically to listen, to peer about him.

Over an hour went by.

Time, he decided. *The belly of the night. Two hundred
paces now. Slow and steady. Patron of Thieves, be with
me. . . .*

It was time to think of nothing, to be an eye, to be an
ear, to breathe just so, to feel vibrations. The hatch *would*
have to be on the side facing Mark's door. . . .

Twenty more paces, ten . . . What are they burning in those factories, anyway? It bites the nose . . .

He circled the vehicle twice, seeking alarms. Finally, he extended his hand, touched the smooth, cold body of the ship . . .

Now, little man, there is no retreat, he told himself.

He cracked the hatch, drawing slowly and steadily upon it. Silently, it came open. A moment later, he was inside, scanning the rooftop, seeking the hatch's interior handle. There would be an unavoidable noise in closing it. He located the handle and pulled downward upon it until it was only opened a crack. . . .

No!

The door to Mark's apartment banged open and the man himself emerged. Mouseglove's fingers outlined and dug for the pistol within his parcel on the seat beside him. There was not time in which he might take off, no way in which he could flee.

Yet, Mark did not immediately advance. He stood with his thumbs hooked behind his belt, studying the sky, the roof. Could it be that it was only the man's insomnia which had brought him outside?

Mouseglove realized that he was holding his breath. He let it out slowly and took the pistol onto his lap. His left arm was beginning to tremble, from holding the door nearly closed against the tension of its spring.

. . . And don't let it rattle, he appended to his latest prayer.

He located the trigger and raised the pistol. Abruptly, Mark buttoned his jacket and closed the door behind him. He began walking across the terrace.

I'd shoot him. Right now. If I could be sure of getting him. But I've never used one of these things. And already my grip is slippery upon it. I'd take the chance with a crossbow, if I had one. If this door were shut and the window down . . . If . . .

Mark passed within five meters, without even glancing at the flier. Mouseglove, deep within his cowl, crouched, arm aching, watched him go.

It was another ten minutes before he dared to slam the hatch and turn his attention to the controls.

*   *   *

Pol did not permit the music to falter. The man-beast's eyes had passed over him several times as it moved slowly back and forth along the hall. It was well over two meters tall, with dark, curved horns. The room stank. Pol wondered what sort of teeth the creature possessed, with the head of a herbivore and the reputation he was still fresh on from his recent readings. He decided that he was willing to leave the question to sorcerers of a more academic bent. He turned his full attention to his playing.

Only his hands moved. He imagined that he plucked strands extending from the instrument to the horns of the beast. The force that grew within his wrist seemed to flow out through his fingertips, into the guitar, across the distance that lay between them.

. . . *Rest. A nervous life such as yours requires some interlude of peace,* he sent within the song. *Not merely sleep, but the deep, muscle-easing joy of total rest that is almost pain, it is so sweet.* . . .

The minotaur slowed even more, finally coming to a standstill beside the wall. Even its awful breathing slowed.

. . . *Forget, forget the moment. The dream-sights dance already behind eyes that would close. Approach the cloud-strewn border of the land where visions dwell. They beckon.* . . .

The minotaur put out his right hand and leaned upon the wall. His head nodded. He snorted softly, once.

. . . *Go, go to that place. There, skiey towers caressed by cool breezes make sweet the forgetting—and in fields of flowing green you wander. Delight spills across your body like a gentle rain. You bathe in the pools of healing. Bright colors fill your vision. There comes a song that brings you peace.* . . .

The creature knelt, lowered himself to the floor. His eyes closed.

Pol continued to play for a long while. There was little expression upon that sleeping face, other than a certain slackness. And the minotaur's breathing had grown much slower and quieter. For the first time, Pol dared to look away from him, to trace with his eyes the path of the strand he had followed.

The green line led to a niche, high in the wall at the far end of the room. There were several clusterings of the darker strands about it, but these were far less elaborate than those he had encountered beneath the pyramid—and apparently cast where they were mainly for purposes of protecting the faintly glowing cylinder from molestation by the minotaur himself.

Pol moved quietly across the stone floor in that direction, his hands automatically continuing the melody as he studied the knottings of the spells. There were three of them, any one of which might have stopped the minotaur or an ordinary man. Yet, their undoing should take a competent sorcerer no more than—

He glanced back at the sleeping creature as he realized that he would have to stop playing in order to unwind the spells.

He reduced the tempo and strummed more softly.

. . . *Sleep, sleep, sleep* . . .

He stopped and lowered the instrument. His left hand twisted forward. When the first spell was undone, he glanced back and saw that the beast still slumbered.

As he worked on the second one, he heard a noise behind him, but at that moment he could not look away. Finally, it fell apart beneath his hands and he turned quickly, strands dispersing all about him.

The minotaur had only turned in its sleep.

He returned to the consideration of the final spell. It was no more difficult than the others. But he could not rush its untwining for the proper pace was as much a matter of necessity as the appropriate movements. His left hand darted, hooked and twisted. These last strands were colder than the others and, correspondingly, released a greater feeling of heat when they were at last undone.

Again, Pol looked back.

The minotaur's eyes were open and staring at him.

Who are you?

A singer.

What do you want here?

A mere bauble.

The thing in the niche? It bites. Take care.
I shall. You do not mind that I take it?
Why should I? It is nothing to me. Where have I been?
Dreaming.
*I had never been there before. There were bright things
I'd never seen. . . .*
Colors?
*Perhaps. Everything was good. Like never before. I
want to go there again.*
That can be arranged.
I want to dwell there forever.
Close your eyes then, and listen to the music.
The minotaur closed his eyes.
Bring this music and send me away. . . .
Pol began to play, recovering all the visions which had
come to him earlier. As he did, his eyes passed over the
second section of the rod in its niche—longer, narrower than
the first segment, bearing a scene of animals and men and
woodland spirits, free of strife, dancing, eating, loving . . .
He struck the strings, reached out, seized the rod-
section and fitted it into the first at his belt. Then he
resumed playing as the minotaur still drowsed. He felt the
increased warmth, the mightily enhanced sense of power
that now twisted about the rod. As he played, he called
upon it for a new usage and he felt that power move
warmly through his abdomen, down his arm, into the
guitar, to be joined with the music itself.
    *. . . Across the fields, where there is no strife, no hun-
ger, no pain, where no one is a monster, where the light is
soft, where the birds call and the brooks burble, where
twilight comes on bringing stars like swarms of fireflies—to
dwell there forever, never to awaken, never to depart—
sleep, bull-man, in the peace you have never known—
always, ever . . .*
Pol turned away from the sleeper. He touched his wrist
to the new section of the rod. Somewhere, buried in his
unconscious, it seemed that there should be a record of
every step, every turning he had taken on the way in.
Therefore—
The dragon-image rose like a phoenix glowing above his

wrist. Surely, it should be able to reach those buried memories.

Go! he commanded. *I follow!*

It darted away from him, to depart the hall from the doorway nearest the niche, rather than the one through which he had entered.

He hesitated only a moment, then followed, smiling. So much for theory. He took it as a message that the forces his special sense reached and manipulated were not to be categorized in so facile a manner.

As he took his first turn beyond the doorway, he had his final glimpse of the sleeping minotaur, over his right shoulder. He saw the knot of his own spell drifting above the prostrate form, like a giant, yellow butterfly.

* * *

Mouseglove's relief was immense as the ship cleared the highest tower and soared out, away from Anvil Mountain. Already, the lights of its city were small beneath him, and he was surprised to be taken by a sensation of beauty viewed as he looked upon it. Turning away, he continued to direct the vessel up past the regions where the dark bird-things wove their interminable patterns. So far, there was no indication of pursuit. He pushed the ship to its ultimate speed and held it there until the mountain was only a dim outline behind him. At last, this, too, faded and only the stars gave him light.

Then he relaxed, unclasping his cloak and letting it fall over the back of his seat. He sighed and rubbed his eyes and ran his fingers through his hair. A great tension began draining away, and the beginnings of delight in the act of flying under his own control came over him.

Soon . . . At this speed, he would be in Dibna before morning. That would provide ample time for hiding the vessel and walking into town. In a day's time, he should be able to locate a buyer or a middle-man for the disposition of the figurines. Unless, of course, the men who had commissioned their theft were still alive, still wanted them. Either way . . . A few days more, possibly, to tie up the deal. Then, his purse full of coins, he would treat himself to a bit of revelry. After that, use the flying machine to travel to another town where no one would know of the

transaction. In fact, it might be best to do that before
celebrating. Then find a place to settle down. A villa on
a hillside, with a view of the sea. A cook, a manservant, a
gardener—it would be pleasant to have a garden—and a
few assorted slave girls. . . .

He turned the control wheel slowly to the right. More,
more . . . Southeast, south . . . He began to wonder why
he was doing it. This was no longer the way to Dibna. He
struggled to halt the motion, but his hands continued to
move the control. Southwest . . . He was almost completely turned around. It would simply have to be cor-
rected. Only . . .

His hands refused to obey, to turn him back. It was as if
the will of another now directed his actions. He fought
against it, but to no avail. He was now headed in almost
exactly the one direction that he did not wish to go. As he
watched himself being directed, the entire sequence of his
actions took on a dreamlike quality, as though he himself
were being forced further and further into the background,
as though . . .

Dreamlike. For a moment, the tiny control lights swam
before him, rearranging themselves into seven flickering
forms. The full memory of his dream crashed down upon
him then, with a feeling that somewhere the last laughter
continued.

He had a strong premonition that he was saying good-
bye to his villa.

*   *   *

Pol's first impulse on reaching the labyrinth's exit was to
rush out through it. Instead, he halted just within the
doorway. Something—he was not certain what—was amiss.
It was as if he had been granted such a brief glimpse of a
danger that he could not name it, could only be aware of
its existence. Had something moved?

He wondered, looking out to the place where Moonbird
watched a sleeping Nora. He took the rod into his hands
and tried to recall elaborate spells from the books he had
read in his father's collection. Everything seemed to be all
right, yet . . .

A slow-moving shadow slid across the ground before
him, twisting itself over every irregularity. Still, it was

easy for him, coming from the world that he had, to recognize the outline as that of a flying machine—a thing larger than the dark birds, if the sound which now reached his ears were any indication of its nearness.

There was a partial spell he had studied, simpler than the complete version of the same thing. It might require considerable energy, but then, he need no longer work solely with his hands upon the fabric of reality. . . .

He raised the rod and began moving it about him, catching and swirling large quantities of the strands, of every color. As the shadow receded, the clot of strands grew before him, assuming a disc-like shape. The colors drained from it as it spun and increased in diameter, until, at length, it was a shimmering shield larger than himself. Objects beyond it rippled and swam and the rod vibrated steadily, silently within his grip.

Now. He took a step forward and the shield advanced a similar distance. Its size seemed sufficient for its purpose and he slowed the swirling movement to restrict its growth, to maintain it at its present size.

The shadow had passed away to his left, and he moved the rod in that direction and tilted it upward. He took another step and scanned the sky carefully. Unlike the complete spell, which rendered its caster entirely invisible, the partial spell he had been able to weave created only a flat screen, capable of blocking observation from a single direction.

Another step, and he caught sight of the battle-wagon, swinging away, farther to the left. Turning sideways, he adjusted the shield and began walking toward the trees. If he were to remain stationary, there was a way to rest his arm. As it was . . .

He crossed the cleared area, turning to follow the movement of the vessel, like some negative-petalled flower after an anti-sun, distorting the light that fell upon it, until finally he was walking backward when he reached the trees.

Standing now before the tree of the girl and the dragon, he spun the shield larger, watching the wavering image of the circling battle-wagon through the upper righthand quadrant of the screen.

He reached out and touched Moonbird.

I am going to awaken her now, he indicated. *When I do, we are going to retreat within the wood.*

And not fight?

We may not have to.

I could barf it to ruin . . .

Not if it gets you first. Trust me.

He turned to Nora and began releasing her from the sleep-spell, reflecting on how much simpler things would have been with the minotaur had he been able to do it at other than close range. Nora stirred, looked at him.

"I've been asleep! You did it to me! I—"

"Shh!" he cautioned. "They're up there!" He gestured with his head. "Sounds carry in a quiet place like this. Save it for later. I've got the second piece. Now we have to get off into the trees. We're invisible from just this one side."

She got to her feet and stood stiffly erect.

"It was not a nice trick," she said, "and you won't catch me that way again."

"I'll bear that in mind," he stated. "Now let's head back that way."

She glanced at the ship in the sky, nodded and turned. Moonbird shifted his great bulk and edged slowly after her.

As he retreated, Pol slowed the swirling motion, withdrew his energies, released the spell. The trees covered them adequately now. It seemed that they had escaped from immediate danger.

Pol seated himself beneath a tree, hands clasped under his chin.

"What now?" Nora finally asked him.

"I am wondering whether I might be able to bring that thing down, as I did that lesser one at the pyramid. Now that I have two of the sections together, it seems possible."

"It sounds worth trying."

"I am going to wait until its course brings it nearer. Distance does seem to be a factor."

For over a quarter of an hour, he watched the vessel, attaching strand after gray metallic strand to the rod that he held. Finally, when the ship swept by them again, he felt ready.

He raised the instrument and stared past it through gaps among the branches, amid the leaves, saw the strands grow taut, imagined that he could hear them singing as if caressed by some cosmic wind. The rod grew warm in his hand as he felt the energies flow forth.

For a time, nothing seemed to happen. Then they heard a cough and a rattle, followed by a sputtering noise. Two of the ship's rotors began to slow. It listed to starboard as a third propellor went out. Immediately, it began to descend, and Pol guessed that this was an action of the pilot's in trying to avoid a crash, rather than an indication that it might not remain airborne a while longer. His knuckles grew white as he gripped the rod, willing more force into his spell. More rattling and coughing noises came from the sinking vessel. A thin wisp of smoke arose from beneath the cowling at its forward end. Two more rotors halted, but by now it was only fifteen or twenty meters above the ground, near to the western perimeter of the labyrinth.

It dropped only a short distance, moments later, and a hatch at its rear fell open. Three men hurried out and another followed more slowly, coughing. Pol saw a darting of flames within and more moving forms beating at and attempting to smother them. He lowered the rod and extended his hand to Nora.

"Let's get out of here," he said. "I've burned out several engines. They won't be able to follow."

They clambered up onto Moonbird's back.

Now! Hurry! Take us away!

We can finish them off first.

They are helpless now. Get us aloft!

Moonbird began a waddling run beneath the trees, fanning the air with his wings. When he broke into the cleared area, he lifted above the ground. A cry came up from somewhere to the right.

Pol saw the three men who had fled the smoldering battle-wagon. They were kneeling and had raised their weapons. White puffs emerged from the muzzles, and he immediately felt a burning pain in the back of his neck and slumped across Moonbird's shoulder. He heard Nora cry

out and felt her catching at his shirt, his belt. His head
swirled through dark places, but he did not immediately
lose consciousness. A distant booming sound came to his
ears. His neck was wet.

We should have finished them first . . . Moonbird was
saying.

Nora was talking as she did something behind him, but
he could not hear the words.

Then his eyes closed and everything diminished.

When the world came back, her hand was on his neck,
holding a cold compress in place. He smelled the sea. He
felt the play of muscles beneath the scales against which
his cheek was pressed. Moonbird smelled a bit like old
leather, gunpowder and lemon juice, he suddenly realized. Somehow the thought struck him as funny and he
chuckled.

"You're awake?" said Nora.

"Yes. How serious is it?"

"It looks as if someone laid a hot poker across your neck
and held it there for a time."

"That's about how it feels, too. What's on it?"

"A piece of cloth I soaked in water."

"Thanks. It helps."

"Do you know a spell to heal it?"

"Not offhand. But I may be able to think of something.
Tell me first what happened, though."

"You were hit by something. I think it might have come
from one of those smoking sticks the men were pointing."

"Yes, it did. But what was the crashing noise? Did their
ship explode?"

"No. It had larger—things—like those pointed by the
men. These turned to follow us, then they began smoking
and making the noise. Several things seemed to explode
near us. Then it stopped."

Pol propped himself and looked back. It hurt to turn his
head. The island was already receding in the distance, its
outline vaguely misted. He looked down at the sea, up
toward the sun.

Moonbird, are you all right?

Yes. And you?

I'll be okay. But we seem to be heading northwest, rather than southwest. Maybe I'm wrong, though. You are the expert.

You are not wrong.

"Let me tie that in place for you."

"Go ahead."

Why? What is the matter?

The place you wish to visit next—it lies a great distance from here, many day's travel.

Yes, I know. That is why it is important that we follow the route I have laid out. Many island stopovers will be necessary.

Not really. Maps mean less to me than my feelings. I realized recently there is a shortcut.

How can that be? The shortest distance between two points is a—a great circle segment.

I will take us the way of the dragons.

The way of the dragons? What do you mean?

I have been that way before. Between some places there are special routes. Holes in the air, we call them. They move about, slowly. The closest one to a place near where you would go now lies in this direction.

Holes in the air? What are they like?

Uncomfortable. But I know the way.

Anything that is uncomfortable to a dragon might prove fatal to anyone else.

I have borne your father through them.

They are much faster?

Yes.

All right. Go ahead.

How far is it?

I may get us there by evening.

Is there a place before that where we can stop for repairs?

Several.

Good.

The sun hung low and red before them. To the right, a fuzzy line of coast darkened the horizon like a rough brush stroke. Mounds and streamers of pink and orange clouds filled the sky to the left and ahead. Moonbird was climb-

ing and the wind seemed to grow colder with each beat of
his wings. Pol stared upward and rubbed his eyes, for his
vision had suddenly blurred.

The blur remained. He moved his head and it stayed in
the same place.

Moonbird . . . ?

Yes, we are nearing it. It will be soon now.

Is there anything special that we should do?

*Do not let go. Mind your possessions. I cannot help you
if we become separated.*

The wrinkle in the sky had grown larger as they climbed,
reminding Pol of the invisibility shield viewed from the
user's side. They reached its altitude and passed it. Looking down upon it, he saw it to be silvery, shining and
opaque, like a pool of mercury, touched faintly pink by the
receding sun. It achieved an even more substantial appearance as they rose higher above it.

Why have we passed it?

It must be entered from the bright side.

"We are going to dive through that?" Nora asked.

"Yes."

Pol touched the back of his neck and felt only a moder-
ate ache. Already, the healing spell he had concocted
seemed to be working—or at least killing the pain. Nora
squeezed his shoulder.

"I'm ready."

He patted her hand as Moonbird achieved a position
above the circle and began to slow.

"Hang on."

They began to drop. Moonbird's wings beat again, driving them faster.

It is not solid, Pol told himself without conviction, as
the shining thing grew before them.

Suddenly, they were past it, and there was no up or
down, only forward. Right and left would not stay put, for
they seemed to be swirling, spiraling about a light-streaked
vortex while a continuously rising scream pierced their
ears. Pol bit his lip and clung tightly to Moonbird's neck.
Nora was hugging him so hard that it hurt. He tried
closing his eyes, but that worsened things, making his

rising vertigo near to unbearable. There did seem to be a bit of brightness far, far ahead. His stomach wrenched, and whatever emerged was mercifully whipped away. Moonbird began expelling flames which fled back past them like glowing spears. The wailing had now reached at least partially into the ultrasonic. If he stared too long at the smears of light they seemed on the verge of becoming grotesque, open-mouthed faces. The one steady patch of brightness seemed no nearer.

Are all of the shortcuts like this? Pol asked.

No. We're lucky, Moonbird replied. *There are some bad ones.*

XVIII

Eyes aching, shoulders sore from the long flight, Mouseglove circled the tumbling stone structure, saw no sign of other visitors and was about to land nearby. His hands jerked, however, swinging the vessel out over the jungle until a cleared area came into sight. His sigh was voluntary as he brought the small ship down for a landing, but when he attempted to utter a choice from his amazing collection of curses, he discovered that his tongue would not respond.

You could at least let me rest, he mentally addressed his unseen manipulators. *Whatever it is that you want of me, you will get a better performance if I am not exhausted.*

We regret the inconvenience, came their first communication since his dream on Anvil Mountain, accompanied briefly by a peculiar doubling of vision, as if the scene about him were momentarily overlaid by the image of a flickering taper, a dark presence moving near it. *But there is no choice. You overtook the other vessels during the night. We gave you a different course, and yours is a faster ship. But your lead is not that great. There is no time to rest. Take the wide, flat blade from the sheath on the door. Go outside. Cut branches, fronds. Conceal this vessel.*

He felt free—free to comply. He did not.

But—

He was seized once again. He felt himself begin to rise, springing the hatch, taking the blade into his hand. There were no replies to his next inquiries.

The great-leaved plants were easy to cut. It did not take him long to cover the small ship. Then he opened a

160

compartment toward the vessel's rear, to strip it, clean it and snap auxiliary fuel cubes into its chambers. The thought of this situation had troubled him during a more alert moment. There was no way the sunlight converters could do the entire job required for the return trip, even if his unwilling hands had not covered over their panels with leaves.

When he had finished the work he stood still for a moment, breathing the warm moist air, listening to the morning calls of the bright parrots, wondering whether he would now be permitted a brief rest. Almost as he thought it, however, his feet began to move, bearing him in what he believed to be the direction of the stone structure with the grotesque carvings. He swung the blade as he went, widening the trail. After only a few paces, he was drenched with perspiration. Insects buzzed about him, and the most maddening part of the entire experience was his inability to brush them away.

At last, he staggered into the cleared area where the stepped structure stood, stylized stone beasts projecting from its vine-covered walls, grinning past him.

I must rest, he tried. *In the shade. Please!*

There is absolutely no time, came the reply, with another flickering image. *You must go around to the other side of the building and enter there.*

He felt himself beginning to move again. He wanted to cry out, but this was still denied him. He moved faster and faster, barely aware of where he stepped, yet somehow he did not stumble.

He was halted again, before the weed-clogged, vine-hung doorway. Then the blade flashed forward and he began clearing it.

Soon he was through the opening and rushing along a corridor. His eyes had not yet adjusted to the gloom, but whatever was in charge of him seemed to know where he was going.

It was only when he neared the head of a wide flight of stairs that he began to slow, finally coming to a halt to regard the scene that lay below and before him, partly illuminated through an irregular gap in the roof where

several stone blocks had fallen—the result of an earthquake
perhaps . . .

At the far side of the chamber below was a low stone
wall. Beyond it was the blackness of a hole. Before it was a
diminutive version of the entire stepped building itself,
complete with tiny statues and carvings. Atop this, in a
crumbling orange basket, lay a narrow cylinder half the
length of a man's forearm. It appeared to be glowing with
a faint, greenish light. Mouseglove took advantage of the
respite to breathe deeply of the moist air, to enjoy the
coolness . . .

That, thief is the object you must steal.

Again, the candle; again, the imperative.

The cylinder?

Yes.

Why bother to tell me? You're pulling all the strings.

*Not any longer. We are about to release you. Your
native wit and reflexes are superior to anything we might
compel you to in such matters.*

Suddenly, he was free. He mopped his brow, dusted his
garments and fell to his knees, breathing heavily. One of
his reflexes kept him silent, if this were indeed to be a
piece of work. Mentally, he framed his most immediate
question:

*What is so difficult about descending these stairs, cross-
ing the room and picking that thing up?*

The dweller in the well.

What is it? What can it do?

*If it detects your presence it will rise up and attempt to
prevent the theft. It is a great feathered serpent.*

Mouseglove began to shake. With his cloak, he muffled
the lowering of the blade to the stone floor. He covered
his face with his hands and rubbed his eyes, massaged his
forehead.

*This is so unfair! I only work in prime form, not when
I'm half-dead with fatigue!*

This time, there is no other way.

Damn you!

We are wasting time. Will you do it?

Have I any real choice? If there is any justice—

Then be about it!

Mouseglove dropped his hands and straightened. He swung into a seated position upon the top step and adjusted his boots. He ran his fingers through his hair, wiped his palms on his trousers and took up the blade. He stood.

With a silent, sweeping movement, he took himself to the left hand side of the stair. Turning sideways then, he began to descend a step at a time, slowly and soundlessly.

When he reached the bottom, he stood perfectly still, listening. Was that the slightest of rustling noises from the well? Yes. It came again, then ceased. Would it be better to dash forward, seize the cylinder and run for it now? Or should he continue to rely on stealth? How big was the creature, and how fast could it move?

As no answers were forthcoming, he took it that his guesses were as good as his tormentors'. He took a single step forward and paused again. Silence. He took another. Yes, the thing was definitely glowing. It was what Pol would be after and apparently would not have time to reach. Why not? Those approaching ships of Mark's . . . ? Probably. So where would that leave him, Mouseglove, even if he succeeded in making off with the bauble? Had the Seven something more in mind for him? Or would he finally be totally free, to go his own way?

Another step . . . Nothing. Two more quick ones . . .

A rustling, as of scales against stone . . .

He controlled a shudder and stepped again, over a small heap of rubble: The rustling continued, as if something large and coiled were unwinding itself.

The grenade! Heave one down the well! Fall flat! Cover your head!

He did as he was told. The grenade was in his hand, then in the air. As he threw himself forward behind the pedestal, he caught a glimpse of an enormous, bright, feather-crowned head rising above the low wall, of huge unblinking eyes, dark as pits, turned in his direction, a green excrescence, like a blazing emerald, set in the brow above them. Then an explosion shook the building.

A large block fell from the ceiling at the corner to the left of the stair, followed by a fall of gravel and dirt, dust particles dancing in the light rays. The orange basket

tumbled from its rest, the rod rolling from it. It struck the
lower step of the small pyramid, bounced and came to rest
beside Mouseglove's elbow.

You've got it! Take it and run!

He looked about, discovered it, seized it, scrambled to
his feet.

Too late! he replied, the rod in his left hand, the blade
in his right. *It's not dead!*

An explosive hissing drowned the final rattlings of the
stonefall. The orange, red and pink-bonnetted head was
swaying as if disoriented, but moving steadily in his direction, too rapidly for him to escape it.

Strike at the jewel between the eyes!

He darted backward, raising the blade, knowing he
would have but one chance.

As the serpent struck, so did he.

                         *   *   *

They burst into the dawn, retching and gasping, ears
ringing, pulses pounding. Pol leaned forward and looked
down at beaches running back to a line of lush tropical
growth.

Down, Moonbird! We can barely hang on!

Moonbird dropped lower, slowing.

On the beach?

Yes. I want to bathe, to eat, to walk.

"Pol, I can't—"

"I know. Neither can I. Just another minute."

Moonbird settled gently. They slid off and lay unmoving
on the sand. After a time, Pol reached out and touched
Nora's hair.

"You did well," he said.

"You hung right in there, too." She patted Moonbird.
"Good show." Then, "Where are we?" she asked.

How much farther?

*We will reach it before the sun stands in the high
places.*

Good.

"We'll be there by noon," he said to Nora.

After a time, they undressed and bathed in the ocean,
then cleaned their garments while Moonbird hunted and

ate things that squealed a lot back among the trees. Their own breakfast was more silent as they watched the sun-dappled waves and the fire-splashed clouds.

"I would like to sleep for an awfully long time," she finally said.

"We have been rather busy."

"When this is over, what are you going to do?"

"If I live," he said, "I would like to read the rest of the books in my father's library."

"And with that knowledge—what?"

"I look upon it as an end, not a means. I don't know what I'll do then. Oh, I want to rebuild Rondoval, of course, whether I stay or move on."

"Move on? To where?"

"I don't know. But I once traveled a golden road that went by wondrous places. Perhaps one day I'll walk it further and see more things."

"And will you be coming back if you do?"

"I think I must. Your land seems more like home to me than any other place I've ever lived."

"It's nice to have such choices," she said.

"If I live," he said.

When Moonbird returned, they stretched, brushed off sand and mounted, holding hands. The sun was higher and the jungle seemed greener now. They rose again, and soon Moonbird was bearing them south.

It was nearly noon when they sighted the stepped pyramid, approached it and began to circle.

You may be too late, Moonbird stated.

What do you mean?

Among the trees there are ships like the one you broke on the island.

I don't see . . .

I see their heat.

How many are there?

I count six.

I wonder how long they have been here? It could be an ambush.

Perhaps. What should I do?

I have to have that piece—

An explosion shook the pyramid.

"What—?" Nora began.

Go low and pass it fast. I want a better look.

Moonbird circled, positioned himself and began to fall. Pol studied the jungle, still unable to detect the vessels of which the dragon had spoken. As they descended, he turned his eyes toward the pyramid itself. Clumps of dirt slid down its sides, and a minor cave-in had occurred at one point. A cloud of dust rose like smoke above the structure.

They passed through the dust and swept in low, regarding the pyramid and the trees beyond it. Nothing stirred. Moonbird commenced climbing once again.

"Gods!" Nora shouted above the wind. "What is it?"

A small man in dark garments had just emerged, running, from an opening in the far side of the pyramid. Moments later, a gigantic feathered head followed him out, to rise, swaying, tongue flashing like fire or blood. It continued to emerge, at great length, with such rapidity that the likelihood seemed strong that it would soon fall upon the man.

Moonbird! Stop! Go back! The jade strand— That man has the rod!

Moonbird was already braking, turning, growing warmer.

It is the serpent of the well! I have always wanted to meet him . . . You must slide off and run as soon as I strike. Take those things you would preserve.

Strike? No! You can't!

I must! I have waited ages for this! It is also the only way to save the man with your thing of power.

Pol struck him with his fists, but it seemed unlikely that Moonbird even felt the blows.

"Get ready to jump down and run!" he cried to Nora, slinging his guitar case, grabbing at the basket of water bottles.

The serpent heard the shout and turned its head upward. Moonbird landed upon its back a moment later. Pol slipped off to the right and began running. A great roaring and a loud hissing rose up behind him. He felt a wave of heat. He saw the giant serpent body twisting toward him. He dodged it, looking about for Nora as he moved. She was nowhere in sight. But the small man with the rod had stumbled and picked himself up again. They sighted one another at the same time, and Pol realized that it was Mouseglove.

"Nora!" he shouted. "Can you see her?"

Mouseglove gestured toward the trees on the other side of the scaly turmoil. Nora had apparently jumped or been thrown in the opposite direction from Pol. He began circling, running toward Mouseglove, well past the place where Moonbird, caught in a colorful coil, had begun to spew smoldering liquids upon his twisting adversary. Ignition followed, and he smelled burning feathers as he ran. At about the same moment, he caught sight of Nora, surrounded by a large body of short, stocky men resembling those he had seen upon Anvil Mountain. Several of them lay unmoving among the grasses and Nora's left shoulder was bloodied. He saw there were dark cords wrapped around her, and that she was being pushed off among the trees.

At that moment, the reptilian combatants rolled toward them and they fled.

They came together among the high growth to the east, gasping, leaning upon vine and fungus-decked trees.

"Hurry!" Pol said, extending his hand. "The rod! I need it!"

Mouseglove passed it to him, a thin, long section, sculpted with clouds, the moon, stars and a celestial palace set above them, angelic spirits passing through the high places. Pol dropped it twice before he succeeded in fitting it into place at the end of the other sections. The feeling of power that washed over him as he did so was immense. It steadied his hands as it made his head swirl. He straightened.

"We have to go after her," he said, facing back toward the sounds of crashing and roaring. He pointed to the left of that place. "We can move faster if we return to the clearing, stay away from the fight, skirt the jungle."

Mouseglove nodded and put up his hand.

"I don't think we'll succeed, but I believe that she is safe for now, anyway."

"What do you mean?"

"I know those dwarves fairly well. She'd be dead by now if they didn't have orders not to kill her. They came here in flying ships and they'll doubtless take her back in one. They must be to them by now."

"I thought it was me they were after—or the last piece of this rod."

"Yes, but they'll avoid you rather than confront you now that you've got it. She was probably second choice—as hostage, possibly."

"What do you mean 'possibly?' "

"Mark likes her himself, you know."

"Yes, I know," Pol said. "Fill me in later. Let's move."

He raised the rod, and a blinding flash of white light leaped from it, cutting a path through the jungle. Without pausing, he headed forward along it.

When they came into the clearing once again, they saw that Moonbird and the feathered serpent were locked together, unmoving, pressed up against the side of the pyramid. The dragon was still caught within a coil, and his teeth were now locked upon the great snake's side. The serpent had his fangs fixed in Moonbird's left shoulder. A portion of the pyramid had collapsed about them.

As they turned and began to pass to their left, a sudden resumption of activity shook the ground. The singed serpent was thown flat as Moonbird, wings freed, rose into the air, his shoulder still in the grip of his dangling adversary. Pol swung about and raised the rod.

No! The word vibrated along a green strand which suddenly sprang up between Moonbird and himself. *This is between us! Stay away!*

Without pausing to acknowledge the message, Pol continued on his way toward the place where Nora had been borne into the jungle, Mouseglove close behind him. There came another roar. Shortly, he smelled the stench of burning flesh. He did not look back.

They reached the spot where the bodies lay among the reddened grasses, Nora's blade protruding from one of them. Now that they were away from the scuffling beasts, other noises came to their ears—mechanical humming sounds from beyond the trees.

A dark shape rose into the air some distance to the south of them. Almost immediately, two more followed it.

"*No!*" Pol cried, and he raised the rod.

Mouseglove caught at his arm, dragging it down.

"You'll kill her if you shoot it down!" he shouted. "Besides, you've no way of knowing which one she's in. You can't afford to hit any of them!"

Pol's shoulders sagged. Two more vessels climbed into the air.

"Of course," he said, his arm falling. "Of course. . . ."

He turned and looked at Mouseglove.

"Thanks," he said. Then, "I've got to go after her. I have to do what Mark wants—take things to a full conflict. He doesn't know what I've got to bring up against him, but he has to find out before he can embark on his campaign. Now he is about to learn. I'm going back there and take Anvil Mountain apart, if Moonbird can still fly. . . ."

"I've got a ship," Mouseglove said. "I stole Mark's. I can fly it. I'll show you."

He took Pol's arm.

As they passed the pyramid again, the struggle was still in progress with neither combatant showing any sign of weakening. Great furrows and pits had been torn in the charred ground; thick, sweet-smelling blood was smeared everywhere, and both dragon and serpent were soaked in it. At the moment, they were so intertwined that it was impossible for Pol to assess their damages, let alone to use the rod on Moonbird's behalf.

He summoned the strand by which Moonbird had addressed him earlier.

I must return to Rondoval now and prepare for battle, he said. *Mark has Nora. Mouseglove can take me there in his flier. I cannot await the outcome of your struggle.*

Go. When it is finished, I will return.

Immediately, the two began to thrash about again. The serpent, half of its feathers missing, began to hiss violently. Flames blossomed about it, upon it, as Pol and Mouseglove hurried by. It succeeded just then in throwing a coil about Moonbird's neck, but the dragon's claws were now raking its midsection.

"Tell him to go for the green jewel in the thing's head," Mouseglove said. "I stunned it for a moment when I hit it there."

Strike at the jewel in its head, Pol immediately relayed to Moonbird, but there was no reply.

They hurried past, coming shortly to the trail Mouseglove had hacked through the brush.

"This way," said the smaller man. "I've concealed it in a place not too far ahead. But—Pol, I'm too tired to make the flight all the way back. I'd fall asleep and kill us both."

"Just get us airborne," Pol replied. "I'll watch and ask questions. We can take turns flying if necessary."

"You look fairly tired yourself."

"I am. But it is not going to be as long a haul as you might think."

They entered a cleared area. Mouseglove paused and gestured, crossed to a green mound, began removing fronds.

"What do you mean?" he asked. "I just made the trip."

Pol moved to assist him.

"You're not going to like it," he said, "but I know a shortcut. . . ."

XIX

. . . He strode past the glassed-in banks of flat-faced machines, their huge metal eyes rotating, stopping, reversing, rotating again, ceaselessly, silently, to his left. To his right, a line of men and women, seated before glowing screens, traced designs with electric pencils upon them. The rug was soft and resilient, making the floor seem almost nonexistent. A gentle light emanated from glowing tubes overhead. The abstract design upon the wall to the right changed as he passed. A soft, characterless music filled the air. . . .

. . . He halted when he came to the large window looking out upon the city. Far below, numerous vehicles passed on the streets. Boats moved upon the distant river, and an airplane was passing overhead. Towering buildings dominated the prospect, and everything was clean and shining and smooth, like a piece of well-tended machinery. A certain warmth grew in his breast as he regarded the power and magnificence of the scene. His fingers tapped at a latch, and he drew the window upward, leaning forward to drink in the full range of sensations which emanated from the city . . .

. . . A heavy hand fell upon his shoulder, and he turned toward the tall, heavyset man who stood smiling beside him, drink in hand, face as ruddy as brick, red hair mingled with white, red scalp showing through. . . .

" . . . Yes, Mark, admire it," he was saying, gesturing with his glass. "One day, all of that will be yours. . . ."

. . . He turned to look again, having drawn back slightly from the aura of power which surrounded the larger man. Something at the left side of his face clicked against the window's frame. Raising his hand to explore, he discovered a huge protruberance above his left eye. Immediately, he remembered that it had been there all along. Turning farther, with something like shame, he reached up and touched it again. . . .

. . . His vision doubled. Beyond the window now, he saw two discrete scenes. Half of the city before him was still bright and beckoning. The other half was gray, drab, the air filled with ashes and yellowish fog-like tentacles. Raucous noises, as of the rattling of heavy machinery rose up on that side of the split scene, accompanied by a wave of acrid odors. Moist, sickly patches of color clung to the buildings. The river was muddy. The ships' smokestacks poured filth into the air. . . .

. . . He drew back, turning again toward the big man, to discover that he, also, had doubled. The man to the right stood unchanged; the one on the left was even redder, his face partly shadowed, eyes flashing baleful lights. . . .

". . . What is the matter, my son?" he was asking. . . . Mark could not speak. He gestured toward the window, turning slightly in that direction, to discover that the scene was no longer split. The left side had superimposed itself upon his entire field of vision. His father merged also at that moment, and only the darker version remained. . . .

. . . Gesturing frantically, Mark tried to inform him as to what had occurred. Suddenly, a dragon appeared above the skyline, Pol mounted upon its back, headed in their direction. . . .

". . . Oh, him," the shadowy figure at his side was saying. "He is a troublemaker. I cast him out long ago. He comes seeking to destroy you. Be strong. . . ."

. . . Mark stared as the figure grew larger and larger, until finally it was crashing soundlessly, through the wall, reaching for him. Then there came a knocking sound, growing louder as it was repeated. Everything began to come apart about him, and he was falling. . . .

He sat up in his bed, drenched with perspiration. The knocking continued. He rose and turned on the light, despite the fact that his left eye saw clearly. Throwing his robe about his shoulders, he moved to the door and opened it. The small man drew back, extending a piece of paper. "You asked to see this as soon as it came in, sir." He glanced at it and lowered it.

"We have Nora, and Pol got away with the magical device," he stated.

"Yes, sir. They're already in the air, bringing her here."

"Good. Notify the force at Rondoval that he may be on his way back there." He looked out, past his new flier, into the night. "I'd better check on the status of our mobilization. Return to duty."

"Yes, sir."

When he had finished dressing, he withdrew the photograph from his night table and stared at it for a time.

"We'll see," he said, "who falls."

*   *   *

Mouseglove was at the controls as they neared Rondoval.

"I don't see how you can seem so rested," he remarked, "after such a short nap. Mine didn't do me that much good —not after that damned shortcut of yours."

He looked about the messy cabin and wrinkled his nose.

"I seem to be drawing some sort of energy from the scepter," Pol answered. "It feels as though I have an extra heart or lung or both. That—"

A puff of smoke appeared above the battlements.

"What was that?" Mouseglove asked, as two more appeared.

"It almost seems as if it could be gunfire. Veer off. I don't want to take—" The ship shuddered, as if from a heavy blow, "—any chances," Pol finished, bracing himself and seizing the rod with his right hand.

A moment later they were falling, smoke coming into the cabin.

"Is it out of control?" Pol shouted.

"Not completely," Mouseglove replied, "but I can't pull it up. I'm trying to miss the rocks, at least. Maybe those trees over there . . . Can you do anything?"

"I don't know."

Pol raised the scepter and strands were drawn to it through all the walls. To his eyes, it seemed again as if he sat at the center of an enormous, three-dimensional spiderweb. All of the strands began pulsing in time with the throbbing that rose in his wrist. The ship seemed to slow.

"We're going to miss the rocks!" Mouseglove shouted.

Perspiration sprang forth on Pol's brow. The lines between his eyes deepened.

"We're going to crash!"

A final burst of power fled from the scepter along the strands. Then there were treetops before them, upthrust branches reaching, then breaking. Abruptly, they came up against one which did not yield and they were pitched forward at the impact. The ship was torn open about them, but they were not aware of it.

Pol came awake with his hands tied behind him and did not open his eyes, as all his recent memories were immediately present within his throbbing head. He heard voices and smelled horses. There followed a sound of retreating hoofbeats. If whoever had shot at them had ridden down from the castle, the fact that they had not killed him immediately seemed to offer some sort of chance. He tested his bonds and found them very secure. He wondered how long he had been unconscious, and he wondered whether Mouseglove had survived the crash. And the scepter . . . Where was it?

He opened his eyes to the barest of slits and began turning his head, slowly.

He flinched, just slightly. But that was sufficient. He had not expected to see a centaur.

"Aha! You are awake!" cried the horse-man, who had apparently been scrutinizing him.

The well-muscled human torso towered above the sorrel horse-body, long, black hair pulled back from the dark-eyed, heavy-featured, masculine face and tied behind the head in something, Pol almost giggled, that he had once known as a pony tail.

"I am awake," he acknowledged, heaving himself toward a sitting position.

He succeeded on the second try. He saw Mouseglove lying on his side, hands similarly bound, still apparently unconscious, perhaps four meters away, beneath a large tree. The guitar case, apparently unscathed, rested against the tree's trunk. Pieces of wreckage lay between them, and when he looked upward, he saw the balance of the flier hanging like a giant, squashed fruit among the branches.

"Why have you tied us up?" he asked. "We've done nothing to you."

"Ha!" snorted his captor, executing a small prancing maneuver. "You call murder nothing?"

"In this case, yes," Pol replied, "since I've no idea what you are talking about."

The centaur stepped nearer, as if considering abusing him. Behind him, Pol saw Mouseglove stir. There seemed to be no other centaurs about, though the ground bore a great number of hoofmarks.

"Is it not possible that you could be mistaken?" Pol continued. "I know of no deaths hereabout—unless a piece of our ship fell on someone—"

"Liar," said the centaur, leaning forward and glaring directly into his eyes. "You came in your ships and slaughtered my people." He gestured toward the wreckage in the treetop. "You even kidnapped one of them. You deny this?"

The hoofs were darting and dancing uncomfortably near him as Pol shook his head.

"I do," he said, staring back, "but I would like to know more about what happened, if I'm to be blamed for it."

The centaur wheeled and paced away from him, kicking dust into his face. Pol shook his head, which had begun aching more severely, and he automatically called for healing strands to wrap it, as he had for his neck wound. They came and attached themselves to his brow, draining away some of the pain. He thought of his wrist then, but it was partly numbed by the pressure of the cord. He wondered whether he could manipulate strands in more complicated patterns without seeing what he was about, or whether there might be some other way to gain control over his captor.

"The others have gone to fetch a warrior to decide what to do with you," the centaur stated. "She may wish to talk about these things. I don't. It should not be long though. I believe that I hear them approaching now."

Pol listened but heard nothing. A purple strand settled near him, its farther end passing across the centaur's shoulder. He willed that it come into contact with his finger-tips. It passed behind him, and shortly he felt a tingling in his left hand. His fingers twisted. There came a familiar sensation of power.

"Look at me," he said.

The centaur turned.

"What do you want?"

Pol caught his gaze with his own. From his left hand, he felt the power move.

"You are so tired that you are almost asleep on your feet," he said. "Now you are, but don't bother closing your eyes. You can hear only my voice."

The centaur's gaze grew distant. His breathing slowed. He began to sway.

". . . But you can move about just as if you were awake, when I tell you to. My hands have been tied by mistake. Come over here and free them."

He rose to his feet and turned. The centaur came up behind him and began fumbling at the knots. Pol recalled seeing a knife at the creature's side.

"Cut the bonds," he ordered. "Quickly!"

A moment later, he was rubbing his wrists.

"Give me the knife."

He accepted the blade, crossed to where Mouseglove lay beneath the tree, watching him.

"Are you hurt?" he asked, as he faced the smaller man.

"I ache all over. But then, I felt that way before the crash, too. I don't believe anything is broken."

Mouseglove stood and turned about, raising his hands. As Pol slit the cord, he said, "Must be Mark's people in your castle. No one else has weapons like that— Uh-oh."

The sound of hoofbeats now came to their ears.

"Shall we run for it?" Mouseglove asked.

"No. Too late. They'd catch us. We'll wait and have this out here."

Pol slipped the knife behind his belt and turned to face the wood. A mental order to the centaur he now con-trolled moved him off to the right.

Shortly, the figures came into sight—four male centaurs led by an older female. She halted, about ten meters from where he stood, and regarded Pol.

"I was told you were bound," she stated.

"I was."

She stepped forward, and Pol started as he saw that she held the scepter in the hand which had been out of sight at her side. She raised it and pointed it at him. He saw a cluster of strands rush toward it. He issued a mental command and the centaur under his spell stepped between them. New spells suggested themselves to him and he summoned strands of his own.

The female centaur's eyes widened.

"What have you done to him?" she asked.

"Return my rod and we'll talk about it."

From the corner of his eye, Pol saw that Mouseglove was edging away.

"Where did you get it?" she asked.

"I recovered it, piece by piece, from the points of the Triangle of Int."

"Only a sorcerer could do that."

"You noticed."

"I, too, have some familiarity with the Art, though only the middle part of this rod will respond to me. Mine is an Earth magic." She gestured upward. "Why then were you riding in that thing?"

"My dragon was occupied. That vessel was stolen from my enemy, Mark Marakson, who has many such, atop Anvil Mountain. Perhaps you have seen his dark birds, who are not of flesh, in the skies."

"I know who he is and I have seen such birds. Some of my people were killed and some injured by men who came in larger vessels such as the one you rode."

The strands came into his hands and Pol felt the power throb in his wrist. Still, he had no wish to face a person who could use even the middle section of the rod.

"Small men, I daresay," he answered, "for such is the stature of the race which serves him. I have never harmed a centaur and I've no desire to. This will be the first time, if you force me to fight here."

"Sunfa, come forward," she said, and a smaller male moved from among those to the rear of the group to a position beside her. There was a long gash upon his left shoulder, and he was missing several teeth. "Were either of these men of the party which attacked you that day?"

He shook his head.

"No, Stel. Neither of them."

Her head snapped forward.

"You know my name now," she said. "So know, too, that I was among the force which stormed Rondoval the day this rod was wrested from Det Morson."

Pol raised his right hand so that his sleeve fell back, revealing the dragonmark.

"I am Pol Detson," he stated. "I have heard stories concerning my father. But I was taken from this land as a child and raised in another place. I never knew him. The past is dead, so far as I am concerned. I have only been back for a short while. I need that scepter for purposes of arousing the forces of Rondoval against those of Anvil Mountain. Are you going to return it to me?"

"In many ways," she replied, "this is even more disturbing than your being what we had thought you. For the moment, it is good if our enemy is also your enemy. But to see the hordes that lie beneath Rondoval roused once again is a frightening thought, especially for those of us who were alive in your father's day. So tell me, what do you propose doing when your battle is over?"

Pol laughed.

"You are assuming that I win and that I live. But, all right . . . I would lay most of my forces to rest again. I would like to be left alone to pursue my studies, and I would be happy to return the favor and leave everyone else in the neighborhood to his own devices. After a time, I may do some traveling. I don't know. I am not attracted by the darker aspects of the Art. I have no desire to conquer anything, and the idea of ruling over anybody bores the ass off me."

"Commendable," she said, "and I find myself wanting to believe you. In fact, it seems likely that you are telling the truth. However, even granting that, people do change. I would like very much to see you deal with the people who feel that they can hunt centaurs whenever they choose. But I would also like some assurance that you will not one day be inclined to do it yourself."

"My word is all that I can give you. Take it or leave it."

"But you could give me more—and in return, your own way might be eased."

"What have you in mind?"

"Swear an oath of friendship with us, upon your scepter."

"Friendship is a thing that goes further than nonaggression," he replied. "It is something that works both ways."

"I will be willing to swear the same oath for you."

"On your own, or on behalf of the other centaurs as well?"

"For all of us."

"You can speak for them?"

"I can."

"Very well. I'll do it if you will."

He looked back at Mouseglove, who was about to slip off among the trees.

"Stay put," he called back. "You're safe."

"For now," Mouseglove replied. But he returned.

Pol moved around the cataleptic centaur who stood between Stel and himself, destroying the spell which held him with a twisting motion of his hand as he passed. That one drew away, eyes shifting rapidly, until Stel spoke some reassurance.

"Tell me the words of the oath," Pol said, coming up before her.

"Place your hand upon the middle section of the rod, and repeat after me."

Pol nodded and complied.

As she began to speak the words, a series of dark strands knotted themselves about them. He felt a vaguely threatening force accumulating within them. When they had finished speaking the knots separated and drifted away, like small, dark clouds. One went to hover behind Stel. He felt such a presence behind himself, also.

"There," she said, passing the rod to him. "We have created our own dooms, should we betray one another."

They clasped hands.

"No problem then," Pol answered, smiling "and it's good to have some friends. I'd like to stay and visit, but now I've some monsters to rouse. Hopefully, I'll be back."

He turned away and fetched his guitar case.

"A weapon?" she asked as he raised it.

"No, a musical instrument. Maybe I'll be able to play it for you one day."

"You are really going to Rondoval now?"

"I must."

"Give me time to raise a force, to rid the place of your enemies. Now we are allies, it is our fight, too."

"Not necessary," Pol said. "They are up in the castle. My destination is far below it. Moonbird—my dragon— showed me a tunnel to the place. I'll go in that way and bypass the bastards. There is no need at all to deal with them now."

"Where does the tunnel open?"

"Down the slope, to the north. I'll have to do a little climbing but I foresee no real difficulties."

"—Unless your enemies see you and go after you in their flying boats."

He shrugged.

"There is always that chance."

"So I will take a small force and lead a diversionary assault from the south. Two of my males will bear you and your friend to the northern slope."

"The enemy has guns, which kill from a distance."

"So do arrows. We'll take no unnecessary risks. I am going to send runners now, to tell the others to arm and to bring them here. While we wait, I would like to hear your music."

"Okay. Me, too," said Pol. "Let's get comfortable."

XX

"You were with him," Mark said to Nora, as they both leaned upon the railing to his roof garden. "What is his power, anyway, now he has that scepter?"

"I don't know," she replied, looking at the flowers. "I really don't know. I'm not even sure that he was absolutely certain. Or else he was being very close-mouthed."

"Well, I think it possible that he is dead. On the other hand, I've no idea how he got across the ocean as quickly as he did. He has something going for him. He was in my flier at one point—and it was shot down near Rondoval. Still . . . Supposing—just supposing—he is still alive? How would he attack me? What sort of forces might he bring?"

She shook her head and looked at him. His lens was a pale blue and he was smiling.

"I couldn't tell you, Mark," she said, "and if I could . . ."

"You wouldn't? I'd guessed that much. It didn't take long did it? For you to fall in love with a flashy traveler with a good story?"

"You really believe that, don't you?"

"What else am I to think? We've known each other most of our lives. I thought we had something of an understanding. Then, practically overnight, you're in love with a stranger."

"I am not in love with Pol," she said, straightening. "Oh, it could happen, very easily. He's quick and strong—clever, attractive. But, really I hardly know him, despite what we've been through together. On the other hand, I thought that I knew you—very well—and now I see that I was mistaken about a great number of things. If you want

181

honesty, rather than sweet words, I am not, at this moment, in love with anyone."

"But did you once feel that way about me?"

"I thought that I did."

He hammered his fist against the rail.

She laid a hand on his shoulder.

"It's this lens, isn't it? This damned, ugly bug-eye!"

"Don't be silly," she said. "I wasn't talking about appearance. I was talking about what you are doing. You've always been different. You've always had a way with mechanical things. That in itself is hardly bad, but what you are doing—what you are planning to do—with your knowledge and your contrivances—that is."

"Don't let's go into it again."

She withdrew her hand.

"You asked me. If he still lives, Pol has to fight you—some way—now. Sometimes it almost seems that a conflict between the two of you was ordained before you both were born. Other times I've thought of it, though, it seemed that it need not be so. You could be friends. He is the closest thing you have to a relative. And it is probably that way for him, also. I will tell you what I told him. I feel like a pawn. You are jealous of him, and he will want to rescue me from you. I almost feel as if my life has been somehow manipulated to bring me into this position, to insure that a battle will occur. I wish that I'd never met either of you!"

She turned away. He guessed that she was crying, but was not certain. He began to extend his hand.

"Sir! Sir!"

A captain of his guard was rushing toward him. Scowling, Mark turned.

"What is it?"

"Castle Rondoval is under attack! The message just came through! Should we send reinforcements?"

"Who is attacking? How? What are the details?"

"There are none. The message was short, garbled. We are waiting for an answer."

"Divert all the nearest birds. Get me a picture of what's going on. I'll be down there shortly. We're going on alert."

He raised his hand and two guards, pretending to study the garden from its opposite end, immediately moved toward him.

"I'd wager your lover lives," he said, "and that this is his doing. At any rate, your talk of pawns has given me an idea. Guards! Take her away. Protect her. Watch her well. She may be of some use yet."

Turning on his heel, he headed toward the elevator. He did not look back.

*   *   *

Mouseglove moved with near-acrobatic skill up the final few meters of the cliff-face, hauled himself into the cave mouth, turned, stooped and assisted Pol.

"All right," he said then, "I am about to keep a promise. I vowed that if they would leave me alone, I would bring them back to Rondoval." He groped beneath his cloak and withdrew a parcel. "They did and I have. So here."

He handed the package to Pol.

"I don't understand. What is it?" Pol asked.

"The figurines of the seven sorcerers I stole from your father. As you gained sections of that scepter, they grew in power until finally they were able to control me. During the trip back here, I told you everything I had done, but I didn't tell you why. They are the reason. Surely, you don't think I'd go and play games with a feathered serpent for laughs? They are powerful, they can communicate if they want—and I have no idea what they are up to. Also, they are all yours now. Don't worry, though. A big part of their purpose in life seems to be taking care of you. I would try to learn more about them soon, if I were you."

"I wish I had time," Pol remarked, "but I don't. Not now." He secured the parcel at his belt and turned. The dragon-light sprang forth to dart before them. "Let's go."

Mouseglove fell into step beside him.

"I wonder how the centaurs are doing?" he said.

Pol shrugged.

"I hope they get the message soon that we made it safely. If the two who brought us hurry, they will. Then they can lay off and return to the woods."

"If you really meant that oath, perhaps you ought to

send something particularly nasty upstairs to clear the halls."

"Why?"

"I've seen how centaurs fight. They're tough, but they also get kind of frenzied after awhile. I've a hunch they won't be falling back."

"Really? I didn't know that."

"Oh, yes. So, surely you could spare a dragon or an ogre or two, to clean house and protect your new friends."

"I guess I should."

They walked on for a time, following the pale light. At several points they had to climb down over rocky irregularities.

"Uh, I guess we'll be parting company soon," Mouseglove said as they entered the first of a series of larger caverns. "I've done what I came back to do, and I promised myself I'd never set foot on Anvil Mountain again."

"I didn't expect you to accompany me there," Pol replied, "and it's not your fight. What have you in mind to do now?"

"Well, after your servant's made it safe for the likes of me upstairs, I'll head in that direction. Be sure to tell him that I'm okay. I'll borrow some fresh garments, if that's all right with you, clean up, have a nap and be moving on."

They passed a large, winged, sleeping form.

"You have my permission, my thanks and my blessing," Pol said. "Also my ogre, to clear your way."

Mouseglove chuckled.

"You are a difficult young man to gull. I'm actually coming to like you. Pity, we'll probably never meet again."

"Who knows? I'll ask the Seven when I get a chance."

"I'd rather you didn't remind them of me."

The next cavern they entered was even larger, though more level. Pol looked at the humped and massed bodies among which they made their way. There seemed to be no way of estimating their number, though the strands ran thick and numerous through the gloom.

As they trudged on, coming at last into the major cavern and starting across it, Pol finally glimpsed the soft glow of the master spell at its farther end.

"Tell me," he asked, "do you see any light in that direction?"

"No. Just the one we're following."

Pol gestured and seized a strand. Soon it took on a pale color and something of incandescence.

"See that?"

"A line of light, running before us."

"Good. I'll give you one of that sort to follow out. What is that thing in your hand?"

"A pistol I've carried since I left Mark's place."

"I thought so. You won't need it here."

"It comforts me."

After a considerable interval, they stood before the pied globe. Pol held the scepter as he faced it.

"I hope this works as I'd anticipated," he remarked.

"I feel some force, but I see nothing special. . . ."

"Go and stand over in that niche." He gestured, and for a moment the scepter blazed like a captive star. "I will tell you when it is safe to depart. There is your strand." He gestured again, and a line of pale fire grew in the air before the niche. "Good luck!"

"To you, also," Mouseglove replied, clasping Pol's hand and turning.

He moved quickly and backed into the opening, unable to take his eyes from the spectacle of the younger man, who had already begun a series of seeming ritual movements, his silhouette distorted by guitar case and flapping cloak, his face pale and mask-like in the blaze of the rod, beneath the dark, silver-splashed wings of his hair. Mouseglove clutched the pistol more tightly as the slow dance of the hand and the rod progressed, for he felt a chill followed by a wave of warmth, another chill . . . and now he had momentary flashes of vision, as of a massive, burning ball of yarn being unwound.

Pol moved his hand deftly, in and out, unwinding unravelling, and old words trapped within the fabric of the structure, came to him and he spoke them as he worked, and the waves of heat came more frequently, till finally he saw through to the center, the core, the end. . . .

He thrust the scepter into the heart of the spell and spoke the final words.

A great wash of forces swept by him and he swayed, striving to keep his balance. The strands now clung to the scepter, obscuring it completely to Pol's vision. His right arm seemed to take fire as he laid his will upon it.

A moaning rose within the cavern, growing to a mighty chorus of sounds, which echoed and reechoed about him, followed by rustling, scraping noises and the falling of stones.

". . . Arise! Arise! and follow me to battle!" he sang, and now there were larger movements within the darkness.

The moaning died down and ceased. The snorts, snarls, roars and rattles diminished. Now the sounds of heavy breathing came to him from every direction.

He plucked a single strand, and soon a huge, gray form moved past him on two legs, hunched forward, arms dragging on the ground, yellow eyes burning within the darkness of a triangular face, scales rustling with each stride. It paused before Mouseglove, who raised the pistol and waited, but it turned and moved on an instant later.

"Give it an hour," Pol stated, "and the upstairs should be cleared. It knows you now and will not harm you."

Mouseglove nodded, realizing as he did that the movement could not be seen, but unable to control his voice. Brief bonfires flared and died at all distances as dragons tested their flames.

Pol turned away, directing all his attention to impressing his identity and his commands upon the awakening creatures.

Arise, I say! We fly south to destroy the city atop Anvil Mountain! Those of you who cannot fly must be mounted upon those who can! I will lead the way!

He cast about for only a moment, and then his fingers moved unerringly to catch at a dark green strand drifting near him.

Dragon! he called. *Name yourself!*

I am called Smoke-in-the-Skies-at-Evening-against-the-Last-Pale-Clouds-of-Autumn-Day, came a proud feminine reply.

In the interest of ready communication, I shall refer to you as 'Smoke.'

That is agreeable to me.

Come to me now. We must lead the others.

For a time, nothing occurred, as he realized that Smoke had slept within one of the farther caverns. All of the stirring sounds grew louder as the other creatures stood, stretched, mounted. Finally, he heard a noise like a rising wind rushing toward him, and a piece of darkness detached itself from the distant shadows, to sweep in his direction and settle silently before him.

Greetings, Pol Detson. I am ready, she said.

He released the strand and moved to touch her neck.

Greetings, Smoke. If I may mount now, we will be on our way.

Come up. I am ready.

Pol climbed toward her shoulders and settled into position. He raised the scepter and lights danced throughout the cavern.

Follow! he ordered. Then, to Smoke, *Now! Let us go!*

Smoke was smaller than Moonbird but seemed faster. In a matter of moments, they were airborne and moving ahead quickly. Pol looked back once. He could not distinguish Mouseglove in his niche, but he saw that dark forms were rising like ashes in his wake.

You will sing us a battle-song? Smoke asked.

Pol was surprised to find it already upon his lips.

XXI

The bird-things sent to determine the nature and progress of the conflict at Rondoval were the first observers of the dragon-flight which began at the northern cliff-face below the castle, spiraling upward, wheeling through the west and falling into a sky-darkening pattern heading southward, led by a man mounted upon a sleek gray dragon, a shining scepter in his right hand. The sun settled as they flew, and the metallic birds climbed and moved far to the right and the left to monitor their progress.

Mark assigned troops to the various stations, and the elevators ground ceaselessly as tanks and artillery pieces were raised from the warehouse areas to the streets of the city proper. Weapons and ammunition were issued to the defenders. All available sky boats were serviced and armed. Assembly lines were shut down, and the workers went to collect their weapons.

Mark studied the array of screens in the surveillance center, showing varied views of the oncoming formation.

"I'd like to know what those things can do," he remarked to the captain who stood at his elbow. "This could be closer than I'd care to see it. Who'd have thought he could raise something like that this quickly? Damned sorcerer! Send a dozen battle-wagons to hit them at dawn. Swing six of them wide to hit their left flank out of the sunrise, and drop six on them from above. We'll probably lose them, but I want to see how it happens."

"Yes, sir."

Mark toyed with the idea of sending for Nora, but dismissed it. He visited the lab instead, to check whether

188

a long-range jumble was yet possible. He doubted it, but something useful might yet be salvaged from that project.

. . . *Damn!* he mused. *A year from now and he'd never make it across the desert. I know about more things than I've got. Can't get them into production fast enough. . . . Damn!*

His lens was a pale yellow beneath a perfectly clear sky. Stars winked at him and a warm breeze licked like an affectionate tiger at his cheek. Suddenly, a meteor shower began, and he watched it for several minutes, dismissing the shaking beneath his feet as the labors of the heavy machinery which had long since been shut down.

*   *   *

Pol fled across the night, the power of the scepter his meat, his drink and his sleep. When the attack came in the morning, he spread the formation, detached two groups of ten dragons each to deal with the sky boats and continued on. Later, sixteen dragons rejoined him, but two of them had to drop out, their injuries preventing them from maintaining the pace of the others. He led the entire formation to a greater altitude after that and began spreading it into a great line. Through the morning hazes, the ground seemed to ripple momentarily beneath them.

He saw the advancing formation of flying things just before Anvil Mountain came into view.

Destroy as many as are necessary to get through, he ordered the leather-winged masses at his back. *But do not remain to toy with them. I doubt they will bomb or strafe once you are into their own city fighting with its defenders. Destroy anything on the mountain that offers resistance. Then burn the place. Only this girl*—and he sent a mental picture of Nora back along the strands—*must not be harmed. If you see her, protect her. And this one*—a picture of Mark followed—*is mine. Call to me if you see him.*

They swept on toward the line of defenders and shortly the firing began. A little while after that, dragon vomit fell like rain upon the sky boats. Fires dotted the ground, wreckage and falling bodies filled the air. There were a great many of the ships, but their crews could not reload the guns quickly and their accuracy was far less than perfect. After several minutes of combat, it was clear that Pol's forces would not be halted here. When they finally passed on toward Anvil Mountain, their force was diminished but the air fleet was broken.

As they came within range of the flat-topped mount, the artillery fire began. But Pol had spread his formation even more thinly by then, having seen evidence of heavy artillery on his earlier visit to the place.

Still, the great guns fired with deadly effect for several minutes, until two of them toppled, one exploded and others began firing wildly.

Sweeping even nearer, through the morning light, Pol saw that the entire mountain was shaking.

It is a mighty magic you wield, Smoke remarked.

That is not my doing, he replied.

A dragon can feel magic, and that which leads to the earthquake I feel upon my back.

I do not understand.

The answer hangs at your belt.

The figurines?

I know not what they are, only what they are bringing to pass.

Good! I'll take all the help I can get!

Even if they control you?

Either way, I have no choice now but to try to win, do I?

They broke through the openings in the artillery screen, dragons landing and discharging the non-winged creatures which immediately turned and sought the defenders. Tanks rumbled along the shaking streets, some of them spewing flames back at the dragons.

A steady crackling of gunfire rose above the city. The metallic worms were out, wrestling with the attackers. Here and there, blades flashed in the hands of men as ammunition was exhausted. The howling, bounding lesser beasts of the caverns tore through the city, killing and being killed. A crack opened, diagonally, in one of the main avenues and noxious fumes rose out of it.

Pol looked about, searching rooftops and opened bunkers, hoping to catch sight of the red-haired man with the eye of many colors. But Mark was nowhere in sight.

He sought altitude again, and he directed Smoke to take him in a wide circle above the city. The screams grew fainter as they rose, and the designs of the buildings and the overall layout of the city impressed themselves upon him for the first time. The place was efficiently disposed, extremely fuctional, logically patterned and relatively clean. He realized that he felt a grudging admiration for a country boy capable of materializing such a dream—and in such a brief while—whether his world wanted it or not. He wished once again that he could have sent Mark back to the place where he himself had been so long the misfit.

They landed upon the vacant roof of a tall building; and there, without dismounting, Pol raised the scepter with both hands and laid his will upon his forces below. They required organization now, not skirmishing. It was time to create groups and direct their efforts toward specific objectives. His wrist pulsed, the rod pulsed, the strands pulsed as he began. There was usually a feeling of elation as he worked with the power. But this time, while the feeling was present, there was little joy accompanying it. He had never wished to be the destroyer of another man's dreams.

He saw tanks torn apart by his creatures, but he also saw dragons beset and hacked apart by the small folk, who, having moved from the wilds to this existence in the span of a few years, still possessed the instincts of pack hunters when reduced to the bloody basics of life. He felt something of an admiration for them, also, though this in no way affected his tactics. He grew more and more dispassionate as the sun climbed and the conflicts progressed. Moving each time artillery pieces were repositioned to bring him down, directing strike forces toward the most troublesome emplacements, he hurled other assaults against what appeared to be nerve centers, breaking down walls and spreading fires, wondering the while whether Mark occupied some similar position elsewhere, and with radio communication directed his forces into the surprising patterns of resistance which kept developing. Most likely. Things were still too closely balanced to permit him to desert his command post and seek the other out, however.

The casualties were heavy on both sides. Pol felt he now had the edge, though, in that he was destroying more and more of his adversary's capabilities as the day progressed, whereas his own foces were not dependent upon things outside themselves. He was slowly reducing them to reliance upon the simplest of weapons, and when this reduction had reached the proper point, a parity of forces would represent no equality whatsoever and the battle would be near to its end.

The mountain gave another shudder, and the opening in the ground grew larger. Steam had emerged from it for a long while, earlier, but with the enlargement flames and pieces of stone shot forth, the buildings nearby suffered partial collapse of their facades and a roaring noise came up, growing until it smothered all the sounds of the fighting.

Pol's aching hands tightened even more upon the scepter, as he said aloud, "Only a fool could call it coincidence. If I've an unseen ally, make yourself known!"

Immediately, seven large flames hovered in the air before him, unsupported by any burning medium. The one to his left flickered, and the reply seemed to come from that source:

It is no coincidence.

"Why, then?"

Now the second flame flickered.

It is a recurring thing, this struggle. Ages ago, the world was split by it, giving birth to the one in which you were raised, where we are legend, and making that one a legend to this. It is an undying conflict and its time has come again. You are the agent of preservation; Mark, the champion of the insurgency. One of you must be utterly obliterated.

"Has he allies such as you?"

The third replied:

Beneath that shrine, far below, is an ancient teaching machine. He bears a small unit within his body which keeps him in constant communication with it.

Pol immediately disengaged a force and directed it against the shrine, with instructions to destroy everything beneath it as well.

"Do you already know the outcome here?" he asked.

It is still undecided, said the fourth.

We distract you, said the fifth.

. . . And your full attention is still required here, said the sixth.

. . . And so we depart, said the seventh, as they faded and dwindled to nothing.

Pol was immediately beset by a fresh artillery barrage, and had to fly to a new vantage while directing attacks against the guns.

Strong fumes reached him before very long and he had to move again, seeing now that the opening below had become a glowing crater, its smoke rising to smudge the sky. Its rumbles continued to grow, also.

Much later, he realized that no one was shooting at him any longer. Suicide fliers had attacked for a time, but he had destroyed them with blasts from the scepter until, finally, they had ceased.

The fighting below had grown more and more disorganized, as both sides suffered massive casualties. The battle for the shrine, far down below the slopes, continued. A remarkably powerful defense had seemed to arise from almost nowhere, and Pol had diverted more forces to deal with it.

. . . And Nora thought herself a pawn, he reflected. *What am I? I exercise all the functions of command, yet I am no freer than any of those below. Unless . . .*

Up, Smoke! Big circles!

I, too, serve, came the reply, and they were rising, turning.

The third time around, he saw them—Nora and Mark atop a high building across the avenue from the crater. It was a flash of sunlight gleaming upon a red lens turned in his direction that drew his eyes to their position.

Over there, Smoke! It still may not be too late to talk to him! If I can just make him see what is happening!

Smoke turned and beat toward the rooftop. Pol waved his dirty handkerchief, doubting that the gesture meant anything in this place, but willing to try anything he knew to gain conversation with the other.

"Mark!" he shouted. "I want to talk! May I come down?"

The other lowered a small unit into which he had been speaking and gestured for him to land.

As soon as Smoke touched the roof, Pol leaped down and headed toward the tall figure with the yellowing eye lens.

"I am only now beginning to realize what we are doing," Pol said, while he was still moving. "It was an encounter such as this, between science and magic, which destroyed a high culture in this land ages ago, which split the continuum into parallel parts. We are doing it again! We are both victims! We've been manipulated. This battle is affecting the land itself! We have to—"

An explosion at his back caused him to stumble forward. Whether the great cry from Smoke was mental or verbal, he never knew.

"Damn you, Mark!" he called as he got to his feet, not even looking back, already knowing what he would see. "I came here to save your life, to stop this thing—"

"How considerate," Mark stated. "In that case, I accept your surrender."

"Don't be an ass!" Pol staggered to the edge of the shuddering building. "Surrender what? Look down there! Both of our armies are almost finished. We can still stop it. Right here. We can still save something. Both science and magic do work here—so it is not an either/or proposition in this place. They must both be special cases of some more general law. Let's work out something compatible. Let's not go the way we're being pushed. If the continuum must be split again, let's split it our way. I'll work with you. But look down there! Look what's happening! Do you want that?"

Mark moved to the low, partly shattered parapet, followed by Nora. Pol saw that he held her wrist in a powerful grip. He looked down again himself, to where a fiery river now flowed along the avenue, away from the still growing crater almost directly below them. Mark's lens flashed green through the smoke and and falling ash. Even at this height, Pol could feel heat upon his face.

"If I have slain your dragon, you have destroyed my shrine," Mark said softly, "just now."

With a sudden movement of his arms, he drew Nora to the edge and held her there. His lens flashed red again.

"I reject your mad offer," he stated. "If I let you go, you can acquire more supernatural assistance and attack me again one day."

"It works both ways," Pol replied. "You can rebuild again—better, stronger. I'm willing to take that chance."

"I'm not," Mark said, twisting Nora's arm. "That rod you hold seems to be the key to your power. Throw it down into the crater or I'll throw her. Try using it against me now and I'll take her along with me."

Pol looked at the rod for only a moment, then cast it out over the edge. Mark watched it fall. Pol did not.

"Let her go," he said.

Mark pushed her back and down, so that she stumbled and fell to the rooftop.

"Now I can face you," he said.

Pol raised his fists and moved forward.

"I am not such a fool," Mark said, sliding an oblong case from a pocket upon his right thigh. "I remember that you've had training with your hands. Try this!"

Suddenly, Pol was able to see the roar from the nascent volcano below, yellow and black-streaked, washing about him. The rooftop buckled beneath his feet, emitting musical tones like spikes, as the sky tipped, becoming a funnel, its terminus his head, down which the sharp-edged clouds and swirls of smoke were pouring. His feet were far away—perhaps in Hell—yes, burning, and when he tried to move, he dropped to one knee and the firmament shuddered and his eyes were moist with gems which sliced his cheeks apart as they descended. Smooth blue notes emerged from his mouth like escaping birds. Mark was laughing purple rings and his orange eye was a rushing headlight. The thing he held before him tore shimmering holes in the air, and—

—and from one of the holes emerged seven wings of flame.

Your guitar, said the first.
Get the case off your back, said the second.
Get it out of the case, said the third.
Play it, said the fourth.

Your hands know the way, said the fifth.
Get the case, said the sixth.
Open it, said the seventh.

A black mountain flew past him, as his hands—unfamiliar things themselves—performed operations they alone understood. Blue sparks flew from three points upon the blackness. A strange and dangerous object was rising out of the shadows before him. . . .

His hands made it move to his knee and began doing things they alone knew. . . .

Constellations bloomed before his eyes. A throbbing began down near the place of movement. . . .

Attack! said the first.
Drive back that which assails you, said the second.
Let him see as you see now, said the third.
. . . Hear as you hear, said the fourth.
You lulled the minotaur, said the fifth.
. . . This one you shall drive beyond the bounds of reason, said the sixth.
Destroy him! said the seventh.

Suddenly, he heard the music. The distortions still played about him, but he pushed them farther off. He changed the beat. He rose slowly to a standing position. The waves from the jumble-box washed over him and reality was troubled each time a portion of the broadcast broke through, reached him. But his vision cleared for longer and longer periods of time. He saw Mark, holding the box, pointing it at him, perspiration like a mask of glass upon his face. His lens was flashing wildly through the entire spectrum. He swayed. The music drowned even the rumbling below, though the smoke came and went between them. Nora knelt, head bowed, hands covering her face. Pol put more force into his strumming, driving the beat into his adversary's brain. Mark took a swaying step backward and halted. Pol advanced a step, colors swirling intermittently in the air before him. Mark retreated another pace, his lens flashing faster and faster from color to color. When the building shook again, slanting beneath their feet, Mark staggered and dropped the box. His lens went black for several pulsebeats. He put out his hands for support, took another step . . . A cloud of smoke swept over him. He fell against the parapet, and it gave way. . . .

Pol stopped playing and dropped to his knees. Automatically, he lowered the guitar into its case. He began crawling toward Nora then, feeling a strong pull to his right as the building canted even more precipitously. When he reached her, he placed his hand upon her shoulder.

"I did try to save him," he said.

"I know."

She lowered her hands from her face and hugged him gently, looking away toward the rail.

"I know."

Hurry, Pol! The building is going!

He looked upward, unbelieving. A vast, dark form was sliding through the smoke.

Moonbird!

Mount as soon as I light. Only moments remaining . . .

The great dragon settled beside them, enormous open wounds upon his sides and shoulders. Pol boosted Nora onto his back, slung his guitar case and followed.

How—? Pol began.

The one called Mouseglove. I can talk with him, Moonbird said as they rose. *He lies injured at Rondoval, attended by centaurs. Your ogre destroyed all the men but the two in the ships. Fortunately, he had a weapon that slays from a distance. He says that he will be your houseguest until he is whole again. He told me to come here.*

As they climbed higher, Pol summoned strands, all that he could, and clutched them for a moment.

It is over, he said. *We are going home.*

From here and there, his surviving minions rose to follow.

He looked down, once, into the raging heart of the crater.

 . . . *If I were to drop the seven figurines into it,* he wondered, *would I be free?*

You are a fool, came a voice out of a sudden flame, *if you think that we—the most bound of all—are even as free as you.*

The flame faded, and Pol turned and watched the smoking mountain grow smaller as Moonbird beat his way into the sky.

I am not finished learning, he said. *But I've had enough lessons for today.*

Nora had slumped before him, but her breathing was regular. He eased her into a more comfortable position. He felt older as he regarded the sinking sun, and very tired, though he knew he could not permit himself to sleep for a long while. He reached out and touched one of Moonbird's wounds.

I am glad that someone I know won something, he said.

Later, the stars came out and he watched them all the way to home and morning.

MADWAND

This one is for Trent

I

I am not certain.

It sometimes seems as if I have always been here, yet I know that there must have been a time before my advent.

And sometimes it seems as if I have only just lately arrived. From where I might have come, I have no idea. Recently, I have found this vaguely troubling, but only recently.

For a long while, I drifted through these halls, across the battlements, up and down the towers, expanding or contracting as I chose, to fill a room—or a dozen—or to snake my way through the homes of mice, to trace the sparkling cables of the spider's web. Nothing moves in this place but that I am aware of it.

Yet I was not fully aware of myself until recently, and the acts I have just recited have the dust of dreams strewn over them, myself the partial self of the dreamer. Yet—

Yet I do not sleep. I do not dream. However, I seem now to know of many things which I have never experienced.

Perhaps it is that I am a slow learner, or perhaps something has recently stimulated my awareness to the point where all the echoes of thoughts have brought about something new within me—a sense of self which I did not formerly possess, a knowledge of separateness, of my apartness from those things which are not-me.

If this is the case, I would like to believe that it has to do with my reason for being. I have also recently begun feeling that I should have a reason for being, that it is important that I have a reason for being. I have no idea, however, as to what this could be.

It has been said—again, recently—that this place is

201

haunted. But a ghost, as I understand it, is some non-physical survival of someone or something which once existed in a more solid form. I have never encountered such an entity in my travels through this place, though lately it has occurred to me that the reference could be to me in my more tangible moments. Still, I do not believe that I am a ghost, for I have no recollection of the requisite previous state. Of course, it is difficult to be certain in a matter such as this, for I lack knowledge concerning whatever laws might govern such situations.

And this is another area of existence of which I have but recently become aware: laws—restrictions, compulsions, areas of freedom . . . They seem to be everywhere, from the dance of the tiniest particles to the turning of the world, which may be the reason I had paid them such small heed before. That which is ubiquitous is almost unnoticed. It is so easy to flow in accordance with the usual without reflecting upon it. It may well be that it was the occurrence of the unusual which served to rouse this faculty within me, and along with it the realization of my own existence.

Then, too, in accordance with the laws with which I have become aware, I have observed a phenomenon which I refer to as the persistance of pattern. The two men who sit talking within the room where I hover like a slowly turning, totally transparent cloud an arm's distance out from the highest bookshelf nearest the window—these two men are both patterned upon similar lines of symmetry, though I become aware of many differences within these limits, and the wave disturbances which they cause within the air when communicating with one another are also patterned things possessing, or possessed by, rules of their own. And if I attend very closely, I can even become aware of their thoughts behind, and sometimes even before, these disturbances. These, too, seem to be patterned, but at a much higher level of complexity.

It would seem to follow that if I were a ghost something of my previous pattern might have persisted. But I am without particular form, capable of great expansions and contractions, able to permeate anything I have so far encountered. And there is no special resting state to which I feel constrained to return.

Along with my nascent sense of identity and my ignorance as to what it is that I am, I do feel something else: a certainty that I am incomplete. There is a thing lacking within me, which, if I were to discover it, might well provide me with that reason for being which I so desire. There are times when I feel as if I had been, in a way, sleeping for a long while and but recently been awakened by the commotions in this place—awakened to find myself robbed of some essential instruction. (I have only lately learned the concept "robbed" because one of the men I now regard is a thief.)

If I am to acquire a completeness, it would seem that I must pursue it myself. I suppose that, for now, I ought to make this pursuit my reason for being. Yes. Self-knowledge, the quest after identity . . . These would seem a good starting place. I wonder whether anyone else has ever had such a problem? I will pay close attention to what the men are saying.

I do not like being uncertain.

Pol Detson had arranged the seven figurines into a row on the desk before him. A young man, despite the white streak through his hair, he leaned forward and extended a hand in their direction. For a time he moved it slowly, passing his fingertips about the entire group, then in and out, encircling each gem-studded individual. Finally, he sighed and withdrew. He crossed the room to where the small, black-garbed man sat, left leg crooked over the arm of his chair, a wineglass in either hand, the contents of both aswirl. He accepted one from him and raised it to his lips.

"Well?" the smaller man, Mouseglove by name, the thief, asked him when he lowered it.

Pol shook his head, moved a chair so that his field of vision took in both Mouseglove and the statuettes, seated himself.

"Peculiar," he said at last. "Almost everything tosses off a thread, something to give you a hold over it, even if you have to fight for it, even if it only does it occasionally."

"Perhaps this is not the proper occasion."

Pol leaned forward, set his glass upon the desk. He flexed his fingers before him and placed their tips together. He began rubbing them against one another with small, circular movements. After perhaps half a minute, he drew them apart and reached toward the desk.

He chose the nearest figure—thin, female, crowned with a red stone, hands clasped beneath the breasts—and began making a wrapping motion about it, though Mouseglove could detect no substance to be engaged in the process. Finally, his fingers moved as if he were tying a series of knots in a nonexistent string. Then he moved away, seating himself again, drawing his hands slowly after him as if playing out a line with some tension on it.

He sat unmoving for a long while. Then the figure on the desk jerked slightly and he lowered his hands.

"No good," he said, rubbing his eyes and reaching to recover his wineglass. "I can't seem to get a handle on it. They are not like anything else I know about."

"They're special, all right," Mouseglove observed, "considering the dance they put me through. And from the glimpses they gave you at Anvil Mountain, I have the feeling they could talk to you right now—if they wanted to."

"Yes. They were helpful enough—in a way—at the time. I wonder why they won't communicate now?"

"Perhaps they have nothing to say."

I found myself puzzled by the manner in which these men spoke of those seven small statues on the desk, as if they were alive. I drew nearer and examined them. I had noted lines of force going from the man Pol's fingertips to them, shortly after he had spoken of "threads" and performed his manipulations. I had also detected a throbbing of power in the vicinity of his right forearm, where he bore the strangely troubling mark of the dragon—a thing about which I feel I should know more than I do—but I had seen no threads. Nor had I noted any sort of reaction from the figures, save for the small jerking movement of the one as the shell of force was repelled.

I settled down about them, contracting, feeling the textures of the various materials of which they had been formed. Cold, lifeless. It was only the words of the men which laid any mystery upon them.

Continuing this commerce of surfaces, I grew even smaller, concentrating my attention now upon that figure which Pol had momentarily bound. My action then was as prompt as my decision: I began to pour myself into it, flowing through the miniscule openings—

The burn! It was indescribable, the searing feeling that passed through my being. Expanding, filling the room, passing beyond it into the night, I knew that it must be that thing referred to as pain. I had never experienced it before and I wanted never to feel it again.

I continued to seek greater tenuosness, for in it lay a measure of alleviation.

Pol had been correct concerning the figure. It was, somehow, alive. It did not wish to be disturbed.

Beyond the walls of Rondoval, the pain began to ease. I felt a stirring within me . . . something which had always been there but was just now beginning to creep into awareness. . . .

"What was that?" Pol said. "It sounded like a scream, but—"

"I didn't hear anything," Mouseglove answered, straightening. "But I just felt a jolt—as if I'd been touched by someone who'd walked across a heavy rug, only stronger, longer . . . I don't know. It gave me a chill. Maybe you stirred something up, playing with that statue."

"Maybe," Pol said. "For a moment, it felt as if there were something peculiar right here in the room with us."

"There must be a lot of unusual things about this old place—with both of your parents having been practicing sorcerers. Not to mention your grandparents, and theirs."

Pol nodded and sipped his wine.

"There are times when I feel acutely aware of my lack of formal training in the area."

He raised his right hand slightly above shoulder-level, extended his index finger and moved it rapidly through a series of small circles. A book bound in skin of an indeter-

minate origin appeared suddenly in his hand, a gray and
white feather bookmark protruding from it.

"My father's diary," he announced, lowering the volume
and opening it to the feather. "Now here," he said, running his finger down the righthand page, pausing and
staring, "he tells how he defeated and destroyed an enemy
sorcerer, capturing his spirit in the form of one of the
figures. Elsewhere, he talks of some of the others. But all
that he says at the end here is, 'It will prove useful in the
task to come. If six will not do to force the wards I shall
have seven, or even eight.' Obviously, he had something
very specific in mind. Unfortunately, he did not commit it
to paper."

"Further along perhaps?"

"I'll be up late again reading. I've taken my time with it
these past months because it is not a pleasant document.
He wasn't a very nice guy."

"I know that. It is good that you learn it from his own
words, though."

"His words about forcing the wards—do they mean
anything at all to you?"

"Not a thing."

"A good sorcerer would find some way to learn it from
the materials at hand, I'm sure."

"I'm not. Those things seem extremely potent. As for
your own abilities, you seem to have come pretty far
without training. I'd give a lot to be able to pull that book
trick—with, say, someone's jewelry. Where'd you get it
from, anyway?"

Pol smiled.

"I didn't want to leave it lying around, so I bound it
with a golden strand and ordered it to retreat into one of
those placeless places between the worlds, as I saw them
arrayed on my journey here. It vanished then, but whenever I wish to continue reading it I merely draw upon the
thread and summon it."

"Gods! You could do that with a suit of armor, a rack of
weapons, a year's supply of food, your entire library, for
that matter! You can make yourself invincible!"

Pol shook his head.

"Afraid not," he said. "The book and the jumble-box are

all I've been keeping there, because I wouldn't want either to fall into anyone else's hands. If I were traveling, I could add my guitar. Much more, though, and it would become too great a burden. Their mass somehow gets added to my own. It's as if I'm carrying around whatever I send through."

"So that's where the box has gotten to. I remember your locating it, that day we went back to Anvil Mountain . . ."

"Yes. I almost wish I hadn't."

"You couldn't really hope to recover his body or your scepter from that crater."

"No, that's not what I meant. It was just seeing all that— waste—that bothered me. I—"

He slammed his fist against the arm of his chair.

"Damn those statues! It sometimes seems they were behind it all! If I could just get them to—Hell!"

He drained his glass and went to refill it.

The sensation ebbed. I did not like that experience. The room and its inhabitants were now tiny within the cloud of myself, and more uncertainties were now present: I did not know what it was that had caused me pain, nor how it produced that effect. I felt that I should learn these things, so as to avoid it in the future. I did not know how to proceed.

I also felt that it might be useful for me to learn how to produce this effect in others, so that I could cause them to leave me alone. How might I do this? If there were a means of contact it would seem that it could go either way, once the technique were mastered. . . .

Again, the stirring of memory. But I was distracted. Someone approached the castle. It was a solitary human of male gender. I was aware of the distinction because of my familiarity with the girl Nora who had dwelled within for a time before returning to her own people. This man wore a brown cloak and dark clothing. He came drifting out of the northwest, mounted upon one of the lesser kin of the dragons who dwell below. His hair was yellow, and in places white. He wore a short blade. He circled. He could not miss the sign of the one lighted room. He began to descend, silent as a leaf or an ash across the air. I believed that he would land at the far end of the courtyard, out of sight of the library window.

Yes.

Within the room the men were talking, about the battle at the place called Anvil Mountain, where Pol destroyed his step-brother, Mark Marakson. Pol, I gather, is a sorcerer and Mark was something else, similar but opposite. A sorcerer is one who manipulates forces as I saw Pol do with the statue, and the book. Now, dimly, I recalled another sorcerer. His name was Det.

". . . You've been brooding over those figures too long," Mouseglove was saying. "If there were an easy answer, you'd have found it by now."

"I know," Pol replied. "That's why I'm looking for something more complicated."

"I don't have any special knowledge of magic," Mouseglove said, "but it looks to me as if the problem does not lie completely in that area."

"What do you mean?"

"Facts, man. You haven't enough plain, old-fashioned information to be sure what you're up against here, what it is that you should be doing. You've had a couple of months to ransack this library, to play every magical game you can think of with the stiff dolls. If the answer were to be found that way, you'd have turned it up. It's just not here. You are going to have to look somewhere else."

"Where?" Pol asked.

"If I knew that, I'd have told you before now. I've been away from the world I knew for over twenty years. It must have changed a bit in that time. So I'm hardly one to be giving directions. But you know I'd only intended to remain here until I'd recovered from my injury. I've been feeling fine for some time now. I've been loathe to leave, though, because of you. I don't like seeing you drive yourself against a crazy mystery day after day. There are enough half-mad wizards in the world, and I think that's where you may be heading—not to mention the possibility of your setting off something which may simply destroy you on the spot. I think you ought to get out, get away from the problem for a time. You'd said you wanted to see more of this world. Do it now. Come with me—tomorrow. Who knows? You may even come across some of the information you seek in your travels."

"I don't know . . ." Pol began. "I do want to go, but—tomorrow?"

"Tomorrow."

"Where would we be heading?"

"Over to the coast, I was thinking, and then north along it. You can pick up a lot of news in port cities—"

Pol raised his hand and cocked his head. Mouseglove nodded and rose to his feet.

"Your warning system still working?" Mouseglove whispered.

Pol nodded and turned toward the door.

"Then it can't be any—"

The sound came again, and with it the form of a light-haired man appeared in the doorway, smiling.

"Good evening, Pol Detson," he stated, raising his left hand and jerking it through a series of quick movements, "and good-bye."

Pol fell to his knees, his face suddenly bright red. Mouseglove rounded the desk. Picking up one of the statuettes and raising it like a club, he moved toward the brown-cloaked stranger.

The man made a sudden movement with his right hand and the thief was halted, spun and slammed back against the wall to his left. The figurine fell from his grip as he slumped to the floor.

As this occurred, Pol raised his hands beside his cheeks and then gestured outward. His face began returning to its normal color as he climbed to his feet.

"I might ask, 'Why?' " he said, his own hands moving now, rotating in opposite directions.

The stranger continued to smile and made a sweeping movement with one hand, as if brushing away an insect.

"And I might answer you," said the other, "but it would take some coercion."

"Very well," said Pol. "I'm willing."

He felt his dragonmark throb and the air was alive with strands. Reaching out, he seized a fistful, shook them and snapped them like a lash toward the other's face.

The man reached out and caught them as they arrived. A numbing shock traveled up Pol's arm and it fell limply to his side. The density of the strands between them increased to a level he had never before witnessed, partly obscuring his view of his opponent.

Pol made a large sweeping motion with his left hand, gathering in a ball of them. Immediately, he willed it to fire and cast the blazing orb toward the other.

The man deflected it with the back of his right hand and then flung both arms upward and outward.

The light in the room began to throb. The air became so filled with the lines of power that they seemed to merge, becoming huge, swimming, varicolored patterns obscuring much of the prospect, including the stranger.

As the pulse in his dragonmark overcame the numbness in his right arm, Pol sent his will through it, seeking a clearer image of his adversary. Immediately, the form of the other man began to glow, as the rainbow-work wove itself to closure. The room disappeared, and Pol became aware that his form, too, had become luminiscent.

The two of them faced one another across a private universe built entirely of moving colors.

Pol saw the man raise his hands, cupping them before him. Immediately, a green serpent raised its head from within them and slithered forth, moving in Pol's direction.

Pol could feel a raw creation force moving all about him. He reached out and up, beginning a rapid series of shaping movements. A huge, gray bird came into being between his hands. He laid his will upon it and released it. It flashed forward and dove upon the snake, catching at it with its talons, striking with its beak. The serpent twisted its body and struck at the bird, missing.

Looking past this contest, Pol saw that the man was now juggling a number of balls of colored light. Even as the bird rose, bearing the struggling snake in its talons, to flap upward and merge with the kaleidescopic field which surrounded them, Pol saw the man cast the first blazing ball in his direction.

Smiling, Pol shaped a tennis raquet and saw a look of puzzlement cross his adversary's features as he regarded the unfamiliar instrument.

He slammed the first ball back at the man just as the second was released. The sorcerer dropped the remaining balls and dove to the side to avoid the return. Pol batted the second one out-of-court as the man rolled forward and came to his feet, his right hand snapping outward, something long and black moving with it.

He swung the raquet and missed as the whip caught him about the neck and jerked him forward. He felt himself falling. Dropping the raquet, he reached for the choking thing that held him, to seize it, unwind it—

It jerked again and the world began to spin and darken. It continued to tighten, and he heard the sound of laughter, coming nearer . . .

"Not much of a contest," he heard the other say.

Then there was an explosion and everything went black.

It was instructive to observe the exchange of forces between Pol and the visitor. Also, mildly unsettling, as it occurred to me that they might be inducing pain in each other. Yet, they had wanted to do it or they wouldn't have. I was more interested in the manipulations than I was in their progressive wearing down of each other, because I felt that I might be able to engage in that sort of activity myself and I wished to be further informed. Its abrupt ending came as a surprise to me. Save for small, less complex creatures, I had not seen one being end another's existence. Indeed, it had not occurred to me that these larger ones could be ended. I felt as if I should have taken a part in it, though on which side and in which direction, I could not say. I was also uncertain as to why I felt this way.

Where there had been three there were now two. I did not understand why they had done it, nor how the lance of force had come from the statuette to terminate the stranger before Mouseglove's projectile reached his head.

Pol shook his head. His neck was sore. He rubbed it and opened his eyes. He was lying on the floor beside the desk. Slowly, he pushed himself into a seated position.

The stranger lay upon his back near the door, right arm

outflung, left across his breast. A piece of his forehead was missing and his right eye was a crimson pool.

To his left, leaning against a bookshelf, Mouseglove stood rubbing his eyes. His right arm hung at his side and in his hand was the pistol he had carried away from Anvil Mountain. When he saw Pol move he dropped his left hand and smiled weakly.

"Are you all right?" he asked.

"I guess so. Except for a stiff neck. What about yourself?"

"I don't know what he hit me with. It affected my sight for awhile. When I came around, the two of you seemed to be pulsing into and out of existence. I wasn't able to get a shot at him till the last time he came through." He replaced the weapon in a holster behind his belt and moved forward, extending his hand. "Everything seems normal enough now."

Pol accepted his hand and rose. They both crossed the room and looked down at the dead man. Mouseglove immediately knelt and began searching him. After several minutes, he shook his head, unfastened the brown cloak and covered the man with it.

"Nothing," he said, "to tell who he is or why he came. I take it you have no idea?"

"None."

They returned to their seats and the wine flask, Mouseglove restoring the fallen figurine on the way.

"Either he had some reason for disliking you and came by to do something about it," Mouseglove said, "or somebody else who feels that way sent him. In the first case, some friend of his might come along later to continue the work. In the second, another may be sent as soon as it is known that this one failed. Either way, it would appear that more trouble will be forthcoming."

Pol nodded. He rose and removed a book from a shelf high on the lefthand wall. He returned to his seat and began paging through it.

"This one got through all of your alarm spells without giving warning," Mouseglove continued.

"He was better than I am," Pol said, without looking up from the book.

"So what is to be done?"

"Here," Pol said, locating the page he sought and reading silently for a time. "I had been wondering about this for some time," he went on. "Every four years there is a gathering of sorcerers at Belken, a mountain to the northwest. Ever hear of it?"

"Of course—as a good thing to stay away from."

"It will begin in about two weeks. I've decided to attend."

"If they're all like this fellow—" Mouseglove nodded toward the form upon the floor. "—I don't think it would be a very good idea."

Pol shook his head.

"The description makes it sound rather peaceful. Advanced practicioners discuss theory with one another, apprentices are initiated, rites involving more than one sorcerer get tried out, exotic articles are traded and sold, new effects demonstrated . . ."

"The person behind this attempt on your life may be there."

"Exactly. I'd like to settle this quickly. It may all be some sort of misunderstanding. After all, I haven't been around long enough to have made any real enemies. And if the one I seek isn't there, I may learn something about him—if there is such a person. Either way, it makes it seem worthwhile."

"And that will be your only reason for going?"

"Well, no. I also feel the need for some formal training in the Art. Perhaps I can pick up a few pointers at something like that."

"I don't know, Pol . . . It sounds kind of risky."

"Not going may prove even more dangerous in the long run."

They heard a scraping noise and a popping sound from the courtyard. Both rose and moved to the window. Looking downward, they saw nothing. Pol seemed to stroke the air with his fingertips.

"The man's mount," he said finally. "It's freed itself of whatever restraints he'd laid upon it and is preparing to depart." He moved his hand rapidly, raising the other one as well. "Maybe I can get a line on it, trace it back to where it came from."

The lesser kin of the dragon rose in the northeast and swept through a wide, rising arc, leftward.

"No good," Pol said, lowering his hands. "Missed him."

Mouseglove shrugged.

"I guess you won't be going with me," he said, "if you'll be heading for that convocation, in the other direction."

Pol nodded.

"I'll leave tomorrow, too, though. I'd rather be moving about than staying in one place between now and then. So we can take the trail for a little way together."

"You won't be riding Moonbird?"

"No, I want to see something of the countryside, too."

"Traveling alone also has its hazards."

"I'd imagine they are fewer for a sorcerer."

"Perhaps," Mouseglove replied.

The dark form of the dragon-mount dwindled against the northern sky, vanished within a mountain's shadow.

II

That night, as I permeated the dead man's body, seeking traces within his brain cells, I learned that his name had been Keth and that he had served one greater than himself. Nothing more. As I slid into and out of higher spaces, as I terminated a rat in a drainage channel in the manner I had recently learned, as I threaded my way among moonbeams in the old tower and slid along rafters in search of spiders, I thought upon the evening's doings and on all manner of existential questions which had not troubled me previously.

The energies of the creatures which I had taken had a bracing effect upon my overall being. I wandered through new areas of thought. Other beings existed in multitudes, yet I had never encountered another such as myself. Did this mean that I was unique? If not, where were the others? If so, why? From whence did I come? Was there a special reason for my existence? If yes, what could it be?

I swirled across the ramparts. I descended to the caverns far below and passed among the sleeping dragons and the other creatures. I felt no kinship with any of them.

It did not occur to me until much later that I must possess some particular attachment to Rondoval itself, else I might long ago have wandered off. I realized that I did prefer it and its environs to those other portions of the countryside into which I had ventured. Something had kept calling me back. What?

I returned to Pol's sleeping form and examined him very carefully, as I had every night since his arrival. And I found myself, as always, hovering above the dragonmark upon his right forearm. It, too, attracted me. For what

reason, I could not say. It was at about the time of this
man's arrival that I had begun the movement which had
culminated in my present state of self-awareness. Was it
somehow his doing? Or—the place having been deserted
for as long as it had been—would the prolonged presence
of anyone have worked the same effect within me?

My desire for purpose returned to me strongly. I began
to feel that my apparent deficiency in this area might have
been accidental, that perhaps I should possess a compulsion, that there was something I should be doing but had
somehow lost or never learned. How significant, I wondered, was this feeling? Again, I was uncertain. But I began
to understand what had produced my present attitude of
inquiry.

Pol would be departing on the morrow. My memories of
a time before his time had already become dim. Would I
return to my more selfless state when he left? I did not
believe so, yet I was willing to concede that he had played
some part in my awakening into identity.

I realized at that moment that I was trying to make a
decision. Should I remain at Rondoval or should I accompany Pol? And in either case, why?

I tried to terminate a bat in flight but it got away from
me.

The two of them took the northern trail on foot that
morning, traveling together through the pass and downward to the spring-touched green of the forest to the place
of the crossroads Pol had marked upon the map he bore.

They rested their packs against the bole of a large oak,
still darkly damp with the morning dew, and considered
the mists which dwindled and faded even as they watched,
while the sun became a bright bulge upon the slope of a
mountain to their right. From somewhere behind them
the first tentative notes of birdsong were commenced and
then abandoned.

"You will be out of the hills by evening," said Pol,
looking to the right. "It will be a few days before I get
down, and then I'll have to climb again later. You'll be
basking in the sea breeze while I'm still shivering my ass
off. Well, good luck to you and thanks again—"

"Save the speech." said Mouseglove. "I'm coming along."

"To Belken?"

"All the way."

"Why?"

"I allowed myself to get too curious. Now I want to see how it all ends."

"It may well end indeed."

"You don't really believe that or you wouldn't be going. Come on! Don't try to talk me out of it. You might succeed."

Mouseglove raised his pack and moved off to the left. Shortly, Pol joined him. The sun looked over the mountain's shoulder and the gates of dawn were opened. Their shadows ran on before them.

That night they camped within a stand of pine trees, and Pol had a dream which felt like no dream he had ever known before. There was a clarity and a quality of consciousness involved which spun it past his inner eye with a disturbing simulation of reality, while in all aspects it was invested with a foreboding air of menace and yet possessed him with a certain dark joy.

Seven pale flames were moving in slow procession widdershins about him, as if summoning him, spirit fashion, to appear in their midst. He rose up slowly out of his body and stood like a bloodless image of himself. At this, they halted and left the ground. He followed them to treetop height and beyond. Then they escorted him northward, moving higher and faster beneath a sky filled with palely illuminated clouds. Grotesque shapes seemed to fill the trees below, the mountains about him. The wind made a whining sound and black forms flitted out of his way. The terrain rippled in dark waves as his speed increased. The wind became a howling thing, though he felt neither cold nor pressure from it.

At last, a huge, dark form loomed before him, set halfway up a mountainside, dotted here and there with small illumination; walled, turreted, heavy, high, it was a castle at least the size of Rondoval and in better condition.

There followed a break in his dream-awareness from which he recovered after an eon or a moment to a feeling of cold, of dampness. He stood before a massive double-door, heavily ironbound and hung with huge rings. It was inscribed with the figure of a serpent, spikes driven through it; the crucified form of a great bird hung above it. Where it was located, he had no idea, but it seemed suddenly familiar—as though he had glimpsed it repeatedly in other dreams, forgotten until this instant. He swayed slightly forward, realizing as he did that the chill he experienced hung about the Gate itself like an invisible aura, increasing perceptibly with each tiny movement he made toward it.

The flames burned silently, sourcelessly, at either hand. He was overwhelmed with a desire to pass through the Gate, but he had no idea as to how this might be accomplished. The doors looked far too formidable to yield to the strength of any solitary mortal. . . .

He awoke cold and wondering, pulling his covering higher and drawing it more tightly about him. The next morning he remembered the dream but did not speak of it. And that night it was partly repeated. . . .

He stood again before the dusky Gate, with the recalled sensations but few specific images of his journey to the place. This time he stood with his arms upraised, pleading in ancient words for them to open before him. With a mighty creaking they obeyed, moving outward a short distance, releasing a small breeze and an icy chill along with tendrils of mist and a sound of distant wailing. He moved forward to enter. . . .

On each night of that first week on the road, he returned to that dream and traveled further into it, losing his flame-like companions when he passed beyond the Gate. Alone, he drifted across a blasted landscape—gray and bronze, black and umber—beneath a dark, red-streaked sky where a barely illuminated, coppery orb hung still in what could be the west. It was a place of shadow and stone, sand and mist, of cold and wailing winds, sudden fires and slow, crawling things which refused to register themselves upon his memory. It was a place of sinister, sentient lights, dark caves and ruined statues of monstrous form and mien. Some small part of him seemed to regret that he took such pleasure in the prospect. . . .

And the night that he saw the creatures—scaled, coarse

monstrosities; long-armed, hulking parodies of the human form—sliding, hopping, lurching in pursuit of the lone man who fled before them across that landscape. He looked down with a certain anticipation.

The man ran between a pair of high stone pillars, cried out when he found himself in a rocky declivity having no other exit. The creatures entered and laid hold of him. They forced him to the ground and began tearing at him. They beat at him and flayed him, the ground growing even darker about them.

Abruptly, one of the creatures shrieked and drew back from the ghastly gathering. Its long, scaly right arm had been changed into something short and pale. The others uttered mocking noises and seized upon it. Holding the struggling creature, they returned their attention to the thing upon the ground. Bending forward, they wrenched and bit at it. It was no longer recognizable as anything human. But it was not unrecognizable.

It had altered under their moist invasions, becoming something larger, something resembling themselves in appearance, while the beast they held to witness had shrunken, growing softer and lighter and stranger.

Nor was it unrecognizable. It had become human in form, and whole.

Those who held the man pushed him and he fell. In the meantime, the demonic thing upon the ground was left alone as the others drew back from it. Its limbs twitched and it struggled to rise.

The man scrambled to his feet, stumbled, then raced forward, passing between the pillars, howling. Immediately, the dark creatures emitted sharp cries and, pushing and clawing against one another, moved to pursue the fleeing changeling, the one who had somehow been of a substance with him joining in.

Pol heard laughter and awoke to find it his own. It ended abruptly, and he lay for a long while staring at moonlit clouds through the dark branches of the trees.

They rode one day in the wagon of a farmer and his son and accompanied a pedlar for half a day. Beyond this— and encounters with a merchant and a physician headed in the opposite direction—they met no one taking the same route until the second week. Then, a sunny afternoon, they spied the dust and dark figures of a small troop before them in the distance.

It was late afternoon when they finally overtook the group of travelers. It consisted of an old sorcerer, Ibal Shenson, accompanied by his two apprentices, Nupf and Sahay, and ten servants—four of whom were engaged in the transportation of the sedan chair in which Ibal rode.

It was to Nupf—a short, thin, mustachioed youth with long, dark hair—that Pol first addressed himself, since this one was walking at the rear of the retinue.

"Greetings," he said, and the man moved his right hand along an inconspicuous arc as he turned to face him.

As had been happening with increasing frequency when confronted with manifestations of the Art, Pol's second vision came reflexively into play. He saw a shimmering gray strand loop itself and move as if to settle over his head. With but the faintest throb of the dragonmark he raised his hand and brushed it aside.

"Here!" he said. "Is that the way to return the greeting of a fellow traveler?"

A look of apprehension widened the other's eyes, jerked at his mouth.

"My apologies," he said. "One never knows about travelers. I was merely acting to safeguard my master. I did not realize you were a brother in the Art."

"And now that you do . . .?"

"You are headed for the meeting at Belken?"

"Yes."

"I will speak with my master, who no doubt will invite you to accompany us."

"Go ahead."

"Who shall I tell him sends greetings?"

"Pol Detson—and this is Mouseglove."

"Very well."

He turned and moved to catch up with the bearers. Pol and Mouseglove followed.

Looking over the apprentice's shoulder, Pol glimpsed the old sorcerer himself before the man addressed him. Swathed in blue garments, a gray shawl over his shoulders, a brown rug upon his lap, it was difficult to estimate his size, though he gave the impression of smallness and fragility. His nose was sharp, his eyes pale and close-set; his cheeks and forehead were deeply creased, the skin mottled; his hair was thick, long, very black and looked like a wig—for his beard was sparse and gray. His hands were out of sight beneath the rug.

"Come nearer," he hissed, turning his head toward Pol and squinting.

After he did so, Pol held his breath, becoming aware of the other's.

"Detson? Detson?" the man asked. "From where have you come?"

"Castle Rondoval," Pol replied.

"I thought the place deserted all these years. Who is lord there now?"

"I am."

There was a stirring beneath the brown coverlet. A big-jointed, dark-veined hand emerged. It moved slowly toward Pol's right wrist and plucked at the sleeve.

"Bare your forearm, if you please."

Pol reached across and did so.

Two fingers extended, Ibal traced the dragonmark. Then he chuckled and raised his eyes, staring at Pol, past him.

"It is as you say," he remarked. "I did not know of you—though I see now that you are troubled by more than one lingering thing from out of Rondoval's past."

"That may well be," said Pol. "But how can you tell?"

"They circle you like swarms of bright insects," Ibal said, still looking past him.

Pol consciously shifted into his second mode of seeing, and while there were many strands in the vicinity, he detected nothing which resembled a circling swarm of insects.

"I fail to observe the phenomenon myself. . . ."

"Most certainly," the other replied, "for it has doubtless been constantly with you—and it would of course seem different to you than it does to me, anyway, if you could detect it at all. You know how sorcerers' perceptions vary, and their emphasis upon different things."

Pol frowned.

"Or do you?" Ibal asked.

When Pol did not reply, the old sorcerer continued to stare, narrowing his eyes to tight slits.

"Now I am not so certain," he said. "At first I thought that the disorganization of your lights was a very clever disguise, but now—"

"My lights?" Pol said.

"With whom did you serve your apprenticeship—and when did you undergo initiation?" the other demanded.

Pol smiled.

"I grew up far from here," he replied, "in a place where things are not done that way."

"Ah, you are a Madwand! Preserve us from Madwands! Still . . . You are not *totally* disorganized—and anyone with that mark—" He nodded again at Pol's right arm "—must possess an instinct for the Art. Interesting . . . So why do you travel to Belken?"

"To learn . . . some things."

The old sorcerer chuckled.

"And I go for self-indulgence," he said. "Call me Ibal, and accompany me. It will be good to have someone strange to talk with. Your man is not a brother of the Art?"

"No, and Mouseglove is not really my man—he is my companion."

"Mouseglove, did you say? I seem to have heard that name before. Something to do with jewels, perhaps?"

"I am not a jeweler," Mouseglove replied hastily.

"No matter. Tomorrow I will tell you some things that may be of interest to you, Detson. But it is still over half a league to the place where I intend to camp. Let us move on. Upward! Forward!"

The servants raised the litter and moved ahead with it. Pol and Mouseglove took up positions behind it and followed.

That night they camped amid the ruins of what might once have been a small amphitheatre. Pol lay troubled for a long while, in fear of the dreams that might come to him. He still had not spoken of these, for in daytime the things of sleep seemed far away. But when the stillness descended and the fire dwindled the deeper places of shadow seemed filled with faces, as if some ghostly audience capable of seeing beyond the cowl of sleep had come together here to watch his journey into the place of baleful lights and screaming winds and cruelty. He shuddered and listened for a long time, his eyes darting. He knew of no magic to affect the content of his dreams. And he wondered again as to their significance, partly with the mind of one whose culture would have seen them in psychopathological terms, partly with the freshly tuned awareness that in this place another explanation could as readily apply. Then his thoughts began to drift, back to the encounter with the sorcerer who had tried to kill him at Rondoval. The dreams had begun almost immediately after that, and he wondered whether there could be a connection. Had the other laid a spell upon him before he had died, to trouble his sleep thereafter? His mind moved away, lulled by the steady creaking of insects in the distant wood. He wondered what Mark would have done. Looked for some drug to block it all out, perhaps. His mind drifted again. . . .

The movement. Now a familiar thing. The fear was gone. There was only anticipation within the rapid and disjointed series of images by which he moved. There was the Gate, and . . .

It stopped. Everything stopped. He was frozen before the image of the partly opened Gate. It was fading, insubstantial, going away, and there was a hand upon his shoulder. He wanted to cry out, but only for a moment.

"It's all right now," came a whisper, and the hand left him.

Pol tried to turn his head, to sit up. He found that he could not stir. A large man, his face more than half-hidden in the shadow of his cowl, was rising from a kneeling position beside him, passing through his field of vision. Pol thought that he glimpsed part of a pale moustache and—impossibly—a shining, capped tooth.

"Then why can't I move?" he whispered through clenched teeth.

"It was far easier for me to lay a general spell upon this entire camp than to be selective about it. Then I needed but arouse you and leave the others unconscious. The paralysis is, unfortunately, a part of it."

Pol suspected that this was a lie but saw no way to test it.

"I saw that your sleep was troubled. I decided to grant you some relief."

"How can you see that a man's sleep is troubled?"

"I am something of a specialist in that matter which confronts you."

"That being . . .?"

"Did your dream not involve a large door?"

Pol was silent for a moment. Then, "Yes," he said. "It did. How could you know this unless you induced it yourself?"

"I did not cause your dream. I did not even come here for purposes of releasing you from it."

"What, then?"

"You journey to Belken."

"You seem to know everything. . . ."

"Do not be impertinent. As our interests may be conjoined, I am trying to help you. I understand more than you do about some of the forces which are influencing you. You make a serious mistake, wandering about the world announcing yourself at this point in your career. Now, I have just taken great pains to remove the memory of your name and origin from the minds of Ibal and everyone in his party. In the morning, he will only recall you as a Madwand traveling to Belken. Even your appearance will be a confusion to him. If he should ask your name again, have another one ready, and use it in Belken, also. Rondoval still has its enemies."

"I gathered something of this with the attempt on my life."

"When was this? Where?"

"A little over a week ago. Back home."

"I was not aware of this. Then it has begun. You should be safe for a time, if you remain incognito. I am going to rinse your hair with a chemical I have here, to conceal that white streak. It is too distinctive. And then we must hide your dragonmark."

"How?"

"A relatively simple matter. How do you see manifestations of the Powers when you are working a spell?"

Pol felt moisture upon his scalp.

"Usually as colored strands—threads, strings, cords."

"Interesting. Very well, then. You can imagine me as wrapping your forearm with flesh-colored strands—so closely as to entirely mask the mark. It will in no way interfere with your workings. When you wish to uncover it you need but go through an unwrapping ritual."

Pol felt his arm taken, raised.

"Who are you?" he asked. "How do you know all these things?"

"I am the sorcerer who should never have been, and mine is a peculiar link with your House."

"We are related?"

"No. Not even friends."

"Then why are you helping me?"

"I feel that your continued existence may serve me. There. Your arm is nicely disguised."

"If you really wish to protect me from something, you might do well to tell me somewhat about it."

"I do not deem that the most fitting course of action. First, nothing may happen to you, in which case I would have exposed you to information I'd rather not. Second, ignorance on your part may actually benefit me."

"Mister, someone's already gotten my number. I don't like the notion of being suddenly engaged in another sorcerous duel."

"Oh, they're all right if you win. That was the nature of the assassination attempt?"

"Yes."

"Well, you're still intact."

"Just barely."

"Good enough, my boy. Keeps you alert. Now, perhaps we'd best coarsen your features a bit and lighten your eyes a trifle. Shall we have a wart beside your nose? No? An interesting scar on your cheek then? Yes, that should do it. . . ."

"And you won't give me your name?"

"It would mean nothing to you, but your knowledge of it might trouble me later."

Pol willed the dragonmark to life, hoping his disguised arm would mask this from the other's second sight. The man voiced no reaction as the throbbing began. Pol sent the force up and down his right arm, freeing it from the paralysis. Then his neck. He had to be able to turn his head a bit. . . . Best to leave the rest as it was for the moment. Catalepsy, he knew, is hard to fake.

The hands continued to move over his face. The other's face remained out of his field of vision. Pol summoned a tough, gray strand and felt its ghostly presence across his fingertips.

"Now they'll all think you've been to Heidelberg. . . ."

"What," Pol asked him, "did you say?"

"An obscure reference," the other offered quickly. "A really good sorcerer has knowledge of places beyond this place, you know—"

Pol let the energy pulse through him, breaking the paralysis entirely. He rolled onto his side and directed a flash movement of the gray strand. It snaked upward and snared the man's wrists. As he tightened it, he began to rise.

"Now I will ask my questions again," Pol stated.

"Fool of a Madwand!" said the other.

The strand writhed in Pol's hand and a feeling like an electrical shock traveled up his arm. He could not release the thing and the dragonmark felt as if it were on fire. He opened his mouth to scream, but nothing came out.

"You are very lucky," was the last thing he heard the man say before the storm reached his brain and he fell.

Dawn had just bruised the eastern heaven when he opened his eyes. It was the voices of Ibal's servants which had awakened him, as they moved about packing their gear, making ready to decamp. Pol raised his hands to his temples, trying to recall how much he had drunk. . . .

"Who are you? Where's Pol?"

He turned his head, saw Mouseglove standing arms akimbo, staring at him.

"Is there a scar on my cheek?" he asked, raising his fingertips to search it.

"Yes."

"Listen to my voice. Don't you recognize it? Is the streak in my hair gone, too?"

"Oh . . . I see. Yes, it is. Why a disguise at this point?" Pol got up and began gathering his things.

"I'll tell you about it while we're walking along."

He searched the ground for signs of his visitor, but it was a rocky place and there were none. As they followed Ibal's servitors back toward the trail, Mouseglove paused and pointed into a clump of withered shrubbery.

"What do you make of that?" he asked.

Three mummified rabbits hung among the tangle of branches.

Shaking his head, Pol walked on.

III

It was more than a little traumatic at the beginning: the sights and sounds—all of the new things we encountered beyond Rondoval. I hovered close to Pol for the first several days, drifting along, sensing everything within range, familiarizing myself with the laws governing new groups of phenomena. Travel, I discovered, *is* broadening, for I found myself spreading over a larger area as time went on. My little joke. I realized that my expansion was at least partly attributable to the increased number of things whose essences I absorbed as we traveled along—plants as well as animals, though the latter were more to my liking—and partly in accord with Boyle's and Charles' laws, which I'd picked out of Pol's mind one evening when he returned in memory to his university days. I cannot, in all honesty, consider myself a gas. Though I am anchored to the physical plane, I am not entirely manifested here and can withdraw partly with ease, entirely with more difficulty. I confine myself to a given area and move about by means of my will. I am not certain how that works either. I was aware, however, that my total volume was increasing and that my ability to do physical things was improving—like the rabbits. I had decided to look upon the entire journey as an educational experience. Any new thing that I learned might ultimately have some bearing upon my quest for identity and purpose.

And I was learning new things, some of them most peculiar. For instance, when that cloaked and muffled man entered the compound, I had felt a rippling as of a gentle breeze, only it was not physical; I had heard something like a low note and seen a mass of swimming colors.

Then everyone, including the camp watchman, was asleep. There followed more movements and colors and sounds. Having recently learned the meaning of "subjective," I can safely say that that is what they were, rather than tangible. Then I observed with interest as he altered the sleepers', memories concerning Pol, realizing from the sensations I had experienced and from my memory of those back at Rondoval during Pol's duel with the sorcerer in brown that I was extremely sensitive to magical emanations. I felt as if I could easily have altered these workings. I saw no reason to do so, however, so I merely observed. From my small knowledge of such affairs, it seemed that this one had an unusual style in the way he shifted forces among the planes. Yes. Sudden memories of a violent occasion reinforced this impression. He was peculiar, but I could see how he did everything that he did.

Then he stood beside Pol for a long while and I could not tell what he was about. He was employing some power different from that which he had used minutes before, and I did not understand it. Something within me jerked spasmodically when he reached out and laid a hand upon Pol's shoulder. Why, I did not know, but I moved nearer. I witnessed the entire conversation and the transformation of Pol's appearance. When the man covered the dragonmark I found myself wanting to cry out, "No!" But, of course, I had no voice. It irritated me considerably to see it done, though I knew that it remained intact beneath the spell—and I was aware that Pol could undo the spell whenever he chose. What this reaction told me about myself, I could not say.

But then, when Pol rose and there was a brief and rapid exchange of forces between the men, I rushed to settle upon Pol and permeate his form, inspecting it for damage. I could discover nothing which seemed permanently debilitating to his kind, and since they generally render themselves unconscious during the night I made no effort to interfere with this state.

Withdrawing, I then set out to locate the other man. I was not certain why, nor what I would do should I succeed in finding him. But he had departed quickly and there was no trace of him about, so the questions remained academic.

That was when I came across the rabbits and terminated them, as well as the bush where they crouched. I felt immediately stronger. I puzzled over all my reactions and the more basic questions which lay behind them—wondering, too, whether I was really made for such a fruitless function as introspection.

No one in the company, Ibal included, seemed to take note of Pol's altered appearance. And none addressed him by name. It was as if each of them had forgotten it and was embarrassed to reveal the fact to the others. Eventually, those who spoke with him settled upon "Madwand" as a term of address, and Pol did not even get to use the other name he had ready. Conceding the possibility of its protective benefit, he was nevertheless irritated that his new identity had caused Ibal to forget whatever it was that he had intended telling him about Rondoval. Not knowing how strong the stranger's memory-clouding spell might be, he was loath to associate himself with Rondoval in his companions' minds by broaching the subject himself.

It was two nights later, as they sat to dinner, that Ibal raised a matter almost as interesting.

"So, Madwand, tell me of your plans," he said, spooning something soft and mushy between what remained of his teeth. "What do you propose doing at the fest?"

"Learning," Pol replied. "I would like to meet some fellow practitioners, and I would like to become more proficient in the Art."

Ibal chuckled moistly.

"Why don't you just come out and say that you're looking for a sponsor for initiation?" he asked.

"Would I be eligible?" Pol inquired.

"If a master would back you."

"What would the benefits be?"

Ibal shook his head.

"I find it hard to believe you are that naive. Where did you grow up?"

"In a place where the question never arose."

"I suppose I can believe that if I try, since you *are* a Madwand. All right. I occasionally find ignorance very refreshing. Proper experience of the rituals involved in initiation will result in an ordering of your lights. This will allow you to handle greater quantities of the energy that moves through all things. It will permit you to grow in power, a thing which might not happen otherwise."

"Will initiations actually be conducted at Belken this time, during the course of the gathering?"

"Yes. I plan on having Nupf initiated there—though Sahay, I feel, is not ready."

He gestured toward the larger of his apprentices, the youth with dark eyes and pale hair. Sahay frowned and looked away.

"Once an apprentice has been initiated he is on his own, so to speak?" Pol asked.

"Yes, though a man will occasionally remain with his master for a period of time afterwards to learn certain fine points of the Art which might have been neglected while he was studying the basics"

"Well, if I can't locate a sponsor I guess that I'll just have to muddle through life on my own."

"If you are aware of the dangers of initiation . . ."

"I'm not."

"Death and madness are the main ones. Every now and then they claim a few who were not quite ready."

"Could I get some coaching so as not to be unready?"

"That could be arranged."

"Then I'd be willing."

"In that case, I will sponsor you in return for future goodwill. It's always nice to have a few friends in the trade."

The dreams of the Gate and the peculiar land beyond them did not return that night, nor on any succeeding night until their arrival at the festival. The days passed uneventfully, routinely, as they hiked along, until only the fact of his changed appearance assured Pol that something unusual had actually occurred. The terrain had altered as they headed upward, though the ascent here was more gradual than the descent from the mountains about Rondoval. Belken itself was a great, black, fang-like peak, dotted with numerous depressions, bare of trees. The evening they first caught sight of it, it seemed outlined by a faint white light. Mouseglove drew Pol aside and they halted to regard it.

"Are you sure you know what you're getting into?" he asked him.

"Ibal has outlined the initiation procedures for me," Pol replied, "and he's given me an idea of what to expect at the various stations."

"That is not exactly what I had in mind," Mouseglove said.

"What, then?"

"A sorcerer tried to kill you back at Rondoval. Another came by, apparently to help you, last week. I get the impression that you are in the middle of something nasty and magical—and here you go, walking right into a den of magicians and about to attempt something dangerous without the normal preparations."

"On the other hand," Pol replied, "it is probably the best place for me to discover what is going on. And I'm sure I will find uses for any additional insight and strength the initiation provides."

"Do you really trust Ibal?"

Pol shrugged.

"It seems that I have to, up to a point."

"Unless you decide to quit the whole game right now."

"That would put me right back where I started. No thanks."

"It would give you time to think things over more, perhaps find a different line of investigation to follow."

"Yes," Pol answered, "I wish that I could. But time, I feel, is something I cannot afford to spend so freely."

Mouseglove sighed and turned away.

"That mountain looks sinister," he said.

"I have to agree with you."

The following morning, proceeding among the foothills, they reached the top of a low ridge and the group halted. Spread out before the eastern base of the mountain was something out of dreamland or fairy tale: a sparkling collection of creamy towers and golden spires amid buildings which looked as if they had been carved out of massive gemstones; there were bright arches over glistening roadways, columns of jet, rainbow-hung fountains . . .

"Gods!" Pol said. "I'd no idea it was anything like that!" He heard Ibal chuckle.

"What's funny?" Pol asked.

"One is only young once. Let it be a surprise," the old sorcerer replied.

Puzzled, Pol continued on. As the day advanced, the dream-city lost some of its glamour. First went the sparkling and the rainbows; then the colors began to fade. A haziness came over the buildings, and within it a uniform grayness settled upon the entire prospect. The structures seemed to diminish in size, and some of the spires and higher columns vanished altogether. Glassy walls grew opaque and took on motion, a gentle, flapping movement. Then the fountains and the archways were gone. It was as if he now looked upon the place through a dimming and distorting glass.

When they sat to lunch, Pol addressed Ibal:

"All right, I'm surprised and I'm several hours older now. What's become of the city?"

Ibal nearly choked on his mush.

"No, no," he finally said. "Wait until dinnertime. Watch the show."

And so he did. As the sun moved westward and the shadow of the peak fell over the hazy outlines of the structures at its base, the flapping movement ceased and the walls began to acquire something of their former sheen. Pol and Mouseglove continued to stare as they approached. As the shadows lengthened, the place seemed to grow, slowly at first, more rapidly as the afternoon faded toward evening. The haze itself seemed to be dimming and the outline of higher structures again became visible within it. Drawing nearer to it, they became aware of the spurting of fountains. The colors gradually reappeared within the still-firming outlines of the buildings. The towers, columns and arches took on a greater solidity.

By dinnertime they were very near, and the city was much closer to its early morning appearance. The haze continued to dissipate as they sat watching it, taking their meal.

"Well, have you guessed?" Ibal asked, spooning in a dark broth.

"It appears to be different things at different times," Pol said. "So obviously it is not what it seems and must represent some sort of enchantment. I've no idea what's really there, or why it changes."

"What is really there is a group of caves, shacks and tents," Ibal explained. "Each time, by lot, various practicioners acquire the responsibility for putting the place into order for the gathering. What they normally do is send their apprentices and some servants on ahead. These clean and repair the structures, raise the tents and set up the various facilities. Then the apprentices usually vie in working out spells to give it a pleasing appearance. However, apprentices vary in ability, and since the thing is only to be temporary first class spells are seldom employed. Consequently, it is beautiful from evening through dawn. As the day progresses, however, it begins to waver. Things are weakest at noon, and then you catch glimpses of what is really behind it all."

"Do the spells hold on the inside as well as the outside?"

"Indeed, Madwand, they do. You shall see for yourself soon."

As they watched, the sparkling began again, faint at first, growing.

They reached the foot of Belken by evening and entered the bright city which had grown up there. The first archway through which they passed might have been made of branches strapped together, but it gave every appearance of gold-veined marble possessed of intricate carvings. Countless lights drifted through the air at several times the height of a man. Pol kept turning his head, assessing the wonders. Unlike any city with which he was familiar, this one seemed clean. The way beneath their feet was unnaturally bright. The buildings appeared almost fragile, with an eggshell translucence to them. Filigreed screens covered fancifully shaped windows in walls sporting designs of glowing gemstones. There were balconies and overhead walkways, arcades through which richly garbed men and women passed. Open-fronted shops displayed magical paraphernalia and exotic beasts were penned and tethered throughout the city—though a few wandered harmlessly, as if taking in the sights themselves. Thick clouds of red smoke rose from a brazier on a corner where a turbanned mage chanted, a demonic face and form taking shape within it high above the street. The sounds of flutes, stringed instruments and drums came from several directions. On an impulse, Pol jerked his guitar into existence, tuned it, slung it and began playing as they walked along. He felt his dragonmark throbbing invisibly, as if in response to the magical ambiance they were entering. Bright birds in cages of silver and gold trilled responses to his song. A few of the passing faces turned his way. High above, the face of the mountain was glowing softly, as if traversed by swarms of fireflies. And even higher, the stars had appeared in a clear sky. Cool breezes moved about him, bringing the odors of exotic incenses, perfumes, of sweet logs burning.

Mouseglove sniffed and listened, fingers twitching, eyes darting.

"It would be difficult to know what to steal, in a place where nothing is what it seems," he remarked.

"Then you might look upon it as a vacation."

"Hardly," Mouseglove replied, eyeing a demon-face which seemed to regard him from behind a grating high in the wall to his left. "Perhaps as an experience in compulsory education. . . ."

Ibal, croaking orders to his servants at every turn, seemed to know the way to his quarters. They were, Pol later learned, the same apartments he had always occupied. Their appearance would be radically altered upon each occasion, one of the older servants informed him. Orientation here was a matter of familiarity with position rather than appearance.

The apartments to which they were conducted as Ibal's guests seemed extensive and elegant, though the eye-swindling shimmer of glamourie lay upon everything and Pol noted that solid-appearing walls seemed to yield somewhat if he leaned upon them, smooth floors were sometimes uneven to the feet and chairs were never as comfortable as they looked.

Ibal had dismissed them, saying that he intended to rest and that he would introduce them to the initiation officials on the morrow. So, after bathing and changing their garments, Pol and Mouseglove went out to see more of the town.

The balls of white light illuminated the major thoroughfares. Globes of various colors drifted above the lesser ways. They passed knots of youths whose overheard conversations were like the ruminations of philosophers and groups of old men who called upon their powers to engage in practical jokes—such as the tiny cloud hovering just beneath an archway which suddenly rattled and drenched anyone who passed below it, to the accompaniment of uproarious laughter from the gnome-like masters lurking in the shadows.

Brushing away the moisture, Pol and Mouseglove continued on to a narrow stair leading down to a winding street less well-illuminated than those above—blue and red lights, smaller and dimmer than the others, moving slowly above it.

"That looks to be a possibly interesting way," Mouseglove indicated, leaning on a railing above it.

"Let's go down and have a look."

It seemed a place of refreshment. Establishments serving food and beverage, both indoors and out, lined the way. They strolled slowly by all of them, then turned and started back again.

"I like the looks of that one," said Mouseglove, gesturing to the right. "One of the empty tables under the canopy, perhaps, where we can watch the people pass."

"Good idea," said Pol, and they made their way over and sat down.

A small, dark, smiling man wearing a green kaftan emerged from the establishment's doorway almost immediately.

"And what will the gentlemen have?" he inquired.

"I'd like a glass of red wine," said Pol.

"Make mine white and almost sour," said Mouseglove.

The man turned away and immediately turned back. He held a tray bearing two glasses of wine, one light, one dark.

"Useful trick, that," Mouseglove observed.

"Private spell," the other replied.

The man grew almost apologetic then as he asked them to drop their payment through a small hoop into a basket.

"All the others are starting it, too," he said. "Too many enchanted pebbles going around. You might even have some without knowing it."

But their coins remained coins as they passed through the charmed circle.

"We just arrived," Pol told him.

"Well, keep an eye out for stones."

He moved off to take another order.

The wine was extremely good, though Pol suspected that a part of its taste was enchantment. Still, he reflected after a time, what difference should it make? Like the entire place about them—if it serves its purpose, appearance can be far more important than content.

"Hardly an original observation," Mouseglove replied when he voiced it. "And it meant a lot to me every time I lifted a bogus jewel I thought was real."

Pol chuckled.

"Then it served its purpose."

Mouseglove laughed.

"All right. All right. But when death gets involved it is better to know which is the real dagger and which the real hand. After what happened that last night in your library, I would be very careful in a place like this."

"By what means that I am not already employing?"

"Well, that magical shower we passed through earlier," Mouseglove began. "I just noticed—"

He was interrupted by the approach of a blond, well-built young man with finely chiseled features and a flashing smile. He was extravagantly dressed and he moved with an extraordinary grace and poise.

"Madwand! And Mouseglove! Strange meeting you here! Waiter! Another of whatever they're having for my friends! And a glass of your best for me!"

He drew up a chair and seated himself at their table.

"It looks as if they did a better than usual job this year," he said, gesturing. "How do you like your accommodations?"

"Uh—fine," Pol replied as the waiter arrived and produced their drinks.

The youth gestured and his hand was suddenly filled

with coins. They leapt upward from it, arched through the hoop and into the basket with a small pyrotechnic display.

"Coloful," Pol said. "Listen, I hate to seem rude since you're buying, but I can't seem to recall . . ."

The youth laughed, his handsome features creasing with merriment.

"Of course not, of course not," he said. "I am Ibal, and you are looking at the finest rejuvenation spell ever wrought." He brushed a speck of dust from his bright sleeve. "Not to mention a few cosmetic workings," he added softly.

"Really!"

"Amazing!"

"Yes. I am ready to meet once again with my beloved Vonnie, for two weeks of lovemaking, revelry, good food and drink. It is the only reason I still come to these things."

"How—interesting."

"Yes. We first met here nearly three hundred years ago, and our feelings have remained undiminished across the centuries."

"Impressive," Pol said. "But do you not see one another in between times?"

"Gods, no! If we had to live together on a day-to-day basis one of us would doubtless kill the other. Two weeks every four years is just right." He stared into his drink a moment before raising it to his lips. "Besides," he added, "we spend a lot of the intervening time recovering."

He looked up again.

"Madwand, what have you done to yourself?"

"What do you mean?" Pol asked.

"That white streak in your hair. Why is it there?"

Pol ran a hand through his still-moist thatch.

"Little joke," he said.

"Not in the best of taste," said Ibal, shaking his head. "You'll have people associating you with Det's Disaster. Ahh!"

They followed a sudden movement of his gaze out along the street, past a halted fat man and a pair of strollers, to where a woman approached under a swaying blue light. She was of medium height, her hair long and dark and glossy, her form superbly molded beneath a light, clinging costume, her features delicate, lovely, smiling.

Following his sharp intake of breath, Ibal rose to his feet. Pol and Mouseglove did the same.

"Gentlemen, this is Vonnie," he announced as she came up to the table. He embraced her, kept his arm about her. "My dear, you are lovelier than ever. These are my friends, Madwand and Mouseglove. Let us have a drink with them before we go our way."

She nodded to them as he brought her a chair.

"It is good to meet you," she said. "Have you come very far?" and Pol, captivated by the charm of her voice as well as the freshness of her person, felt a sudden and acute loneliness.

He forgot his reply as soon as he uttered it, and he spent the next several minutes admiring her.

As they rose to leave, Ibal leaned forward and whispered, "The hair—I'm serious. You'd best correct it soon, or the initiation officials may think you flippant. At any other time, of course, it would not matter. But in one seeking initiation—well, it is not a time for joking, if you catch my meaning."

Pol nodded, wondering at the simplest way to deal with it.

"I'll take care of it this evening."

"Very good. I will see you some time tomorrow—not too early."

"Enjoy yourselves."

Ibal smiled.

"I'm sure."

Pol watched them go, then returned his attention to his drink.

"Don't look suddenly," Mouseglove whispered through unmoving lips, "but there is a fat man who has been loitering across the way for some time now."

"I'd sort of noticed," Pol replied, sweeping his gaze over the bulky man's person as he raised his glass. "What about him?"

"I know him," Mouseglove said, "or knew him—professionally. His name is Ryle Merson."

Pol shook his head.

"The name means nothing to me."

"He is the sorcerer I once mentioned. It was over twenty years ago that he hired me to steal those seven statuettes from your father."

Pol felt a strong urge to turn and stare at the large man in gold and gray. He restrained himself.

". . . And there was no hint from him as to what he wanted them for?" he asked.

"No."

"I feel they're very safe—in with my guitar," Pol said.

When he did look again, Ryle Merson was talking with a tall man who wore a long-sleeved black tunic, red trousers and high black boots, a red bandana about his head. The man had his back to them, but a little later he turned and his eyes met Pol's in passing, before the two of them moved on slowly up the street.

"What about that one?"

Mouseglove shook his head.

"For a moment I thought there was something familiar about him, but no—I don't know his name and I can't say where I might have seen him before, if indeed I did."

"Is this a coincidence, I wonder?"

"Ryle is a sorcerer, and this is a sorcerers' convention."

"Why do you think he chose to stand there for so long?"

"It could be that he was simply waiting for his friend," Mouseglove said, "though I found myself wondering whether he had recognized me."

"It's been a long time," Pol said.

"Yes."

"He could simply have come over and spoken with you if he wanted to be certain who you were."

"True."

Mouseglove raised his drink.

"Let's finish up and get out of here," he said.

"Okay."

Later, the edge gone from the evening, they returned to their apartments. Not entirely because Mouseglove had suggested it, Pol wove an elaborate series of warning spells about the place and slept with a blade beside the bed.

IV

Enough of philosophical rumination! I decided. It is all fruitless, for I am still uncertain as to everything concerning my existence. A philosopher is a dead poet and a dying theologian—I got that from Pol's mind one night. I am not certain where Pol got it, but it bore the proper cast of contempt to match my feelings. I had grown tired of thinking about my situation. It was time that I did something.

I found the city at Belken's foot to be unnerving, but stimulating as well. Rondoval was not without its share of magic—from utilitarian workings and misunderstood enchantments to forgotten spells waiting to go off and a lot of new stuff Pol had left lying about. But this place was a veritable warehouse of magic—spell overlying spell, many of them linked, a few in conflict, new ones being laid at every moment and old ones dismantled. The spells at Rondoval were old, familiar things which I knew well how to humor. Here the power hummed or shone all about me constantly—some of it most strange, some even threatening—and I never knew but that I might be about to collide with a deadly, unsuspected force. This served to heighten my alertness if not my awareness. Then, too, I seemed to draw more power into myself just by virtue of moving amid such large concentrations of it.

The first indication that I might be able to question someone concerning my own status came when we entered the city and I beheld the being in the tower of red fumes. I watched it until the manifestation dissipated, and then was pleased to note that the creature assumed a form

241

similar to my own. I approached the receding thing immediately and directed an inquiry toward it.

"What are you?" I asked.

"An errand boy," it replied. "I was stupid enough to let someone find out my name."

"I do not understand."

"I'm a demon just like you. Only I'm doing time. Go ahead and mock me. But maybe someday you'll get yours."

"I really do not understand."

"I haven't the time to explain. I have to fetch enough ice from the mountaintop to fill all the chests in the food lockers. My accurséd master has one of the concessions here."

"I'll help you," I said, "if you'll show me what to do—and if you will answer my questions as we work."

"Come on, then. To the peak."

I followed.

As we passed through the middle reaches of the air, I inquired, "I'm a demon, too, you say?"

"I guess so. I can't think of too many other things that give the same impression."

"Name one, if you can."

"Well, an elemental—but they're too stupid to ask questions the way you do. You've got to be a demon."

We got to the top where I learned how to manage the ice. It proved to be a simple variation on the termination/absorption techniques I employed on living creatures.

As we swirled back down toward the lockers—as two great spinning towers of glittering crystals—I asked, "Where do we come from? My memory doesn't go back all that far."

"We are assembled out of the universal energy flux in a variety of fashions. One of the commonest ways is for a powerful sorcerous agency to call one of us into being to perform some specific task—tailor-making us, so to speak. In the process we are named, and customarily we are released once the job is finished. Only, if some lesser or lazier mage—such as my accurséd master—later learns your name he might bind you to his service and your freedom ends again. That is why you will find quite a few of us doing jobs for which we are not ideally suited. There just aren't that many top-notch sorcerers around—and some of them even grow lazy, or are often in a hurry. Ah, if only my accurséd master could be induced to make but the smallest mistake in one of his charging rituals!"

"What would happen then?"

"Why, I'd be freed in that moment to tear the son of a bitch apart and take off on my own, hoping that he had left no magical document mentioning my name nor passed it along to some snot-nosed apprentice. To be safe, you should always destroy your accurséd former master's quarters to take care of any such paperwork—burning is usually best—and then go after any apprentices who might be in the vicinity."

"I'll remember that," I said, as we reformed our burdens into large chunks in the lockers and headed back for more.

"But you've never had this problem? Not even once?"

"No. Not at all."

"Unusual. Perhaps you had your origin in some massive natural disaster. That sometimes happens."

"I don't remember anything like that. I do seem to recall a lot of fighting, but that is hardly the same thing."

"Hm. Lots of blood?"

"I suppose so. Will that do it?"

"I don't think so, not just by itself. But it could help if something else had started the process."

"I think there was a bad storm, also."

"Storms can help, too. But even so, that's not enough."

"Well, what should I do?"

"Do? Be thankful that no one knows your name."

"*I* don't even know my name—that is, if I have one at all."

We reached the peak, acquired another load, began the return trip.

"You must have a name. Everything does. One of the old ones told me that."

"Old ones?"

"You really are naive, aren't you? The old ones are the ancient demons from the days that men have forgotten, ages ago. Fortunately for them, their names have also been forgotten, so that they dwell largely untroubled by sorcerers, in distant grottoes, upon far peaks, in the hearts of volcanoes, in places at the ocean's bottom. To hear them tell it, no accurséd master could oppress you like the accurséd masters of long ago. It is difficult to know whether there really is any difference, since I know of none so unfortunate as to have served under both ancient and modern accurséd masters. The old ones are wise, though, just from having been around for so long. One of them might be able to help you."

"You actually know some of them?"

"Oh yes! During one of my intervals of freedom I dwelled among them far below, in the Grottoes of the Growling Earth, where the hot magma surges and steams—a most wondrous and happy place! Would that I were there now!"

"Why don't you return?"

"Nothing would please me more. But I am bound not to wander too far by my accurséd master's accurséd spell, and he is not in the habit of granting vacations."

"How unfortunate."

"Indeed."

We entered the lockers again and finished filling the ice chests.

"Now, thanks to you, I am finished ahead of schedule," the demon said, "and my accurséd master will not summon me to another accurséd task until he realizes that this one is finished. Therefore, I have a few minutes of freedom. If you would like, we will return to the heights where we can see for a great distance and I will attempt to give you directions for reaching the Grottoes of the Growling Earth—though their entrance lies on another continent."

"Show me the way," I said, and he soared upward.

I followed.

The instructions were complicated, but I set out immediately to follow them. I fled far to the northwest until I came to a great water heaving regularly toward the stars it imaged. There, unaccountably, I slowed. I knew that I had to cross it as the next stage of my journey, but I was drained of all will to begin. I drifted northward along the coastline, puzzled. What was it that was holding me back?

Finally, I sought full control of my nebulous person. I attempted to consider the situation in a totally rational manner. I saw no reason for hesitation. I ignored the strange lethargy which had taken hold of me. Forcing myself forward, I passed over a narrow, pebbly strand of beach and on out above the splashing swells.

I felt my new resolve waver almost immediately, yet I struggled to continue, to break through whatever odd barrier it was that had been raised against me.

It was then that I heard the voice, mixed in with the booming of the surf.

"Bell, or," it said. "Bell, or . . ."

And I listened and grew afraid.

"Bell, or," it repeated, "bell, or, bell, or, bell, or," over and over again.

I realized that some part of me had immediately understood something of what lay behind those utterances. And I knew they meant that I was defeated in my quest.

I summoned my last bit of will to oppose the force which held me, for here at last was something I might query.

"Why?" I hurled at the waves and the sky. "Why? What is it that you want of me?"

There was a moment of silence, and then the voice returned:

"Bell, or, bell, or . . ."

I felt defeat wash through me, a dark, cold thing like the waters below, as I saw that those strange words were to be my only answer.

Turning, I rushed back to the shore then fled southward, knowing I would have to look elsewhere for my answers. The words faded gradually wtthin my being. My thoughts became focussed upon Pol Detson.

Once I reached glowing Belken and the magic-infested city at its foot, I proceeded unerringly to the building and the room where Pol lay sleeping. How I achieved this with no real effort, I could not say, unless some bond had grown between us as a result of our association.

As I inspected the defenses he had reared, I heard him moan softly. I entered his sleeping mind and saw that he had passed beyond a door in his dreams into a place which both delighted and repelled him. I had never intervened in his affairs before, but I recalled that he had seemed to be relieved when awakened by the nameless sorcerer that last time he had dreamed such a dream. So I caused him to awaken.

He lay there for a long while, troubled, then drifted into a more peaceful slumber. I departed then to seek my demon acquaintance and see whether there was anything else I might learn.

I drifted over to the accurséd master's quarters, but my friend was neither there nor in the vicinity. Then, faintly, I detected the glitteing trail such as had occurred behind us during the ice-hauling expeditions. I hurried to follow, as it had faded further even as I had considered it.

I sped along the skiey trail as rapidly as I could conduct myself. The distance proved to be great, but a slight brightening of the way indicated that I was gaining.

Many leagues farther to the south and the west, the trail arced downward toward a riverside town. It ended at a house which was vibrating and from which a series of crashing noises could be heard. I passed into the place and noted that blood was smeared everywhere—the walls, the floors, even the ceiling. My friend had hold of a male human whose limbs were broken and whose brains had been dashed out against the fireplace.

"Greetings! You're back so soon! Was there some problem with my directions?"

"No, but some force I do not understand prevented me from departing this continent."

"Strange."

The human flew across the room to crash against the far wall.

"Do you know what I think it is?"

"No. What?" I said.

"I believe you are under a spell that you do not even know about—bound in a particular way to some very special duty."

"I have no idea what it could be."

"Give me a hand with the entrails, will you? They should be strung about."

"Sure."

"Well, I think that you ought to find out what the thing

is and discharge it. Maybe the accursèd master who laid it on you is dead now or demented. In either case, you're very lucky. Once you've done whatever there is to be done, you'll be free."

"How do I find out what it is?"

"I guess that I am going to have to instruct you further in these matters. Since I am prepared to count you as a friend, I am going to tell you something in strictest confidence—my name. It is Galleran."

"That's a nice name," I said.

"It is more than just a word. It summarizes me when it is fully understood."

We finished the stringing and Galleran dismembered the body, passing me a leg and an arm.

"Do something artistic with these."

I hung one over a rafter and placed the other in a large kettle.

"Because I know my name I know all that there is to know about me," Galleran said. "You will, too, as you begin to understand it. Now, what you must do is discover your own name. When you learn that, it will also bring you knowledge of the task with which you have been charged."

"Really?"

"Certainly. It must follow."

Galleran placed the head upon the mantelpiece.

"How am I to find it out?" I asked.

"You must search your earliest memories—many times, perhaps. It is there, somewhere. When you find it you will know it. When you know it, you will know yourself. Then you can act."

"I will—try," I said.

Galleran proceeded to strew embers from the fireplace about the room.

"Help me to fan these to flame now, will you? It is always best to leave the place burning after your work is done."

"Surely."

As we strove to set the room to fire, I asked, "Why is it that your accursèd master wanted this man destroyed?"

"One of them owed the other money, I believe, and did not wish to pay it. I forget which."

"Oh."

We waited about until we saw that we had a good blaze going. Then we rose into the night with the smoke and headed back toward Belken.

"Thank you for all that you have taught me this day," I said as we parted later, "Galleran."

"I am glad to be of help. I must admit that you have roused my curiosity—mightily. Let me know when you have learned your story, will you?"

"Yes," I said. "I will do that."

Galleran returned to the accurséd master's quarters to report the completion of the assigned task. I rose into the air, heading toward a place high upon the western face of Belken. Earlier, on our ice-gathering expedition, I had noticed an opening there heading into the heart of the mountain, strange lights and vibrations all about it. I had grown very curious as to where it led and was determined to explore there. One never knows where one's name might lie.

V

. . . Pol drifted again through the great Gate and into the land beyond. Moving more rapidly than in the past, he viewed another hunt, transformation and pursuit with growing amusement. On the second capture, however, the victim was cannibalized and another had to be sought. Pol experienced a psychic tugging which drew him away from the scene and on out across the wasteland. For what seemed to be days he traveled, in a dim, indeterminate form, over the unchanging deadlands, coming at last to a worn but high range of black mountains which extended from horizon to horizon. Three times he assailed its heights and three times he fell back; on the fourth occasion, the dry, howling winds forced him toward a gap through which he fled. He emerged on the other side above a terraced city which covered this entire face of the range. This slope, however, continued to a far lower level than that on the opposite side, dropping at last to the shore of an ancient, waveless, tideless sea and continuing on below its surface. Circling, he saw the outlines of buildings beneath the waters and the dark, moving forms of the beings who dwelled there. Through the always-evening haze, he saw the creatures of the upper terraces, gray, long-limbed, ogre-like, slightly smaller versions of the things he had seen in the wastes. Human-appearing beings also were there, moving freely among them.

He descended very slowly, coming to rest atop a high spire, where he perched and regarded the figures below. A great number of these congregated quickly at the base of the structure. After a time, they built a fire, brought forth a number of bound people, dismembered them and burned

249

them. The smoke rose up, he breathed it, and it was pleasing to him.

Finally, he spread his wings and spiralled downward to where they waited upon the lowest terrace. They made obeisance to him and played him music upon instruments which wailed, thrummed and rattled. He strutted among them, occasionally choosing one to rend with his great beak and talons. Whenever he did this, the others watched with awe and obvious pleasure. Later, one who wore a brass collar studded with pale, smouldering stones approached, holding a three-pronged iron staff surmounted by a sooty white flame.

He followed the light and the one who bore it into the shadowy interior of one of the buildings—a lopsided metal structure of tilted floors and slanted walls. It was windowless and damp; it smelled of stale perfumes. Deep within the place, cold and still upon a high marble slab, lay the woman, candles burning at her head and her feet, her only garments garland and girdle of red flower petals already touched with brown. Her hair was a soft yellow verging upon white. Her lips, nipples and nails were painted blue. He uttered a soft trilling note and mounted the stair, the slab and the woman. Raking her once with claw and slashing her twice with his beak, he began to sing. He enfolded her then with his wings and began a slow movement. The one who bore the iron staff struck it in slow, regular rhythm upon the cold stone floor, its flame making dancing shadows upon the weeping walls.

After a long while, the woman opened her pale eyes, but they did not focus and she did not move until many minutes had passed. Then she began to smile.

When the three of them came forth, others had assembled and more were rising from the depths and moving downward from the higher levels. The thrumming, wailing, dry rattling of the music had grown to massive proportions, and a steady clicking sound which came from the chests of the assembled creatures themselves rose in counterpoint to it. Then began a slow procession, led by the light-bearer, which moved over many levels of the world-circling, sea-dipped city. They stayed in red chambers during their journey, and the sea changed color six times as they moved both above and beneath it. Massive russet worms swam to accompany their passage—eyeless, humming, streaked and rotating—and space was folded, that prospects came and went with great rapidity. The notes of a mightly gong preceded them and signed their departures.

The sky grew even darker on the day of his daughter's birth. Nascae tossed, moaned and cried out, afterwards lying as still and cold as she had that day upon her slab. The mountains shouted thunder and a red rain fell, flowing like waterfalls of blood down the terraces to the sea. The child was named Nyalith, to the sounds of tabor and bone flute. When she spread her wings and soared above the world there was a sound like thunder, and horns of yellow light preceded her. She would rule them for ten thousand years.

He flew to the highest peak of the black range and turned himself to stone, there to await Talkne, Serpent of the Still Waters, who would come to contest the land of Qod with him. The people made pilgrimages to that place, and Nyalith offered sacrifices at his feet. Prodromolu, Father of the Age, Opener of the Way, they called him in tireless chant, bathing him in honey and spices, wine and blood.

He felt his spirit rise, singing, to flash beyond the mountains. Then the deadlands twisted and churned beneath him. He dropped through a fading night toward brightness.

Pol awoke with a feeling of well-being. He opened his eyes and regarded the window through which the morning light leaked. He drew a deep breath and flexed his muscles. A cup of steaming coffee would be delightful, he decided, knowing full well that such was not attainable upon this world. Not yet, anyway. It was on his list of things to look into when he had the chance. Now . . .

At that instant, his dream returned to him, and he saw it to be the source of his pleasure. With it came remembrance of other dreams of a similar nature, dreams—he realized now—which had come to him every night since the nameless sorcerer had visited him on the trail and changed his appearance. But these, unlike the others, were uniformly pleasant despite a certain grotesqueness.

He rose, to visit the latrine, to wash, to dress, to rinse the streak in his hair with a jar of liquid he had purchased from an apothecary on the way home the previous evening. While he was about these things, he heard Mouseglove stirring. He dismantled the warning spells while he waited for the man to ready himself. Then the two of them stopped by Ibal's quarters but were told by a servant that the master could not be disturbed.

"Then let's take a walk and find some breakfast," Mouseglove suggested.

Pol nodded, and they made their way back to the small street with the cafes. The night's sparkle and sheen faded as they dined; and as the sun climbed higher a certain dinginess appeared here and there in the brighter quarters about them.

"Sleep well?"

"Yes. Yourself?"

Pol nodded.

"But I—"

Mouseglove's eyes shifted sharply to his left and he nodded in that direction. Pol leaned back in his chair and stretched, rolling his head as he did so.

The man who was approaching down the narrow street was clad in black and red as he had been the previous evening. He was looking in their direction.

Pol leaned forward and raised his mug of tea.

"You still can't recall . . .?" he asked.

Mouseglove shook his head.

"But he's coming this way," he muttered without moving his lips.

Pol took a sip and listened for footfalls. The man had a very soft tread and was almost beside him before he heard a sound.

"Good morning," he said, moving into view. "You are the one called Madwand, of Ibal's company?"

Pol lowered the mug and raised his eyes.

"I am."

"Good." The other smiled. "My name is Larick. I have been appointed to conduct the candidates for initiation to

the entrance on the western height of Belken this afternoon. I will also be your guide through the mountain
tonight."

"The initiation is to be tonight? I'd thought it was not
held until near the end of things?"

"Normally, that is the case," Larick replied, "but I had
not been reading my ephemeris recently. I only learned
last night when I was appointed to this post that there will
be a particularly favorable conjunction of planets tonight—
whereas things will not be nearly so good later on."

"Would you care for a cup of tea?"

Larick began to shake his head, then eyed the pot.

"Yes, I am thirsty. Thanks."

He drew up a chair while Pol signaled for a fresh pot.

"My friend's name is Mouseglove," Pol said.

The men studied each other and clasped hands.

"Glad."

"The same."

Larick produced a piece of parchment and a writing
stick.

"By the way, I do not really have your name, Madwand,
for the list of candidates. How are you actually called?"

In instant reaction Pol's mind slid over the present and
back to an earlier time.

"Dan," he said, "Chain—son."

"Dan Chainson," Larick repeated, writing it. "You are
fourth on my list. I still have six to go."

"I take it that the rescheduling is as much a surprise to
all those involved?"

"I'm afraid so. That's why I have to find everyone in a
hurry."

The tea arrived and Pol poured.

"We will meet at the Arch of the Blue Bird," Larick
said, gesturing. 'It is the farthest archway to the west. It is
somewhat south of here, also."

Pol nodded.

"I'll find it. But when do we meet?"

"I was hoping we could all get together by noon," he
answered. "But that seems unrealistic, the way things are
going. Let's say by the time the sun lies midway between
noon and sunset."

"All right. Anything special I should bring?"

Larick studied him for a moment.

"How much preparation have you had for this?" he asked.

Pol wondered whether the flush he felt in his cheeks was visible through his magical disguise, scar and all.

"It depends upon what you mean by preparation," he said. "I've had some instruction as to the metaphysical side of things, but I was counting on more time here for learning something of the practical aspects."

"Then you did not—as your nickname implies—serve what might be referred to as a normal apprenticeship?"

"I did not. I know what I know by means of aptitude, practice and some study—on my own."

Larick smiled.

"I see. In other words, you have had as little preparation as one can have had and still be said to have had some preparation."

"I'd say you've put it properly."

Larick took a drink of tea.

"There is some risk, even for those with full training," he said.

"I already know that."

"Well, it is your decision, and I will have time to go over things somewhat during the climb and while we wait for sundown outside the entrance. To answer your first question, though, bring nothing but the clothes you wear, one small loaf of bread and a flask of water. These may be consumed at any time during the journey, up until the actual entry into the mountain. I would suggest you keep most of it until near the end, as we maintain a total fast during the night's progress through Belken."

Larick finished his tea and rose.

"I'll have to be locating the others now," he said. "Thanks for the tea. I'll see you at the Blue Bird Archway."

"A moment," said Mouseglove.

"Yes?"

"At what point on the mountain will you be emerging in the morning?"

"We'll come out of a cave low on the eastern face—this side, that is. You can't see the place from here. If you want to walk along with me I'm going up to a higher level now. I might be able to point it out to you from there."

"Yes, I'll come."

Mouseglove rose. Pol did also.

A flight of tarnished butterflies swept by as they mounted the stair. When Pol rested his hand against an ornamental column, it felt more like the trunk of a tree than cold stone. The huge gems set into walls had lost much of their brilliance in day's hard glare. But Pol smiled, for the impression of beauty still held despite all of this.

They climbed a hill and Larick pointed at the mountain.

"Yes. Over there," he said. "Near the base—that triangular, darkened area. You can see it if you look closely."

"I see it," Mouseglove said.

"Yes," said Pol.

"Very well. Then I must be on my way. I will see you later."

They watched him head off toward a group of buildings to the south.

"I'll be waiting there when you come out," Mouseglove said. "Don't trust anybody while you're inside."

"Why not?"

"I've gotten the impression here and there that Madwands are looked down upon and resented by those who have served regular apprenticeships. I don't know how strong the feelings might be, but there'll be nine of them in there with you. I wouldn't turn my back on them in any dark corridors."

"You might have a point there. I won't give them any opportunities."

"Shall we stroll back and see whether Ibal is receiving company yet?"

"Good idea."

But Ibal was not yet receiving. Pol left a message that the schedule had been advanced and that he would be leaving that afternoon. Then he returned to his own quarters and stretched out upon his bed, to rest and meditate. He thought over the entire story of his life as he now knew it—the story of the son of a powerful and evil sorcerer, his life preserved in exchange for his heritage as he was exiled to another world, one which knew no magic. He recalled the day of his return, his bitter reception in this world when he was recognized by means of the dragon birthmark upon his right wrist. He remembered his escape, his flight, his discovery of the ruined family seat at Rondoval and all that went with it—his identity, his powers, his control over the savage beasts that slept there. He relived his conflict with his brilliant but warped step-brother, Mark Marakson, in the anomolous center of high technology which that one had resurrected atop Anvil Mountain in the south. He thought of his brief but doomed affair with the village girl Nora, who had never stopped loving Mark. And now . . .

The Seven. The peculiar manipulation of his life by the seven statuettes, which seemed to have ended that day atop Anvil Mountain, returned to plague his thoughts. He still had no notion as to their true functions, purposes, aims. He felt that he would never enjoy full freedom from apprehension until he came to terms with them. And then the recent unexplained attempt upon his life, and the midnight encounter with the sorcerer who seemed to have answers but did not care to share them . . .

About the only personal thing that did not pass through his mind was a consideration of his recurrent dreams. Soon he fell asleep and had another.

He took his loaf and his water flask with him to the Arch of the Blue Bird. Mouseglove accompanied him to that point. Larick and six of the others were already present. The westering sun had encountered a cloudbank and the city took on its evening sheen prematurely. The other candidates were uniformly young and nervous; and Pol forgot their names—except for Nupf, with whom he was already acquainted.

The sky continued to darken while they waited for the others, and Pol idly let his vision slip into the second seeing. As he cast his gaze about he noted a blue-white pyramid or cone near the center of town, a thing which had not registered itself upon his normal perceptions. Continuing to watch it for a time, he gained the impression that it was growing. He moved his seeing back to its normal mode and the phenomenon faded.

Making his way past the other candidates, he approached

Larick who stood, obviously impatient now, watching the massing clouds.

"Larick?"

"What do you want?"

"Just curious. Would you know what that big cone of blue light growing up over there is?"

Larick turned and stared for several moments, then, "Oh," he said. "That is for our benefit—and it reminds me again just how late things are getting. Where the devil are the rest of them?" He turned, looking in several directions, and then a certain tension seemed to go out of him. "Here they come," he said, noting three figures on a distant walkway.

He turned back to Pol.

"That cone you see is the force being raised by an entire circle of sorcerers," he explained. "By the time we enter Belken, it will have reached the mountain and filled it, attuning all ten stations within to greater cosmic forces. As you move from one to the other, each a symbolic representation of one of your own lights, the energies will flow through you and you will thereby be shaped, reshaped and attuned yourself."

"I see."

"I am not certain that you do, Dan. The other nine candidates, serving proper apprenticeships, should have developed their lights properly, in the natural order. For them, tonight's experience should only be an intensification with some minor balancing. With you, though—a Madwand may take any path. It could prove painful, distressing, even maddening or fatal. I do not say this to discourage or frighten, merely to prepare you. Try not to allow anything that occurs to cause you undue distress."

Here Larick bit his lip and looked away.

"Where—where are you from?" he asked.

"A very distant land. I'm sure you would never have heard of it."

"What did you do there?"

"Many things. I suppose I was best at being a musician."

"What about magic?"

"It was not known in that place."

Larick shook his head.

"How could that be?"

"It is just the way that things were."

"Then yourself? How did you come to this land? And how did you become a Madwand?"

For a moment, Pol found himself wanting to tell Larick his story. But prudence put a limit to his desire.

"It is a very long tale," he said, looking back over his shoulder, "and the other three are almost here."

Larick glanced in that direction.

"I suppose that you had some interesting experiences once you discovered your abilities?" he said hurriedly.

"Yes, many," Pol replied. "They might fill a book."

"Do any stand out in your memory as particularly significant?"

"No."

"I get the impression that you do not like to talk about these things. All right. There is no requirement that you do so. But if you would tell me, I would like to know one thing."

"What is that?"

"A white magician may on occasion use what is known as black magic, and vice-versa. We know that it is all much the same and that it is intent that makes the difference— and that it is from intent alone that the magician's path might be described. Have you yet chosen one path or the other?"

"I have used what I had to use as I had to use it," Pol said. "I like to think that my intentions were relatively pure, but then most people so justify themselves in their own eyes. I mean well, most of the time."

Larick smiled and shook his head.

"I wish that I had more time to talk with you, for I feel something very peculiar behind your words. Have you ever used magic with great force against another human being?"

"Yes."

"What became of that person?"

"He is dead."

"Was he also a sorcerer?"

"Not exactly."

" 'Not exactly'? How can that be? A person either is or is not."

"This was a very special case."

Larick sighed and then smiled again.

"Then you are a black magician."

"You said it. I didn't."

The three final candidates now approached the group and were introduced. Larick looked them all over and then addressed them:

"We are late getting started. We will head along this way immediately and then proceed until we have departed the city. The trail will commence shortly thereafter and we will begin our climb. I do not know yet how many—if any—rest stops we may make along the way. It depends on our progress and the time." He gestured toward a heap of folded white garments. "Each of you pick up a robe on the way by. We'll don them right before we enter."

He turned and passed under the arch, moving away.

Mouseglove approached Pol.

"I'll be at the exit point in the morning," he said. "Good luck."

"Thanks."

Pol hurried after the others, moving toward the head of the group. When he glanced back, Mouseglove was gone. He continued his pace until he caught up with Larick, falling into step beside him.

"I am curious," he said, "why you are trying so hard to make me out a black magician."

"It is nothing to me," the other replied. "Those of all persuasions meet and mix freely in this place."

"But I am not. At least, I don't think I am."

"It is of no importance."

Pol shrugged.

"Have it your way, then."

He slowed his pace and fell back among the group of apprentices. Nupf came up next to him.

"Bit of a surprise here, eh?" the apprentice said.

"What do you mean?"

"The suddenness of it all. Ibal doesn't even know I'm on my way. He's still—" he paused and grinned "—occupied."

"At least he got my name onto the list before he turned his attention to other matters."

"It was not entirely altruistic of him," Nupf replied. "I envy you considerably, should you come through this intact."

"How so?"

"You don't know?"

Pol shook his head.

"Madwands—particularly those who make it through initiation," Nupf explained, "are, almost without exception, the most powerful sorcerers of all. Of course, there aren't that many around. Still, that is why Ibal would like to have you remember him with a certain fondness and gratitude."

"I'll be damned," Pol said.

"You really didn't know?"

"Not in the least. Could that have anything to do, I wonder, with Larick's efforts to find out whether I'm black or white?"

Nupf laughed.

"I suppose he hates to see the opposite side get a good recruit."

"What do you mean?"

"Oh, I don't really know that much about him, but the rumor going around among the other candidates has it that Larick is so lily white he spends all of his free time hating the other side. He is also supposed to be very good—in a purely technical sense."

"I'm getting tired of being misjudged," Pol said. "It's been going on all my life."

"It would be best to put up with a little more of it, for now."

"I wasn't thinking of disturbing the initiation."

"I'm sure he'll run it perfectly. Whites are very conscientious."

Pol laughed. He adjusted his vision and looked back at the cone of power. It had grown noticeably. He turned away and moved on toward the mounting clouds. Belken had already acquired something of radiance beneath them.

VI

Seated upon the wide ledge outside the cavemouth, three-quarters of the way up the mountain's western face, Pol finished his bread and drank the rest of his water while watching the sun sink beneath the weight of starless night. There had been only one brief break on the way up and his feet throbbed slightly. He imagined the others were also somewhat footsore.

There came a flash of lightning in the southwest. A cold wind which had followed them more than halfway up made a little whistling noise among rocky prominences overhead. The mountain had a faint glow to it, which it seemed to acquire every night, only tonight it continued to brighten even as he watched. And when he shifted over to second seeing it seemed as if all of Belken were afire with a slowly undulating blue flame. He was about to comment upon it to Nupf when Larick rose to his feet and cleared his throat.

"All right. Put the robes on over your clothes and line up before the entrance," he said. "It will be a bit of a walk to the first station. I will lead the way. There is to be no talking unless you are called upon for responses."

They unfolded the coarse white garments and began donning them.

". . . And any visions or transformations you may witness—along with any alterations of awareness—are occasions neither for distress nor comment. Accept everything that comes to you, whether it seems good or bad. Transformations themselves may well be transformed before the night is over."

They lined up behind him.

261

"This is your last chance for questions."

There were none.

"Very well."

Larick proceeded at a deliberate pace into the cave-mouth. Pol found himself near the middle of the line which followed him. His vision slipped back into its natural range. The bluish glow diminished somewhat but did not depart. The narrow, high-walled cave into which they entered pulsated in the same fashion as the outer slopes of the mountain, giving sufficient, if somewhat unsettling, illumination to light their progress. As they passed further along, the brightness and movement intensified to the point where the walls were submerged within it, vanishing from sight, and it was as if they walked a fire-girt avenue out of dream between celestial and infernal abodes, its direction being a matter of conjecture as well as mood.

A distant rumble of thunder reached them as the way curved to the left, then to the right, slanting upward. It steepened rapidly after that, and in a few step-like places the worn floor seemed to show evidence of human handiwork.

Another turn and it steepened even more sharply, and heavy guide-ropes appeared at either hand. At first, the candidates were loath to take hold of them, for the action was tantamount to placing one's hands among leaping flames; but after a time they had no choice. There was no sensation of warmth; Pol felt only a vague tingling on his palms, though his dragonmark began to throb beneath its disguise after several moments. The air grew warmer as they mounted, and he could hear the sounds of his companions' labored breathing as they hurried to keep up with Larick.

Abruptly, they entered a grotto. The guide-ropes ended. The floor of the landing on which they halted was more nearly level. Immediately before them lay a large, circular pool blazing with white light as if illuminated from below. Low-dipping stalactites shone like icicles above it. The walls came down almost to its edges, save for the stony tongue on which they stood. Almost, for a narrow ledge seemed to circle that entire bright lens of still liquid.

Larick motioned them out upon the ledge immediately. They edged their way out and around, backs brushing against the rough rock. After several minutes, Larick began signing them to halt or move on, until all of them were distributed in accordance with some plan known only to himself. Then he moved out to the edge of the spit from which he had conducted the arrangement and stared down into the radiant waters. The candidates did the same.

The light dazzled Pol's eyes at first, but he soon became aware of his own bleached reflection, the irregular sculpture of the roof like some fantastic landscape behind it. He looked into his own eyes; a stranger, for this was the face of the disguise he still wore—heavier brow, scar upon the left cheek.

Suddenly, his reflection melted, to be replaced by the image of his true face—leaner, thinner of lip, possessed of a higher hairline—with the white streak running back through his dark locks. He tried to raise his hand to his face and discovered that a strange lethargy with a dull species of sluggishness had come over him. His hand only twitched slightly and he made no further effort to move it. Then he became aware of a voice speaking the words he had but recently learned. It was Larick's, and when he had finished speaking they were repeated by the first candidate upon the far edge of the pool. They echoed through the chamber and tolled inside his head. A faint, sweet scent rose to his nostrils. The next candidate began speaking the same words, and in a part of his mind Pol knew that when his turn came he would be repeating them. Yet, in a way, it seemed as if something within him were already saying them. He felt himself in some way detached from time. There was no time here, only the light and the reflected face. The words rolled toward him, awakening things deep within his being. Then he saw that the reflection was smiling. He was not aware of any movement of his own face. As he watched now, the image wavered and divided itself. It was suddenly as if he had two heads—one which continued smiling to the point of a sneer, the other bearing a massively sad expression. Slowly, they turned to face one another. He was riven by peculiar emotions. How long these persisted, he could not tell, as he observed the two who were one in their archetypal debate. It was only slowly that a vague feeling of wrong-ness began to come over him.

Then he realized that he was indeed speaking. His turn had come and he had begun his part in the circle without being aware of it. The words vibrated within him, and the world seemed oddly altered—distanced—about him. The light from below his feet grew even brighter. The images within the pool were warped, folded back upon them-selves. The two heads of his reflection merged, to become his solitary, unsmiling countenance. A feeling of exhilira-tion grew within him now and the sense of wrongness was swept away. His head seemed full of light as he uttered the final syllable.

It passed then to the woman to his left, who began the intonation. Pol lost all sense of self now, as well as time and place, and merely existed within the sound and the light, feeling changes pass through him, until it was over.

Without any word or visible sign, he knew when they were finished. The light in the depths coalesced, seemed to take on the form of a great egg, while the final speaker went through his part. Then, for a long while they stood in silence regarding the depths. Without cue, Pol suddenly raised his head and looked toward Larick. As his gaze moved across the chamber, he saw that all of the others were looking up and turning simultaneously. Slowly then, the candidates moved on along the ledge.

When they reached its end and came onto the pier, Larick raised an arm, gesturing toward his left, then turned and led them through a very narrow cut behind a screen of rock which none had noticed before. After several paces, moving sideways, it widened. Almost immediately, Larick dropped to his hands and knees and crawled into a small, black hole. One by one, the others did the same. The pale, flame-like light and the undulance were present there, also, but inches away in any direction.

Progress was slow, for they worked their way down-ward, fighting against slippage, crawling flat-bellied through particularly low places, twisting and scraping themselves as they negotiated turns.

The candidate before and below him halted suddenly, and Pol did the same. He heard a grunt from the rear as the one behind him was drawn up short. The walls had paled somewhat to a grayish tone with a pink cast to them.

The candidate before him began inching forward again and Pol did the same, slowly. This continued for approximately one body-length, then was followed by another halt. Pol, still giddy from the opening experience, felt unable completely to control his thoughts. He alternated between mild distress and resignation over this.

After a brief pause, they advanced again, a similar distance. Several more such, and Pol saw its cause. There was a circular opening in the floor. The candidates eased themselves down through it, hung at arm's length and then dropped.

He waited for a time after the one before him passed through, then lowered himself, hung a moment and let go.

It was not a long drop. He landed with his knees bent and immediately moved to the side. Shortly, he joined the others, who stood near the center of the chamber where the roof was high, arranged in a circle in accordance with Larick's gesturing, around the most prominent object in sight—a pink stalactite several times his own height, rising from a large, bumpy, roughly rectangular piece of rock.

When they were all in position about it, Larick motioned them back, spreading the formation to positions as far away from the towering object as the geometry of the cavern permitted. For a moment, the man's eyes met his own, and Pol, unaccountably, felt that there was pain within them. Then Larick moved away, to mount a rock at the far corner of the chamber. Shortly, everyone's gaze left him and returned to the object before them.

Pol relaxed, assuming a contemplative state of mind once again. He looked up and then down the monolith. He felt the power in the place. He slipped his vision into the second seeing for a moment, but there was no change other than an increased brightness to the stalactite. There were not even any drifting strands in the vicinity, a phenomenon which struck him as somewhat odd when he thought about it much later.

At the first slow words from Larick he returned his sight to normal, feeling only the physical sensations which the sounds and their echoes stirred within him. The experi-

ences of timelessness and distancing came over him more
quickly than they had on the previous occasion. Now, as
he watched, the light on the surface of the towering formation began shifting. It seemed almost as if the thing
were moving slightly.

Larick grew silent and some member of the circle began
the intonation. The cavern slowly faded about him as this
occurred. Pol felt that the huge form was the only tangible
object in existence. The words followed him, however,
filling this version of the universe which he now occupied.
Then, suddenly, the monolith seemed larger, its shape
indefinably altered.

Another voice took up the words. Pol watched, fascinated, as the object moved and shifted its appearance. The
lumpy base seemed more and more to be the knuckles of
three folded fingers, the single upright a forefinger extended, a small, low prominence on its other side the joint
of a bent thumb. Of course . . . It had been a hand all
along. Why hadn't he noticed sooner?

The voice moved nearer. The hand was indeed stirring,
turning in his direction. The finger began to dip, slowly.

His breathing ceased and a sense of awe came over him
as it continued to descend toward him. The narrowing
distance between them was filled with power. Unaccountably, his right shoulder and arm began to tingle.

The finger, large enough to crush him, reached—gently,
delicately—and brushed very lightly against his right
shoulder.

He almost collapsed, not from any weight but from the
feelings which invaded him at that moment. He steadied
himself as the source of the words came even nearer. The
finger was retreating now, moving back toward its upright
position.

The tingling continued in his arm and shoulder, to be
succeeded first by a dull ache and then by a numbness
when it came his turn to speak the words. The cavern
returned, however, and the hand became once again a
stalactite upon a rough rock.

The words went full circle, they meditated in silence for
a spell and Larick then motioned them to follow him through

an opening in the wall behind the rock upon which he stood.

Pol moved slowly, awkwardly, puzzled by the dead weight which hung at his right side. He reached across and seized his right biceps with his left hand.

His upper arm felt swollen, immense; it was tight against the cloth of his sleeve.

He ran his hand down his arm. The entire limb seemed suddenly grown oversize. Also, it was uniformly diminished in sensitivity. With great effort, however, he found that he could move it. When he lowered his eyes, he discovered that his hand—still normal in appearance and feeling—hung far lower than usual, in the vicinity of his knee. He felt for the power of his dragonmark, but it, too, seemed to have been numbed. Then he recalled Larick's words on the matter of transformations this night—that they should be accepted without distress and not be permitted to interfere with the business at hand. Nevertheless, he glanced surreptitiously at the others, to see whether he could detect any malformations. The few he was able to view before entering the tunnel did not exhibit any gross impairments. And no one seemed to notice his own.

They walked. The way was level, straight and sufficiently wide. The illumination persisted. They passed through an empty chamber without halting—where it seemed that a high-pitched musical tone was being constantly sounded, just beyond the bounds of audibility—and they continued until another grotto opened before them.

Here they entered. It was a rounded chamber with a curved roof, almost bubble-like in appearance. Larick spaced them about a rock formation resembling a cauldron, near its center. Again, a chanting commenced and again Pol knew the oceanic feeling, the detachment he had experienced at the other stations, though here it was mixed with something of depression, sadness. His left arm acquired the tingling sensation at this point, and when his turn had come and passed and all was done it resembled the right exactly in its transformation.

This time he accepted the change with less distress, as part of the total experience. The others must be undergoing similar experiences, he decided. He followed them to a well-like depression across the way, discovering as he did that sensation, mobility and control were returning to his arms.

He watched the others. A knotted rope fastened about a nearby rock hung down into the hole. One by one, the candidates took hold and climbed down it, vanishing into the darkness. When his turn came he did likewise, with great ease, pleased with the enormous strength which now resided in his arms and shoulders.

In the yellow-blue cavern to which they descended the now-familiar ritual formation was established and the rite carried out about a large, spherical crystal set upon a pedestal. Before it was concluded, Pol's left hand felt as if he had dipped it in boiling water. He gave no outward evidence of this, not even looking down upon it, until after this phase, too, was completed and Larick led them out through an opening in the wall to the left.

The hand still throbbed, but the sensation of heat had vanished. When he viewed it, he saw that it had grown massive, purplish, scaly; the nails were thick, dark, triangular, hooked, at the ends of long, powerful-looking digits which reached almost to his ankle. The robe he wore concealed much of the change within its folds, its long, wide sleeves. Still . . . He looked about again. None of the other candidates seemed to have noticed his discomfort. Again, he forced the thought of it away. He trekked after the others along a broad, level tunnel, his gait somewhat disturbed, as if by overbalancing and compensation.

A sword hung from a chain midway between floor and roof at the near end of the next chamber. This, in its turn, became the object of their meditation, swinging and glinting redly as the words circled it. The visions which swam through his mind at this, as at the previous station, barely registered themselves on his consciousness, as the feeling of the power of his new limbs came to occupy his awareness with the burning pang in his right hand—this time a thing of masochistic pleasure to him. He spoke the words in a ringing voice and did not even look down, already knowing what he would see.

When it was over, he turned and joined the line filing

out through another opening and into a downward-slanting tunnel, moving now as if within a dream, his actions determined by some a-logical pattern he could feel about him, no longer wondering whether the others' notions of personal transformation coincided with his own.

The way was steep; sweet odors rose up it. The walls were a living net of pale fire. The floor sparkled, almost moistly. They continued downward for a long while, coming at last to a small chamber into which they were crowded about a simple, unadorned cube of stone. The place was strewn with flowers, accounting for the odor he had detected on the way down. Here he found the smell almost sickly sweet in its intensity. When the words were spoken in these close quarters they hurt his ears. He felt excessively warm and became very conscious of the beating of his heart. A wave of dizziness passed over him, but he knew that even if he fainted there was no place to fall, so closely were they packed together. Later, he believed that he had actually succumbed to unconsciousness briefly, for there was a gap in his memory up until he found himself speaking. It seemed that there had been another vision, one which had partly numbed his senses. He could not recall the details. His heart was beating rapidly now, with an unusually heavy throbbing. He became peripherally aware that the candidates who stood at either hand were removed a greater distance from him than they had been the last time he had been aware of their presence. The aroma of the flowers had diminished sharply, or else he had become accustomed to it.

He lowered his head as he finished speaking and saw that his robe was torn. Then he became aware of the enormous breadth of his shoulders, the barrel-like girth of his chest. No wonder his garment was rent. How could this be an illusion? He glanced at the nearest candidates. Wrapped in their own meditations, none of them seemed to be paying him any heed.

Slowly, he raised his right hand. He reached inside through the torn place, groped about until he located an opening in his own garments which lay beneath. His heavy fingers explored below them, encountering a tough, hard, bumpy surface. He explored further. From navel to neck, it felt as if he were covered with scales. He withdrew his hand and let it fall. When he looked up again, he saw that Larick was staring at him. The man looked away immediately.

When they departed the room, it was as if they followed a continuation of the tunnel which had brought them to that place, still slanting downward, headed in the same direction. He controlled his breathing carefully as they walked, for its sounds came heavy and stertorous when he drew deep breaths.

There came a cooling for which he was grateful, as they continued down the long shaft. The next chamber was much larger than the one they had quitted, its floor of a greenish stone. A heavy oil lamp was suspended by chains from its roof, and its flames waved as the words were spoken.

This time it was his left leg. The moment that the tingling began he knew what was to follow. When it finally came, he almost collapsed. The leg seemed to have grown much longer and heavier than the right one. He was almost completely unbalanced and had to keep that knee bent and the other straight. But, if anything, the dream quality he was experiencing was enhanced by this phase of the ritual progress. As they turned and he lurched his way along a mercifully level tunnel, visions, like objectified free associations, were everywhere. He could not place his hand against the swimming wall for support without seeming to touch some beast-face or a woman's breast, a flower or the feathers of a bird.

In this frame of mind, he was not even certain what he saw in the next chamber. That it was large and scented, he was aware. The images seemed everywhere dense. Zodiacal beasts moved in procession before him. If he fixed his eyes upon one, it dissolved into an entirely new series of forms. After a time, he gave up. He almost welcomed the tightening and the warmth in his right leg when it came, for his balance was finally restored when that one matched the other.

His mind a chaotic jumble now, he departed with the others, moving surely and swiftly down another long steep way.

They came at last into a very dark chamber where

stalactite and stalagmite were joined to form a towering silver pillar about which Larick led and placed them. Pol's mind cleared momentarily, and he wondered what had actually been happening and for how long the ceremony had been going on. The images were dispersed. There was only the shining pillar here, lovely and bright. With his elongated reach, he felt that he could almost extend his arms and embrace it. The thing seemed to reflect power. He felt some sort of stability returning. He raised his massive hands and stared at them. Where had he seen their like before? He adjusted his vision for the second sight, but they remained unchanged when this occurred.

He let his hands fall as the memory came to him. They were like the hands of those demonic creatures he had seen in his dreams of the land beyond the Gate. What could this mean? Why were they being objectified in this fashion during this ritual of a supposedly beneficial nature? Was this truly the sort of transformation of which Larick had spoken, or was he undergoing something else?

He raised a hand to his face, ran his fingertips across his features. They seemed unchanged, yet—

He was seized by an abdominal cramp which bent him partway forward. Involuntarily, he clutched at his midsection. In that instant, Larick began speaking again, yet another sequence of the words. He felt the pressure of his belt and unfastened it. He heard the sound of cloth tearing beneath his robe. When the pains had passed, he was aware of a widening in the pelvic area, a spreading of his hips. It was difficult when he attempted to stand fully upright. His spine now seemed to possess a curvature which bore him forward so that his hands rested upon the ground. His feet began to ache.

Then it did not matter. The moment of full rationality passed, and he was caught up in another sequence of visions and feelings of power. It seemed that a very long time had passed. His mind drifted through the repetitions and his own part in them. When they moved again, he followed, slouched far forward, oblivious and ignored.

Larick led them to an opening in the floor through which the top of a ladder protruded. He motioned for them to follow after and proceeded to descend it.

Pol waited until all of the others had gone down before beginning his own clumsy descent.

The ladder creaked beneath him and one rung came loose. But he clutched its sides tightly and kept going. It was a long descent, finally taking him directly into the midst of the others, who stood within a circle drawn upon the floor of this chamber. He noted that two of the other candidates had collapsed and that Larick was kneeling, massaging the chest of one of them.

He jumped down the final few feet and waited. The man on whom Larick had been working moaned after a time and sat up. Larick immediately moved to the other—a small, red-haired man, whose teeth seemed tightly locked together—and listened for a heartbeat. Apparently there was none, for he abandoned that one immediately and returned to the other. After several minutes, he helped that other to his feet and checked the red-haired man again. The second form remained still. Larick shook his head and rose, leaving the man where he had fallen. He motioned the others into a formation around himself, then raised both hands.

Pol's feet began to ache as the power was raised within the circle. The pain grew so severe that he had to tear off his boots seconds later. He held them beneath his arm inside the robe as the ritual progressed. He dimly recalled that this was the final stage of the initiation. Everything would be over soon and he could go somewhere and sleep. . . .

He found himself saying the words, his voice normal, steady. When he had finished, he closed his eyes. An extraordinarily vivid image immediately arose. He saw Rondoval beseiged, a storm raging about it. The image flowed. A man stood upon the main balcony, a black scarf about his neck, the scepter of power in hands. His hair was frostwhite save for a black streak running back through it. He was singing orders to his unearthly hordes and causing flames to rise before his enemies. But a sorcerer all in white—old Mor!—came to duel with him. The older man prevailed, the defense slackened, the man on the balcony slumped and withdrew.

Inside, he raced to a nearby chamber and began manipulating magical paraphernalia. The action was telescoped.

Moments later, it seemed, scepter held high, he stood at the Circle's center, voicing words of power that rang through the room, causing a twisting, smoky shape in a corner near the ceiling to vibrate in resonance.

"Belphanior ned septut!" he cried. "Bel—"

The door burst open and a messenger entered and collapsed as the forces swept over him.

"The gate has been breeched . . ." he said, before he expired.

The sorcerer spoke a word of protection, thrust the scepter into his sash and broke the Circle.

He departed the chamber, raced up the hall and entered another room, where he seized and braced a powerful bow which hung there. He chose a single arrow from a soft leather quiver and took it with him.

Below, Pol saw him use the weapon to slay the leader of the attacking forces. Then he fought a duel with old Mor, was bested and died, buried beneath a heap of rubble.

Things blurred. The storm had passed. The fighting had ceased. He saw Mor mounted upon the back of a centaur, riding into the west, the dead sorcerer's body tied across the back of another of the horse-people.

Another blur.

Within a cavern, illuminated by his glowing staff, planted like some unnatural tree, Mor was alone with the dead sorcerer. The body was laid on its back upon a slab of stone, arms folded. Leaning above the corpse, Mor was doing something to the face—rubbing, pressing. At some later point he raised his hands and seemed to pull the face away.

No. It was a deathmask that he held upraised, and in that moment Pol noticed how closely the features resembled those of Mor himself.

He began speaking softly, but Pol could not distinguish the words. The second seeing came over him and he beheld a fine, silver strand attached to the mask.

Everything came apart and trailed away then, as visions do.

Pol opened his eyes. Everyone was standing in meditation and there was an echoing sound in the air, Larick's hands were raised and he was clapping them together slowly, speaking certain final words.

When he had finished, Larick passed among them, stopped and raised the dead man, positioned him across his back, moved to its perimeter and broke the Circle. He turned then and gestured for the others to follow him.

They exited the chamber and moved along a widening tunnel, passing at length into a large, irregularly shaped, unadorned cavern cluttered with rock and stalagmite, hung with huge stalactites. The air there was cooler still. Pol's head began to clear.

Larick picked his way across the cavern and found a place to deposit the body. Then he returned, mounted a small prominence and addressed his followers:

"Krendel was the only candidate who succumbed to the forces," he said. "The rest of you may be said to have passed, in one fashion or another. It could be several weeks before the new alignment of your magical states has stabilized. Because of this, I caution you against any operations of the Art for a time. Things could go very much awry, with unpredictable results. Wait, rest, confine your activities to the physical plane. When you feel ready, begin your workings in a very small way—and wait after each step, to be certain that things are proceeding properly."

He turned and looked back over his shoulder. He gestured in that direction.

"That tunnel leads back into the world," he said. "It is long. I will conduct each of you up it personally, to meet the dawn.

"You will be first," he told the nearest. "Go and wait for me over there. I will join you in a moment."

He stepped down from the mound and headed toward Pol.

"Come over here," he whispered, and he led him into a side passage behind a fat stalagmite.

"Something is wrong," Pol said. "I've become a monster and no one seems to notice."

"That is true," Larick answered, raising his voice to a normal pitch.

"Should this not pass, now the initiation is over?"

"Madwand," he replied, "your transformation had nothing to do with the initiation. Can you say you know nothing of the House of Avinconet?"

"Yes. I've never heard of it."

"Nor of the great Gate to a dark and sinister world? A Gate you would fling wide?"

Pol frowned.

"I see," Larick said, sighing. "What I did to you was indeed necessary. I took the opportunity afforded by your state of mind at each stage of the initiation to lay powerful spells upon you—exchanging your body, piece by piece, for that of one of the dwellers in that accursed place. Save, of course, for your head."

"Why?" Pol asked. "What have I done to you?"

"Personally, nothing," Larick answered. "But the evil you would work is so great that everything I have done is warranted. You will learn more of what lies before you by-and-by. Now I must get back to the other initiates."

Pol extended one massive, taloned hand to seize him. Larick gestured briefly and the entire limb was instantly paralyzed.

"What—?"

"I have complete control of your new body," the other stated. "I have enfolded you in a series of virtually unbreakable spells. See how I lay my will upon you, totally immobilizing you now? There is also a masking spell. It even compensates for your ungainliness. Only you see yourself as you truly are—a necessary reminder, I'd say. You are now, in all ways, my creature."

"And you were so concerned about black magic," Pol said. "Perhaps you feared competition?"

Larick winced and looked away.

"It was necessary, this time," he said, "to combat a greater ill."

"Don't preach me that line. I've done nothing wrong. You have."

Larick turned away. Pol screamed at him.

His cry was cut short as the man turned back and gestured again. Now Pol could no longer speak at all.

"I'll come for you last and we will journey to Castle Avinconet," Larick said, and then he smiled. "Don't go away."

He passed the rocky corner and was gone.

Pol heard a drop of water fall from a stalactite into a nearby pool. He heard the sounds of his own shallow breathing. He heard the distant voices of the other initiates, doubtless discussing the night's experiences.

If magic had bound him, then magic could free him, he decided. But he could not locate the sources of his own power. It seemed as if that part of him were somehow asleep. He brooded over Larick's words, over the fact that his dreams were apparently a nasty reality to someone else. He sought through his memories for some clue as to why this should be so. He wondered whether his present situation were in any way connected with the attack of the sorcerer Mouseglove had dispatched back at Rondoval. He strained to move, but no movement followed.

Then there came the sound of a footstep beyond the passage. It seemed too soon for Larick to be returning, but—

A large man, as tall but wider than Larick, turned the corner and advanced. His face was a constantly shifting thing, as if seen through a multi-phase refracting medium. The eyes drifted, the nose swelled and shrank, the mouth twisted through ghastly parodies of human expressions. But when he opened it to speak, Pol still saw that there was a shining, capped tooth. He tried the second seeing but was unable to penetrate the distortion spell the person wore like a mask.

"I see that my disguise still holds for your features," came the familiar voice. "But what have you done with the rest?"

Pol found that he could not even snarl.

"Actually," the man went on, "that is a terrific body. You could wreak all sorts of havoc with it, if you'd a mind to. I suppose you're rather attached to your own, though, eh?"

He raised his head, one huge eye and one small one focusing upon Pol's own, shifting relative sizes even as he stared.

"Forgive me," he said then. "I'd forgotten you can't answer."

He raised one hand and slapped Pol lightly across the

mouth. It stung for only a moment, and something seemed to be released with the stinging. Pol found that his jaws were unlocked, that he could move his head.

"What the hell is going on?" he asked.

"I haven't the time to tell you, even if I wished to," the other replied. "It's a long story and there are other considerations of much greater moment just now. Everything seems to be coming along nicely, though. I wouldn't worry too much."

"You call this 'nicely'?" Pol said, casting his gaze down over his monstrous form.

"Well, not necessarily from an esthetic standpoint, if you happen to be human," the man said. "I was referring to the progression of events. Larick thinks he's got you now."

"Offhand, I'd say he's right."

"That might be remedied, if you're willing to play the game out."

"I don't even know the stakes, or the rules."

"That will be a part of your reward if all goes well: answers to your questions—and answers to some you haven't even thought of yet."

"Such as who you are, and what you're after?"

"That will almost assuredly come out."

"Will I like what I discover?"

"In matters of taste, each person is of course the only judge."

"What choice have I?"

"You may act, or be acted upon."

"What do you want me to do?"

"Go along with things, find out what it is that your captor desires and decide whether that is what you also want. Then you act accordingly. Larick feels that he has you under complete control, but in a moment I will break his infantile spells. I will also reverse the moderately clever body exchange he has worked upon you, restoring to you your own vigorous, youthful—if fatigued—carcass. Then will follow the work of a true master. Freed and restored, I will disguise your body as I disguised your features, giving to it in every respect the semblance of the monster you now are. For an encore, I will then cloak you

in a masking spell in all ways identical to the one which
now hides your hideous appearance from most mortal
eyes—"

"A disguise within a disguise?"

"Precisely."

"To what end?"

"At some point, those who desire you in the reduced
state will be sure to strip away the outer layer to behold
the captive monster within."

The large sorcerer strode forward and clasped him by
the shoulders. Instantly, Pol felt something like an electric
shock pass through him. His arm dropped. He sagged
forward. His boots fell to the floor from where he had
clutched them beneath his left arm all this long while. The
sorcerer seized that arm and an agonizing pain ran through
it. Before Pol could examine it, he had hold of the other.
He was humming as he worked. Whether or not this was a
part of his procedure, Pol could not tell.

As he raised his hands and realized that they were
indeed *his* hands again, the man struck him a mighty blow
across the back with his left hand and upon the chest just
above the heart with his right. Even within the well-muscled and heavily armored form that he wore, Pol could tell
that the man was no weakling.

He felt the air rush out of his lungs as his chest cavity
was returned to normal. He began to straighten and the
sorcerer struck him a terrific blow in the abdomen, well
below the belt. The change continued in that region, and
he straightened fully, massaging, slapping himself, as much
for the joy of feeling his own form again as to ease the
omnipresent aches.

The big sorcerer kicked him in the shins and he felt the
aches, straightening and shrinkage begin in his legs.

"I must say you have a violent approach to these matters," he remarked.

"Perhaps you'd prefer a six-hour incantation with incense?"

"I never argue with success."

"Prudent. I now begin the first masking spell, causing
you to look as you just were."

The illusion began, growing like a gray mist about him,
shaped by the flowing gestures of the face-changer's hands.

Pol felt his hidden dragonmark throb in the presence of this magic. Soon it cloaked him completely, coalescing, sinking through his garments.

The sorcerer sighed and straightened.

". . . And that will be all they see, if they pierce your outer guise, soon to be supplied by me. I must caution you concerning the obvious, however."

"That being?"

"You must act as if you are still under control. Be standing paralyzed in the same position in which he left you when Larick returns. Follow all of his orders as if you had no choice. The moment you deviate, you lose your chance to learn anything further. You will probably also have a fight on your hands."

Pol nodded. He looked down at himself as he did, seeing the monstrous appearance once again but not feeling it.

"I'll mask this illusion for everyone else now, as Larick had it," the sorcerer said, "but leave the appearance for you, as he also had it, as a reminder to act in keeping with it—with clumsiness and obedience."

Pol watched the man's hands as they commenced an intricate series of gestures.

"Do you see strands when you work?" he asked him suddenly.

"Sometimes," the sorcerer replied. "But right now I see beams of colored light, which I intercept. Hush. I'm concentrating."

Pol fixed his eyes on the man's changing face, trying to guess at his true features. But there was no pattern to the changes.

When the movements ceased and the man straightened, Pol said, "You told me on that night you came to me in our camp that our interests might not be entirely conjoined."

"Oh, there is a possibility that we might wind up at odds," the other replied. "I hope not, but there you are. It could happen. If so, it won't be because I didn't try, though. And at least for the moment we want the same thing: to get you out of here intact, to deceive your enemies, to position you strategically."

"Have you any idea what will happen when I leave here?"

"Oh, yes. You will be spirited away almost immediately—to Castle Avinconet."

"Larick did say that much. But who else is involved. And what will I meet at that end?"

"It is far better for you to learn these things yourself, to keep your responses normal."

"Damn it! There's more to it than that! You're hiding something!"

"In what way does that make me different from other men? Play your part, boy. Play your part."

"Don't patronize me. I need more information to carry this thing off."

"Bullshit," the sorcerer replied and turned away. "And strike your pose again. I believe I hear someone coming."

"But—"

"The rest is silence," the changing man said, as he vanished around the corner.

VII

Mouseglove hunkered in a rocky recess to the left of the cavemouth, his hood raised and cloak drawn about him against the morning's chill. To his right, the fresh-risen sun constructed morning above the foothills, skimming a layer of glory from the magical city he had quitted hours before. Eight of the initiates had so far passed him, each in the company of Larick, to salute the dawn, then make their ways back toward the town, alone, or in the company of a servant or former master. When he heard footsteps once again, Mouseglove stirred slightly, turning his head toward the opening. When he saw Pol approaching with the leader, he rose, joints creaking, but did not immediately depart his station.

Unlike those who had preceded him, Pol had already removed his white robe. His gait was slower and more awkward than usual. Larick, too, was dressed only in his day garments and head cloth. His face bore a far less solemn aspect than it had when he was bringing the others forth from Belken. He was snapping orders at Pol as they emerged. The two immediately turned to their left and began walking quickly in that direction.

Puzzled, Mouseglove stepped out from his niche and hurried after them.

"Good morning," he said. "How did you fare during the night?"

Larick almost stumbled in halting, and he placed his hand upon Pol's arm. By the time he turned, his face was composed. Pol, moving more slowly, was without expression.

"Good morning," Larick replied. "Your friend is well enough physically, but some who go through initiation

281

experience mental disorganization in varying degrees. This
has occurred with him."

"How serious is this thing?"

"That depends upon a great many factors—but it is
generally treatable. I was hurrying him off right now with
that end in mind."

"That is why you skipped the dawn salutation?"

Larick's eyes narrowed for the briefest moment, as if
assessing the other's knowledge of the matters involved.

"We were not going to dispense with it entirely," he
said. "But perhaps you are right, since this is the traditional spot."

He turned toward the place where the others had stood
to perform the final ritual function.

"Pol! Do you at least understand me?" Mouseglove said.

Larick turned back.

"I am certain that he does," he told him. "But, techni-
cally, he should not address anyone until he has finished
with this part of things. You can see in a few minutes what
his response will be."

He led Pol over to the place, speaking softly and rapidly
to him. Mouseglove shifted about, glancing in every direction. A little later, he saw Pol raise his arms and lift his
face toward the light in the east. As Pol began to mutter,
Larick moved a short distance away from him. Mouseglove
watched carefully, hands beneath his cloak.

When Pol had completed a hurried version of the sun-
rite, he turned toward the smaller man.

"It may not be all that serious," he said then. "But I
must go away with Larick for a time. I can afford to take
no chances in something like this."

"How long?"

"I do not know. For as long as is necessary."

"It could take a week or two," Larick put in. "Possibly
even longer."

"Where is it that you are taking him? I'm going with
you."

"I couldn't tell you that until I have conferred with
some experts. Perhaps he can be treated here. Then again,
he may have to go away."

"Where?"

"That remains to be determined."

"Pol," Mouseglove said, "are you certain that this is what you want to do?"

"Yes," Pol replied.

"Very well. We will go and find out. If it is to be here, I will wait. If it is to be elsewhere, I will accompany you."

"That will not be necessary," Pol said, and he turned away. "I don't need you."

"Nevertheless . . ."

"You are an encumbrance!" Larick said, and he raised his hand.

Mouseglove moved, but not fast enough. All strength and sensation fled his limbs. He fell, his hand still gripping the butt of the pistol he had been unable to draw.

For some time before he opened his eyes, Mouseglove was marginally aware of a slow, intermittent, shuffling sound. When finally he did open them, his field of vision was occupied by a small, gray, mossy rock and a scattering of gravel. He noted that the day had grown perceptibly brighter.

He moved his left hand slowly, placing its palm flat upon the ground near to his shoulder. It remained there for long seconds before he became aware of the coldness of the stone. The shuffling sound came again and he raised his head a few inches, suddenly aware of a stiffness in his neck. He pushed hard with the hand, heaving himself upward, rolling into a seated position, fighting a tendency to slump forward. As his gaze moved across the area, passing the place where Pol and Larick had stood, his memory of the morning's events poured into his mind. He turned his head to the east. The station of the sun told him that an hour or more had passed since that encounter. He rehearsed the entire exchange, seeking clues as to what had occurred within the mountain and what might now be afoot. He resolved that the next time he argued with a sorcerer he would have the weapon drawn and pointed at its target.

A series of small sounds reached him from within the cave, turning itself into several rapid footfalls and then halting. He drew one knee beneath him and pushed him-

self up into a crouch. He rose slowly as the footfalls came
again, nearing the mouth of the cave. He drew the weapon
and pointed it at the opening, the hammer making a
clicking sound as he set it.

The steps grew stronger, steadier. A moment later, a
small, red-haired man appeared within the opening. He
was wearing a dirt-streaked white robe. He leaned against
the rock, eyes rolling and blinking, head turning. When
his gaze swept over Mouseglove, it did not pause. His
complexion was dead white. He twitched and jerked, as
though he were having a minor seizure.

Mouseglove watched him closely for a long while before
he spoke.

"What is the matter?" he asked, weapon still steady.

The head rolled again, the eyes passing over him, then
back again, back again, their orbit narrowing, a rapid
scanning motion. At last, they seemed to focus upon him,
but the look they held caused him to suppress a shudder.

"What is the matter?" he repeated.

The man took a step forward, raised a pale hand, opened
his mouth and inserted the fingers. He made a gargling
noise, then withdrew his fingers slightly, pinching the tip
of his tongue. He took another step, released the tongue,
held both hands at shoulder level. He took another step,
and another, his right hand moving from side to side,
gradually reaching forward. He continued to make gasping, rattling noises, and his tread grew more steady.

"Hold it!" Mouseglove said. "What do you want?"

The man roared at him and rushed forward.

"Stop!" Mouseglove cried, and when the man did not he
pulled the trigger.

The round struck the man in the left arm, turning him
sideways. He swayed for a moment, then dropped to his
knees, making no effort to reach for the area of impact. He
rose again almost immediately, turning back toward
Mouseglove, voicing a new series of gutturals.

"Don't make me shoot again," Mouseglove said, setting
the hammer. "I recognize you. I know you're one of the
candidates. Just tell me what you want."

The man kept coming, and Mouseglove fired again.

The man jerked and was turned sideways again, but this

time he did not fall. He straightened and resumed his progress, his steady stream of sounds acquiring more and more inflection.

"Aaalll riight . . ." he said.

Mouseglove licked his lips as he readied the weapon once more.

"For gods' sakes, stop!" he cried. "I don't want to do this to you!"

"Not im—por—tant. Listenlistenlistenlisten," the other said, face totally devoid of expression, eyes still rolling, hands still extended and twitching.

Mouseglove backed off three paces, but the other hastened once more, Mouseglove hafted then and shot him squarely in the chest.

The man was jolted by the blow. He fell backward, caught himself in a seated position and began to rise again.

"No!" Mouseglove cried. "Please! Stop!"

"Stop," the man repeated without emotion. "Listen, listen, listen. Pol. Im—por—tant. You."

"Pol?" Mouseglove said, cocking the weapon again. "What about him?"

"Yes. Pol. Yes. You un-der-stand—me—now. Yes?"

"Then stay put and tell me! Don't come any nearer!"

Slowly, the other rose again, and something which had registered without Mouseglove's realizing it, came into his consciousness at that moment.

The man was not bleeding from any of his wounds. The garment was torn, darkened, slightly damp-looking where each round had penetrated—but there were no bright red splotches.

"Stay—put?" he said. "Stand—here?"

"Yes. You make me very nervous. I can hear you clearly. Tell me from there. What about Pol?"

"Pol . . ." said the other, swaying. "In trouble, Mouseglove. Listen."

"I am listening. What sort of trouble is it?"

"Larick—placed him—under a spell."

"What sort of spell? I'll find someone who can lift it."

"Not necessary. It has been removed. But Larick—does not—know this."

"Then Pol's mind is all right?"

"As always."

"But Larick thinks he is under a spell?"

"Yes. As Pol wishes."

"Where is he taking him?"

"Castle Avinconet."

"That's Ryle Merson's place! I might have known. I will go there and help him in whatever he is about."

"Not yet. You would be of little help and likely be destroyed. There is a better course of action."

"Name it."

"Go to Pol's patron."

"Ibal?"

"That one. Tell him what has occurred. Ask him for speedy transportation back to Rondoval."

"Say he grants it. What then?"

"You can speak with dragons."

"I'm afraid so."

"Tell the old one—Moonbird—to take you to the dead crater on Anvil Mountain and there help you to recover the magical tool."

"The scepter?"

"Yes."

"Say this can be done."

"Then take it to Pol at Avinconet."

"He will be all right in the meantime?"

"They may see fit to destroy him at any time. I do not know. If they do not, however, he may well need it soon."

"Who are you?"

"I do not know."

"How do you know all these things?"

"I was there."

"Why do you wish to help Pol?"

"I am uncertain."

"How is it that I could not kill you?"

"A corpse cannot die."

"Now it is I who do not understand."

"You know enough. Good-bye."

The red-haired man collapsed and lay still. Mouseglove approached him cautiously. There was no sign of breathing, and he considered the man's waxy pallor at closer range. He reached out and touched a cheek. It was cold.

He raised the right hand. It was cold, also; and a certain stiffness had already come into the limb. He pressed upon the fingernails one after the other. They all grew white and remained so. Finally, he leaned forward and lay his ear upon the chest near to the bullet hole. He discovered it to be a quiet place.

He arranged the body, crossing the arms upon the breast. He drew the white cowl up over the head and down across the face. He rose and moved away.

Crossing to the place where Pol and Larick had stood, he located their tracks and began following them. They disappeared quickly, however, in the rocky terrain. He halted there and spent several minutes pondering. Then he turned to the city of illusion and began his descent toward its flickering towers.

VIII

Wind whistling past him, cloak flapping behind him, Pol leaned forward upon the shoulders of the lesser dragon— a lithe, brown creature of similar mien and considerably less mass than the giant beasts of Rondoval—his legs gripping the sides of its back-ridge, hands upon a leather harness it wore. Twenty meters to his left and a few higher, Larick was similarly mounted upon one of the leathern-winged creatures. He glanced occasionally at Pol, who maintained an impassive attitude. A number of bright strands, visible at the second seeing, ran between them. Pol wondered how difficult it might be to kill the other when the time finally came. He decided that magic was too slow and uncertain a thing when employed against another sorcerer. He decided to strike quickly, with full violence and without warning once he had learned what he needed to know and could afford to dispense with the man. It would be foolhardy to leave enemies of his sort alive.

The sun was about to cut the throat of another day in the west and the moon had long since risen—a pale rag tossed above cloud-crests, brightening now over rough and shadowed land—as north and west they headed, long necks of their dark mounts extended, vanes outstretched and occasionally booming against gusts.

They had changed mounts four times during the day, finding the fresh ones magically tethered at a series of high locales. Pol's shoulder and leg muscles had long before ached themselves to the point of numbness. He stole a glance at Larick, who seemed tireless, bent forward and urging his mount to greater efforts. He stared ahead as if trying to burn holes through the darkening air.

Avinconet, Avinconet . . . He had repeated the name to himself for hours, in time with the rhythms of the flight. He had answered truthfully in telling Larick he had known nothing of it, yet—

It seemed now as if there might be some small familiarity attached. It seemed possible that there had been references in some of his father's earlier journals, though he could not recall anything specific.

Avinconet. Avinconet and Rondoval . . . Had there been some sort of tie?

The sun dipped lower and the moon grew brighter—and then, splashed with daysblood, he saw it, spread across the face of one of the more prominent peaks of a distant range. And he knew that he knew it.

Avinconet was the castle of his dreams, through which he had passed on his way to the Gate. Somehow, he had known all along that it was a real place. But seeing it . . . Seeing it gave rise to a train of disturbing sensations. He found himself anxious to enter the place, to locate the Gate. There was something that he had to do there, wanted to do, despite a reflex squeamishness at the very thought of the Gate. Yet, precisely what that action was, he could not say.

He watched the grim architecture grow before him, paling to yellow, silver, gray-white—a huge, central keep, stepped like a terrace, bristling with towers at many levels, flanked by long ranks of attached side-buildings—surrounded by high, wide ramparts, battlemented, possessed of numerous angles, a squat tower atop each turning. Windows were lighted at several levels toward the right side of the main structure. He shifted to the second seeing and immediately noted a tremendous massing of strands high in the air above the rear of the keep. He also noted a small, pale light drifting along the forward wall from left to right, pausing occasionally, wavering.

When they reached a position above the place, Larick swung his mount into a huge circle and Pol's followed, buffeted by strong winds. They commenced a slow, downward spiral.

As they descended toward the larger of a number of courtyards toward the rear, Pol continued to study the small light, visible only with the second seeing. It appeared human in form from this nearer distance, and there was a long, pale strand attached to it. Something about its aspect at this level touched him with a vague feeling of mournfulness.

As they dropped lower, Pol saw that the rear wall of the enclosed area was rough rock—a part of the mountainside itself—pierced by a number of irregular dark openings, several of them barred. It was at about this point that the light upon the ramparts disappeared from sight.

They touched down roughly and Larick alit at once. Moments later, Pol felt his strings jerked and he followed him. Larick unharnessed the beasts, shouted an order and watched them shuffle off into one of the cave-like openings. He followed them and drew upon something in the shadows. A metal grillwork dropped into place with a clang which echoed through the court.

Larick returned to Pol.

"We made excellent time because of the tailwinds," he commented. "I didn't think we'd be getting in till after midnight. He might be able to see you now. I don't know. I'll have to check."

"Who is 'he'?" Pol asked.

"Ryle Merson, the master of Avinconet."

"What does he want with me, wizard?"

"That is really for him to tell you. Come this way."

Pol felt a tugging upon the strands Larick had affixed to his person. He made no resistance but followed their lead toward an open archway to what he judged the northeast. They passed through into a flagstoned corridor where Larick led him about a series of turns.

Left, right, left, left, Pol memorized.

And then they halted before a low doorway. Its heavy wooden door stood ajar and Larick pushed it the rest of the way open. Pol noted that it could be secured from the outside by means of a heavy wooden bar.

"Inside," Larick said, and power pulsed in the strands.

Pol moved forward, stooped and entered. A bench ran along the righthand wall of the small, low-ceilinged room. There were no windows, only a few air-slits at the upper corners. A ragged blanket and a heap of sacking lay upon the bench. There was a chamber pot upon the floor nearby. An empty candle-bracket was affixed to the wall above the bench.

Pol turned back after he had passed over the threshold and the compulsion ceased.

"What's for dinner?" he asked.

"If he can't see you now, I'll have something sent over," Larick replied.

"I'll study the wine list while I wait."

Larick stared at him, shook his head.

"You could use a few more restraints. I don't want you tearing this place apart," he said. "Go sit down on the bench."

"All right, wizard. Not much to tear, though."

Pol crossed the room and seated himself. He could feel the working of the strands about him almost immediately.

"You do that very well," he said.

"Thanks."

". . . But I don't believe it will save you in the end."

Larick chuckled.

". . . So long as the end is a great way off."

"Don't buy any long-playing records," Pol said.

"What does that mean?"

"Even if you find out, it will be too late."

"Have it your way, Chainson."

"I may."

The door closed. The room became very dark. Pol heard the bar slide into place. He shook off the restraining strands.

He had toyed with the idea of trying to get a strand onto Larick while Larick was restraining him, a thing which would permit him to follow the other's progress about the place, seeing some of the things which he regarded. He had dismissed the notion as too risky, but now he wondered . . .

When he switched to the second seeing, the room was bathed in a pearly glow. A pale golden strand hovered near the door. He raised his right hand and exerted his will. Beneath multiple layers of illusion his dragonmark throbbed. The filament drifted toward him.

When it made contact with his fingertips he felt a tiny,

near-electrical tingling. When he blanked his mind and drew upon it for impressions, the sensation spread and he realized quickly that he was indeed reaching the other. Larick might be accused of carelessness, he mused, save that he had no way of knowing that Pol could still function in any magical capacity.

He followed Larick's progress through several turnings and up a long flight of stairs. There was a wide window at one turning, and he saw stars beyond it. Larick made his way through progressively more sumptuous areas of the keep, coming at last to a long gallery leading to a pair of ornate double doors. A liveried servant sat upon a bench to the right of the entrance. He rose as Larick approached, his face bearing a smile of recognition.

"Is he awake?" Larick inquired.

The man shook his head.

"I doubt it," he replied. "It's been awhile—and he said he did not want to be disturbed."

"Oh. Well, if he should wake up, Mak, tell him that I've brought him the man he wanted."

"If he does, I will. But I don't think he'll be about again tonight."

"Then I'm going to see about getting the fellow fed now. Do you want anything sent up?"

"A bit of beef and bread would be nice, and maybe some beer."

"Ryle's turned in a little early. . . ."

"The trip back tired him. He came rather fast."

"Don't tell me about it. All right. I'm for the kitchen. Good night."

" 'Night."

Pol followed him away from the place, step slower now, and down a back stair. He overheard him order the meals from a tired-looking fat woman of more than middle age, whom he had interrupted at a meal of her own, and then watched him prepare a light, cold dinner for himself and eat it quickly. Pol maintained the contact, his own hunger growing. On the fringes of things, he could see the woman preparing the trays.

Larick lingered over a second glass of wine, then sighed and rose slowly to his feet. He bade the woman good night, visited the latrine and made his way on, and downward, for a long distance into what must have been the northeastern wing of the place.

Pol continued his efforts to commit the route to memory, thinking that it must lead to Larick's own quarters. But it dropped lower and lower and seemed to lead farther and farther back toward the mountainside. All traces of splendor were gone here, and the area through which he passed bore the dustiness of disuse and seemed in places to have become a repository of damaged furniture.

Beyond this was a zone of dark emptiness where Larick created a light upon the tip of his blade and bore it overhead like a torch, coming at length to a bare and sweating rock wall over which he ran his hand. He followed this for a time, then turned into an opening in the rock, descending a steep slope into which rough steps had been hacked.

The way narrowed, grew level, turned. Larick began to slow. Twice again, it turned, and by then his steps were faltering. He was approaching a high, massy prominence with something possibly large and somewhat reflective atop it.

His hand wavered and the blade was lowered as he began to climb. Pol became aware that his breathing had deepened. Just as he reached the top he dropped to his knees and remained still. Pol could not make out what it was that lay before him, for something had suddenly gone wrong with the man's eyes.

He waited for a time, but nothing more happened, and then his food arrived and he released the contact.

When he finished eating, Pol pushed the tray away and sought the golden strand again. But it had either drifted off or dissipated. He realized then that he should have affixed it to something, pending his later attention. Yet, he was tired, and he knew that he would not be disturbed again till morning. He assembled a bed of the sacking on the bench and stretched out, covering himself with the blanket. He dozed almost immediately, myriads of images from the past several days flashing behind his eyes.

These faded quickly, and that other consciousness came

over him again. There was a moment of intense cold, and
then he stood before the great Gate. He felt other pres-
ences at his back, but he was unable to turn and look at
them—nor did he desire to do so. The right half of the
Gate swung outward a sufficient distance for him to angle
through, tiny wisps of smoke or fog emerging from it. This
vision had occurred with a sharpness and a rapidity which
surpassed all earlier versions, and this time there was no
ambivalence, no hesitation on his part. He moved forward
immediately and entered the land which lay beyond.

The first thing that he saw, facing him, a short distance
across the blasted landscape, was the head. Impaled upon
a sharpened pole, eyes still open, the head of one of the
demon creatures leered in his direction. He felt that there
was almost something personal in this display, a very
specific caution which he could only at this time find
amusing.

As he felt the transformation come over him, he winked
at the grisly visage and rose, wraith-like into the wan air.
Wind-stirred sands shifted snake-like among the rocks below him. He drifted southward, gaining momentum rapidly. As he did, a sense of jubilation grew within him until
he wanted to proclaim it in a voice like a thousand trumpets across the land. He spread his dark wings, vast as the
sails of some mighty vessel, and beat his way over the
deadland, rising to such an altitude that his mountains
finally became visible.

He, Prodromolu, was filled with the dream-memory of
his other life, and he forgot the head and the Gate and the
small human thing named Pol Detson, of whom he might
once have dreamed. He needed none of these.

When he reached that range, he hurled himself upon it,
fighting the hurricane-force winds that would dash him
against it. Six times he assailed those heights and was
beaten back.

On the seventh he prevailed, and his statue—dripping
of honey and spices, of wine and of blood—was shattered
at the Note that he uttered. Wherever his shadow passed,
buildings toppled and his worshippers faded and died.
Nyalith rose like a tower of dark fires before him. They
met over the waters of the stilled ocean and commenced

the dance that would take them around the world. Stars fell like burning souls about them, as the roaring winds bore them along the jewelled girdle of the planet. Their movements grew more savage with the deaths of kings and the fall of temples. He spoke again at the Mountains of Ice, and the Spell of the Gateway was wrought as Talkne, Serpent of the Still Waters, completed her journey of ten thousand years and rose from the depths to seek him—

Pol, for a moment, knew of the Keys and the dark god's promise as he was jerked suddenly alert there in his cell. The dream still vivid within him, he sat bolt upright and regarded the ghostly image of the woman who stood beside him, gesturing, lips moving, colorless eyes focussed upon his own. He half-rose, putting forth his hand.

She retreated, a look of sudden alarm upon her pale countenance. He withdrew, composing his face and making reassuring gestures. She halted. She appeared to study him. Slowly, she raised her arm and pointed at him. Then she turned and pointed toward the rear of the cell, turned back toward him and shook her head in the negative. He furrowed his brow and she repeated the motions. Suddenly then, she raised all five digits of her left hand and two upon her right. She shook her head, then went through the first series again. He shrugged and turned his palms upward.

She began to wring her hands. He rose, and she backed away. He took a step toward her, and she continued to retreat. He watched as she reached the far wall and passed through it, leaving behind perhaps the faintest trace of an exotic perfume.

He returned to his bench and seated himself, the entire sequence merging with his interrupted dream into a kind of hallucinatory half-world. Perhaps he had imagined it, he considered. Only her high cheekbones, large eyes, small chin and narrow span of brow beneath wide-swept wings of hair made such a strong, such a definite image. He sought, but she had left no strands behind by which he might test her reality.

He crossed to the door of the cell. For how long he had slept, he was not certain. He was still tired, but felt a little more rested than he had earlier. It seemed likely now that

most others in the place would be asleep. Therefore, the
time seemed good to depart, to commence investigating.
He shifted to the second seeing to study the area about
the door.

The response was slow, murky. It was as if he were
wearing smoked glasses on a foggy day. He concentrated
on the bar outside, on locating a connecting strand by
which he might draw it.

Slowly, very slowly, a greenish strand came into focus—
and passed out of it again. He called upon his dragonmark
for power and willed that it return.

But the dragonmark did not throb. There was only a
tingling, an itching sensation upon his forearm. The strand
swam back into view and he reached for it. There was no
contact. It passed through his fingers as if they were not
present. Then it faded again. His eyes began to ache.

He lowered his hands. What was happening? he wondered. This was the first time in all of his experience in
this land that the power had failed him. Could Larick have
done something to block its flow?

Then he remembered what Larick had said about the
initiation rite—that it might have this effect, that one
should refrain from even the simplest workings for several
weeks. Yet it had worked earlier, when he had followed
Larick about Avinconet. It must be erratic during this
period, he decided with a sigh. Somehow, he could hardly
think of the injunction as applying to himself. His initiation had been a sham, a trap. Or had it? He had gone
through all the motions, had undergone consciousness-
heightening experiences at the proper times. Could it be
that he had actually passed his initiation while being transformed into a monster?

He shook his head and tried again. His eyes ached more
and his temples began to throb. There was a burning
sensation along his right forearm. Once more, he saw the
strand dimly, but he was unable to influence it.

He returned to the bench and covered himself. He
thought of the woman for a long while before he slept
again. And this time the only dream-image that he could
later recall was the demon head on the stick, grinning.

IX

In some ways I suppose that it was illuminating, though I am not actually certain how. It did something for me or to me, but I do not know what. It also served to make my nature more obscure to me in certain areas. Yet—

I had entered Belken, that great, dark, glittering, stone hulk, moving along the high tunnel I had found within. In the topmost chamber I brooded for a time, in the place of the waters. I felt a kind of power there, reverberating all about me. It was, in some ways, very disturbing; yet I found it soothing at other levels. I decided then to investigate the entire psychic structure within the mountain.

The route that the would-be sorcerers would take from station to station was clearly marked in non-physical terms. I proceeded to the second area and meditated for a long while in that place, also. If it did good things for them, charged as it was with a kind of ordering power, I reasoned that it might benefit me, too.

How long I took at that and the next station, I do not know. A long while, I believe, for I was lost in long reveries and quickly forgot all about time as I regarded their progressions. It only occurred to me that it might be growing late when I felt an increase in the levels of intensity of those forces in which I was basking. I quickly traced it back to its origin in a circle of sorcerers in the glittering city below. At that time I also learned that it had grown dark outside. I knew this meant that the initiation was about to begin and that the power would continue to rise all night long. I moved on to the next station to maintain my lead. I wanted to complete the thing now, for I felt it

297

possible that it might shake something loose in my memory, giving me what I sought.

Something strange happened at that fourth station, for I heard a voice—tantalizingly familiar—speaking as if addressing me personally, intimately even.

"Faney," it said. "Faney."

It was a masculine voice, and it seemed to me as if I should understand exactly what it meant by that pronouncement. It was spoken fairly sternly, as if some order were being laid upon me. Faney. Was this my name, summoned from my faded past by the charged ambiance? No, that did not seem quite right. Faney . . .

"Faney!"—even stronger tones this time, and with them a roused sense of duty, a desire to follow the incomprehensible order and a sense of frustration at not being able to.

I expanded and contracted. I darted fitfully about within the chamber, seeking some means of discharging the injunction.

"Faney!"

Nothing. There was nothing that I could discover to do which would satisfy what was rapidly becoming a compulsion without an object.

So I moved on. And the power kept growing within the mountain. But the pressure was eased a bit in the next place, and I remained there for a long while. Again, I lost track of time and was only roused from a trance-like state into which I had lapsed by the sounds of the approaching candidates. Almost sluggishly, I drifted down to the next station so as not to be disturbed by them.

The sixth seemed more peaceful than any so far. I spread myself out and absorbed the good vibrations.

It did not seem that long before I heard them approaching again. This time I did not stir. I had no desire to depart and it occurred to me that it could be instructive to witness what went on in the course of the rites.

I watched them enter and take their positions. When he began speaking, I found myself peculiarly attracted to the one called Larick. I studied him, and then I realized why. It was an extraordinary discovery and I was still considering its effects when my attention was drawn to Pol. I was startled by the change in his appearance.

He was slouched well forward and his hands were enormous and scaly. A quick investigation beyond his garments showed me that his arms, though very attractive in their massive, dark fashion, were no longer *his* arms. Still he could not be unaware of this, and if it did not bother him I did not see why it should bother me.

But it did.

Further examination showed me that he was the only one of all those present whose anatomy had been altered. As I puzzled over this, another transformation began in the area of his shoulders and breast. This time I was able to trace it to its source, and I saw that Larick was causing it. I was unable to discover its motive in his mind, for a sorcerer's thoughts become impenetrable when he is working with the stuff of his trade. And none of the others' minds contained anything worth knowing; they were uniformly rapt in a kind of trance state.

I waited until they were finished there and moved on with them to the next station. Whether or not the motive would become clear to me, I was determined to investigate the method of the magical operation being practiced upon Pol.

I observed the next transformation very carefully and saw that it might more truly be considered a transference. As Pol's leg was replaced by a larger, more powerful version, I was able to trace the shifting of materials beyond the mountain. I followed, speeding and spinning down avenues where space was wrinkled and time a stream with many bends and some few oxbow lakes. I followed to the place of the Gate—that dream of Pol's which I had glimpsed. And I followed beyond, into the deadlands where I found a wailing creature whose body was now half-human, dragonmark upon the arm.

"Brother," I addressed it, "wear them well this short while, for it is but some human rite."

But it either could not or would not understand me. It continued its outcry and began beating at the transformed portions of its own person. So I laid a deep sleep upon it, there in the lee of a triangle of standing gray stones,

serving both Pol and itself with little real effort on my own
part. I told myself at the time that this was a necessary
personal involvement—my first—in the affairs of others,
for purposes of assuring that things be played out smoothly
in their entirety, so as to satisfy a number of purely
intellectual needs of my own.

But even then I was beginning to wonder.

I regarded that fascinating land for several extra instants
before I swirled and began the long journey back, bright
thunder and loud lightning oxymoronic over oxbows as I
passed, passed I negative to reverse point and back, finding thoughts this time in Larick's head, of Avinconet and
those he served. The first glimmer of understanding came
to me.

I rotated with a certain satisfaction, then followed them
to the next station. There, I saw the transference repeated
with Pol's other leg. This annoyed me more than a little.
His mind was as far asea as any of the others', convincing
me that he was being victimized. It did not seem a very
fair thing, judging from the little I knew about humans,
especially coming from Larick the way that it was.

When we moved on to the next one, several things
occurred in addition to the alteration of Pol's abdomen.
The one candidate dropped dead. He, of course, was
nothing to me; but at approximately the same moment
there came a repetition of the word "Faney". I studied the
others for reactions to this, but there were none. Of course,
they had just acquired a dead man which might have
proved distracting; still, it had sounded very loud, and
after a few moments I heard it again.

And then again.

It became steady, relentless in repetition. At first I
cowered, but then I listened. How silly of me to have
thought that the others could hear it when it was so
obviously addressing me and me alone. I felt that at some
level I was beginning to understand it. And then something else occurred.

The body was moved, the ritual proceeded, Pol was
altered. But none of these seemed particularly important
at just that moment. I was undergoing a change, far less
physical in nature than Pol's, a thing which raised fascinat-

ing and involved speculations on the subjects of free will and determinism. Unfortunately, I did not have time to pursue them just then, for my full attention was required by the change itself: I had changed my mind. I had taken an unstated, barely realized position of not interfering in the affairs of others for as long as I could remember. I suddenly brought it into focus, examined it and decided that the time had arrived to make an exception.

I did not like what was being done to Pol, but I did not possess the expertise necessary to reverse the phenomenon. I would do something, though—what, I was not certain—something to help him return to what was normal for him, so that he could deal with his own enemies as he saw fit.

I thought about it as we descended to the final station. The voice repeating "Faney" had faded. Pol predictably lost his feet at the next stop. I studied Larick in those moments when he was not conducting operations. I saw that he intended to spirit Pol off to Avinconet, where he would be a prisoner, as soon as the night's work was concluded.

When we departed the last station and moved on into the big cavern, I watched as he laid the paralysis upon Pol and began conducting the others outside. It seemed that I might be able to lift the spell which held him there in the alcove, but I was uncertain as to what could be done next.

I followed the first initiate outside, to witness the last phase of things. Then I saw that a number of the masters had come up to accompany their people back into town. Lurking in a secluded spot, Mouseglove watched the cavemouth.

Of course.

I was already working on my plan as I returned to the cavern. When I discovered the sorcerer of the midnight visitation with Pol, however, I halted and observed. There was a great feeling of power about the man.

He began using that power. I saw that he was employing it to reverse the transference. I moved immediately to interfere in a fashion which could not be detected. It was pure impulse on my part, not to see such good materials wasted. The creature's head could be mounted upon a stick by its fellows for all I cared. I made use of the drawstring space pocket as I had seen Pol do for storage purposes.

I saw Pol returned to himself and disguised. It in no way affected my plan when I realized what he intended to do. He would still be operating in an area of considerable danger.

So I sought the body of Krendel, the red-haired man who had died earlier. In that no one else was using it at the moment, I permeated it and set about studying how it worked. I wanted to have it ready soon to run the errand I had conceived of, to Mouseglove, who waited without.

X

The small man slipped through the golden hole in the center of the room and it began to close behind him. A contracting halo, an optical aberration, the view through the opening was not that of the far side of the sumptuous apartment. Instead, the eye followed the dwindling form of the dark-clad man who had passed that way across a high tapestry-hung hall as it approached an arched gallery past pillars dark and light.

Then the wavering lens closed upon itself, flickered and was gone. Ibal slumped back upon the heap of cushions on which he had been sitting bolt upright. His breathing was suddenly deep and rapid; perspiration dotted his brow.

Vonnie, kneeling beside him, delicately blotted his face with a blue silk kerchief.

"There are not many," she said, "can do the door spell well."

He smiled.

"It is a strain," he acknowledged, "and, to tell the truth, not something I'd ever intended to work again. This time, though . . ."

". . . it was different," she finished.

He nodded.

"What are you going to do now?"

"Recover," he answered.

"You know that is not what I mean."

"All right. Recover and forget. I've given him a hand. My honor is satisfied."

"Is it? Really?"

He sighed.

"At my age, that is all the honor I can afford. The days

are long gone when I would care to get involved in something like this."

Her hands passed through his hair, dropped to his well-muscled shoulders, rubbed there for a time, then led him back to a seated position. She raised a cool drink to his lips.

"How certain are you of your assessment of the case?" she finally inquired.

"The gods know what else it could be!" he said. "Something not at all natural sends Mouseglove to me, with the story that the young man I'd sponsored is old Det's son and that he's just been kidnaped by Ryle Merson. Honor says that I should do something because Ryle has made off with the man I sponsored. So I have. Fortunately, all Mouseglove wanted was a fast trip back to Rondoval—and I've just provided it."

"Is that really enough?"

"It is not as if he were my apprentice. I was only doing the man a favor. I barely know him."

"But—" she began.

"That is all," he replied.

"But it was not what I meant."

"What, then?"

"The things you said at first—could they be true?"

"I forget what I said."

"You said that it is a continuation of something that began before Pol was born . . ."

"I suppose that it is."

". . . the thing that had led to the wars."

He took the goblet into his hands and drained it.

"Yes, I believe so," he said then.

"Something that could reopen that whole business?"

He shrugged.

"Or close it. Yes. I think that might be the case—or that Ryle believes it might be the case. Same thing."

He set the goblet aside, raised his hands and looked at them.

"Pol has apparently aroused the concern of something poweful and supernatural," he said, "and he also has the good offices of the friend we just sent on his way."

"I was not talking about Pol. I am thinking of the entire

situation of which that is but a part. This place is full of important practicioners of the Art. It is the only occasion in four years when they will all be together like this. I would almost say that it seems more than coincidental. Don't you feel that we ought to bring this to their attention?"

Ibal began to laugh.

"Stop and think about it for a minute," he said later. "I think it would be the worst possible thing to do. There were attractive things about both sides in that conflict. Some stood to benefit, some did not. Do you really think we'd get a concensus? We can start the next war right here, if you'd like."

She had stiffened as he spoke and her eyes widened slightly.

"Gods!" she said. "You may be right!"

"So why don't we forget about the entire thing?" he finished. He reached out and took her hand. "And I know exactly how to go about it."

"I believe I'm getting a headache," she said.

Mouseglove did not look back. He accepted the sorcery which had brought him to Rondoval as a part of life. If magic were used against him, things could be very bad. If it worked to his benefit, he was grateful. Until he had met Pol, he had generally attempted to avoid the notice of sorcerers, counting them—usually correctly—as an untrustworthy lot. He mouthed a few words of thanks to Dwastir, patron of thieves, that this one had been helpful, as he hurried into the great hall and made his way down the stairway.

He located the bundle of faggots Pol had charmed for him, raised one and spoke the necessary words over it. He turned then and headed without hesitation along the confusion of tunnels, moving back toward the caverns where he had obtained more than one's normally allotted span of rest.

For a long while he passed through the cool places of dancing shadows before he reached the entranceway where the great slab Pol had toppled lay in shattered ruin all about.

Picking his way among the rubble, he continued into a

place where the echoes died in the distance and the walls
and roof were no longer visible, a place where the odor of
the beasts hung heavy and the torch flickered in vagrant
drafts. Here, too, he knew his way, and he proceeded
along it with much less trepidation than he would have
experienced some months earlier.

The vast, still mounds of scaled and furred bodies were
sprawled casually about, many of them sleeping in the
depths of magical charges as they had, he had, before.
Some few others slept out their natural daily, weekly or
monthly spans.

He wondered, as he made his way to the familiar niche,
whether the one he sought would indeed be resting there.
He might be anywhere in the world, his absence necessi-
tating Mouseglove's rousing another—a thought he did not
relish. Having been trapped for twenty years in the same
version of the sleep spell as Moonbird, he had developed a
peculiar link—a thing even verging on friendliness—with
the giant dragon. With any of the others, he would have to
attempt a complicated explanation, possibly beginning with
his own identity. No, he did not like that thought at all.

As he came near to the place where Moonbird normally
rested he grazed his shoulder against an unremembered
rocky prominence.

Mouseglove! It has been long!

He stumbled back. It was a shoulder of dragon rather
than a shoulder of stone against which he had brushed. He
recovered almost immediately and moved to lay his hands
upon the beast.

"Yes, I am back," he replied. "There is trouble. We
need your help."

The great bulk shifted beneath his hands, causing them
to slide along the hard, smooth scales. Moonbird began to
rise.

What is it? he asked.

"We must go to Anvil Mountain, find Pol's scepter, take
it to him."

He cast it into the fiery hole. He told me this.

"He told me, also—"

But I have been back, and the fires have died. All is

gray rock now. I do not know how far I could dig in it. Get tools.

Mouseglove thought for a moment.

"There is a room off the main courtyard," he said, sending along the image. "I will return and look over the tools there. Meet me in the yard."

It will be faster for me to take you there.

"Well . . ."

Mount!

Mouseglove scrambled onto his back. Minutes later, they were gliding through the darkness.

XI

Pol was awakened by the light shining upon his face. He tossed his head several times to avoid it, then sat suddenly upright, eyes opened.

The door of his cell stood wide.

Had someone come for him, then met with some momentary distraction? He listened. There were no sounds from the corridor.

Cautiously, he rose to his feet. He crossed the cell to the place where he had stood earlier, conjuring ineffectively, eyes throbbing.

Some illusion? To torment him?

He extended his hand beyond the door frame, touched the door. It moved slightly. At that moment, he felt the essence of mocking laughter, soundless. It was as if something vaguely sinister were amused at his puzzlement, his trepidation—something inhabiting a level of reality which did not coincide with his own. He stood frozen, waiting, but it did not occur again.

Finally, he moved forward, passing out into the corridor. It was deserted.

What now? he thought. Should he set out upon the route along which he had followed Larick? Should he strike out and explore elsewhere within the castle? Or should he head back to the courtyard, take one of the flying beasts and flee?

The latter course struck him as the most sensible: Flee, hide and wait for the return of his powers. Then he could go back to Rondoval, rouse his bestial minions and come back here as he had come to Anvil Mountain—to tear the

308

place apart. It made better sense than remaining, power-less and outnumbered, in the citadel of an enemy.

He turned in the direction of the courtyard with the cages. Then he stood still.

His way was barred by a sheet of pale flame.

"And so my choice is not really a choice," he said softly.

Is it ever? came the familiar, ironic notes in his head.

"I guess that remains to be seen."

Like most things, came the reply, accompanied by slightly conciliatory sensations.

"I've never been able to figure out whether you're an enemy or an ally."

We are agents. We aided you once.

"And the next time . . .?"

Why should you have any reason to doubt those who have helped you in the past?

"Because I came away with the feeling that I'd been pushed into something."

I would say, rather, that we pulled you out.

"That is a debatable point. But you say that you are agents. Agents of what?"

Change.

"Much is encompassed by that word. Could you be more specific?"

Two of the forces at work upon this world are science and magic. At times they are opposed to one another. We are on the side of the magic.

"This place hardly seems a stronghold of technology."

It is not. There is no direct confrontation involved here.

"God damn you! Getting a straight answer out of you is like milking a wildcat! Why can't you just tell me what is involved?"

The truth is such a sacred thing that we guard it well.

"I believe that you want my cooperation."

That is why we are assisting you again.

Pol tried shifting to the second seeing. This time it seemed to work smoothly. With it, he detected the out-line of a human form within the flame—small, masculine, head bowed, hands hidden within the long sleeves which overlapped near its dark center. An orange strand drifted near Pol's right hand, the far end of it vanishing within the

flame. He caught it with his fingertips and twirled it. The
dragonmark throbbed upon his forearm.

"Now you will tell me what I wish to know—" he
began.

His hand felt as if it were on fire. He stifled a scream
and dropped to one knee in his agony. His second vision
departed. His entire arm ached.

We will not be coerced in such a fashion, came the
reply.

"I'll find the right way," he said through clenched teeth.

*It would be so much easier and would save so much time
if you would let us show you rather than spend the night
telling you what is involved.*

Pol rose to his feet, holding his aching right hand in the
other.

"I suppose that's the best deal I'll get from you tonight."

It is. Turn and follow the other.

Pol turned and beheld another tongue of flame. This
one was only the size of his hand, and it hung in the air in
the middle of the corridor about eight paces before him. A
moment after his gaze fell upon it, it began to drift away
from him. He followed.

It led him through a hall filled with grotesque statues,
both human and non-human, a low, red brilliance, a soft,
almost vibrant glow lying upon the whole setting, cast
perhaps by the flame itself, giving the impression that all
of the stone forms were beginning to stir. The air there
was stale in his lungs, and he found himself holding his
breath until he had departed the place. The luster was
present in some of the other chambers and hallways, yet
somehow it lacked the sinister character it had given to
that room and those representations. The dragonmark had
begun throbbing when they had entered the place and did
not grow still until they were well away.

He moved down a series of stone stairways, each rougher
than the preceding one, passing through damp chambers
and long passageways, which, judging from the descent he
had made, must be well beneath the castle itself and
hacked from the living stone of the mountainside. At some
point, Pol ventured a look behind him and saw that the
other flame was nowhere in sight. He also saw, however,

that the shadows seemed to slide in a liquid, almost sentient fashion at his back, in a manner he found m———than a little unsettling. He hurried to keep pace with his guide.

The rooms and corridors through which he passed bore the dust of disuse in heavy layers, a thing he found mildly heartening when he moved through a series which could only be torture chambers—equipped as they were with chains, racks, tongs, pincers, weights, flails, whips, mallets and a great variety of oddly shaped blades. All of these bore stains, rust marks or both, along with the comforting coatings of dust. There were bones in odd corners, all of them gnawed long ago by rodents, now dry, brittle, cracked and discolored. Pol brushed a wall with his fingertips and heard the echoes of screams from long ago. When he switched to the second vision, he caught near-subliminal glimpses of atrocities enacted in times gone by, the traumas of which had etched themselves into the setting. Hastily, he reverted to the normal mode of seeing.

"Who . . ." he whispered, more to himself, "was responsible for these things?"

The present lord, Ryle Merson, came the reply from ahead.

"He must be a monster!"

Once, such things were routine here. But he ceased all such activities nearly a quarter of a century ago, claiming that he had repented. It is said that he has led a relatively blameless, possibly even virtuous life since.

"Is it true?"

Who can say what lies in a person's heart? Perhaps he cannot even say himself, for certain.

"You are making this all totally enigmatic to me. I confess to being prejudiced, but in no way can I see his treatment of me as virtuous or blameless—and that goes for his lackey, Larick, as well."

People have reasons for things that they do. Motives and objectives are seldom of matching moral color.

"And what of yourself, whatever you are?"

We are neither moral nor immoral now, for our actions contain no element of choice.

"Yet something set you upon the course you follow. There was a decision there."

So it would seem—a touch of irony to these words?

"Still not giving anything away, are you?"

Nothing.

They moved past a fetid-smelling cistern in which something was splashing. The floor of a recess near an adjacent airshaft was heavy with the droppings and fragile, hieroglyphic skeletons of what might have been bats. Indentations in the floor contained small pools of water. The walls were slimy in this area, and Pol felt as if a great weight of earth and rock hovered just above his head, groaning the long, slow notes of timeless stresses.

He wondered at the brief conversation, recalling the allegations of the Seven after the battle at Anvil Mountain, giving the impression then that their actions were determined. At least they were consistent in what little they did say. There was something more about them which he felt that he should remember, something almost dream-like in texture. . . .

His efforts at recollection ended as he turned a corner and halted. Whether it was a corridor or a room which he now faced, he could not tell. The way ahead was misty—almost smoky—though he detected no odors about it. The flame had halted when he did, and it seemed much nearer now; its brightness had increased, and it had acquired something of a greenish cast.

"What the hell," Pol asked, "is that?"

Just a local etheric disturbance.

"I don't believe in ether."

Then call it something else. Perhaps you will be footnoted by some future lexicographer. We know that things were different where you grew up.

"I'll be damned. That's the closest I've come to getting a rise out of you. So you know my history?"

We were present when you departed this world. We were present when you returned.

"Interesting. Your remarks almost lead me to believe that you do not know what things were like in the place where I was raised."

True, though we are able to conclude a number of things about it from examining your actions and reactions since your return. For example, the familiarity with technology which you demonstrated—

The light before him was extinguished. Pol stood still in the semi-darkness, staring into the faintly luminous mist. He listened to his heartbeat and considered calling upon the dragonlight.

An instant later a blue leaf of flame appeared in the air before him, near to the place where the other had been.

Come now!

The tone was feminine, imperious.

"What became of my other guide?" he asked.

He talked too much. Come!

Pol wondered at this. Had he finally glimpsed a chink in their armor?

"Getting near something you don't want me to know, eh?"

There was no reply. The blue flame began drifting slowly away from him. Pol did not move to follow it.

"Do you know what I think?" he said. "I think that you've got to use me because I am my father's son and he created you. You have some special connection with Rondoval, and only I can serve your purpose."

The flame halted and hovered.

You are wrong.

"I do not believe that you like this," he went on, ignoring the response, "because, for all your talk of determinism, I was raised on another world about which you know little or nothing, and you cannot account for me as you might someone who'd spent his life in this land. I am more of a random factor than you would like me to be, but you have to deal with me anyway. Tonight you will attempt to impress me in some fashion so that I will be more amenable to your purposes. I tell you now that I have seen things beside which the display at Anvil Mountain was very small beer. I am prepared to be unimpressed by any efforts on your part."

You have finished?

"For now."

Then let us continue this journey.

The flame drifted on, slowly. Pol followed. It seemed to be bearing to the left, but there were no other objects in his field of vision against which he might track its motion. He plodded along, and the palely illuminated mist rolled and boiled about him. Unaccountable shadows began to move within it.

He kept changing direction. Echoes were muffled. Pol could not tell for certain whether he was moving through a long, twisting corridor or whether he was backtracking, turning, wandering within one large room. As he was unable to locate any walls, he suspected the latter. But there seemed no way to tell for certain.

The shadows which tracked him grew darker, their outlines becoming more distinct. Some were definitely human in form; others were not. The silhouette of a dragon flickered overhead as if passing at a great height. It seemed as if a great number of people were now moving, silently, at various distances, about him. He tried turning to the second seeing, but there was no change in the prospect.

Suddenly, a figure loomed directly before him—big, ruddy, balding, with large, capable hands. The flame darted past, and perhaps it took up a station somewhere nearby.

"Dad!" Pol said, halting.

His step-father's mouth twisted into a half-grin.

"What the hell do you think you're doing in this backward place?" he said. "I really need you at home, in the business, right now."

"You're not real . . ." Pol said.

But Michael Chain looked solid. His facial expressions—his speech inflections—were exactly those of Michael Chain with a few drinks under his belt and a load of impatience about to break loose.

"You're a disappointment to me. Always were."

"Dad . . .?"

"Go on with your silly games then. Break your mother's heart."

A gesture of dismissal. The large man turned away.

"Dad! Wait!"

He vanished into the mist.

"It's a trick!" Pol said, glaring at the flame. "I don't know how you did that or what it's all about, but it's a trick!"

Life is full of tricks. Life itself may be a trick.

He turned away.

"Why are we standing here in the gloom? I thought you were taking me someplace important?"

You are the one who halted.

"Okay! Let's get going!"

He turned back.

Betty Lewis, wearing a tight, low-cut dress, stood frowning at him off to the left. The texture of her familiar flesh looked so real. . . .

"You could have called," she said. "Maybe it wasn't that big a thing between us, but you might at least have said good-bye."

"I couldn't," he answered. "There was no way."

"Just like all the others," she said, and the mists moved between them and she was gone.

"I see what you are doing," Pol said to the flame. "But it won't work."

It is the condition of this place. You are doing it to yourself.

Pol took a step forward.

"You brought me here!"

"Pol?" came a familiar voice from his right, sending a shiver along his arms.

"The hell with you!" he said, not turning. "Let's go, flame!"

Obediently, the bluish light moved away, and he followed it. The shadow remained to his right, drew nearer.

"Pol!"

He did not look. But an arm was extended into his field of vision—muscular, covered with heavy, rust-colored hair, a thick, wide bracelet at the wrist, studded with control buttons, indicators, lights—and even when he saw it, he did not believe that it was real.

Until the hand fell upon his arm, gripping it, halting him, turning him.

"I feel your hand," he said slowly.

"I felt your wrath," said the other.

Pol raised his eyes to regard the once handsome, rugged features of Mark Marakson, marred by the eyepiece to the left, its lens a deep, glittering blue.

"You gave me no choice," Pol replied.

"You had my name, my parents. You took my girl . . ."

"This can't be!" Pol said.

". . . my life," Mark finished, and then the lens went black and his flesh reddened and charred and began to peel away.

Pol screamed.

The hand, through which the bones were now visible, fell away from his arm. The figure backed off into the mist—the black-lensed prosthetic now affixed to a skull— and then it was gone.

Pol began to shake. He raised his hands to his face and lowered them again.

Nora now stood where Mark had been. Her face was expressionless.

"It is true," she said. "You killed the man I loved."

She turned and walked away.

"Wait!"

He ran, reaching for her, but her shadow was lost among others. Still he groped, turned, moving in one direction and then another.

"Come back!"

Pol! Stand still! Do not lose yourself in this place!

He turned again, and old Mor stood before him, leaning upon his staff.

"For that which I see before you, I would that I had never brought you back," the sorcerer said. *"Better Mark had prevailed than that you do the thing you would do."*

"I don't know what you're talking about," Pol said. "Tell me, if there is something I should know!"

Mor vanished in a burst of fire.

Stay with me! came the words out of the flame. *This could get out of control!*

"Whose control?" Pol asked, turning away.

Stel, the centaur, stood looking into his eyes.

"You would break faith with us," she said, "though you swore by your scepter not to."

"I have not broken faith with you," he replied.

". . . And the doom which walks always at your back will move forward."

"I have not broken faith," he repeated.

"Evil son of an evil father!"

Pol turned and strode away.

Come back!—almost, a pleading note now.

The giant dog-headed figure he had faced beneath the pyramid rose suddenly before him.

Thief! Breaker of the Triangle of Int! came its mental message.

"I stole nothing. I took what was mine," Pol said.

I've curses for thieves, to hound them to the ends of the earth!

"Piss on your curses!" Pol replied. "I beat you once. I'm not afraid of you now!"

He took a step toward the menacing figure.

Stop! They're gaining power! It really can hurt you! came the words out of the flame which had just appeared between them, sounding frantic now.

The dog-headed one raised his right arm. Pol wheeled and ran.

Stop!

A small shape rushed into view. It was white, had long ears, was wearing a waistcoat. It's nose twitched.

"Late again!" it said. "It'll be my head, sure as hell!"

It looked up at Pol.

"Yours, too," it said, before it scurried off.

Pol kept moving.

Stand still! In this place—

He almost bumped into the man. It was the nameless sorcerer he had fought back at Rondoval. Pol backed away from him.

The sorcerer raised his right hand and a fiery knife appeared within it. He cast it directly at Pol's breast.

Pol threw himself to the side and hit the ground rolling. He continued the movement until he was well away from the place.

He lay panting for several moments, then moved to regain his feet. Another man approached as he did so, moving quickly, halting before him. It was a tall, regal figure, with a single black streak running back through a mane of white hair. Pol realized immediately that the features were very similar to his own.

"You are . . . ?" Pol said.

"Det Morson, your father," came the reply.

"Well curse me and be on your way," Pol said, standing. "That's the game here, isn't it?"

"I am not a part of the game here. I am merely taking advantage of it." His right hand rose and brushed Pol's cheek lightly. "Whichever way you turn, no matter what your decision, no matter how things break," he said, "your real enemy will be the Madwand."

"What Madwand? I thought that was a general term for—"

"Henry Spier is the greatest of the Madwands, and he is known only as that."

"What kind of name is Henry Spier? In this place—"

The tongue of flame flared into being between them.

Back, Det! Back to your special hells! came the voice out of fire. *Your power over us has passed!*

Det raised his hands. crossing his arms upon his breast. As if by contagion, flames violated his outline. Suddenly, however, he raised his head and stared at Pol.

"Belphanior." he said. "Remember that in time of need."

Pol opened his mouth to question him, but Det was gone in a rush of fire and wind.

The flame which hung before him began to contract, resuming its former, smaller size and shape.

What did he mean by that? it asked him.

"I have no idea," Pol answered.

What else did he tell you?

"Nothing. There wasn't time."

You are lying.

"The truth is such a sacred thing that I guard it well."

The flame did not move. He felt sensations of puzzlement and of anger, but no words came with them. Long moments passed.

Finally, with a movement almost like a shrug, the flame drifted leftward. Pol followed. There were still shadows in the mist, but they did not draw near. The flame moved quickly now, and Pol increased his pace.

The mist began to thin. Pol saw a wall to his left, nothing to his right. Shortly, an archway appeared before him. He followed the light through it and felt as if he had returned to normal space. There was no mist on this side, only dimness and a faint odor of mildewed tapestry.

"We were really just moving around inside one big room, weren't we?" Pol asked.

There was no reply.

"It was a kind of downbeat Rorschach-thing, wasn't it?" he said. "Everything in there came from me, one way or another. Didn't it?"

Silence again.

"Okay," he said, as they approached a stairway leading upward. "If whatever you want from me requires my cooperation, just remember that you haven't been keeping the customer happy."

He reached the stair and began to mount it.

A ripple of amusement passed back down over him. His dragonmark throbbed intermittently. They reached the top of the stair and passed through a better-furnished, though apparently long-unused room. After exiting, they came upon another stair, again leading upward. As he climbed it, Pol reflected that they had probably come into that eastern or northeastern wing of the place into which he had followed Larick's progress earlier.

"We've taken a kind of roundabout course, haven't we?" he said.

It was necessary.

"Why?"

To avoid the inhabited sections.

"Is that the only reason?"

Why else?

"Not to condition me or impress me in any fashion?"

You flatter yourself.

"Have it your way."

We will.

He took a lefthand turning and headed along a narrow corridor. Then a right into a room with a single, large window which faced out across the ramparts onto a bleak, starlit landscape. The room itself contained old and damaged furniture not arranged as if for use. He exited at its farther end and entered another room also obviously being used for storage. Pol brushed away the strands of a spiderweb as he passed. A rat dashed across his path and crouched, staring, beneath an armchair.

Two rooms later, in a place with several doors, a feeling

of familiarity came over him. He felt certain that Larick had passed this way earlier.

His feelings of fatigue were rising again as they headed leftward and back from corridor to tunnel to a place where rough-cut steps led downward. The flame moved faster, grew brighter now. He increased his pace to match it, reaching out as he passed to touch the rock wall, discovering it to be as moist as it appeared. Yes, this was the way that Larick had come.

He hurried about the turnings and there, finally, before him, was the dark, stony rise with the shining thing atop it. The flame rose toward it. Pol climbed after.

"What is it?" he said under his breath.

Something we'll need.

"You're so damned helpful."

Far more than you seem to realize.

A little later, he saw that it was a casket with a bulging, transparent cover. And when he came up beside it, he drew in his breath sharply, for he saw that it held the body of a woman, perfectly preserved. Her high cheekbones, small chin and wings of hair he now saw to be of a light brown color in the glow shed by his guide, were not unfamiliar to him.

"The ghost . . ." he breathed.

Her spirit is said to wander these halls. It is of no importance. Remove the lid.

"How?"

There are fasteners along the sides and at either end.

Pol continued to regard the pale features.

"Why the Snow White bit?" he finally asked.

Pardon? I do not understand the reference.

"Why is she on display?"

Her father, Ryle Merson, wishes to view her upon occasion.

"Morbid son of a bitch, isn't he? I suppose he's laid a preserving spell on her—if she's been dead very long."

It has been a long while. Remove the lid.

"Why?"

In order to move her.

"Why move her?"

Her presence is required elsewhere. Do as we say!

"All right. It was a pretty steep climb, though."

You will bring her this way.

The flame brightened and Pol could see a level ledge beyond the casket, leading back toward a tunnel. He leaned forward and sought the fastenings. One by one, he undid them and slipped them. He seized hold of the lid's frame then and strained to raise it. For a time, it resisted his efforts. Then, with a creaking sound, it slid slowly upward.

He eased the transparent cover back and lowered it to the ground. Only then, did he pause to scrutinize the woman with more than clinical concern.

"What's her name?" he asked.

Taisa. Pick her up. Bring her this way.

The flame advanced along the level route beyond the casket. Pol stooped, raised the woman in his arms. The faint, familiar aroma of a delicate perfume reached his nostrils.

"How did she come to this end?" Pol asked, as he moved around the catafalque and followed.

A victim of circumstance, in a long and involved struggle.

He crossed the ledge and entered the tunnel behind the moving light.

It turned abruptly to the left after a few paces, and Pol found himself traveling upslope. The feeling of anticipation which had been his companion since he had awakened, was heightened now. He felt that he was nearing the heart of a mystery, a mystery made very personal, a mystery in which he would be playing a significant role.

Anoter turn, and he was in a wide, high, partly furnished room carved out of stone. A large rectangular opening in the lefthand wall showed stars in a now pale sky, and the upper slopes of the mountain. There were heavy chairs and a long table toward the front of the place. To the rear. . . .

He halted and stared.

Bring her over here.

Slowly, almost mechanically, his limbs moved to obey. He was barely aware of the motion, his eyes locked upon the revelation set into the far wall.

Set her down there. No. The head at the other end.

Pol placed Taisa's body atop a slanting stone slab, her feet at the higher end. Her head fell into place within a wide channel which had been cut into the hard, gray surface. Automatically, he adjusted her long, simple, blue garment about her. As he did, he noticed a wide, shallow basin below the end of the groove. A dagger of black stone lay upon its rim. These things registered but made no real impression upon him, for his attention was focussed elsewhere.

He stared at the wall before him, at the great double doors set within it. Perspiration dampened his brow, and his hands possessed a slight tremor as he moved away from the woman and the stone, staring.

They were the Gate of all the forgotten dreams which fell like bright cloaks upon him now.

He drew nearer. The doors were solid, massive, iron-bound, and of a dark, metallic-looking wood. There seemed to be no locking mechanism, no handles, only the inter-mittently spaced rings.

Carved and burned into the Gate in an elaborate coiled pattern, rising from the base to the midpoint, was the form of an enormous serpent, drawing itself high above a styl-ized line of waves. Three heavy spikes had been driven into it—one at the neck, one at the tail and one at the body's middle.

Then, raising his gaze to the top of the frame and above it, he beheld the familiar form of a great, black bird-like thing, wings outspread, carved into the rock. And into this figure, also, spikes had been driven—one into either wing.

Pol took another step and halted, breathing heavily. He was again Prodromolu, Opener of the Way, coursing the heavens of Qod, while below him, mounting steadily up-ward from the depths, the serpent Talkne moved upon the final circuit of her eons-long journey in search of him. Nyalith shrieked a warning which shattered mountains and revealed the secrets at their hearts. Wheeling, he dove toward calm sea-surface. . . .

He came to himself once more, remembering the Keys and the dark god's promise to lead the people from the devastated land, to merge that place with another by opening the way between the worlds. And the Keys . . .

The Keys!

The statuettes were the Keys. Strangely living Keys . . . And—

He lowered his eyes.

Yes . . .

Incised into the floor and painted in fading yellow, red and blue was a large, irregularly shaped diagram. A section of it swept back to encompass the slab upon which Taisa lay; another portion projected far forward, touching the Gates' heavy frame at the left. A number of sharp, near-triangular segments were extended, thorn-like, from the main body of the design. Suddenly aware that his dragonmark was throbbing slowly and heavily, Pol counted them.

". . . Five, six, seven."

Exactly.

He barely glanced at the flame, which hovered now above Taisa.

Bring our physical representations into being upon this plane now, and place each of us at one of the points. You know the order.

"Yes."

Pol shifted his vision, raised his right hand, caught one of the seven ebon strands leading back over his right shoulder. He rotated his hand, winding the filament about it until he felt a tension upon it. The power flashed from his dragonmark back along the line and he jerked upon it.

He held one of the statuettes in his hand—tall, slim, feminine, sharp-featured and imperious. Its cloak bore a patina of beaten gold and it was girdled with orange, red and yellow stones. A single green gem was set into its forehead.

It felt warm and grew warmer yet as Pol held it, turning his head.

Yes . . .

He moved to his right, setting it at the tip of the second peak from the end, facing toward the Gate.

As he straightened, he saw that the stars were fading, the sky growing brighter.

He raised his hand, seeking the strands again. They were not apparent. He realized then that his vision had slipped out of the second seeing. He strove to shift it back, but to no avail.

His dragonmark, he noted then, had lost its recent throbs of power. He massaged his forearm. He tried again to recall his vision.

What is the matter?

"I don't know. I can't do it."

What do you mean you can't do it? You just did.

"I know. But something's slipped again. The power has been coming and going since I went through Belken. Right now it's gone."

The flame moved toward him, hovered directly before his eyes. He closed them against the brightness.

Keep your eyes open.

He obeyed, squinting. He saw that the flame was growing, was becoming a vast sheet of fire, now his own size, now larger.

It advanced and he drew back.

Stand still. We must investigate.

It wrapped him like a cloak, it settled upon him. He felt that it was penetrating his body, his very being. There was no sensation of heat, only an odd, vibrating feeling, as when one steps ashore after several days at sea.

Abruptly, it was gone and a shrinking flame swayed before him.

It is true. You are not at the moment capable of functioning at a magical level. There is no way of telling how long this will last, and the night is almost ended. Ryle Merson may send for you in the morning. We must abandon the project for now and secure you once more within your cell. Return the statuette and—

Pol shook his head slowly.

Of course. In your condition, you cannot return it; and we are barred from exercising any direct control over our analogues. Pick it up. We passed a number of rocks and niches on the way in here. You will have to hide it.

"What about Taisa?"

Leave her.

"What if someone finds her here?"

Not important. Come.

The flame moved past him. He picked up the statuette and followed it. Back in the tunnel, he found a place to cache it in a cleft in the rocky wall.

They made their way out of the cave and back into the palace proper. After a few turnings, Pol realized that they were moving along a different route than they had taken earlier. Their progress was much more rapid this time, avoiding the misty chamber and the dark tunnels entirely.

In a short while, he found himself back at his cell and he entered there, drawing the door closed behind him.

"The journey over was just for show, wasn't it?" he said.

Go back to sleep now.

The flame winked out. He heard the bar slide into place. Suddenly overwhelmed with fatigue, his head spinning, he staggered to his bench and collapsed upon it. There was no time to think before the dark waves took him. . . .

XII

Henry Spier disguised himself anew as he departed the caves of Belken and returned to the enchanted city at its foot. There he spent the day in celebration among his fellow sorcerers, none of whom knew his true identity. He delighted in walking among them bearing a great, dark secret none of them shared. He drank wine spiced with delicate narcotics and he worked wonders and avoided only the greatest among his colleagues. There were none that he feared in a conflict of wills, but he did not wish to come under the scrutiny of any master great enough to pierce his disguise. No, that would be a premature revelation.

He walked, scattering curses and dooms upon those of whom he disapproved, tossing in an occasional boon for one who had won his respect. It pleased him no end to play this secret, god-like role. He had refrained for so long. But now—now he saw the future loosening upon its branch above his outstretched hand. He felt a strange, overwhelming kinship for those who were about to benefit from his labors, all unknowing.

The city expanded in magnificence as the day waned. He had not felt this fine in years. His powers reached an incredible pitch, but he restrained himself from demonstrating more than a fraction of their potency to new comrades gathered round for games and trials.

He hummed and danced as the night descended. He labored over an enormous and elaborate dinner until well past midnight. He brushed sleep away and renewed his vigor with a spell of high order, realized simply and quickly. He drifted upon a silver barge on the town's circular canal,

326

taking with him a courtesan, a catamite, a succubus, a bowl of smouldering dream-leaf and a jug of his favorite wine, which renewed itself as rapidly as its master. After all these years of obscurity and disguise, there was call for celebration, for the Balance was about to tip.

The night wore on, and the city became a fantasia of light and color, sound and senses-dazzling magic. He continued his revels until the sky paled in the east and a momentary hush fled like a phantom wave across the shapes-shifting jewel of the city to break at the foot of Belken. The night's activities commenced again immediately thereafter, but a certain spirit had gone out of them.

Shaking the dust of dream and passion from his person, he rose from his scented cushions and put aside the lighter pastimes of the night. Shedding all frivolity and growing in size as well as regality of mien as he walked, he departed the livelier precincts of the city, heading northward. When he reached the fringe of the city's charmed circle he passed on, climbing a low hill. At its summit, he paused, head lowered, turning.

Finally, he stooped and picked up a dry stick with a number of small twigs still attached. He caressed it and began speaking softly, introducing it to the four corners of the world. Then he stared at it in silence for a long while, still stroking it slowly. The morning grew brighter as he did this, and when he knelt to place the stick upon the ground, it appeared that it had altered its shape, coming now to resemble the form of a small animal. He commenced a low chant.

"Eohippus, Mesohippus, Protohippus, Hipparion . . ." it began.

Dust and sand rose from the ground to swirl about the small figure in a counterclockwise direction, obscuring it completely. As he continued, the spinning tower rose and widened into a dark vortex far larger than himself. It produced a low moaning sound which rapidly became a roaring. Materials from greater and greater distances were sucked into it—shrubs, gravel, bones, lichen.

He stepped back away from its tugging force, arms raised to shoulder level, hands rising and falling. A long, wavering cry came from its center, and he moved his hands downward.

The roaring ceased with a blurt. The swirling curtain began to fall away, revealing a large, dark, quadrapedal outline, head high and tossing.

He moved forward and placed his hand upon the neck of the creature, unfamiliar to the inhabitants of this world. It whinnied.

A moment later, it grew calm, and his hand slid back to the pommel of the saddle with which it had come equipped. He mounted and took up the reins.

They were at the center of a crater which had not been present when he had begun his spell. He spoke to the sand-colored beast, rubbing its neck and its ears. Then he shook the reins gently.

It climbed slowly out of the depression and he turned its head northward. He smiled as they began moving in that direction. Scarlet fingers reached above them from out of the east as they made their way down to a more level area and located a trail. He squeezed with his knees and rustled the reins again.

"Hi-yo, Dust!" he shouted. "Away!"

His tireless mount shot forward across the dawn, quickly achieving a blinding, unnatural pace.

XIII

They had arrived in the afternoon, Mouseglove and
Moonbird, circling above the wreckage atop Anvil Mountain. Looking downward, Mouseglove, who had spent so
much time there, found it difficult to recognize those
features he had known. But he saw the one huge crater,
still now, beside the wreckage of a tall building.

"That has to be it," he stated, "the place where Pol said
he cast the rod."

It is, Moonbird replied.

"It is said that the eye of a dragon sees more than the
eye of a man."

It is said correctly.

"Any of the machines or the dwarves still active down
there?"

I see no movements of either sort.

"Then let us go down."

To the crater?

"Yes. Land beside the cone. I'll climb it and have a
look."

It is quiet within it. And I do not see excessive heat.

"You can see heat?"

*I ride on towers of heat when I soar. Yes. I am able to
see it.*

"Then take us down inside, if you know it is safe."

Moonbird began a downward spiral toward the flared
opening. He tightened his turnings as they drew nearer,
then drew in his wings and dropped, spreading them at
the last moment to ease the landing slightly. Gritting his
teeth, Mouseglove had watched the rough gray walls rush
by. He was jolted forward and to the side when they

329

struck the irregular surface. Clutching at Moonbird, he turned a fall into a dismounting movement, then stood upon the slag heap, leaning against the dragon's swelling rib cage. There was a great silence, and shadows already cloaked the declivity.

Moonbird turned his head from side to side, then looked up, then down.

I might have made a small miscalculation, the dragon confessed.

"What do you mean?"

The size of this place. I may not have sufficient room to climb into the air.

"Oh. Then what are we to do?"

Climb out when the time comes.

Mouseglove cursed softly.

There is a brighter side to the matter.

"Tell me."

The scepter is definitely here. The massive head turned. *Over that way.*

"How do you know?"

Dragons can also sense the presence of magic, of magical items. I know that it is below the ground. Over there.

Mouseglove turned and stared.

"Show me."

Moonbird moved with a slithering sound across the gray roughness, the rubble. Finally, he halted, extended his left forelimb and with an enormous black claw scored an X upon the dark surface.

You must dig here.

Mouseglove unloaded the digging implements, selected the pickax and attacked the spot indicated. Chips flew in all directions, and he coughed occasionally from the dust he raised. He removed his cloak and finally his shirt, as the perspiration flowed freely. After a time, he assumed a statue-like aspect as a layer of gray dust clung to his body. His shoulders began to ache and his hands grew sore, as he drove the pit to a shin-deep level.

"Does your dragon-sense," he asked then, "tell you how deeply it is buried?"

It lies somewhere between two and three times your height in depth.

The crater returned ringing echoes as Mouseglove threw down the pickax.

"Why didn't you tell me that sooner?"

I did not realize it was important. A pause. Then, *Is it?*

"Yes! There is no way I can dig down that far in any reasonable period of time."

He seated himself on a mass of rubble and wiped his brow with the heel of his hand. His mouth tasted of ashes. Everything smelled of ashes. Moonbird moved nearer and stared into the shallow pit.

Might there not still be strong tools about? Or weapons? From the time when Red Mark ruled here?

Mouseglove raised his eyes slowly until he was staring directly overhead.

"I suppose I could climb out and go looking," he said. "But supposing I found some explosives—or one of those throwers of light beams which cut through things? It might destroy what I am seeking."

Moonbird snorted and his spittle flew about. Wherever it struck it began to boil and smoulder. After several seconds, each moist spot burst into flame.

The thing was once hidden because no one knew how to destroy it.

"That is true . . . And I'm certainly not making much progress this way."

He picked up his cloak and began wiping the dust from himself on its inner surface. When he had finished, he donned his shirt again.

"All right. I think I remember where some of the things were stored. If they are still there. If I can still find my way—in all this mess."

He moved to what appeared to be the most negotiable face of the crater wall. Moonbird followed him, with rough sliding sounds.

I had better begin climbing out myself.

"It looks pretty steep, for one of your bulk."

You go now. I will come up in my time. I wish to be away from the disturbance.

"Good idea. I'm on my way."

Mouseglove found a handhold, a foothold, commenced his climb. Later, when he paused to rest upon the rim and

looked back down, he saw that Moonbird had made scant
progress in his attempt to scale the wall. He groped slowly
and carefully for the perfect hold, then dug in with his
powerful talons, improving each niche or shelf with deep
gouges before trusting his weight to it.

Mouseglove turned away, surveying the area once again.
Yes, he decided. Over there to the southeast . . . One of
the places where I hid was beneath that leaning monolith.
And . . .

He glanced at the sinking sun to take the measure of
remaining daylight. Then he moved with speed and grace,
descending, circling, every step of his route already in
mind.

He moved among twisted girders and blocks of stone,
craters and smashed war machines, heaps of rubble, shards
of glass, the skeletons of dragons and men. The ruined city
was very dry. Nothing grew. Nothing moved but shadows.
He remembered his days as a fugitive in this place, still
reflexively casting an eye skyward for signs of the birdlike
mechanical flyers, still sliding about corners and automatically checking for spy devices. For him, the giant figure of
Mark Marakson still stalked the broken landscape, his one
eye clicking and flashing through all the colors of the
rainbow as he moved from darkness to light to shadow and
back again into darkness.

Crossing the fire-scored pavement beside one of the
fallen bridges, he ducked through a twisted door frame into
a roofless building. Within, he passed the shriveled bodies
of half-a-dozen of Mark's diminutive subjects. (He resented the term "dwarf" by which the others referred to
them, since he was approximately the same height himself.) He wondered as he went by what it might be like for
any survivors of that engagement—to be raised from bar-
barism to a highly organized level of existence and then to
be cast back down again to subsisting as in days gone by,
all the machines stopped. Perhaps it had been too brief an
interlude, he told himself. They would not yet have lost
their primitive skills. This entire experience might merely
turn to the stuff of legend among them one day.

But from somewhere—he was never to be certain
where—he seemed to hear the sound of hammering; and

twice, he heard the chuffing noises which made him think of attempts to start one of the great machines.

He located the stairwell he had been seeking and spent ten minutes clearing it for his descent. Below, he followed a series of twisting tunnels down into the mountain itself, the turnings as fresh in his memory as if he had traversed them but yesterday, despite the fact that he moved now through regions of absolute blackness—the generators which had provided their minimal lighting having long since failed. He moved with a certain deliberation, his pistol in his hand. But nothing threatened him here.

The door to the arsenal was locked, but he was able to pick it in the dark, his sensitive fingers faultlessly manipulating the small pieces of metal he had always with him. They had a memory of their own, his fingers, and he had opened this lock before.

Inside, then. And he crossed the room and sought the racks. He filled a grenade belt and slung it, pausing only to acquire an extra supply of cartridges for his pistol after this was done.

Departing the place, he halted, and for reasons not completely clear to himself, locked the door. Then he hurried back along the tunnels, gripping the pistol once again.

As he mounted the stair, a touch of panic—immediately suppressed—followed by a full measure of heightened alertness, came to him. What subliminal cues might have triggered this response, he did not know, but he trusted it fully because it had served him well in the past. He halted, pressed against the wall, then commenced moving slowly up the stairway, his footsteps grown soundless through deliberate placement.

When his head cleared floor level, he halted again and studied the interior of the wrecked room. Nothing stirred. The place seemed unchanged since his earlier passage.

He drew a deep breath, mounted the remaining steps quickly and headed toward the doorway.

There was a rapid movement to his right.

He halted when he saw that it was one of the short, heavily muscled aboriginals who had manned this place, emerged from behind a slanting piece of cracked ceiling material, moving so as to bar his way. The man had on the tattered remains of the uniform those in Mark's service had worn.

Mouseglove raised the pistol and hesitated.

The dwarf was armed with a long, curved blade. But it was not the inequality of arms which stayed Mouseglove's trigger finger. The man appeared to be unaccompanied, but if there were others about the sounds of gunfire might summon them.

"No problem," Mouseglove ventured, lowering his weapon and thrusting it away. "I'm just leaving."

Even before the other's wide mouth shaped a grin, he'd a feeling that he would not be able to talk his way out of this one.

"You were one of them," the man said, moving toward him, blade twitching. "Friend of the sorcerer . . ."

Mouseglove dropped into a crouch, his right hand falling upon the hilt of the dagger which protruded from his boot-sheath, his thumb unfastening the small strap which held it in place.

Still bent far forward, he took the weapon into his hand and began a sidewise, shuffling movement toward his right. The other advanced and slashed at his head with the curving blade. Mouseglove avoided it and raised his own weapon quickly, to nick the man's forearm. He sidled faster and feinted twice toward the man's chest, dodged a thrust he knew he would be unable to parry and produced a small laceration in the other's brow above the right eye with the crosspiece of his own blade. It should have been a neat slash, but he had underestimated the man's speed. The sudden contact with the horny brow-ridge threw him slightly off-balance and he retreated, stumbling.

He recovered his balance, but continued the stumbling movement to scoop up a handful of broken masonry.

Straightening, he cast the pieces at the other's head, danced to the right and thrust. He attempted to twist the blade as it entered the man's left side but found that he was unable to withdraw it.

The man pushed him away and swung his own blade. Mouseglove darted out of range, snatched up another piece of masonry, hurled it and missed. The man moved toward him, the dagger protruding from his side, his blade still raised, his face expressionless. Mouseglove could not tell how much strength remained with him. Another rush, perhaps . . . ? It would be too risky to turn his back on him now, or attempt to dart by—and he still effectively barred his way to the door. He considered simply attempting to avoid him until the injury took its toll. The man had not raised an outcry, and Mouseglove was still determined not to use the pistol unless all else failed or an alarm was given.

The other seemed to smile, tight-lipped, as he came toward him, and Mouseglove realized that he was being backed toward an outhouse-sized slab of roofing material.

"I will live," the dwarf said. "I will recover from this. But you—"

He rushed, blade raised high, careless of any openings now.

Mouseglove gripped the heavy grenade belt which hung from his shoulders, dropped low and swung it with all of his strength toward the other's legs.

The man toppled and Mouseglove moved. He did not spring, because the other had managed to raise his blade. But he seized the extended wrist and threw his weight upon it, covering the fallen man with his own body, pushing downward. With his other hand he caught hold of the other half of the blade and twisted, so that the cutting edge was turned.

As he leaned, pushing it toward the other's throat, the man's left hand clawed upward toward his face. He ducked his head and drew back; as he did this, he felt the other's legs locking about him. They tightened almost immediately, achieving a painful pressure. As this occurred, the left hand assailed his face again, fingers raking toward his eyes.

He removed his right hand from the blade and raised it to fend off the attacking hand. As he did so, the right hand began to move upward against his pressure, the blade slowly turning. The other's legs continued to tighten until he felt that his pelvis would surely crack. Now, slowly, teeth clenched, the man began to raise his wide shoulders from the ground.

Mouseglove dropped his defending right arm and drove

the elbow down and back against the haft of his blade
which protruded from the other's side.

The man shuddered and fell back, the grip of his legs
loosening. Mouseglove repeated the blow and a moan
escaped the man's lips.

Then Mouseglove's right hand was upon the other's
blade again, as he dragged himself free and threw his
weight forward. The blade sank rapidly, its cutting edge
touching the other's windpipe and continuing downward.

As the blood spurted, he dragged the weapon across the
throat and still held tightly to it, afraid to let go until long
after a series of spasms had shaken the man, to be followed
by a stillness, despite the fact that his hands, arms and
shirtfront were spattered and in places soaked by the
other's blood.

He wrenched the blade away then and cast it aside. He
rose, and placing his foot upon the body, drew his dagger
from it and wiped it upon the man's garments. He sheathed
it, picked up the grenade belt and slung it over his shoulder, drew his pistol again and departed the wrecked building.

Nothing barred his way as he headed for the crater, and
he began feeling that his assailant had been a solitary
survivor, half-crazed perhaps, scratching out a living and
leading a reclusive life among the remains of the previous
year's debacle. But then he began hearing noises—a falling stone, a metallic creaking, a scratching, a shuffling
sound—any one of which might, by itself, be taken as the
action of settling, or wind, or rodents. Together, however,
and coming upon the heels of his struggle, they acquired a
more sinister aspect.

Mouseglove hurried, and the sounds seemed to follow
him. He scrutinized every bit of cover as he went, but
detected no one—nothing—of a threatening nature. The
sounds, however, increased in frequency behind him.

He was running, however, by the time he reached the
base of the cone, and he commenced climbing immediately, not even looking back. And though he scanned the
rim of the crater, there was no sign of Moonbird at the
top.

As he climbed, he heard the footfalls below, behind him.
A backward glance took in six or eight of the small people,

emerging from the ruins, running after him now. While they bore clubs, spears and blades, he was slightly relieved to see that none of Mark's advanced weapons appeared to have survived for their use. Several of them, he noted, wore bits of machined metal, like amulets, about their necks. At that moment, he wondered how much they had really understood of the technology into and out of which they had been so quickly propelled. The speculation was only a fleeting thing, however, accompanied as it was by the acknowledgement that primitive weapons render one just as dead as the more sophisticated variety.

Climbing, he wondered then concerning the ghostly bond which permitted him to communicate with Moonbird. Their proximity and spell-involvement in the caves of Rondoval during the two decades of the spell's effect had worked that linkage. He had never communicated with the dragon except at close range, though it occurred to him that now only a thin layer of rock might be all that separated them.

Moonbird! Do you hear me? he cried out in his mind.

Yes, came a distant-seeming reply.

Where are you?

Climbing. Still climbing.

I'm in trouble.

What kind of trouble?

I'm being pursued, Mouseglove told him, *by those people who worked for Mark.*

How many?

Six. Eight. Maybe more.

How unfortunate.

There is nothing that you can do?

Not from here.

What shall I do?

Climb fast.

Mouseglove cursed and looked back. All of his pursuers were nearing the cone's base—and one heavily muscled man was drawing back his spear for a cast. Mouseglove drew his pistol and fired it at him. He missed, but apparently spoiled the other's aim. The spear flew wide, clattering against the cone far off to his right.

He fired again, and this time the nearest of his pursuers dropped his club and clutched at his right shoulder.

What was that?

I had to shoot at a couple, Mouseglove replied, remaining low, continuing up the slope.

Did you find what you sought?

Yes. I have explosives. But my pursuers are too scattered to make them an effective weapon.

But you can use them from a distance?

Yes.

When you reach the top throw them down to the place you dug.

How far up are you?

That is not important.

They make quite a blast.

It should be amusing. Not worry.

Mouseglove looked back again. Three of his pursuers had reached the base of the cone and were beginning to climb. Halting, he took careful aim and fired at the foremost. The man fell.

He did not pause to assess the effect of this upon the others, but turned and put his full strength into his ascent. He was nearing the top now. His pursuers were strong and agile, but so was he. He also weighed less and was faster, so he had managed to acquire a good lead.

Finally, he reached the rim and mounted it, passing over its lip immediately, for cover. Only then did he look down. He made a soft noise at the back of his throat.

Moonbird, dragging his ponderous bulk slowly up the steep wall, had only succeeded in climbing about a quarter of the distance to the top.

I can't throw these things, he told the dragon. *You're too near.*

I have flown through thunderstorms, came the reply, *when the heavens came apart all around. Yet I lived. Throw them.*

I can't.

We die if you do not. And Pol . . .

Mouseglove thought of his pursuers, primed one of the grenades and hurled it down toward the now darkened area where he had been digging earlier. He covered his ears. He heard the blast and felt the vibration. Afterward, he heard the sounds of falling and shifting rocks.

Moonbird! Are you all right?

Yes. Throw another. Hurry!

Mouseglove complied and braced himself again. After the second explosion, he inquired: *Moonbird?*

Yes. Another.

The reply seemed slightly weaker, or could it but have been the roaring in his head, submerging it? He threw the third explosive, pressing himself back against the stone until the detonation occurred and the force of the aftershock had abated.

Moonbird?

There was no answer. He peered downward, through the clouds of dust and the shadows. The area where Moonbird had clung was now totally obscured.

Answer me, Moonbird!

Nothing.

As the ringing in his ears subsided, he thought that he heard scraping noises of ascent from the outer surface of the cone, though they could possibly have been the sounds of falling rocks. He dared not cast a grenade back over the lip of the crater because of its possible effects upon himself, there on the inside.

Quickly, he began his descent.

The dust irritated his eyes and nose, though he was able to refrain from sneezing. He tasted it and he felt particles of grit when he clenched his teeth. He spat several times but could not rid himself of it completely. His way darkened perceptibly with every movement of descent.

His eyes turned regularly in the direction of the area Moonbird had occupied, but he could detect no sign of the great dragon in the darkness below.

Mouseglove continued his descent, wishing, as he groped after a new foothold, that there were some manner in which he could manage to move more rapidly. For now the foremost of the small men was lowering himself over the edge above and two others were moving to follow. Just as he was about to look away, he saw a fourth figure come up and join them.

Cursing, he reached for the next lower hold. Before his

hand located it, however, the rest of his body detected a faint, general vibration in the rock to which he clung. A rumbling sound followed.

Below him, waxing and waning but brightening in the overall process, an orange glow had begun in the heart of the crater. The growling noise came again, accompanied by a wave of heat.

There was a shout above him. His pursuers—five now—had halted. They began climbing upward as he watched, their movements touched with panic.

My bombs tore something loose, he decided. *It's starting again. Can't go up. Can't go down. Wait and die.*

Come down. You will not be harmed.

It's going to erupt!

No. Come down. You will be safe.

What—what is happening?

Can't talk. You come.

Mouseglove's hand continued its long-interrupted motion, coming to rest upon a stony knob to which he transferred his weight.

As he descended, the light grew brighter. The vibrations continued, but they were extremely mild, almost an effect of the echoes which bounced about him. Suddenly, with a roar, a bright fragment of something shot upward past him, followed almost immediately by another, tracing glowing trails through the twilight high above.

Are you sure it is safe? he asked, pressed tightly against the rock wall.

But there was no reply.

Continuing downward, he realized that the temperature had not risen excessively, as might be expected this near the point of an eruption. Could Moonbird be playing games with his own flames, to frighten off the enemy?

No, he decided, looking down into the glow. *It covers too large an area and burns too regularly to be dragonfire.*

He reached the floor of the crater unharmed. Clots of fire continued to flee upward, but none rose from points near him. Walls and pillars of flame came up in great number here, though what it was they fed upon, he could not discern. There was a clear aisle through their midst,

however, heading in the direction he intended to take. He
followed it.

The floor of the crater was even more ravaged than he
remembered it, as a result of his bombing. He picked his
way through heavy rubble toward the heart of a large
depression as he headed for the site of his earlier digging.
After several more steps, he realized that a vast shadow
loomed at its center, below him.

He took another step.

Moonbird . . . ?

It swayed in his direction, and he saw the great head of
the dragon nodding toward him, an ornate rod held between the enormous teeth.

The scepter! You've found it!

Mouseglove extended his hand.

Get onto my back.

I do not understand.

Talk later. Mount!

Mouseglove advanced and climbed upon Moonbird,
scrambling toward his shoulders. Immediately, the dragon
began to move, climbing out of the pit, heading toward
the northern wall, almost exactly opposite the place he
had climbed earlier.

When they reached the crater wall, Mouseglove suddenly caught hold more tightly as Moonbird reared and
commenced climbing.

*Moonbird! You can't get to the top from here! It gets
almost vertical about halfway up.*

I know.

Then why are we climbing?

It is easier here. Till then.

But—

Wait till we reach the ledge.

Mouseglove recalled the rocky shelf to which he referred. It had looked wide enough to support Moonbird—
barely—but it was, in effect, a dead end.

Moonbird was climbing much more rapidly here than
he had up the other wall. The way was less steep, more
rugged. As they mounted higher, Mouseglove glanced
back down. The glow from the fires below seemed to be
spreading, intensifying. He felt a wave of heat upon his

face. It was followed almost immediately by another, much
warmer.

At last, Moonbird reached the rocky shelf, hauled himself onto it, turned and looked downward. As he did so,
the brightness and the heat increased again.

"What is happening?" Mouseglove asked aloud.

The last explosion shook me from the wall, Moonbird
replied. *After I fell I sensed the rod nearby.*

"And the fires started about that time?"

I started the fires. To drive off your pursuers.

"How did you do that?"

*I used the bottom segment of the rod. It is for fire
magic.*

"You can use the rod? I had no idea—"

*Only the bottom segment. Dragons understand the se-
crets of fire.*

"Well, we seem to be safe now, but the fires keep
getting stronger. You might turn them off now—if you
can."

No.

"Why not?"

I will need a tower of heat. To rise out of here.

"I do not understand."

*I will dive from here toward the fires. It is easier to ride
the warm air upward.*

Shadows were dancing all about them now. Mouseglove
felt a fresh wave of heat.

"It's not all that far to the bottom . . ." he said. "Are
you sure you can get yourself airborne in that distance?"

Life is uncertain, Moonbird replied. *Hold tightly.*

He spread his wings and plunged into the blazing crater.

XIV

The depth of my philosophical speculations as to the nature of my own being and that of the universe only increases the more I see of the world. And no real answers seem to occur, either practically or on a more general level. I now find myself wondering whether a state of uncertainty might not be the lot of all sentient beings. Still, it strikes me that there are reasons I do not fully comprehend underlying the actions of others. Their activities seem directed toward creating certain situations, whereas I have no real—objectives. I circulate. I obtain information. But I have no idea what it all means. I do not have an objective, only its mysterious ghost—something which keeps haunting me with the notion that I should have more.

Despite my perplexity in the face of existence, I continued to obey the small imperative which had accompanied me since my departure from Rondoval. I saw Mouseglove off on his errand and watched to see that Ibal did indeed possess the means to deliver him to his destination expeditiously—not to mention the will to do it. I observed Mouseglove's departure and then returned to the place at the foot of Belken where I had obtained my first lessons in animating a body. I tried it again with the spare, with good results, frightening a group of hikers made up of a number of the younger apprentices.

Then I hovered undecided. Should I follow the still-discernable emanation trail of that strange sorcerer back into the city, to discover what he was about? Or should I undertake the pursuit of Pol and Larick toward Avinconet in the north? Almost immediately, that small imperative resolved the matter.

I rose, achieving some altitude, resolved myself into a tighter form, then headed approximately northward. I overtook them in their flight and simply paced them then, drifting, for the rest of the day. Nothing was answered for me by this, but I no longer felt the pressures I had experienced earlier. For this time, I was as content as I had been in the old days, moving aimlessly about the ruins of Rondoval.

Of course it could not last. I realized this as the day wore on and the light was squeezed from it and the great castle, Avinconet, loomed before us in the darkening distance. In that moment, I learned the feeling of fear.

A strange foreboding came over me—a dark premonition, if you like—accompanied by the seeming sourceless knowledge that I could die, that my existence could be terminated and that this thing could occur within that place. It was something which had never occurred to me before, and it came as an awful revelation—for even as I considered it along with what I knew of myself, I saw that it could well be true. It would seem that a life as aimless as mine, more filled with questions than anything else, might not be worth much. I realized in that same moment that this was not the case. More than anything else, I felt, I wanted to continue it, as purposeless and puzzling as it seemed.

I drew nearer to Pol. I wrapped myself about the warmth of his being. Why the thought of flight did not even occur to me at that time, I had no idea. I clung to him as a child to a parent as we rushed nearer that dark citadel.

I remained with him after we landed, accompanying him to the cell in which he was confined. I remained there with him for some time—until his food arrived and I realized that it was unlikely he would be disturbed for the rest of the night. While my earlier fears had not been abated, they had receded sufficiently by this time to permit more rational considerations to come to the fore. Now, while all was still and nothing seemed afoot, would actually be the best time for me to survey the place, to locate whatever menaces might be lurking and consider the best means to nullify them.

Accordingly, I drifted away, leaving Pol in his safe and uninteresting quarters. I moved about various chambers, terminating rats and mice, observing sleepers, seeking signs of dark magics or dangerous forces.

I moved very slowly, not wishing to be surprised. The night wore on, and I came gradually to feel that I had suffered a false augury. Nothing threatened, nothing loomed. It seemed just another pile of rocks made suitable for human habitation by the application of a few simple construction principles and the installation of simple plumbing, some rude pieces of furniture and garish hangings of a nonfunctional nature. The only traces of magical doings seemed painfully innocuous.

Yet, feeling what I had felt, I was not to be so simply discouraged. The middle of the night drew on and passed. I explored each high tower. I—

An indescribable pang passed through my being. It was like nothing I had ever experienced before, unless it be the unremembered shock of my own birth. Something had suddenly changed, something affecting me to the depths of my personality. But even as it occurred, I grew doubtful that it was the fearful thing I'd sought. No tone of dark magic accompanied it. Its ultimate result was a sense of something having been settled in my own case. If I could but discover what it was, I felt that a part of my personal mystery might be solved. I drifted for a long while, meditating, but no illumination ensued and I could not determine the source of whatever it was that had come over me. It was almost as if, somewhere, my name had been spoken, just out of my hearing.

I settled, descending from floor to floor. I had investigated most of what lay above the ground and I decided to regard the areas below the castle, within the mountainside. There were a number of openings, both natural and artificial, and one by one I invaded them and explored.

It was in one of these recesses that I came upon the sleeping woman. She lay unmoving within a container, her spirit wandering, a very pale light of life still visible about her. I moved nearer, to inspect her further, and a trap was sprung. It was a subtle spell, designed to ensnare any less than material being such as myself who might venture too near the lady—presumably to protect her against possession.

So I was caught, several body-lengths from her, in what might best be described as a gigantic, invisible spiderweb. I struggled briefly and saw that it was to no avail. I relaxed against my bonds and tried altering my shape. This did not work either, nor did my attempts to shift away to another plane. The web of forces held me tightly.

I hung, spread out there, trying to analyze it. It had a certain aura of venerability about it, of the sort humans ascribe to vintage wines. I was familiar with this effect from my experience with certain old spells which remained about Rondoval. The good ones, such as this, unfortunately grow better with age, because of the counter-current entropy on the plane where magic operates. This spell, as nearly as I could judge, went back fifteen or twenty years. I tried sending charges of energy through it, a small segment at a time, hoping to locate a weakness at which I might work, from which I might unravel the thing like a stocking. All to no avail. It was of a piece, and it had me.

I remained there for a long while, recalling everything I knew that might be applied against it. When I tried them all and nothing worked, I decided that it might be time to cultivate philosophy to a greater extent. I began musing upon existence and non-existence, I reexamined my premonition, I reconsidered my pang. . . .

I heard footsteps.

It is generally easy to remain inconspicuous when you are invisible and soundless, but I made extra efforts to achieve stillness on all levels, including the mental, when I saw Pol approaching led by a peculiar palm of light as immaterial as myself.

There was something familiar about the flame-like thing, something I did not like at all. I felt, without knowing why, that it had the power to harm me.

I sensed some exchange going on between Pol and the brightness. I heard only Pol's half of it, not willing to try attuning myself to listen in fully, fearing that this might somehow make my presence known to the fiery one.

Finally, Pol unfastened the lid of the container, removed it and set it aside. There was another long pause, and then he removed the woman, crossed a ledge and entered a tunnel, following the flame.

Suddenly, I was free. The spell must have been centered upon the woman, not the locale, not the container.

I hung back. I wanted to see where they were going but I did not wish to get too near, lest I be trapped again. I drifted slowly behind them, leaving myself ample leeway, well aware now of the effective range of the spell.

I recognized the big chamber as soon as I entered it. The last time I had passed this way, I had been moving at metaphysical speeds and following a magical trail, so there had been no need for noting landmarks. Consequently, I'd had no idea that this was where the Gate was located.

The Gate . . .

Just as I remembered it, from Pol's dreams and from my own fast passage, the Gate loomed huge, threatening and fortunately, closed. It had never been opened upon this plane, I guessed, though its ghostly version had been ajar many times, permitting the passage of sendings, essences, spirits. Had its physical self stood so, it might not be possible to close it again, for I could see how an interpenetration of the worlds would begin, the strangely structured, more ancient forms of that other with its vastly stronger magics flowing through to dominate this younger, magically weaker land, changing it into something of its own image, revivified by the raw, natural forms of this newer place. Stronger in magic, weaker in general vitality. The magic would dominate, I was certain . . .

Pol deposited his burden upon the stone with the aura of death about it. His movements were slow, irresolute, as if he were walking in his sleep. I reached out carefully then, more carefully than anything I had ever done before, and I touched his mind, just skimming his surface thoughts.

He was bewitched. He was not aware of it, but the flame had him in thrall.

I saw no way that I might interfere successfully. I knew without knowing how I knew that the thing was stronger than me. I felt totally helpless as it led Pol about, as it directed him to produce the statuette. I was more than a

little pleased when Pol's power failed and the project had
to be abandoned. The flame's frustration gave rise to the
closest thing to joy that I had ever known.

I watched them depart. I doubted that Pol was in any
immediate danger, and I wanted to explore the chamber a
little further. A large, rectangular piece of morning decorated the wall to my left. I began to feel a fresh premonition, concerning this room.

XV

Pol was awakened from a dreamless sleep by the sound of his cell door being unbarred. At first he felt leaden-limbed, hung over, ragged about the edges of his mind, almost as if he had been drugged. But then, within moments, before Larick had even set foot in his cell, the dragonmark began to throb wildly, heavily, in a way it had never done before, sending an adrenalin-like shock through his entire system, clearing his head instantly, informing him with a sense of wild power unlike anything he had known previously.

"Get up," Larick said, approaching him.

Pol felt that he could strike the man dead with a single gesture. Instead, he complied.

"Come with me."

Pol followed him out of the cell, adopting the cumbersome, lumbering gait suitable, he'd judged, for a disguised monster. Through the first window they passed, Pol saw that full daylight now lay upon the world, though he could not see the sun to judge the hour. They took a different route than that upon which he had magically followed Larick the previous evening—different, too, than the way upon which the flame had led him.

"If you cooperate," Larick said almost casually, "it is possible that you will be released unharmed."

"I do not consider myself unharmed," Pol said, mounting a stair.

"Your present situation might be remedied."

"What's in this for you?" he asked.

The other was silent for a long while. Then, "You would not understand," Larick said.

"Try me."

"No. It's not for me to explain things to you," he finally answered. "You will have your explanations shortly."

"What is the price for betraying the trust of the initiation committee?"

"Some things are more important than others. You'll see."

Pol chuckled softly. The power continued to spiral within him. He was amazed that the other could not feel its presence. He had to restrain himself from lashing out with it.

They traversed a lengthy corridor, mounted another stair, crossed a wide hall.

"I would like to have met you under different circumstances," Larick said then, as they reached a downward stair.

"I've a feeling that you will," Pol replied.

He recognized an area through which he had passed during the night. He realized then that they had come into the northeastern wing of the building. They approached a dark, heavily carved door. Larick moved ahead and knocked upon it.

"Come in," came a voice slightly higher in pitch than Pol had expected.

Larick opened the door and stepped across the threshold. He turned.

"Come along."

Pol followed him into the room. It was a study in rough timbers and stone, with four red and black rugs upon the floor. There were no windows. Ryle Merson was seated at a large table, the remains of his breakfast before him. He did not rise.

"Here is that Madwand we discussed," Larick said. "He is completely docile in all but spirit."

"Then you've got the part that counts," Ryle replied. "Leave him to me."

"Yes."

"I mean it literally."

Pol saw the look of surprise which widened Larick's eyes and parted his lips.

"You want me to go?"

Ryle's broad face was expressionless.

"If you please."

Larick stiffened.

"Very well," he said.

He turned toward the door.

"But stay within hailing distance."

Larick looked back, nodded curtly and departed the room, closing the door behind him.

Ryle studied Pol.

"I saw you at Belken," he said at length.

"And I saw you," Pol said, returning the older man's stare. "On the street, talking with Larick, in front of the cafe where I sat."

"You have a good memory."

Pol shook his head.

"I can't recall giving you cause for abduction and abuse."

"I suppose it must look that way to you."

"I suppose it would look that way to anybody"

"I don't want to start off with you on the wrong foot—"

"I didn't want to start off with you on any foot. What do you want?"

Ryle sighed.

"All right. If that is the way it must be. You are my prisoner. You are in jeopardy. I am in a position to grant you any discomfort, up to and including death."

The fat sorcerer rose, moving around the table to stand before Pol. He made a simple gesture and followed it with another, his movements similar to those Larick had used. Pol felt nothing, though he realized what was occurring and he wondered whether the disguise within the disguise would hold.

It did.

"Perhaps you have grown fond of your present condition?"

"Not really."

"Your face is masked by your own spell. I will leave it in place, since I already know what you look like. I suppose we could start with that."

"You've a captive audience. Go ahead."

"Last year I heard a rumor that Rondoval was inhabited again. A little later, I heard of the battle at Anvil Mountain. By magical means, I summoned up your likeness.

Your hair, your birthmark, your resemblance to Det—it was obvious that you were a member of that House, and one of whom I had never heard."

"And of course you had to do something about it, since nobody likes Rondoval."

Ryle turned away, padded across the room, turned back.

"You tempt me to agree and let it go at that," he said. "But I have reasons for the things that I do. Would you care to hear them?"

"Of course."

"There was a time when Det was a very good friend of mine. He was your father, wasn't he?"

"Yes."

"Where did he have you hidden, anyway?"

Pol shook his head.

"He didn't. As I understand the story, I was present at the fall of Rondoval. Rather than slay a baby, old Mor took me to another world, where I grew up."

"Yes, I can see that. Interesting. For whom did he exchange you?"

"Mark Marakson, the man I killed at Anvil Mountain."

"Fascinating. A changeling. How did you get back here?"

"Mor returned me. To deal with Mark. So you knew my father?"

"Yes. We engaged in a number of enterprises together. He was a very accomplished sorcerer."

"You speak as if there was a point where you ceased being friends."

"True. We finally disagreed on a very fundamental issue concerning our last great project. I broke the fellowship at that time and sent him packing. It was then that he initiated the actions which led to the conflict and the destruction of Rondoval. The third party to our enterprise left him when things began looking bad on that front."

"Who was that?"

"A strange Madwand of great power. I don't really know where Det found him. A man named Henry Spier. Odd name, that."

"Do you mean that if you both hadn't deserted him Rondoval might have stood?"

"I am sure that it would have, in a cruelly changed world. I prefer thinking that Det and Spier deserted me."

"Of course. And now you want some extra revenge on the family, for old times' sake."

"Hardly. But now it is your turn to answer a few. You say that Mor brought you back?"

" 'Returned me' is what I said. He did not accompany me. He seemed ill. I believe that he went back to the place where I had been."

"The exchange . . . Yes. Were you returned directly to Rondoval?"

"No. I found my own way there, later."

"And your heritage? All the things that you know of the Art? How did you come by this?"

"I just sort of picked it up."

"That makes you a Madwand."

"So I've heard. You still haven't told me what you want."

"Blood tells, though, doesn't it?" Ryle said sharply.

Pol studied the man's face. Gone now was the bland expression which had accompanied most of their earlier exchanges. Pol read menace in the narrow-eyed look now focused upon him, in the rising color and the tightness about the mouth. He noted, too, that one pudgy hand was clenched so tightly that its rings cut deeply into the flesh.

"I don't know what you mean," Pol said.

"I think you do," Ryle replied. "Your father tipped the Balance which prevailed in this world, but did not succeed in his attempt. I stopped him here and Klaithe's forces finished him at Rondoval. There had to be a reaction sooner or later. Mark Marakson brought it into the world at Anvil Mountain, where you stopped him. Now it must tip in the other direction again—your father's way—toward total sorcerous domination of the world. It can be stopped for good at this point, or it can go all the way—your father's dream realized. I have been waiting all these years to stop it again, to end it, to see that it does not come to pass."

"I repeat. I don't know what—"

Ryle came forward and slapped him. Pol fought down an impulse to strike back as he felt a ring cut his cheek.

"Son of a black magician! You are one yourself!" he

cried. "It can't be helped! It's in your blood! Even—" He grew silent. He stepped back. Then, "You would open the Gate," he said. "You would complete your father's great work for this world."

Pol suddenly felt that this was true. The Gate . . . Of course. He had forgotten. All those dreams . . . They began phasing now into his consciousness. With this, a certain wiliness came over him.

"You say that you were party to the entire business, at its beginning?" he asked softly.

"Yes, that is true," Ryle admitted.

"And you were talking about black magic . . ."

Ryle looked away, walked back to the table, drew the chair farther back and lowered himself onto it.

"Yes," he said, his eyes directed toward the remains of his breakfast, "in both senses, too, I suppose. Black because it was being used for something that was morally objectionable, and black in the more subtle sense of its deepest meaning—the use of forces which must warp the character of the magician himself. The first is always arguable, but the second is not. I admit that I was once a black magician, but I am no longer. I reformed myself long ago."

"Employing Larick to perform the actual spells for you hardly seems to avoid the spirit of black magic. As in my case . . ."

His words trailed off as Ryle raised his eyes and fixed him with them.

"In your case," he said, "I would—and will, if necessary—do it myself. It would at worst be an instance of the first sort—employed to prevent a greater evil."

"On the general theory of morals—that others need them?"

"I am thinking of more than the two of us. I am thinking of what you would do to the entire world."

"By opening the Gate?"

"Exactly."

"Excuse my ignorance, but what will happen if the Gate is opened?"

"This world would be flooded, submerged, by the forces of a far older world—in our terms it is an evil place. We would become an extension of that land. Its more powerful, ancient magic would completely overwhelm the natural laws which hold here. This would become a realm of dark enchantment."

"The evil may well be relative then. Tell me what objection a sorcerer could have to something which would make sorcery more important."

"You use the argument by which your father first swayed me. But then I learned that the forces released would be so strong that no ordinary sorcerer could control them. We would all be at the mercy of those others from beyond the Gate and those few of our own kind to whom it would not matter, in league with those others."

"And who might those few of our own kind be?"

"Your father was one, Henry Spier another; yourself, and those others like you—Madwands all."

Pol repressed a smile.

"I take it that you are not a Madwand?"

"No, I had to learn my skills the hard way."

"I begin to understand your conversion," Pol said, instantly regretting the words as he saw Ryle's expression change again.

"No, I do not believe that you do," he answered, glaring, "not having a daughter bound by the curse of Henry Spier."

"The ghost of this place . . . ?" Pol said.

"Her body lies in a hidden spot, neither dead nor alive. Spier did that when I broke the fellowship. Even so, I was willing to fight them."

Pol wanted to look away, to shift his weight, to pace, to depart.

Instead, "What exactly do you mean when you say Madwand?" he asked.

"Those like yourself with a natural aptitude for the Art," Ryle said, "those possessed of a closer, more personal relationship with its forces—its artists rather than its technicians, I suppose."

"I appreciate your explaining all these matters," Pol told him, "and I realize you are not going to believe any denials I might make concerning my intentions, so I won't make any. Why not just tell me what it is that you want?"

"You have had dreams," Ryle said flatly.

"Well, yes . . ."

"Dreams," he continued, "which I sent to you, wherein your spirit traveled beyond the Gate to witness the starkness and desolation of that evil place, wherein you saw the creatures who dwell there, engaged in depravities."

Pol recalled his earlier dreams, but he thought too of the later ones, showing him the cities beyond the mountains, neither stark nor desolate, but holding a culture so complex as to surpass his understanding.

"That is all that you showed me?" he asked, puzzled.

"All? Is that not enough? Enough to persuade any decent man that the Gate must not be opened?"

"I suppose you made a good case then," Pol said. "But tell me, are dreams all that you sent to me?"

Ryle cocked his head to one side, frowning. Then he smiled.

"Oh. That," he said. "Keth . . ."

"Keth? He was the sorcerer who attacked me in my own library?"

Ryle nodded.

"The same. Yes, I sent him. A good man. I thought he'd best you and settle things then and there."

"What things? For all your talk about the Gate and my father and Madwands and black magic, I still do not know what it is that you want of me."

The fat sorcerer sighed.

"I thought that by sending you the dreams—showing you the menace of the thing—and then by explaining the situation carefully, as I have just done, that I might—just possibly might—win you over to my way of thinking and persuade you to cooperate with me. It would make life so much easier."

"You didn't exactly start off on the right foot by playing monster games with my anatomy."

"It was also necessary to show you the extent to which I will go if you do not choose to help me."

"I'm still not sure of that. What's left—besides death?"

Ryle rubbed his hands together and smiled.

"Your head, of course," he said. "I have begun in the easiest manner possible. But if, after suitable painful practices upon the body you are now wearing, you refuse to give me what I want, then I will complete the transfer. I will send your head to join the rest of you in exile beyond the Gate. I will be left with a somewhat maimed demon servant, and you—you have seen that place—you will have an unfortunate existence before you for all your remaining days."

"It sounds very persuasive," Pol observed. "Now, of what might it be the consequence?"

"You know where the Keys are—the Keys that can open the Gate or lock them forever. I want them."

"Presumably to do the latter?"

"Certainly."

"I'm sorry, but I don't have any such Keys. I wouldn't even know where to look for them."

"How can you say that when I saw them on the table in your study numerous times—and even as I watched your struggle with Keth?"

Pol's thoughts went back, both to that scene and to one of his dreams. He felt the resistance building within him.

"You can't have them," he said.

"I'd a feeling this was not going to be easy," Ryle remarked, rising. "If opening the Gate means that much to you, it just shows how far gone you really are."

"It is not opening the Gate," Pol replied. "It is having something taken from me in this fashion that rankles. You are going to have to work for anything you get out of me."

Ryle raised his hands.

"It may be easier than you think," he said. "Painless, in fact—if you're lucky. We'll learn in a moment how far-sighted you might have been."

As Ryle's hands began moving, Pol fought down the desire to strike back. A small voice seemed to be saying, "Not yet." Perhaps it was himself. He shifted his vision to the second seeing and saw a great orange wave rolling toward him.

When it struck, he felt a certain slowing and then a rigidity of his thought processes. A genuine stiffness came over his body. Gone was any certainty as to what he wanted or did not want.

Ryle was speaking and his voice seemed somehow more distant than their proximity indicated:

"What is your name?"

It was with a peculiar fascination that he felt his lips move, heard his own voice reply, "Pol Detson."

"By what name were you known in the world where you grew up?"

"Daniel Chain."

"Do you possess the seven statuettes that are the Keys to the Gate?"

Suddenly, a sheet of flame hung between them. Ryle did not seem aware of its presence.

"No," Pol heard himself reply.

The fat sorcerer looked puzzled. Then he smiled.

"That was awkwardly phrased," he said, almost apologetically. "Can you tell me the location or locations of the seven magical statuettes which once belonged to your father?"

"No," Pol answered.

"Why not?" Ryle asked.

"I do not know where they are," Pol said.

"But you have seen them, handled them, had them in your possession?"

"Yes."

"What became of them?"

"They were stolen from me, on the way to Belken."

"I do not believe that."

Pol remained silent.

". . . But you are to be congratulated for your foresight," Ryle continued. "You have guarded against self-betrayal with a very powerful spell. It would take me a long time to ascertain its exact nature and to break it. Unfortunately for you, I have neither the time nor inclination, and you must be forced to speak. I have already mentioned the means which will be employed."

The man began another series of gestures, and Pol felt a certain clarity return to his consciousness. As this feeling grew, the image of the flame faded.

"I have also restored your appearance, for esthetic purposes," Ryle said. "Now that you are yourself again, is there anything that you would care to add to what you said?"

"No."

"I didn't think so."

The fat sorcerer turned away, crossed the room, opened the door.

"Larick?" he called.

"Yes?" came a distant voice.

"Take this man back to his cell," he said. "I'll send for him when the interrogation room has been made ready."

"You tried a coercion spell?"

"Yes. A good one. He's protected. We'll have to go the other route."

"A pity."

"Yes."

Ryle turned back.

"Pol, go along with him."

Pol moved, turning, advancing slowly toward the doorway. He wondered as he did . . . He would be passing very close to Ryle. If he were to turn suddenly and attack the man, he felt that he could deal with him fairly quickly, before the other could bring any magic into play. Then, of course, he would have to fight Larick, and he wondered whether he could dispatch Ryle before the younger sorcerer was upon him. For that matter . . .

A vision of the flame flashed before him again.

"Not yet," came the voice in his mind. "Wait. Soon. Restrain yourself."

Nodding mentally, he passed Ryle and stepped out into the corridor where Larick waited.

"All right," Larick said, and he commenced walking, heading in the opposite direction from which they had come.

Pol heard the door of the room he had quitted close behind him. One quick rabbit punch, he decided, just below that kerchief he always wears, and Larick will be out of the picture . . .

Almost predictably, the image of the flame passed before his eyes once again.

"Turn here."

He turned, then said, "This isn't the way we came."

"I know that, you son of a bitch. I want to show you what your kind have done."

Suddenly, they passed into a familiar area, and with a touch of panic Pol realized where they were headed and what it was that he was being taken to see. He slowed his pace.

"Come along. Come along."

No plan presented itself to him, but the pulse of power still throbbed in his disguised arm. He decided to rely upon the guidance of the invisible flame. Something would provide him with an opportunity, very soon, he felt, an opportunity to smash Larick and—

Of course. His future actions came into perfect focus. He was suddenly certain as to what was going to occur, knew exactly what he was going to do when it did.

They entered the cavern. Larick produced a magical light which traveled on before them, illuminating their advance. Pol readied himself as they made their way around to the place where the opened, empty casket lay. Just a few more steps . . .

He heard Larick cry out. The sounds echoed from the rocky walls. His vision swam through the second seeing. Bands of bright, colored light moved everywhere. When he tried, he was able to resolve them into strands, but the moment he relaxed this effort they became bands again— horizontal, not drifting, but moving slowly upward, of various widths. After a moment, he saw that they overlay a field of vertical bands, and beyond them, diagonals. The world had acquired a peculiarly cubist structure. And he realized in that instant that he had but shifted to another mode of seeing the same thing which had always been presented to him as the strands—and he knew that there were others beyond it and that, somehow, in the future, he would always view the magical world in the mode most appropriate to his needs of the moment rather than the more restricted vision his power had brought him in the past. And he knew, intuitively, how to use these bands just as he had known in the past what the strands were for. It took a great effort to restrain himself from reaching out to manipulate them as Larick turned toward him, teeth bared.

"She's gone!" he said. "Stolen! How—?"

Then his eyes took on a strange cast and his head slowly turned to his right. Pol was certain that he, too, was now into the second seeing and something in his version of it was indicating to him the direction in which Taisa had been taken.

Larick turned suddenly and moved rapidly, heading off along the ledge. The light which had guided them remained stationary, somewhere behind Pol, spilling its pale light into the empty casket.

Pol advanced, moving onto the ledge, holding his second sight in focus, ready to utilize his new understanding of magical processes. He hurried toward the natural light at the end of the tunnel, rushing past the place where he had hidden the statuette.

When he came into the chamber, a chorus of voices burst upon his consciousness: "Now! Now! Now! Now! Now! Now! Now!"

Larick, his back to him, was bent over Taisa's still form upon the sacrificial stone, perhaps ten paces before him. Pol reached up with both hands and seized upon an orange band, feeling his will go forth through the dragonmark.

In a moment, it was loose and swinging freely, like a long, bright pole, sweeping toward Larick.

Even as he made the gesture, however, Pol saw Larick stiffen and begin to turn, knowing that the other sorcerer had heard the sounds of his entrance. He saw the look of astonishment upon his face, succeeded immediately by one of apprehension.

But Larick managed to move, and he moved quickly. His left hand shot upward, fingers knotting. He seized upon a red diagonal and jerked it into the path of Pol's attack.

The force of the blow knocked him sprawling upon the floor, but he had managed to keep it from striking him. Pol turned the long shaft which he still held, and with a chopping motion of his left hand shortened it to a javelin. Larick shook his head and began pushing himself up from the floor. His gaze locked with Pol's as Pol was drawing back his right arm to hurl the gleaming shaft.

Larick pushed himself back onto his heels and raised

both arms high up over his head. Pol cast the spear of light directly toward him and Larick dropped his arms. The bright bands which lay before him jumped and seemed to turn on their longitudinal axes.

It was like the sudden snapping shut of a Venetian blind. Larick was momentarily invisible behind a rainbow wall. Pol's lance struck against it and both the shaft and the wall seemed to shatter in a fountain of sparks. As these fell away, he saw Larick standing, moving his hands crossbody.

His peripheral vision warned him, barely in time. Larick was operating two lateral diagonals like a bright pair of scissors. Pol extended both hands before him and rushed forward.

He seized upon a vertical and thrust it before him into the jaws of the light-spell. The diagonals closed upon it, their edges halting inches from his waist. He saw a slight sign of strain upon Larick's face as the man's hands tightened further. The diagonals jerked nearer. He pushed even harder himself, holding them back. Larick leaned forward, straining against the pressure.

Abruptly, Pol heaved forward with all of his strength, throwing himself backward, dropping to the floor and rolling to the side as Larick staggered back and the bands closed above him.

Regaining his feet, he faced Larick again, watching his hands. He began circling the other at a distance of about fifteen feet and Larick turned slowly, accommodating his position to the movement. Slowly, the other sorcerer's hands began to move in an elaborate pattern. Pol followed them as closely as he could but was unable to detect any manipulation of the magical materials as he now perceived them.

Suddenly, Larick's foot passed through a wide, sweeping gesture and one of the lower bands took Pol across the ankles and he pitched sideways to the floor. Cursing himself for being misdirected so easily, he struggled to rise.

But the floor seemed to ripple and heave, preventing his recovery. As he fought against it, he realized that his weight no longer rested upon the floor, but that he now rode upon a rippling wave of the bands several inches above it. It was then that he began to realize that technique in these matters could be more important than raw energy. He could not regain his footing, but supported himself on his knees and left hand. He saw Larick's right foot moving rapidly up and down as if pumping a piano pedal, keeping the surface in agitation beneath him. It seemed that Larick's facility so far exceeded his that effective countermeasures were a matter of reflex to him, whereas Pol had to think for several moments to decide upon each attack and defense.

He wondered then whether a magical attack was the ultimate answer in dealing with the man. If he could only get near enough to land a blow capable of distracting Larick from magical manipulations, he felt confident that his own boxer's reflexes would be sufficient to deal with him in hand-to-hand fighting. If they were not, then he'd a feeling that he'd simply met a better man . . .

The bands! They could obviously be employed to support one's weight. So . . .

Reaching upward, he took hold of the higher, rising bands and drew himself upright, continuing the motion until he swung free above the heaving layer. Larick's right hand was already moving, out to the side, at shoulder level.

Pol reached far forward, took hold of another horizontal, swung upon it, directly toward Larick.

He was able to twist his body aside at the last possible moment, release himself and drop.

Larick had held a three-foot blade of green light, swordlike, swung ready to impale him.

He felt the normal floor beneath him again, and he snatched at a diagonal band of yellow light, willing it into blade-form, dragging it into an *en garde* position as he struggled for footing. It was the first time in this world that he had held anything like a blade in his hands—and also the first time since the end of the previous fencing season at the university.

He parried a head cut and leaped backward, not having sufficient footing and balance to venture a riposte. As he recovered and Larick advanced, he became aware of two things simultaneously: Larick was facing him full-body rather

than sidewise, and a dark oblong several feet in length had
taken form upon his left arm.

He backed away as Larick came on. Blade and shield
was not normal collegiate fencing. It was something medieval—slower, more ponderous, entailing different foot-
work. He was not about to materialize a shield of his own
and face Larick on terms with which the other man had to
be more familiar.

Larick swung his blade through a chest cut and Pol
leaped backward, entirely avoiding any engagement. Larick continued his advance, Pol his retreat.

Quickly, he reviewed everything he knew concerning
the other's techniques. Larick should be unfamiliar with
the lunge; also, most of his bladework should involve the
edge rather than the point of the weapon. Pol maintained
a saber en garde, but began thinking in terms of the épée.

He halted his retreat and feinted a chest cut. Larick
raised his shield slightly and moved to ready his blade for
a slashing riposte. Pol did not follow through, and he saw
that Larick was beginning to smile.

He adopted a low stance and beat once upon the other's
blade. The attack followed.

The moment Larick's blade moved, Pol was back and
up, very straight and high, his weapon describing a clock-
wise semicircle into an overhand position, from which he
executed a stop-thrust to the other's forearm. Larick made
a small noise in his throat as Pol then continued the
movement through a full bind in anticipation of going in
for the body past the edge of the shield.

But the weapon spun out of Larick's hand, and he
stepped backward, covering himself more fully. Pol smiled,
stamped his foot and rushed him.

Larick raised his right arm, but Pol ignored it and threw
a head-cut. The green blade came flying back from the
floor into Larick's hand, and he parried it. Pol could not
check his momentum, so he increased it, crashing into
Larick's shield before he could riposte.

As Larick staggered back, Pol chopped heavily at his
weapon, knocking it aside, then kicked as hard as he could
squarely against the center of the shield. Larick stumbled
and Pol chopped again, knocking the blade from his hand

once more. The shield swung aside and Pol was no longer in any orthodox fencing posture, but was near enough to drive his left fist into the other's midsection.

The shield fell away as he struck, and he cast his own weapon aside to throw a right at Larick's jaw.

Larick recovered, and raising his hands before his face, his elbows together over his midsection, rushed directly toward him. Pol stepped to the side and threw a left toward his head but did not connect.

Larick dropped and seized him about the knees. Pol felt himself go off balance; grabbed for Larick's shoulder, caught only a handful of his shirt and fell backward to the accompaniment of a tearing sound.

"Kill him! Hurry!" the voice came into his head.

As Pol fell, Larick attempted to hurl himself upon him but was met with a crosscut that knocked him off to the side. At that instant, Pol knew exactly what he must do.

He raised his right hand to shoulder level, palm upward, as he rolled to straddle Larick's supine form. His dragonmark throbbed as the blackness of the lines which separated the bands about him fled toward his hand and coalesced into a dark ball of negation, cancellation, death.

As he swung the ball downward toward Larick's face, his eyes jerked once and he barely had time to twist his body and hurl the death-sphere across the room, away.

Larick struggled to rise, and he clipped him once, hard, on the point of the chin and felt him grow slack. Then he rocked back onto his heels, brushed his hair out of his eyes and stared.

He reached slowly forward. There, where he had torn away the sleeve . . . Larick's right arm lay bare.

His hand trembled slightly as he touched the exposed dragonmark above Larick's right wrist.

XVI

Ryle Merson's voice filled the chamber:

"Is he still alive?"

Pol ignored it, reached up and removed the bandana from Larick's head. A single streak of white ran through his dark hair, front to back.

Only then did Pol turn his head and regard the heavy figure which had just come into the chamber.

"Have you slain him?" Ryle asked.

Pol stood and took a step toward the man.

"I haven't killed anyone here, yet," he said. "Who is Larick, anyway? And what is he to you?"

"How did you come free of the spell which bound you?"

"No. You answer me. I want to know about Larick."

"How quickly you forget your position," Ryle said softly. "You may have freed yourself from direct control, but your leash is short."

He spoke then the words which dissolved the spell of illusion, and the human guise slipped from Pol to reveal the monster body.

"The spell stands ready for the final transfer of which I spoke," he said, "requiring but the proper guide-word."

"I think not," Pol replied, and his will flowed forth through the dragonmark, shattering the image of the monstrous form which hung over him; his features flowed back into their normal pattern, and his hair was stirred as by an invisible wind, its natural color returning, the white streak reappearing.

His garments hung in rags upon him and he breathed heavily for several moments, but he smiled.

"Answer me now," he said. "Who is Larick?"

Ryle's face grew pale.

"Back when your father and I were still on friendly terms," he said, "he gave his young son into my care, as an apprentice."

"Larick is my brother?"

Ryle nodded.

"He is about five years older than you."

"What have you done to him?"

"I taught him the Art and I raised him to be a good man, to respect the decent things—"

Pol did a quick calculation.

"He was perfect insurance, too—when you broke with my father—wasn't he? You had a hostage then, against the wrath of your former friend."

"I am not ashamed to admit it," Ryle replied. "You never knew your father. The man was a devil. And he was one of the best sorcerers around. I had to have some protection."

A sudden flash of inspiration possessed him and Pol asked, "Could it be that Spier, who was still on good terms with my father, did what he did to your daughter in order to assure Larick's safety?"

The color returned heavily to Ryle's face.

"You think just like them, don't you?" he said. "Yes. Even your father hadn't pierced my defenses, but that bastard got through and did that thing to her. Larick has felt guilty about it all his life."

"With no small help from you, I'd guess. That's how you keep him in line, huh? The old guilt trip?"

"Something you've never felt, I'm sure. You're ready to cut a helpless girl's throat. You'd have done it by now if I hadn't heard Larick's cry."

"I'd rather cut yours," Pol said, moving forward. "You're a damned hypocrite. You're no better than my father or Spier. Maybe you're worse. You were ready to go along with their plan when you thought there was something in it for you. When you saw you had something to lose you became a white magician and a defender of righteousness. It's a lot of bullshit! You haven't changed. Now you make my brother do your dirty work, to keep your own hands

clean. But they're not. You're not a big enough fool to
believe they are, are you?"

Ryle moved his hands into the beginning of a warding
gesture, and Pol slipped immediately into the second seeing,
dragonmark still pounding with his pulsebeat.

"You talk to me of morality when you hold the Keys to
the Gate and my daughter lies ready for your blade? Who
is the hypocrite, Detson?"

An arc of fire passed between the man's fingertips, and
Pol looked about for strands or bands, in vain.

But then, suddenly, it seemed as if great clouds of
colored fog were drifting into the chamber.

Pol extended his hand and a blue mist was there when
he needed it. He felt the condensing moisture upon his
fingers. A moment later, he passed a globe of water the
size of a basketball, dripping, from hand to hand. Fire.
Water. It seemed he had the logical remedy ready for
whatever Ryle had in mind.

As he waited for the older sorcerer to make the first
move, he thought back over his battles with Keth and with
Larick, wondering again why his perception of the magical
world had altered in each instance. Then it occurred to
him that on each occasion his vision could have been
colored by the other's magical world-view. Perhaps, now,
Ryle's world was somewhat more cloudy than most.

"We change each other's way of seeing, don't we?" he
said, half-aloud.

"I am here to kill you, not to instruct you," Ryle replied, and the fires he held became a curved dagger which
he cast toward Pol's breast.

Pol willed coldness and felt it flow through his fingertips. The watery sphere clouded and grew solid, covered
with frost. The blade gouged ice chips from it when it
struck, and then fell to the floor. Pol hurled the ice ball at
Ryle, but the sorcerer stepped aside and it shattered against
the wall behind him.

Ryle raised both arms and lowered them suddenly. The
room vanished. They inhabited a region composed entirely of themselves and the colored clouds. Pol took another step forward. As before, he reasoned that if he could
get within striking distance with his fists he could become

a sufficient distraction to dispense with the magic and then, of course, with Ryle.

He moved to take another step forward and his way was blocked by the abrupt appearance of a low wall. He began to step over it and its top was suddenly studded with tall shards of glass. He withdrew and bumped against something. Glancing quickly to the rear, he beheld another wall. And then there was one to his right, and his left. Almost simultaneous with his awareness of their existence, they began to move nearer. Ryle was staring intently toward him, the palms of his hands facing one another and moving slowly together.

But there was no up, no down here. He willed the fogs to boil beneath him, to levitate him as the bands had done earlier.

He rose out of his prison then and passed over its forward wall. It seemed almost too easy . . .

Studying Ryle then, he saw traces of concern about those probing eyes. The man did not know his strengths or his weaknesses yet, knew only what he had accomplished thus far. And so there was fear. So he was fighting a very conservative duel at this point, testing him, watching him, keeping his distance. Such seeming the case, Pol was suddenly apprehensive himself. Ryle was doubtless very good at this sort of thing. In a little while he would realize the limits of Pol's experience and would likely unleash a devastating attack. Pol was not at all certain that he could survive it. Therefore, he ought to act quickly and decisively. But how? He could not think of an appropriate offense in this silent, dreamlike place of deadly cotton candy. Unless . . .

Perhaps he might change the rules, change the milieu. Perhaps he had, in some fashion, been guilty of letting the other man choose his own battleground. There was so much that he still did not know . . .

He felt that he had to finish with Ryle as quickly as possible. Beyond the possibility of Larick's recovering at any time and coming to the aid of his adversary, Pol feared a recurrence of the effect he had already experienced several times—that unpredictable, intermittent failing of his powers.

He had wondered several times since he had fought
Keth whether all of the symbolic byplay was truly necessary in a magical encounter. Since it was will against will,
force manipulation against force manipulation, and perhaps, personal energy against personal energy, it would
seem that it might be stripped to its barest essentials and
Devil take the hindmost. It occurred to him immediately
that this was an untutored, Madwand way of thinking. But
he was slowed whenever he tried to imitate the refine-
ments the others had developed in the long courses of
their studies, and he knew that he was handicapped when
he was forced to play their games. There were obvious
advantages in doing things that more subtle way, but he
had no time to learn it at the moment. Therefore, he
determined to attempt the alternative as he tried to move
nearer.

With some trepidation, he blanked the second seeing.
The fogs vanished. The room returned to normal, Ryle
standing near its entrance, a faraway look in his eyes.

Pol raised his right hand, directing it toward Ryle, and
willed that the other fall down, shrivel and die. The dragonmark seemed suddenly icy and he felt the power leap
forth. He continued to focus his will and a steady flowing
sensation moved, wavelike, down his arm.

Ryle swayed for a moment, then steadied himself. Suddenly, Pol found himself standing on a spit of land, his
stance unaltered, a mighty torrent of water rushing past
him at either hand. Ryle stood upon a small island down-
stream. Even as he watched, the nearer edge of Ryle's
islet was being eroded away and the man was forced to
draw back upon it.

But Ryle raised both hands, a look of intense concentration upon his face. The movement of the water began to
slow. A tremor shook the land upon which Pol stood. The
water lashed about for several moments, then grew still.
This did not last long, however. Shortly, it began moving
again. But this time it was flowing toward Pol. He watched,
fascinated, as its velocity increased and the land began to
wear away before him.

He shook his head as if to clear it. Ryle had drawn him
back into a symbolic situation. He dismissed the waters for

a moment and bent his efforts toward reestablishing his
presence in the chamber.

The river vanished. They were back in the room again.
Nothing had changed. Only now Pol felt a pressure, a
pronounced squeezing sensation all over his body. It was
increasing by the moment.

He refocused his energies.

"Burn, melt, fall down . . ."

The pressure vanished and Ryle staggered, as from a
sudden blow. Pol maintained his own pressure now, his
entire will behind it. Ryle began to sway, as if caught in a
heavy wind.

Then, suddenly, there were flames between them, fanned
as if by a great gale blowing in Ryle's direction. They rose
from a wide chasm which divided a rocky landscape between them.

Even as he watched, the winds died down and the
flames became vertical. Then he felt the warm touch of a
breeze upon his face. The tongues of fire began to bend
toward him . . .

"No!" Pol cried, and the vista was swept away.

The breeze and the heat remained until he gained control of his forces once again. Then they fell, and he hurled
his energies at the other with renewed vehemence.

. . . He stood upon a mountain peak, Ryle atop another. A storm was raging between them. Bolts of lightning fell upon both slopes—

"No," he said softly, "not this time," and he stood again
in the chamber and continued the pressure.

. . . Each of them stood upon a floe of ice, tossed by a
gray choppy sea—

"No."

They were in the chamber and Ryle was glaring at him.
His arm was beginning to ache, but the wavelike sensation
continued to pulse through it.

. . . There was darkness all about them, and the meteor
shower began—

"No."

He maintained the focus of his concentration, ready to
dismiss any new distraction. It had to be will against will.

The room began to fade and he restored it immediately.

"No."

He smiled.

For half-a-minute he maintained his assault, and then he felt the pressure beginning to mount against him. He drew upon his reserves of determination, but it continued to build.

Even this way, he realized then, Ryle had the edge. The man had played a careful game but it had not really been necessary. He knew that he could not hold him back much longer. Ryle really was stronger. Of course, he had no way of knowing that.

Pol took another step forward. If he could just reach him, could just use his fists again . . .

But the pressure grew excruciating with the next step. He knew that he would never make it across the chamber. And now the fat sorcerer was beginning to smile . . .

"Father?"

Ryle turned his head and the pressure was gone. Off to his left, Pol could see that Taisa was sitting up upon the slab of stone.

"Taisa . . . ?"

The man took a step forward.

Pol gathered his forces and struck. Ryle fell like a poled ox.

"Father!"

Taisa slumped back upon the stone. Larick, who had been stirring, grew still.

Gargantuan peals of laughter shook the room.

XVII

The wolf paced and turned in the great cavern, below the Face, before the frozen forms of the other beasts and the men. He slipped out only briefly to find something to eat, unable to go too great a distance from the lair, and a part of his mind always kept watch upon the entrance. He made his kill quickly and took it back with him into the grotto. He lay before the shadowy forms of the other hosts, crunching bones. Beyond this, there was only silence.

When he rose again, his movements were less rapid and they continued to slow, as did his heartbeat and his breathing.

Finally, he was barely stirring, and at last he came to a halt. His eyes grew glazed. He became totally immobile.

Slowly then, a serpent uncoiled itself upon a ledge near the place of the Face. It twisted its way down the rough, rocky wall, tongue darting, eyes bright. It slithered across the floor. It fell upon the remains of the wolf's meal and consumed them.

It mounted the wall again, exploring ledge after ledge, entering each cranny and crack, eating any insects it came upon. Tongue darting, it tested every stirring of the air.

Hours passed, its movements slowed. At length, it stopped within a night-dark crevice.

The big cat awakened and stretched. She went to regard the still and expressionless Face high upon the wall. She patrolled the cavern. She left briefly to feed, as the wolf had done, returned and grew stiff as she licked her rectum, one leg high overhead.

A man awakened. He cursed, drew his blade and inspected it, sheathed it. He began to pace. After a time, he spoke to the Face. It never replied, but he was not misled. He could feel the intelligence, the power within it. The sightless eyes seemed to follow him wherever he went.

At last his words trailed off and he became a part of the scenery.

The Harpy awakened and uttered a cry and a curse. She flapped in quick patrol about the cavern, defecating profusely, imaginatively.

Then she considered the Face and grew silent. She went to feed at the remains of the cat's meal.

All were as one before the Face.

XVIII

Pol turned toward the doorway. An unnaturally-cast shadow covered the large figure of the man who stood there. As soon as Pol's gaze fell upon him, that one moved forward and entered the chamber. The shadow went away.

Pol stared. The man wore a yellow cloak, darker garments beneath it. He was blue-eyed, with sandy hair white at the temples. His features were rugged, his expression almost open, almost honest. He smiled. He had a shiny, capped tooth.

"There is a lesson there for you, lad," he said, and Pol recognized the voice. "He had you, but he allowed himself to be distracted. I lifted an old spell, to give you an opening, to see what you would do." He shook his head. "You shouldn't have allowed yourself to be distracted, also. You should have struck instantly, not stood gawking. A better man could have killed you in that interval—would have."

"But the distraction itself might have represented a threat," Pol replied.

"If a building is falling on you, you don't concern yourself with the horn of an approaching car. You deal with the most immediate peril first. That's survival. You were good, but you hesitated. That can be fatal."

"Car? Who the hell are you, anyway?"

"You know my name."

"Henry Spier?"

The man smiled again.

"So much for introductions."

From somewhere, he produced a black cigarette holder, screwed a cigarette into it and raised it to his lips. Smoke drifted upward from it before it reached his mouth. He puffed upon it and looked about the chamber.

"Things seem to have worked themselves out just about as I'd calculated them," he observed.

He reached beneath his cloak and produced the statuette Pol had hidden in the tunnel.

"You found it. . . ."

"Of course."

Henry Spier walked past him and placed the figure at the second point from the right in the diagram upon the floor.

"Six to go," he commented as he straightened and turned.

"That is the first cigarette I've seen in this world," Pol said.

"A man of perception may choose his pleasures from many places," Spier replied. "I'll be happy to teach you all about them later. But now we have some important business to conclude."

"My dreams," Pol said. "You released me from what I might call the first series, that night on the trail . . ."

Spier nodded.

". . .But then there were more—set in the same world, but very different."

Again Spier nodded, and the smoke curled above his head.

"Since you were being propagandized in the first instance," he stated, "I felt it only fair that you should be granted a somewhat fuller picture when the opposition had its opportunity."

"I must confess that the fuller picture was not entirely comprehensible to me."

"It would be surprising if it were," said Spier, "since it was an alien and vastly older civilization that you viewed. What is far more important, though, is whether or not you found it attractive."

Spier's eyes suddenly met with his own and Pol looked away.

"I found it—fascinating," he said, and when he looked back he saw that Spier was smiling again.

"Excellent," the man replied. "I believe that finds us in

basic agreement as to values. What say you produce the other six Keys now and we be about our business?"

Pol looked about the chamber. He gestured.

"You cautioned me against inattention and distraction. What of these?"

"My power would have to be broken for these three to awaken," he said. "It would require a faltering of my will, and I doubt the sufficiency of anything I propose doing now to work that end."

Pol shook his head and turned away. He regarded the still form of Taisa upon the block of dark stone.

"Your gaze follows the direction of your thoughts, I see."

"Does this thing really require a human sacrifice?"

"Yes. So be of good cheer that you now have a choice. We can save the girl for your later pleasure and use Ryle, who would be most happy to kill you if it would serve his ends."

"What of—my brother?"

"He would not go along with our plans. Ryle has warped his thinking. I suggest you permit me to banish him, perhaps to the world where you yourself grew up."

"He is a sorcerer. He may find his way back."

"It will be a simple enough matter to inflict a loss of memory."

"That could be kind of rough."

"His treatment of you was somewhat less than exemplary."

"But as you said, Ryle influenced him."

"Who cares what the reason may be? I am only willing to spare him at all because he is your brother."

"Say that I give you what you want. What assurance have I that I will be of any use to you afterwards?"

"There will be massive changes, and I cannot control an entire world by myself. There are not that many Madwands about. I would not dispense with any of them unnecessarily. And you, of course, will always hold a special place, because of this assistance."

"I see," Pol said.

"Do you really? Are you aware what will come to pass in this world when the Gate is opened?"

"I think so. Or at least I have my suspicions."

"It will become our plum. With the power at our disposal, we will be gods of the new world."

Pol's eyes moved toward the Gate, where some trick of the light made the figure of the nailed bird seem to jerk forward.

"Supposing I said 'no'?" he asked.

"That could cause us both considerable inconvenience. But what possible reason could you have for not agreeing?"

"I don't like being pressured into things, whether it's by you or Ryle or the statuettes themselves. I've been manipulated ever since I set foot in this world, and I'm tired of it."

"Well, as in most major matters there is only a limited number of choices. In this case, you are with me, you are against me or you want to walk away from me. Two of those responses are unacceptable and would require action on my part."

"I wouldn't like that," said Pol. "But then, you might not either."

"Are you threatening me, lad?" Spier asked.

"Just stating a possible consequence," Pol replied.

The big man sighed.

"You're strong, Pol," he said, "stronger today than you ever were before in your life. You've passed your initiation, and your lights are all shining as pretty as can be—for the moment. No telling how long it will last, of course. But be that as it may, I am stronger still. There would be no contest whatsoever between us. You would be as a candle's flame before the hurricane of my will. Now, I could force you to produce the Keys. But I would far rather you did it willingly, for I want you alive and on my side and wearing no special enchantment."

"Why?"

"I've my reasons. I'll tell you later, after I'm sure of you."

"You foresaw a possible conflict between us. Something you'd said . . ."

"Yes, I did. But it need not be. If you're squeamish, I'll even do the sacrificing myself."

Pol laughed.

"That's not it. I'd have killed Ryle only a little while ago if I could have. As I said, you're pressing me, you're manipulating me."

"I have no choice."

"The hell you don't."

Spier turned away, staring for a moment at the Gate.

"I wonder . . . ?" he began.

"By the way," Pol said, "if you were to kill me, how would you get at the Keys?"

"Only with great difficulty, if at all." Spier said, "since you are carrying them around in what is practically a private universe. If you die, it would be a hell of a problem piercing it."

"Then your 'candle in the wind' metaphor isn't quite apt, is it? You'd have to pull your punches if it came to throwing any."

"Perhaps. Perhaps not. I wouldn't count on it, though. The Gate could be opened with just one Key—but it might take me a couple of years and an awful lot of trouble. Good thing we're just speaking hypothetically, isn't it?"

Pol crossed the chamber and touched the Gate for the first time. It felt cold. The eyes of the nailed serpent seemed to be fixed upon him.

"What would happen if the statuettes were destroyed?" he asked.

"That would be a very difficult thing to accomplish," Spier replied, "even if one knew how."

"But we're being hypothetical, aren't we?"

"True. The Gate would fade away from this plane, and you would be standing there looking at a raw piece of mountain."

"But it is open now—or can be opened without the Keys—on another plane?"

"Yes. But only tenuous things can take that route, as you did in your dreams."

"What brought it here in the first place?"

"Your father, Ryle and myself—with great exertions."

"How? And how are the statuettes involved?"

"That's enough for being hypothetical—or anything else of an interrogatory nature," Spier said. "There were three choices—one good one and two bad ones. Do you recall?"

"Yes."

Pol turned toward him, leaned back against the door and folded his arms across his breast. Immediately, he felt the coldness along his spine, but he did not move. The power was still there, moving within his right forearm.

Spier's eyes widened, slightly and but for an instant. He glanced upward and then back down at Pol again.

"I know your answer," he said, "but I have to hear you say it."

"You ran out on my father and left him to face an army."

Spier frowned, looked puzzled.

"He acted against my advice," he said. "The army was there because of his actions, not mine. There was no sense in my dying with him. But what is all of this to you? You never even knew him."

"Just curious," Pol said. "I wanted to hear your side of it."

"Surely you are not going to use that as a basis for refusing me? You were only a baby."

Pol nodded. He was thinking of the thing that might have been his father's ghost walking beside him in the misty chamber.

"You're right. But humor me with one more question, if you will. Would the two of you have fought one another eventually, for hegemony in this new land?"

Spier's face reddened.

"I don't know," he said. "Perhaps . . ."

"Had it already begun? Were you on the threshold and was this your way—"

"Enough!" Spier cried. "I take it that your answer is 'no'. Would you care to tell me which is your real reason for denying me?"

Pol shrugged.

"Choose any of the above," he said. "Maybe I'm not certain myself. But I know there is a sufficiency."

The coldness had invaded his entire body now, but he made no move to withdraw from the serpent figure of the Gate against which he leaned. It was almost as if it had invited him to position himself just there . . .

"It's a shame," Spier said, "because I was beginning to like you. . . ."

Pol hit him. He summoned up every bit of the power he could muster, backed it with all of his will and hurled it at the man.

Very slowly, Henry Spier unscrewed the cigarette from its holder, dropped it upon the floor and stepped on it. He replaced the holder in some hidden pocket beneath his cloak. It had to be sheer bravado. Pol knew that the man must be feeling the force of his attack. But the display was effective. Pol felt a tremor of fear at Spier's power, but he maintained the siege and reached for even more force to back it. He was committed now, and he felt as if he were sliding down a long tunnel which ended in blackness.

Spier raised his eyes and they bored into his own. Pol suddenly felt a resistance rising.

Spier took a step toward him.

It was as if he suddenly faced a heat backlash, as if the target of his exertions stood directly before him rather than some distance away.

Frantically, he switched to the second seeing. His vision focused upon Spier, advancing upon him, fists raised. The image of Spier, still standing in the distance, faded. The man's face was twisted into a smirk and perspiration dotted his brow. His fist was already moving.

Pol's concentration was broken. He ducked forward, raising his hands to protect his face. He heard a solid *thunk*, followed by a brief cry and realized immediately that Spier's blow had fallen upon the Gate.

He dropped his hands and drove his left fist, followed by his right, into Spier's abdomen. The blows had surprisingly little effect. The man was solid.

Even as he swung a left uppercut and felt it connect, he realized that the main pain the man seemed to have felt was in the bloodied knuckles of his right hand, which he now held in an awkward position. Pol immediately threw a right toward his face, but this blow was blocked. Then Spier rushed him.

Spier's bulk crashed into him, driving him back against the Gate. Pol was dazed as his head struck upon it. Then Spier stepped back and their eyes met again.

He called upon the dragonmark to raise a defense as a shock ran through his entire system like a jolt of electricity. He struck out with the power he had wielded earlier, but it barely seemed to shield him against the forces the other was turning against him. He felt a pressure beginning to build, not unlike that which Ryle had turned upon him. Both he and Spier stood absolutely still now, and though he threw everything he had into the defense, the pressure continued to mount.

A throbbing began in his temples and his breathing became labored. He grew damp with perspiration, though he still felt abnormally cold. A wave of dizziness came and went, came again. He felt that he might only be able to hold Spier off for a few more seconds. His defenses would crumble, the man would place him under control, force him to produce the statuettes and then possibly use him for the sacrifice. Where was the flame which had guided him, protected him?

He seemed to hear faint, mocking laughter. In that instant he realized that this was the end toward which they had guided him. They wanted the Gate opened. If he were not willing, then they would not protect him against the one who would.

His vision began to fade as the vertigo retuned. If this were to be the end, then at least he ought to try inflicting a final hurt upon his enemy.

He placed his right foot flat upon the door behind him and thrust himself forward toward Spier, striking outward and upward with both fists.

He was surprised that his blow actually landed. The last thing that he saw before he fell was the look of astonishment on Spier's face as the man toppled over backwards.

A wave of darkness rushed through Pol's head. He felt nothing as he hit the floor.

XIX

Drifting. He was drifting through blackness and silence. His only other sensation was a feeling of intense cold, but after a time this passed.

For how long he drifted, he could not tell—moments, ages . . . The sensation was not unpleasant, now that the coldness had passed. Memory required too much effort. He only knew that it was good to know something of rest, of an end to all exertion.

A gentle rocking motion began. Even so . . . It was hardly disturbing. But then motion commenced in a single direction. He rode with it, still feeling the rocking as he was drawn along.

He perceived a faint light. It seemed to be coming from all directions, but he did not wonder at the variety of sensory apparatus the sensation might require. His consciousness was growing, but portions of his mind were numb.

The light grew and the motion continued. Whatever was below seemed a pale yellow with smoky patches.

Now the prospect grew clearer, but his sense of perspective was warped. The light values were strange, and there was no way of determining his distance from the slowly resolving objects below. It was a broken land, rocky, sandy, shadowed, with wind-borne clouds of dust and low-lying, snaky mists. But there was nothing recognizable for contrast, nothing to provide a scale. Yet the place was familiar. Where? When?

He dropped lower. Were they mountain peaks or low ridges above which he moved?

And where was he going? Was he controlling his own

movements, only drifting, or both? Or neither? It almost
seemed—

He was moving alongside one of the larger stone prominences. Suddenly, he rounded it and the matter of relative proportions was resolved.

About ten feet below him, high on a stake, a demonic
head was impaled. Something which might be classifiable
as a grin drew the dark, scaly face tight. The eyes were
fully opened, very black and appeared to be staring directly at him.

He felt something akin to a shudder as he was swept on
past the grisly thing, with the distinct impression that it
had winked at him. The wasteland fell farther below him
as he soared into a twilit area of pale stars in a pale sky
above the level of blowing dust. Here the wind still blew,
cold, with a moaning sound, empty of everything.

Far below now, the features of the landscape fled backward. A fountain of sparks rose as if to intercept him, but
he veered far wide of it. Shortly afterwards, a crashing
metallic note filled the air, as of the striking of a great
gong, the reverberations of which seemed to remain with
him for many long minutes.

A bright meteor cut a long, slow trail above and before
him; and he heard a sound like thunder though there were
no clouds in the sky. His velocity seemed to increase, and
the moaning of the wind rose in pitch. Far below him, the
dark and light patches of the land moved in a sea of
distortions, rendering themselves into momentary faces—
elongate, twisted, beautiful, alien, angry, composed, be-
reft. He passed over a shattered city above which dark
forms hovered and turned. Small blue lights darted amid
the ruins. Occasionally, the dark things fell upon one and
extinguished it. He passed above a black tower from whence
a lovely, liquid-voiced singing emerged. A squat, many-
legged creature with a juicy, cracked skin, lay like a rotten
plum atop it. A brazen chariot passed silently through the
middle air, driven by a dead-white being muffled in saf-
fron, drawn by long-tailed creatures whose breath emerged
in white clouds to congeal and fall as crystals upon the
winds. In a moment, the apparition was gone, and he
began to doubt whether he had actually seen it.

A tinkling, as of hundreds of tiny bells, accompanied his passage above a gray plain where armies of humans and demons stood frozen in martial attitudes beneath some ancient enchantment whose fringes he had touched. Ahead of him then, the horizon was broken along its entire length—a thin, irregular edge of the world, rising. He focused his attention upon it.

It grew into a saw-toothed band and then a rampart—mighty, towering and black. For a long while it seemed that at any moment he might be dashed against the great range. And then a shifting of light lay a new perspective across the land, and he realized that it was incredibly distant, incredibly huge. Something tightened within the cloud of his being as he realized intuitively that he must pass over it.

Below, the hidden features of the land were still revealed in fragmentary flashes. He no longer had vision to the rear, but he felt, vaguely, that something was following him. Briefly, he assaulted the frozen part of his own mind, with inquiry as to what he was, where he had come from. Nothing yielded, the brief frenzy passed and forgetfulness of its occurrence ensued. He continued his contemplation of the world before him, realizing that he had come this way before, knowing that this time it was different, knowing that he had a mission to fulfill.

The mountains loomed even larger, and he knew that—no matter what the nature of his form—their traversal would not be easy. He began studying their silhouette, looking for a low area, a gap—anything that might ease his passage. He thought that he detected such a place off to the left, and he made an effort to direct his course toward it.

He was surprised when this actually occurred. It was his first voluntary act that he could recall since coming into consciousness, and it pleased him to see it prove fruitful. Immediately, however, he wondered what had been directing him up until this time.

He became aware then of a kind of tugging, of the sensation of being drawn onward by something beyond the mountains, something which was willing to give him a little leeway, that he come more rapidly and safely into its lands. He exerted himself again, and his velocity increased.

As he drew nearer to the mountains it seemed that he grew more tangible than he had been earlier. For now he began to meet with resistance, to feel the buffeting of the winds.

The mountains towered above him, their peaks vanishing in the darkness overhead. He rose to an even greater altitude as he came nearer, approaching the gap. The winds caught him and cast him back down, screaming now in their passage.

He stabilized himself and mounted again, moving even nearer to the rocky face as he ascended. This time he rose higher before the screaming winds forced him back.

On his third attempt, he moved more rapidly, driving himself upward with great force, the slope of the mountain becoming a dark blur before him. When the winds finally took hold of him, he fought them, almost reaching the level of the bright gap before he was forced downward yet again.

The fourth time he tried a different angle of attack and was beaten back almost immediately.

He hovered at a lower altitude, recovering orientation and stability, mustering fortitude. He massed his energies once more. Then he began to rise.

This time he followed the best course he had taken earlier, close to the face of the mountain. He hurled himself upward, attempting to exceed all earlier velocities.

The wind curled about him and played upon him as on the string of some musical instrument. He throbbed to its vibrations as he fought it. He continued to rise against its pressures, but he felt the rapid dissipation of the energies which composed his being. A feeling came over him that if he did not make it up and through this time, he would be swept away to drift for perhaps half of an age before he recovered sufficient strength to try again.

As the battering increased and he felt himself slowing he invested all of his remaining strength in an attempt to continue the upward drive. A momentary lull permitted him a great gain, but the assault began again just as he neared the gap.

"Whoever you are that calls," he cried wordlessly toward the gap, "if you really want me, then lend a hand!"

Almost immediately, he felt the tugging—and for the first time it seemed a physical sensation rather than a psychical leading-on. He added his own energies to it and felt himself rising at a more rapid rate. He swept past the highest point he had achieved with his earlier efforts. The gap was before him if he could but bend his course and strike a proper passage now.

He exerted himself again, and the steady pull—from ahead now—assisted him. He came into the gap.

He had hoped for some sheltering from the winds once he achieved the cleft in the mountains, but now he faced a gale blowing through it. Fighting his way to the shelter of an opening in the righthand wall, he gathered his forces and considered the way ahead. He had seen prominences before him and other openings in the walls.

Braving the winds, he advanced and took shelter in the lee of a rocky rib to the left. The wind whistled by him and icy crystals sparkled in long streaks within dark grooves amid the stone. He made another effort, advancing a small distance and sheltering again. The tugging had subsided—or, rather, reverted to the mental level, as a summoning.

When he felt that he had regained sufficient strength, he entered the blast and moved forward once more. In such fashion, he traversed the long defile, finding himself at last in the final protected area, adjacent to the forward opening of the pass. As he waited there, he considered his course of action upon emerging. He decided to move immediately to the nearer side—this being the left—upon departing the gap to prevent his being swept back into it.

As he traveled that final distance, he caught a glimpse of a dark and ancient sea, far ahead, before he slipped to the side, was taken by the winds and felt himself hurled skyward.

He rose at a rapid rate, and the world spun kaleidoscopically through whatever senses he possessed. He was tossed upward and outward away from the mountain and then found himself falling, to be caught and dragged through a washboard-like trough of turbulence. When this ended, he fell again, his senses in total disarray.

After a time, he slowed, and he became aware of the tugging once again. He drifted away from the region of high winds, continuing to lose altitude. Gradually, what passed for vision reasserted itself.

Below him, sweeping down to the still sea and seeming to continue beneath its surface, was a fantastic, terraced city of asymmetrical buildings, many of them of a darkly burnished metal, extending on to the right and the left to vanish at the horizon. He was drawn nearer to this place. Towers of colored smoke redolent with heavy perfumes drifted by him. His vision was constantly tricked by the unusual perspectives, the pale light. He drifted lower and saw where demons walked with their human lovers; he heard the strange, slow music from the revolving pentagons. He moved above an avenue lined with grotesque statues, all of them turning slowly in a centuries-long figure-dance. An enormous being, chained among russet pillars, wept continually into a stone basin from which green chalices were filled by the passersby. Faint flashes like heat lightning colored the somber sky far out over the sea. He grew dizzy at the prospect; there was something new and not quite comprehensible in every direction that he looked. Such as the high, yellow tower near the seaside with the statue of the dark woman-like bird-thing crouched atop it . . .

Then it stirred and he knew that it was no statue.

Nyalith's voice went forth like trumpets across the land and the sea.

All motion below him was frozen for an instant.

And he knew.

He turned toward the waters and directed his course out over them, his velocity mounting steadily, the world becoming a gray, tunnel-like blur about him. He moved along that line of force which had drawn him across the world. He felt, for the first time, the presence toward which his flight was bearing him.

Before him, there occurred a darkness at the end of the tunnel. Then, for one flashing moment, he caught sight of the great black-winged form, limned against a violet sky, lightnings flickering about it. A moment only, and then he was swept to that destined rendezvous, his newly awakened consciousness shifting and breaking apart, merging.

He opened his beak and sent forth his answering cry across the still waters, a cry of exultation in the knowledge that he, Henry Spier, had been joined with the ancient consciousness of Prodromolu, Opener of the Way.

He rode the winds to a great height, then dived down to regard his own reflection in the waters—shadowy birdform haloed in baleful light. Here was the power, he knew. He would summon his people and lead them across the land to the place of the Gate. There he would arouse his human body on the other side. It mattered not that but one Key was in place. This would prove sufficient with the Opener of the Way as aid, once the blood of any of the fallen was added to the spell. There was nothing now to stay the merger of the planes, the salvation of his world. He beat downward once with his wings, feeling their strength, grazing the surface of the water beneath which bright things moved.

Then, sea-splitting tower of scale and mud, it rose before him, red eyes unwinking, wrack of the depths adorning its horns, upon whose back the rock-shelled scavengers danced among skeletons of ships and shards of dead things' bones. And even as it reared, it swayed, the dragger-back-into-the-mud of primordial creation, Talkne, Serpent of the Still Waters, who had for eons awaited this passage and the renewal of their eternal conflict.

Prodromolu's wings went wide, scooping at the air, slowing his forward progress. In that instant before recovery, Talkne struck.

Hammerlike, the head of the serpent fell against the fluttering bird, driving it down among the waves amid a flurry of feathers. Talkne plunged after him.

Prodromolu's talons extended like switchblade scimitars, to gouge long furrows in the serpent's side. His beak slashed as Talkne threw a coil over his back.

Then they were rolling over and over in the water, sending up mighty showers of spray, their blood darkening the foam as it billowed in all directions. His talons continued to slash against the side of the snake, seeking purchase there, as the coil tightened across his back and

Talkne's head darted from side to side, moved forward, moved backward, seeking an opening for a deadly strike. Above them, the skies darkened and lightened again. Far across the water, the cry of Nyalith was repeated.

"It is a summons you will never answer, Bird," hissed Talkne.

"We've had this conversation before, Snake," Prodromolu answered.

For the first time, their eyes met, and both stared for a long, peculiar moment.

"Pol?" the bird croaked.

"Henry . . . ?"

And then Prodromolu struck, overwhelming the slower, human personality within. Talkne writhed in the sudden spasm of his talons, but the dark wings were already shrugging water as they beat with a sound like wet sails aluff, and the serpent was rolled onto her back, tail thrashing, as Prodromolu mounted the air and strove to raise the other into his own element.

Talkne fought back, heaving coil after coil toward the bird. But Prodromolu avoided them or slashed with his beak, never missing a beat with his pinions as he commenced a slow movement in the direction of the land, dragging the serpent after him, half-in, half-out of the water.

The bird uttered a triumphant cry as his velocity increased and more and more of Talkne's bulk was drawn into the air, dangling and writhing. After a time, the mountains came into view, and the world-city upon their slopes. It was then that the serpent struck again.

Talkne's head flashed upward, mouth wide. But the fangs closed only on feathers. The tail swung then like a great club, battering the bird. Prodromolu reeled and jerked at the blow but did not lose altitude. Three times the serpent attempted to catch him in a coil and three times failed. Again, the head came up and back, but Prodromolu parried the strike with his beak and strove for a greater altitude.

They mounted higher into the streak-shot air. The land was nearer now, and Talkne's weight hung limp and heavy in the dark bird's claws. The wing-beat tempo increased and a steady wind fanned the snake.

"Out of the water," Prodromolu said, "you are nothing but a stuffed skin, a sausage."

Talkne did not reply.

"I am Opener of the Way," he said after a time. "I go to throw wide the Gate, to bring the breath of fresh life."

"You will not depart this world," Talkne hissed.

Prodromolu swept on toward the land, its music and incense now reaching him across the water, a crowd of its orange-robed inhabitants waiting near the shoreline to be slain, singing and swaying as his shadow drew near. He opened his beak again and cried out to them.

As he approached the land he chose the spot with care, fled across the lower terraces and opened his claws as he banked and commenced a wide circle.

The serpent body writhed, twisting as it descended upon the city. Where it struck, buildings collapsed and people and demons were crushed, fountains were broken and fires sprang forth from the rubble. Prodromolu's head dropped and his wings swept back. He plunged toward his fallen adversary.

As he struck with his talons, Talkne's still body suddenly responded like a broken spring. A coil fell across his back and tightened immediately. Off balanced, one wing pinned, feathers flying, Prodromolu was wrenched to one side and then over, and over again. More of the buildings collapsed, statues toppled, as they turned, rolled, fell. They descended the terraces, the ground shaking beneath them. The singing grew louder as they dropped toward the lowest level.

As the constriction of Talkne's body increased, Prodromolu tightened his own grip upon it and continued to strike and tear with his beak. Their blood mingled and spread in a series of coin-like pools. Orange-clad bodies lay all about them as the bird continued to hammer at the scaly form which imprisoned him in massive bands. At last there came a slight loosening of the serpent's coils, and the bird struck with renewed energy, tearing out chunks of flesh and dashing them aside into a small ornamental garden of silver-leafed shrubs.

He felt the serpent go limp. Dragging himself free, he struck once again, then threw back his head and uttered a piercing shriek. Then he spread his wings slowly, painfully, and lifted himself into the air.

The head of the serpent flashed upward and the mouth snapped shut upon his right leg. With a whiplike movement, Talkne cast Prodromolu through the air and into the water, not letting go the leg, slithering immediately after to wind about the dark bird again.

"You will not depart this world," Talkne repeated, driving them out into deeper water.

"Pol!" said the other, suddenly. "You don't know what you're doing. . . ."

There was a long pause, as the serpent dragged him even farther away from the shore. Then, "I know," came the reply.

Talkne dove, bearing Prodromolu along with him.

The bird tore partway free for an instant and drove his beak down upon the back of the serpent's head a bare instant before the fangs found the side of his neck and closed there.

As the waters roiled about him and the blow from that great beak fell upon the head of the serpent, Pol felt his consciousness fading and then everything seemed distant. Even as he locked his fangs more tightly upon the other, he felt insulated from the event, as if it really involved two other parties. . . .

Thrashing frantically, he could not free himself from the grip upon his neck. As he was drawn ever more deeply beneath the water, Henry Spier felt the blackness rising and covering him over. He wanted to cry out. He reached to summon his powers, but he was gone before the necessary movement of Art could be completed.

XX

He was walking. The mists were rolling all about him and the figures came and went. There was one very familiar one, with a message . . .

It was cold, very cold. He wanted a blanket, but something else was thrust into his hands. A warmth seemed to flow from it, however, and that was good. The moaning sounds ceased. He had barely been aware of them until then. He clutched more tightly at the object he held and something of strength came into him from it.

"Pol! Come on! Wake up! Hurry!"

The message . . .

He was aware that his face was being slapped. Face?

Yes, he had a face.

"Wake up!"

"No," he said, his grip continuing to tighten upon the staff.

Staff?

He opened his eyes. The face before him was out of focus, but there was something familiar about it even then. It moved nearer to his own and the blurring vanished from its features.

"Mouseglove . . ."

"Get up! Hurry!" the small man enjoined him. "The others are stirring!"

"Others? I don't . . . Oh!"

Pol struggled to sit up and Mouseglove assisted him. As he did so, he saw that it was his father's scepter which he held clutched in his hands.

"How did you come by this?" he asked.

"Later! Take it and use it!"

Pol looked about the chamber. Larick had rolled onto his side, facing him. His eyes were open, though his expression was not one of comprehension. Across the chamber, near the door, Ryle Merson was moaning and beginning to move. From the corner of his eye, Pol saw that Taisa's arm was rising. He remembered Spier's words concerning a lapse of will, and he stared at the man, just as Spier began to sit up.

"Are they all enemies?" Mouseglove asked. "You'd better do something to the ones who are—fast!"

"Get out of here," Pol said. "Hurry!"

"I'll not leave you now."

"You must! However you came in—"

"Through the window."

"Back out it then. Go!"

Pol got up onto one knee and raised the scepter before him, staring at Henry Spier across it. Mouseglove moved out of sight, but Pol could not tell whether he had fled or only retreated. From somewhere, the smell of dragons came to his nostrils.

His arm was already throbbing, and he gave a grateful shudder that the power had not again deserted him. The statuette still stood in position upon the diagram, facing the Gate. He rose to his feet and sent his will into the scepter. There was an answering tingle in the palms of his hands. A sensation as of a protracted, subauditory organ note passed through him.

He felt no doubt whatsoever that Spier must die. If he let him live, he decided that he would be guilty of a greater offense than if he killed him, becoming himself responsible for any evil the man would work.

With a sound like a thunderclap, a sheet of almost liquid flame leapt from the scepter's tip to fall upon Henry Spier. The chamber was brilliantly illuminated and shadows ran relay races about the uneven walls.

Then the flame parted like a forked tongue, to reveal Spier standing beyond the bifurcation, right arm upraised.

"How'd you manage to get your hands on that thing?" he said, above the fire's roar.

Pol did not reply but bent all of his efforts to closing the fiery gap. Like a bloody pair of scissors in a shaky hand, it commenced swaying toward, then away from the man in its midst. Pol felt the counterpressure growing and then waning, as Spier mustered his forces with occasional lapses.

"Your dragon outside the window, eh?" Spier said. "Must have him well-trained. Can't stand dragons myself. Smell like stale beer and rotten eggs."

The flames suddenly flew wide apart, like a letter Y, then a T. They began retreating toward Pol, the arms of the T slowly curving back around in his direction.

Pol gritted his teeth, and the flames' progress toward him was halted. He was seized with the sickening realization that even with his powers augmented by the scepter, Spier seemed to hold the edge. And Spier's strength was continuing to grow as he recovered, whereas his own appeared to have reached its limit. The flames began to sway again, but they were edging closer toward him. He knew that it was too late to shift to a different mode of attack, and he knew also that it would not make any difference if he could.

"It is a powerful tool that you hold," Spier stated slowly, as if reading his mind. "But a tool, of course, is only as good as the man who uses it. You are young, and but recently come into your powers. You are not sufficient to the task you have set yourself." He took a step forward and the flames roared ominously. "But then, I doubt that any man in this world is."

"Shut up!" Pol cried, and he tried to banish the flames, but they remained.

Spier took another step and halted as a surge of effort accompanying Pol's anger flicked them back a span in his direction.

"There can be only one outcome if you persist," Spier went on," and I do not want that. Listen to me, boy. If you are good enough to give me as much trouble as you have, you are very good. I would regret very much having to destroy you, especially when there is no reason for it."

There came a loud report from the direction of the window, and a bullet richocheted about the chamber. Spier glanced in that direction at the same time Pol did.

Mouseglove, standing outside, had rested his elbows upon the wide, stony sill. The pistol, pointed toward Spier, still smoked in his hand. He seemed to stiffen, and he slid away out of sight, the weapon clattering against stone as it fell.

Pol turned back in time to see Spier completing an almost casual gesture.

"Had I a moment or so more, I would have made him turn it against himself," he said. "But I can do that afterwards. Firearms are such a barbaric intrusion in this idyllic place, don't you think? I approve of your actions at Anvil Mountain, by the way. The Balance must be tipped toward more magic, where we will be supreme."

Panting now, Pol fended off the return of the flames, his dragonmark feeling as if it were itself afire. He knew that without the scepter he would be dead in the face of the present onslaught. Spier seemed to be increasing even in stature now, as he recovered, an aura of poise and command growing about him.

"As I said, there is no reason for this," Spier continued. "I am willing to forgive our archetypal struggle beyond the Gate and what passed between us here before then. I feel that you still do not understand. I am also more convinced than ever of your suitability as an ally." He took a step backward and the pressure diminished. "A sign of my good faith," he said. "I have made the first move toward our easing away from this in stages. Let us call a halt and work together to our mutual benefit. I'll even teach you some unusual things about that staff you hold. I—"

Pol screamed and fell to his knees as his entire left side was seized and twisted by a hideous series of spasms. He thought that he felt his lower ribs give way.

Summoning all of his remaining energy, he drove it toward Spier in a gigantic psychic wedge, powered by fear, hate, a sense of betrayal, shame at his own gullibility . . .

"It wasn't me!" Spier cried—half in anger, half in surprise—as he was driven, tripping, back against the wall.

"Larick! Stop it . . ." came a weak voice from off to the right, as Ryle Merson struggled to his feet.

Instantly, the seizure halted, though its aftereffects left Pol kneeling, aching, shaking.

"Help him! Damn you!" Ryle cried, advancing. "That's Spier he's got against the wall!"

The fat man suddenly moved quickly and placed his hand upon the scepter below Pol's own. Immediately, Pol felt a partial easing of the tension which had held him for so long.

Spier's eyes, which had been wide, suddenly narrowed. Larick came up beside Pol on the left, his hand, also, coming to rest upon the scepter.

"You say I would use you," Spier said, "and this is true. But they are also guilty—of the same thing."

Pol bore down with his will, augmented by the others'. The flame leaped forward again—and halted, as if it had met an invisible wall.

He strove to increase his efforts and felt the others doing likewise, yet the situation remained unchanged. In fact, Spier was smiling—a small, almost sad smile.

"What's happening?" Pol said in a hoarse whisper.

"He's holding us," Ryle replied.

"All three of us?" Pol asked. "I almost had him myself before!"

"My little serpent," Spier said from across the chamber. "Although you surprised me several times, I was but testing your strength and letting things run long enough to give me the opportunity to speak with you. I see now that I have failed, and I must conclude things, though it really does my heart sore to see you put to waste. Good-bye— until some more agreeable life, perhaps."

He began to walk toward them. Immediately, the scepter became burning hot in Pol's grip. He clung to it despite this, however, and directed all of their energies toward halting the man, who now seemed the embodiment of strength and assurance. He felt some resistance, but Spier did not stop, and the smell of burning flesh came to his nostrils. His head swam, and for an instant the mists seemed to roil about him and the figure to his right was no longer Ryle Merson. What was he saying?

Spier doubled forward as if experiencing a sudden stomach cramp. He waved both his hands in small circles, frantically, the right before him, the left far out to the side.

After a moment, he straightened, the hand movements

continuing but becoming more regular now, the circles growing. He looked ahead and then to the left.

"They're coming out of the woodwork now," he said ruefully.

Pol, who could no longer tell whether the scepter was hot, cold or lukewarm, turned his head toward the chamber's entrance.

Ibal and Vonnie stood there. He bore a white wand. She held what appeared to be a brass hand mirror, crosswise and close to her breast.

"You've roused the bloody geriatrics ward," Spier added, glaring now and appearing fully recovered. "We'll just have to retire them again."

His left hand changed its pattern, altered its rhythm. The metal mirror flashed as Vonnie swayed. Ibal laid a hand upon her shoulder and displayed his wand like an orchestra conductor at the opening of Brahms' Second Symphony.

"There *was* a time when you were good, old man," Spier said. "But you should have stayed retired . . ."

He flicked his right hand suddenly and Ryle Merson cried out and fell.

"A little misdirection never hurts," he said. "And then there were four . . ."

But his face showed signs of strain, and the mirror flashed again.

"Damned witch!" he muttered, retreating a step.

A needle-fine line of white light fled from the tip of Ibal's wand and pierced Spier's right shoulder. Spier bellowed as the arm fell to his side and a wave of fire and force from the scepter swept over him.

Clothing smouldering, he gestured wildly and the scepter was torn from Pol's and Larick's grip, spinning across the room and striking Ibal about the chest and shoulders as it turned. The white wand dropped to the floor as the sorcerer fell, his face already twenty years older.

The mirror flashed again and Spier seemed to catch its light with his left hand, from whence it was reflected upon Pol and Larick.

Pol felt it as a blow and was momentarily blinded. Falling, he struck against Larick, who was not strong enough to hold him. Both of them went down as Spier, his arm dripping blood, hair and eyebrows singed, face bright red, cloak smoking, turned toward the woman. He was muttering—whether profanity or the beginning of a spell, she was not certain.

"My dear lady," Spier said, advancing upon her, swaying. "It is all over."

Distantly, Pol heard her reply: "In that case, behold yourself."

He heard Spier's scream and thought that she had finished him. But then, at an even greater distance, he heard the man's weak answer: "Good. But not good enough."

But Pol was already walking through the place of mists, the form of the man so like himself at his side, telling him something, something to remember, something important . . .

"Belphanior!" he said aloud, half-raising his head.

And then he slumped and the mists rolled over him.

XXI

My world was torn apart and reassembled in an instant. Possibly I, too, was subjected to the same process. My existential yearnings were redefined and satisfied by that single gesture. The perturbations of my spirit subsided. Everything—for the first time in my existence—was made clear to me. I reveled in the moment.

"Belphanior!"

Belphanior. Yes, Belphanior. It fit so beautifully, like an exquisite garment tailored just for me. I turned before the mirrors of my spirit, admiring the cut and the material.

I had been hurriedly assembled from the raw stuff of creation in this world by the sorcerer Det Morson on the day of his death—almost within minutes of it, actually. So rushed had he been by the unusually speedy advance of his enemies that he had been unable properly to conclude the work, to charge me in full with all of the necessary restrictions, compulsions and promptings. He rushed off to tend to his death without quite completing his spell and setting into motion all of those reflexes he had instilled. Or telling me who I was. Conscientious in the extreme, I realized, I had been trying to figure these matters out for myself.

It is very pleasing to learn of one's importance in the scheme of things.

And it is a good thing, in a very real sense, to have made one's own way in the world, unlike those others who came full-furnished with stocks of intellectual and emotional equipment suiting them for their comfortable niches in life and requiring never a second thought. Consider . . .

Det rushed off. I see now why he did not release me.

400

Not only was I incomplete, without that final pronunciation of my name, but my infant strength would have been of small use against that army of besiegers and their wizard would doubtless have put me aside, likely rendering me useless for my true purposes. For how long after the fall of Rondoval I remained, trapped by the paraphernalia of the spell in that small chamber, I do not really know. Years, perhaps; until the natural erosions of time wore away the designs which barred my exit from that room. No true hardship this; for my existence at that time was next to vegetable in character, not at all the inquiring and highly sophisticated state of mind I now enjoy. In the years which followed, I learned the geography of the place thoroughly, though I never questioned the nature of the force which kept me anchored to it—not even when I found that my modest forays into the countryside were invariably accompanied by an apprehension which was only allayed when I returned to the castle's confines. But I was young and naive. There were so many questions I did not yet ask. I slithered along rafters. I danced among moonbeams. Life was idyllic.

It was not until Pol's arrival and all of the activities which ensued that anything like a true curiosity was aroused in me. Beyond the vermin and some then incomprehensible dwellers upon other planes, my only experience with sentients had come from the minds of the sleeping dragons and their companions—hardly the most stimulating intellectual fare. But I was suddenly deluged with thoughts and words, and the ideas which lay behind them. It was then that I came into self-consciousness and first began to explore the enigmas of my own condition.

I know now that I was drawn to Pol because of his dragonmark, and any of the horde of other cues which served to identify him to me at some primal level with my first accurséd master. I did not know, however, that this was a part of the design of my existence. In light of it, certain of my other actions became even more intelligible. Such as my animation of the corpse for purposes of conveying a message to Mouseglove. Such as my decision to depart Rondoval and follow Pol.

"Belphanior." Delicious word.

As Pol lay semiconscious, gasping, aching, suffering from
a number of burns, broken bones, sprains, abrasions, con-
tusions and near-total fatigue, I realized that an important
part of my mission in life involved his protection and I was
pleased to have succeeded as well as I had, considering
the handicap under which I was working. It gratified me
that I had occasionally relieved the pressure of some of his
more distressing dreams, not to mention sending Mouseglove
after the scepter, without which he would almost certainly
by now have been dead.

Yes, it pleased me that I had done the right things when
I had acted, had reached so many proper conclusions by
virtue of my own initiative rather than because of any
standing order I was obliged to follow. As I considered the
fallen form of Larick—also under my protection—as well
as those of Ryle, Ibal and the rapidly failing lady Vonnie, I
was happy to know that by extension, as allies, I could also
count them as being in my care. The philosophical vistas
now opened to me seemed almost limitless.

Yes.

With the pronunciation of my name I was immediately
aware of who and what I was:

I am the Curse of Rondoval (a technical term, that),
existing to defend both the premises and the members of
the House, and failing that, to avenge them.

I look upon it as a challenging, exciting and wonderful
occupation.

It is with extreme gratitude that I now consider the fact
that Det Morson, hard-pressed as he was there at the end,
yet managed to find time for the creation of a good Curse.

As I watched Henry Spier and Vonnie swaying and
staggering back and forth, hurling their remaining energies through intricate and deceptive patterns at one another in a conflict to determine the fate of my charges, not
to mention that of the world, I realized that, despite the
forces which had been thrown against him, the man had
the edge and would doubtless in a few moments emerge
victorious. It was instructive to follow his magical manipulations. There was genuine artistry there, as I understood
it. The man had, after all, once been a peer and close
friend of my accursèd master. It was, in this sense, unfor-

tunate that he had become an enemy of Rondoval and, hence, the designated recipient of my wrath.

Which led me to another important train of considerations: With Det Morson dead these two decades and two heirs of Rondoval visible on the floor, who was his proper successor as my accursèd master? Larick was Pol's senior, yet he had forsaken the family precincts to dwell at Avinconet. Pol, on the other hand, maintained his residence at the family seat and thus was more sensitive to the needs of Rondoval itself. Witness, his ongoing program of repair and renovation. The matter could, over the years, become very important when it came to the assigning of priorities in my work-schedule.

I resolved it finally in Pol's favor. Possibly, ultimately, a sentimental choice. While I allowed myself to be swayed by the argument from residence, I was not unaware that my decision could easily have been colored by the fact that I knew Pol better than I did his brother and that I had not approved of Larick's earlier actions against him. Or, to put it more simply, I liked Pol better.

I drifted near his twitching, recumbent form, and for the first time attempted direct communication with him.

Everything is all right now, accursèd master, I reported, *except for a few details.*

He began coughing just as Vonnie screamed, interfering with his acknowledgement.

I regarded Henry Spier once more, his face twisted and blackened, as he tied the final knots of his spell. I noted, too, that Ryle Merson was awake and struggling to raise one arm. Larick and Ibal were likely to remain unconscious for some time longer. Taisa was sitting up and looking very bewildered.

I reviewed a number of possible actions I might take against Spier, rejecting many—even the one which involved flooding the chamber by diverting a nearby underground stream, a course which possessed a great esthetic appeal for me.

Finally, the choices were narrowed to one and the only remaining detail involved my decision as to the proper color scheme.

Avocado, ranging to a very pale green, I finally decided.

XXII

When Pol heard the voice in his head, he rolled onto his side and opened his eyes. He lacked the strength to do anything more. The situation appeared virtually unchanged so far as he could tell. Vonnie seemed no longer a young woman, but middle-aged and tired-looking. Spier also looked worn, but there was still some vitality in his gestures. A moment more and it appeared that the man would win.

There came a loud hissing sound from the back of the chamber. Spier glanced in that direction and his face froze. His hands halted in mid-gesture. Vonnie also looked that way, with identical results.

Pol struggled to turn his head, and when he succeeded he beheld a particularly ghastly materialization. It appeared to be the demon body he himself had briefly worn, taking rapid shape beside the table—headless. In place of a head, it wore a crown of flames—avocado, ranging to a very pale green.

Pol heard Taisa shriek. And from their changing expressions, it appeared that Spier and Vonnie each thought the other responsible for the phenomenon.

In that moment, a bit of light fled from between Ryle Merson's cupped hands to fall upon Spier's breast. Spier staggered back, gesturing as if to brush it away and casting a quick glance in Ryle's direction.

Pol raised his hand and moved it as if engaged in a sorcerous manipulation, though the power was gone, the dragonmark still once again. Spier made a warding movement just as the voice boomed out:

"The Curse of Rondoval is upon you, Henry Spier!"

The flame-headed demon-form lurched forward, and

Spier—all color fled from his face—turned and seized the statuette, which he raised before him.

"I have served you!" he cried. "Now it's your turn! Now, or never!"

There came a flash of light from Vonnie's mirror, directed toward Spier, simultaneous with a heavy scraping sound from the direction of the table.

The light from the mirror did not reach Spier. Somewhere in the vicinity of the figurine—at arm's length before him—it appeared to be absorbed. The jewels in the statuette suddenly shone like tiny, colored fires.

A dark shape rushed forward, racing the demon-form toward Spier. It passed the creature—a heavy wooden armchair from beside the table—passed Spier also, pivoted in midair, dropped and pushed forward, striking Spier behind the knees.

The sorcerer collapsed into the chair, still clutching the blazing icon.

The chair tilted backward and levitated rapidly, just as the Curse of Rondoval sprang toward it. It swung in a wide arc about the room and the fire-crowned avenger bounded after it.

It rushed at the wall, banked suddenly, then shot directly toward the window.

Belphanior recovered his balance, turned, and sprang after it, talons extended. He caught the edge of Spier's long yellow cloak which trailed behind.

The chair jerked and Spier made a gagging sound, clawing at his throat with one hand. Then its clasp tore loose and the cloak fell away. The chair resumed its forward motion, picking up speed, and passed out through the window.

Pol heard a startled cry followed by a dragon's roar. A moment later, there were gunshots. Then he heard Mouseglove cursing. He propped himself with one stiff arm and started to sway. He felt Ryle's hand upon his shoulder, steadying him.

"Easy . . ." Ryle said. "He's been checked. We're safe."

Ryle helped him into a sitting position, then looked toward Taisa, Larick, Vonnie.

The old woman was sitting upon the floor, the mirror at

her side. She held Ibal's head in her lap and was speaking softly, almost crooning, above him. When she felt Ryle's gaze, she raised one hand to cover her face. Ryle quickly looked away.

Larick was stirring again. Ryle rose slowly, ponderously, to his feet and made his way toward his daughter. Pol caught only one brief glimpse of his face.

"Accurséd master," Belphanior said then, prostrating himself before him. "I have answered your summons. I apologize that the man escaped my wrath."

"What—who are you?" Pol asked, moving his suddenly warm foot back from the bowed, avocado to pale green-flamed head. "And please rise."

"Belphanior, the Curse of Rondoval, your servant," he said, raising himself into a semi-erect stance.

"Really?"

"Yes. You called and I answered. I would have dismembered him for your delight, save for that unfair chair trick."

"Perhaps you'll have another opportunity one day," Pol said. "But thank you for this service. It was timely, and well done."

Belphanior handed him the yellow cloak.

"Your own garments are in need of repair. Perhaps the sorcerer's robe . . ."

"Thanks."

Pol took it into his hands. The light fabric felt strange, yet at the same time familiar. There was a small patch of white on the inside, below the collar. He raised it and looked more closely.

CUSTOM-MADE IN HONG KONG ran the words upon it.

He almost dropped the cloak as he was taken by a sudden chill.

"May I assist you, accurséd master?"

"No. I'll manage."

He drew it about his shoulders and fastened it at the neck. He straightened his legs painfully, rising upon them. The ache in his left side grew stronger. Larick, too, was attempting to rise. He extended his hand. Larick looked at it for a moment, then took it and pulled himself up. He did not release it for a moment, however, but continued to stare at the dragonmark. Then he looked up at Pol's hair.

"I never knew," he said at last.

"I only learned at the last possible moment myself," Pol said.

Over his shoulder, Pol saw that Mouseglove was seated upon the windowsill, staring. A moment later, the small man shouted something out the window and dropped to the floor.

"Moonbird couldn't follow the chair," he called out. "It was moving too fast."

Pol nodded. As Mouseglove came toward him, he saw that Ryle and Taisa were also approaching.

Larick turned toward the woman, smiling. She moved past him, placed her arms about Pol's neck and kissed him.

"Thank you," she said, at last. "I thought this day would never come, till wandering in spirit I saw you brought here. I knew somehow that you would free me."

As he gazed past her, Pol saw a peculiar look pass over Larick's face. He disentangled himself quickly, pushed her gently back and bowed despite his aching side.

"I am pleased to have helped," he said, "but it was hardly my doing alone. It was simply—circumstance."

"You are modest."

Pol turned away.

"We'd best see to Ibal and Vonnie immediately."

The old sorcerer looked young again but was still unconscious. Vonnie's beauty had for the most part returned and its enhancement continued as Pol watched. She smiled up at him.

"He'll be all right," she said. "I just wanted to keep him from awakening until the cosmetic spell was in place. We can repair the rejuvenation spells later."

She picked up the magic mirror and regarded herself in it. She smiled.

"Vanity, I know," she said. "Delightful thing."

"Let us," Ryle said, coming up beside them, "repair to more congenial quarters. Perhaps your servant can bring Ibal, Pol."

"That will not be necessary," Vonnie answered, holding the mirror before Ibal's face.

Ibal's eyes opened. He considered his reflection, then began to rise.

"Lead on," she said. "We will follow."

XXIII

Night had fallen. In a large chamber in the castle Avinconet, six jeweled figurines were grouped at the center of a series of concentric circles painted upon the floor; among these circles and about them various Words and Signs had also been executed. It had taken the entire day to situate them so, for every possible thing that could have gone wrong—from spilled paint, mispronounced Words, incorrectly drawn figures, a series of earth tremors and troops of marauding vermin who had marred the pattern—had gone wrong.

At last, however, the final spell had been pronounced, the final line drawn, the final gesture executed. Immediately, the interference had ceased. The Keys were contained.

Now Pol, Larick, Ibal, Vonnie, Ryle, Taisa, Mouseglove and Belphanior sat, reclined, stood, paced, drifted as an invisible cloud, took refreshment, rested and conferred at the farther end of the large room.

". . . Then I don't understand why they didn't help Spier," Mouseglove was saying.

"I believe that they were helping Spier all along," Ryle replied, "but we finally exhausted them, too, for a little while. Long enough, though. Almost."

"You say that, theoretically, he could still open the Gate with the one Key?" Mouseglove asked.

"He told Pol that he could, and I believe that he's right. It would probably take a lot of effort, though. I just don't know for certain. He's the greatest living authority."

"What now?" Larick asked, from where he sat beside Taisa who was looking at Pol who was looking at the book he held in his lap.

"They're neutralized now, but I will not rest until all seven Keys are destroyed," Ryle said. "They could still be stolen or freed somehow and the thing could start all over again."

"I can guard them against mortal thieves for a time," Mouseglove offered.

. . . *And I against those of the other variety*, Belphanior said from somewhere.

"But *can* they be destroyed?" Taisa asked. "After everything we tried on them earlier . . ."

"Everything that exists has some weakness." Ibal said, lowering his goblet. "We will have to explore carefully."

"It's in here," Pol said. "Far back, and scattered, but our father did leave some clues. I've already come across a few new ones. I am going to have to read through the entire thing now and put them all together. It will take a while . . ."

"It must be done," Larick said.

"Yes."

"I cannot help but admire their vision," Ibal said. "You know, if I were Madwand rather than a traditionally trained man of the Art, I don't believe that I would be sitting here with you."

Ryle looked at him sharply.

Ibal chuckled.

"Don't give me that look," he said. "You were in on it at the beginning, till you learned that one important fact. And if you had been Madwand, what then, Ryle?"

Ryle looked away.

"I can't deny it," he said. "It's wrong, but I hate them as much for shattering that vision as for anything else."

"I did not say it just to irritate you," Ibal continued, "but as a caution: Trust no more Madwands than those here present—unless they be well-proven."

"You think Spier may now seek allies?"

"Wouldn't you?"

"I believe I am onto something," Pol said, turning a page. "I don't think this is going to be easy . . ."

A feeling of tension came into the room, as if the air pressure had suddenly been raised. It built for several seconds and then subsided.

"What was that?" Mouseglove asked.

The Keys attempted to shatter their confines, Belphanior announced. *But they failed. Your spells proved more than adequate.*

"Very promising." Larick said. "Keep reading, brother. And mark that passage."

Later, invisible and drifting, I was the only audience save for a drowsing dragon, when Pol sat upon the ramparts of Avinconet and played his guitar, slowly, with bandaged hands. I counted myself fortunate to have gained my name and found my calling in life that day. As I listened to his song, I decided that he must not be too bad, as accursèd masters go. I rather liked his music.

Then a strange thing happened, for my perceptions are not as their perceptions and I like to feel that they are far less readily tricked. The moon broke forth from behind a cloud, infusing the land with its pale light; and falling upon him there, it made it seem for a moment that Pol's hair was white with a dark streak down the middle, rather than the other way around. In that moment, I recalled an infant perception of my creator, and it seemed that I looked again upon the face of Det overlaying Pol's own, masklike. The image had a more than natural strength in the impression it made upon me, and the memory it created was somehow an uncomfortable thing.

But it was gone in an instant, and the music continued. *Is life a quick illusion or a long song?* I asked myself, as I was in need of new philosophical pursuits.

ELIZABETH MOON

THE DEED OF PAKSENARRION